A
Garland Series

VICTORIAN
FICTION

NOVELS OF FAITH
AND DOUBT

A collection of 121 novels
in 92 volumes, selected by
Professor Robert Lee Wolff,
Harvard University,
with a separate introductory volume
written by him
especially for this series.

NO CHURCH

Frederick William Robinson

Three volumes in one

Garland Publishing, Inc., New York & London

1976

Bibliographical note:

this facsimile has been made from a copy in the
New York Public Library

Library of Congress Cataloging in Publication Data

Robinson, Frederick William, 1830-1901.
   No church.

   (Victorian fiction : Novels of faith and doubt ;
v. 50)
   Reprint of the 1861 ed. published by Hurst and Black-
ett, London.
   I. Title. II. Series.
PZ3.R56No5 [PR5233.R16]   823'.8   75-499
ISBN 0-8240-1574-6

NO CHURCH.

BY

THE AUTHOR OF

"HIGH CHURCH."

[F. W. Robinson .]

" And as we fall by various ways, and sink
  One deeper than another, self condemned
  Through manifold degrees of guilt and shame
  So manifold and various are the ways
  Of restoration, fashioned to the steps
  Of all infirmity, and tending all
  To the same point, attainable by all—
  Peace in ourselves, and union with our God."
                                    WORDSWORTH.

IN THREE VOLUMES.

VOL. I.

LONDON:

HURST AND BLACKETT, PUBLISHERS,
SUCCESSORS TO HENRY COLBURN,
13, GREAT MARLBOROUGH STREET.
1861.

LONDON:
PRINTED BY R. BORN, GLOUCESTER STREET,
REGENT'S PARK.

THE PROLOGUE.

PRISON-BORN.

NO CHURCH.

THE PROLOGUE.

PRISON-BORN.

"If you please, sir, Hannah Calverton's worse."

"Confound that woman—she's always worse!"

"Mrs. Withers thinks she's really very ill, sir."

"Mrs. Withers has no business to think anything of the kind. Tell Mrs. Withers to give another dose of the mixture at once—I'll be round first thing in the morning, Miss Edmonds."

"But, sir, I think it will be necessary to see her !"

"I think not," was the curt reply.

The above dialogue was held one dark, rainy, windy December morning, at the early hour of two ; the speakers were a young woman and a middle-aged man ; the young woman huddled in the shelter of a doorway; she, her bearskin cloak her brown uniform and her paralytic umbrella, struggling against the wind and rain ; the middle-aged man on the weatherproof side of the door, shivering on the hallmat, in dressing gown and slippers. In December, with the wind blowing and rain slanting down, and the day scarce two hours old, not an enviable position for either of these public servants—still the odds in favour of the doctor who was out of the wet, and intended to keep so, the fates permitting.

The doctor, after his last observation, shuffled upstairs again, in a temper the reverse of amiable. He was angry with the woman of the name of Calverton for becoming, or shamming worse, vexed with the prison matron who had awakened him from a pleasant dream of a rise in salary and a vote of thanks from the Directors, and downright savage with his deaf old housekeeper who had not heard the bell ring, though it might have roused the dead. That housekeeper should have warning in the morning, and that Hannah Calverton should have a dose that would do her good in the morning, and that Miss Edmonds should be severely reprimanded in the morning for her abrupt manner of addressing a gentleman so high in office as himself. What business had that Miss Edmonds to think differently from him — a poor devil working sixteen hours a day—it was very wrong and disrespectful of Miss Edmonds. Memorandum—to report Miss Edmonds, and have five shillings stopped from the wages for which she was slaving out her life. A reverence for prison authorities was a rule that must be stringently enforced, an unseemly manner of speaking——" A thousand thunders, there's the bell again! "

Mr. Dabchick had slipped off his dressing-gown, kicked his slippers divers ways, extinguished his night-lamp, and was in the act of creeping into bed, when the house-bell rang furiously once more. Mr. Dabchick waited for the housekeeper above-stairs to hear something of the clamour; but she was a woman of the world, and not to be roused at two in the morning on any pretence whatever. *Anathema maranatha*, let him descend again, and be again tormented by these prison officers.

" If you please, sir, Mrs. Withers thinks the woman is dying, and you had better come, sir."

" Very well, very well, Miss Edmonds; I'll be round in a minute. If the woman's *not* dying, mind, I shall be very angry! "

And with this kind assertion, Mr. Dabchick shuffled upstairs again, dressed himself
with great coolness and deliberation, took the
trouble to ascend another flight of stairs and
deliver a piece of his mind to his deaf housekeeper; finally descended to the hall, shut himself out, went a little way down the dark lane,
rang the bell of the great prison gate, was admitted by a sleepy man in uniform, who touched
his hat, crossed the paved yard, rang another
bell at another gate, was admitted by a sleepy
young woman, who had no hat to touch and
an umbrella to hold ; crossed a third yard, or
airing ground, passed into the infirmary, where
Mrs. Withers, infirmary matron, pale and nervous, awaited his arrival with Miss Edmonds,
pale and firm.

"Oh! Mr. Dabchick, Calverton's so very ill!"

"So I have been told before," snapped the
doctor, as he tramped down the corridor towards the infirmary quarters, followed by the
female officer.

In the infirmary, a long narrow room, lighted by gas, and containing some twelve or fourteen beds, eight of which were tenanted by prisoners whose ill health had necessitated a removal from their cells. Heavy-browed, scowling female prisoners, the majority of whom sat up in bed, and nursed their knees, and cursed Hannah Calverton for robbing them of their night's rest and dying at unseasonable hours; or pretending to die, and waking honest folk, and bringing the good doctor out of his warm bed, and worrying the infirmary nurse, and Mrs. Withers, and Miss Edmonds, with her " goings on ;" for she was always a " going it " this Hannah Calverton, and up to a hundred tricks. This was her sixth time in prison ; and her prison life had been a troubled one to herself, her fellow-prisoners, and her officers. She had smashed more windows, and been carried more often to *the Dark* than any two of her contemporaries ; " she had had her fling," her co-mates and sisters in exile asserted, and having flung away all health and strength, had come at last to die. And there she lay on her iron bedstead near the fire, the wreck of a bold, handsome woman, whose defiant looks were even not yet quenched.

"Well, doctor, where's the child? If you don't bring the child, I'll scream—by God, I'll die screaming!"

The surgeon made no answer, but placed his fingers on her wrist, which a moment afterwards was wrenched suddenly away from him.

"What's the good of it," she cried, as she thrust her hand beneath the bed-clothes. "You can't make me better, doctor; you don't know any more than I; there's nothing you can do or say that can keep me alive till daylight. I'm sinking, ain't I?"

"You are very weak," the doctor said evasively.

Mr. Dabchick's tone had altered in the

sick woman's presence; his irritability had softened down; his manners were less brusque. There was a heart somewhere about him, although prison service had hardened it, and prisoners whims and caprices rendered it sceptical. This was a case that called for his attention, and he pardoned Miss Edmonds for entrenching on the happiest dream he had had for some time past.

" I want to see the child," she said again.

" Don't bring a child in here," grumbled one old woman of seventy, " at this time of the morning. We can't get too much rest at any time, the Lord knows, and it's precious hard that ——."

" Hush !" cried Mrs. Withers.

" Shan't hush !" was the rejoinder. " It isn't time to hush when ——"

" If that woman speaks again," said Mr. Dabchick, " give her no port wine till Saturday, and double the bark."

Mr. Dabchick had studied character, and

knew the weak points of his patients—port wine and bark had been necessary for this querulous prisoner, who liked port wine and abhorred bark like poison. The hint was effectual; the old woman gave a snort like a sea-horse, lumped down in her bed, and drew her counterpane over her head. .The rest of the women who were awake sat still and watchful; only one of the number, a young woman crying in an adjacent bed, was at all affected by the scene. It was she who said, somewhat indignantly—

"Surely she may see the child, doctor? Mrs. Withers, you'll send for the child, won't you?"

Mr. Dabchick whispered a few words to Mrs. Withers, which were repeated to Miss Edmonds who departed.

The dying woman had watched them anxiously with her two dark, restless eyes, and as Miss Edmonds left the infirmary, she said—

"I thought you'd let me see her. I daresay by law now, you couldn't help yourselves, although I am a poor prisoner. Here, you may feel my pulse now."

And a long thin arm was stretched from the bed towards the doctor.

"I'm terribly ill," she said with a shudder; "doctor, I'm awfully ill! Such a catching here," grasping her throat with her other hand, "like the devil getting a grip of me before his time. The parson," with a strange, weak laugh, "wanted to frighten me about the devil yesterday,—good Lord, how he preached and went on and told me all I knew before. As if I hadn't been—as if I—wait a moment."

The woman stopped and panted for breath; the doctor released her hand, and Mrs. Withers offered her something in a glass which she pushed angrily away.

"As if I hadn't been brought up better, or wasn't a fairly married woman, or known what was right once," she continued; "as if my family hadn't been a respectable family, and earned money honestly—not like these creatures' families," she said, disparagingly.

One woman who had been crouching in her bed, sullen and observant, flashed up at this, and wanted to know what *she* meant by that "imperence," and would have argued the point at the top of her voice if Mrs. Withers had not looked her down.

"The parson was coming again in the morning—he may save himself the trouble, I'm thinking. Doctor," cried Calverton with a sudden eagerness, "Mrs. Withers, what will they do with Bessy when I'm gone? Good heaven, I've never thought of that before—what will they do with Bessy?"

"Send her home of course."

"Home. *Home!*" she cried—"wait a moment, that's worth thinking of."

The wasted hands were spread before her face, and the woman shivered as she lay.

Mr. Dabchick walked to the fire and stood looking at the red coals and debating within himself whether there were any further necessity to remain. The woman must die, and there was no skill on earth could save her. It was half-past two in the morning, and he should be glad to get to bed again. He was moving towards the door when the woman said—

"Wait one moment, doctor; just another moment."

The doctor looked towards her; the face was covered by the thin hands still, and the form was shivering yet.

Of what did she wish to think at that time, and at so late an hour? What had she neglected to think of during that long prison life, shut within the four walls of her cell and with so much time before her? Was it of the past, or the present, or the future, the grim reality of which was troubling her?

"Home to Wales is a long journey for a

child," she remarked at last; "you'll see, doctor, that she reaches my brother's safe."

"Your brother's?"

"Ay, her next relation, my husband being across the seas and never likely to come back. My brother, Matthew Davis, near Aberogwin—who'll remember that?"

"I will," said the infirmary matron, kindly.

"Thankee, you're a Christian woman— you've been kinder to me than I deserve, take it all together. I should like to shake hands with you, if you'll be good enough."

Mrs. Withers put her hand in that of the prisoner's, which held it fast.

"Don't forget Aberogwin, two miles from the Penberriog Quarries, where he works; everybody knows him there. He's a man that will take care of her, and do his best for the poor prison-born I leave behind. She'll grow up better than her mother—she can't grow worse!" she added, bitterly.

The doctor stole out of the room on tiptoe,

at the same moment as Miss Edmonds returned with a dark-haired, dark-eyed child of
four years old. The woman dropped Mrs.
Withers' hand and made an effort to sit up in
bed as the child entered, then let her head
fall back heavily again.

" Weak as a rat," she murmured ; " Bessy,
Bessy ! "

The child was at her mother's side at last,
looking at that mother with a scared expression of countenance.

" Bess, do you remember what you and I
were talking about, a little while ago?"

The child nodded her head.

" About going away, you and I, when I
got my *ticket*—about the world you know
nothing about, where there are no high walls,
no locks and keys, or women prowling about
and reporting you for this and that, as if you
daresn't call your soul your own ! About—
what a noise you make Jane—what's all this
to you?"

Jane was the prisoner in the next bed, who had betrayed some little emotion before, and was now inclined to be hysterical.

"I know I'm a fool—but we were pals once, you see," said Jane.

"Ah! yes—and I was jealous of you once, don't you remember?"

"Yes—*what fun!*" sobbed the woman.

"Bessy's going home to Wales; her nearest relatives are in Wales, and Government is bound to send the children home. It's a good job her father's in Australia, Jane?"

"Yes," said Jane, "in Australia. Poor Dick Calverton, I think I see his yaller gipsy face!"

And Jane laughed and cried at the reminiscence till she tired Mrs. Calverton's patience.

"Ah! you always were a weak fool. You'd better try hard for your ticket, and go out after Dick; there's no one in the way now. Don't patter any more—I'm sick of it!"

The woman spoke with greater difficulty, and fought harder with her breath. The prisoners round her, tired of watching, had resumed their recumbent positions, and were most of them snoring heavily. The fire burned brightly; the wind was boisterous in the airing yard, and sighed, and moaned and howled; and the rain beat heavily against the thick coarse glass behind the iron bars. The child stood by her mother's side, betraying some emotion, but more of wonder; she could not understand for what she had been brought thither, unless it was to see how ghastly white her mother looked. Born within those prison walls six months after the mother's last incarceration, she had been reared in a hard nursery, seen much tribulation; mixed with a crowd of callous and half-demented women, had even during the last three months been schooled with them, and taught her alphabet by the schoolmistress of the establishment. Prison-born, but no prisoner, little Bessy Calverton had passed four years of life in her mother's cell, in the prison nursery, and airing grounds—lately, of a Sunday, experiencing a little liberty by accompanying the national school in the neighbourhood to church, and having many things to wonder at—ladies and gentlemen bravely dressed walking about the streets, and no one in a brown uniform following them with a key; horses, and carts, and omnibuses; green trees and fine houses, with flower-gardens in the front thereof. A strange world, that set her thinking why mother should live in a little room with an iron door, perhaps, although too young to argue the matter at present.

"I have been lucky to keep the child so long here. I've known the time when two years was the extent, and off they'd pack the young ones—anywhere. Bessy, you've come to say good-bye, girl—ain't you sorry?"

"Good-bye ? — yes," the child repeated.
"Are you going away ?"

"Ay, both of us—both off to new worlds,
Bessy, and quit of this great prison — this
black home. Why, Mrs. Withers, half my
life's been spent here."

"Ah! more's the pity."

"I was twenty years of age when I was
here first. Good Lord! what a time ago—
what changes! You weren't here then,
hardly any of you. This is a place that cuts
you matrons up as well as us ; you can't
stand it long. Where's Bessy ?"

"Don't you see me mother ?" whispered
the child.

"Bessy must grow up a good girl," said
the mother; "when she's old enough, she'll
make amends for all—my evil ways. My life
may be a warning to her, perhaps : if it's a
warning, why, so much the better for me.
You're going into the country, Bessy, amongst
the mountains—such a pret—pretty place !"

"She's going!" cried Jane, leaping up in bed again.

"Tell Uncle Matthew — tell him — I'm sorry for a good deal of the past—some one tell him that. Tell Dick Calverton — ah, Dick's at the gold diggings, making his for— tune, so there's no—thing to tell him. I'd have sent my curse, if I — if I had known his address. A black villain, a crafty, two-faced—two-faced—Bessy, kiss me!"

By an effort she flung one arm round the child, and drew her to her wasted form. The old defiant look, the impress that many years of sin had left there, seemed to soften as she clasped the child, that one link to her better self.

"Only this—one—left—to say good-bye! Where's Lotty, I wonder? Well, I—I don't care! I never did care for any—anything: I never stood for anything in my life. It would have been the same over again, once quit of this place!"

" Don't say that," whispered the chief matron of the infirmary—" not at this time, in such an awful moment! Think for the little while still left of a merciful Redeemer, and try to pray ! "

The woman shook her head restlessly to and fro, to and fro upon the pillows.

" Don't tease me—don't worry—what's the good? I *did* try to pray before the doctor came, but the words stuck in my throat, though they weren't for me. Only for Bessy here—poor Bessy !"

The mother sighed ; and Bessy, guessing all too well now, began to sob passionately.

" Do you think, Mrs. Withers—she'll—she'll grow up good now ? " was the anxious question.

" Why should she not, in good hands."

" Ah ! in good hands. The Lord keep her out of Dick's clutches, then, or—but he's fortune hunt—ing—it's all square! I wonder when they'll write to Mat—thew Davis, with my best wishes—blessing, if it'll sell for any—thing. He'll take her—I'm—sure—of it."

The voice was very weak and low; the matron of the prison had to bend her head down to catch the words; Jane had stolen from the next bed in her night-dress, and was leaning over her; the rain beat more furiously against the glass, the wind rioted more without as if exulting in the human misery within. The woman murmured " Bessy" again, and then died calmly in her prison bed. The world was over with her—her strange, ill chosen, mis-spent life met with its natural termination, within a prison walls; but little sympathy or hope or confidence to make her dying hours more light.

So die every week some poor unfortunate like unto this erring woman; so every day some friendless, motherless child stands alone amidst strange faces, seeking her fortune as early in the day as this dark-eyed daughter of the woman lying there sought hers.

PART THE FIRST.

CONCERNING MOUNTAINS AND METHODISTS.

CHAPTER I.

BEFORE THE CURTAIN.

HALFWAY up a Welsh mountain stood the cottage of Matthew Davis, quarryman. In the heart of Wales, in one of its fairest resting-places, and shadowed by one of the boldest and most rugged mountains on the summit of which rumour said the Welsh had encamped in old times, and fought and worried Longshanks the Plantagenet.

As pleasant a spot as any in glorious old Wales was this Aberogwin, lying a little out of the beaten track of tourists, and therefore all the more delightful to the few sturdy pedes-

trians and the handful of artists who contrived
to find their way thither in the summer
months.   There are no first-class hotels within
a good fifteen miles of Aberogwin ; no guides
prowling at the foot of the mountains, or
the edge of waterfalls, to show you a way
and point you a beauty you are sure not to
miss; and there are no coaches rattling through
it twice a-day.   Wales has its lions elsewhere,
and the lion-seekers find Aberogwin in very
small letters on their ordnance maps, and go
elsewhere for pleasure.   A mile-and-a-half
from Aberogwin is a straggling village, built
for the accommodation of the quarrymen who
work at Penberriog quarries, which village is
tabooed by guides and guide-book also—there
being larger quarries, requiring three, four, or
five thousand men in more northern parts of
Wales, and travellers like the largest of everything as well as the rest of mankind.   There
are a dozen mountains from which a finer view
can be obtained than from the summit of

Snowdon ; but Snowdon is so many
feet higher, and all who set foot in Wales
struggle up to its summit, and cry, *un fait ac-
compli.* Is the largest mountain, the widest
lake, the broadest fall ever the best, O blundering brother tourist; or may we not be as
deceived in the colossal, as in the biggest ap-
ple we cried to have when we were boys? For
in Aberogwin are all the elements of gran-
deur—all the true light and shade, rock and dell,
hill and vale, that the eye loves to dwell on and
the artist to depict. Sketch the old cottage
of Matthew Davis from the west, backed by
the mountain on which the mist wreaths are
hanging, aud one might look at it and cry
Switzerland. Paint it from the east, where
the cottage only peeps through a forest of
larches growing half-way up the mountain,
and the stream comes leaping, plashing down
the mountain side, and falling over the moss-
grown rocks twenty feet at a time, and one
might cry Arcadia, and die believing in it.

Shepherds in blue satin doublets, and shepherdesses in worked flounces, dotting the landscape here and there, and talking or singing *à la* Philip Sidney, would not be out of place in such a picture. It looks a happy land, on which peace and harmony and human love seem resting like a blessing.

Eight years of Bessy Calverton's life have been spent in this mountain home—a great and a grand change from the stifling London prison where the mother died. The mother had been a true prophet; Matthew Davis had been written to by the prison authorities, and had expressed his willingness, with a few texts, to take care of his unfortunate little niece; and presto the cells, and the infirmary wards, and the prison nursery, vanished away, and mountain, lake, and vale were stretching around the wondering child.

The change was for the better; and though life was dull and monotonous amongst the mountains, and Matthew Davis and his daughter were not the most cheerful beings on the face of the earth, Bessy had considered it home, and settled down therein pretty content with the world and its inmates.

Of this father and daughter with whom the greater part of Bessy Calverton's childhood was passed, let us speak a little ere we raise the curtain.

Matthew Davis was a wisp of a man, who had had an arm blown off and an eye blown in, one unfortunate day at the quarries, during blasting operations,—a thin, diminutive, white-faced man, with sandy hair and sole's eyes. Looking at him in the rear, in his white jacket, trousers, and straw hat, one might have taken him for a little boy,—right about face, and he made you jump with that worn, cadaverous old face of his. Matthew Davis was a religious man, who carried hymn books in his pocket, and studied his bible at the works, and lived upon religion till it disagreed with him. He was a stanch

Methodist, who could never leave his religion alone, but dragged it in by the ears at every opportunity, fitting or unfitting; and worried more people to death than we intend —the Fates permitting—to worry readers. He was a man of long-winded graces and extempore prayers; justice demands that we should add, that he was an earnest man—one of those men who *do* make a show of their religion, and are vain of their good works, and yet no hypocrite. Narrow-minded, as are most men who believe in no creed save their own, and base every action of their lives upon a bible text, but meaning well, and, like many better, wiser, failing sometimes in his best intentions. Not a pleasant man by any means, either in chapel or out of it, Sundays or week days—a man who seldom smiled, and seemed with his fishy eye to be looking over your shoulder for something— mayhap the arm and eye which were blown away when the powder charge was eccentric, and he was younger and more rash.

A good servant to his master, and one who had been rewarded for faithful service by being made an overlooker after his accident, and who did overlook—with a vengeance ! The Welch quarrymen are a peaceable, honest race of men, but I do not believe the quarrymen of Penberriog would have torn their hair with despair if another premature explosion had extinguished the remaining optic of Matthew Davis of Aberogwin. He was not a lenient man ; he looked after his employer's interests, and he was not blind to his own. When he took visitors over the quarries, that one eye looked sharp after his fees, as he bowed them out of the gate.

Matthew Davis had worked at Penberriog slate quarries five and thirty years, and saved money, and invested money in a variety of ways. A shrewd, calculating, money-scraping individual, who had a few hundreds in the bank at Carnarvon, and some five and ten pound shares in half a dozen public companies.

The cottage up the mountain side was his own, and so was the little bit of fat, fertile land that stretched therefrom to the broad, well-made Government road; and so was the sleepy cow, and the fifty wild, bony sheep that scrambled up and down the mountain all day, and appeared to feed on slate and iron stone, and were more agile than graceful under that course of diet.

He was not a proud man, however, although it was something akin to pride in his spotless character that placed the name of her who died in prison under ban and interdict. In the early days the child had spoken much of her mother, till the stern and constant HUSH! from the father and daughter had checked her in that reminiscence.

That daughter, Mary Davis, was twenty-four years old, only child of her father's first wife, and now sole housekeeper at the cottage, Mr. Davis having lost and decently buried both his relicts. Mary Davis was as diminutive in proportion as her father, not unlike him in features, which were more sharply cut than ugly, but brighter about the eyes, which were quick and restless, and not unpleasant eyes either. A busy, careful little housekeeper, with Welsh bluntness of manners, and not too much good temper on washing and butter-making days—a young woman who worked hard, and was school-mistress to her little cousin, and came out strong in slaps.

Such were father and daughter when Eliza-beth Calverton, late of Brixbank Prison, was twelve years of age, and resident in Aberog-win. Bessy had made considerable progress in her studies under Mary Davis's tuition; she had evinced a shrewdness in her inquiries that often puzzled her governante, and a self-will at times that often aggravated her, and had even struggled to be lively under difficulties at times that did not succeed very well. Her uncle and cousin, however,

objected to high spirits, and kept them down
and put a curb on a certain spasmodic wilful-
ness, that flashed out occasionally and reminded Matthew of her mother, and made
her old-fashioned before her years, and
dosed her with texts and bible lore, and
punished her when necessary with a chapter
or two of the Testament to learn.

And yet Bessy Calverton would escape at
times, and no sharp words or harsh measures
keep her in the cottage. Bessy was high-
spirited and wilful, we have said; more, she
would exhibit periodical fits of resistance
that astonished her cousin, and made her nervous, though Mary understood the admirable
art of repressing her emotions. Cross Bessy
Calverton too much, damp her young ardour,
stand between her and the fields in the hay-
making time, between her and "the torrent
path" when the rains had swollen the lake
and the fall was heavy, and Bessy would
burst into passionate tears, and stamp her

tiny feet, and tear her pinafores, and sulk
with an obduracy there was no softening for
several days. At those times Bessy had to
be carefully watched, lest she should resist
the interdict and escape to the fields,
or the waterfall, and brave the matter out.
There were struggles even between Matthew
Davis and his niece, in which neither
gave way—in times lying wide apart, and
gradually becoming less as the child grew
more old and thoughtful—and which inwardly
troubled Matthew Davis despite the invaria-
ble expression of his austere countenance.
He was a narrow-minded man, who had had
but little experience in children ; his daughter
Mary he had trained after his own manner,
and she had become the model of all that was
dutiful, filial, and religious : he had but one
method of training up children in the way
they should go—plenty of religion, plenty of
work, no playfellows, and no pocket-money.
It kept children quiet, and brought them up

steady and God-fearing; it made them a comfort to their parents and guardians when they arrived at man's estate. He did not understand that there are many ways to many natures necessary; that there are natures that may be rigorously trained and every twig nailed to the wall of some bigoted opinion, but there are also natures that should run wild a little, and have their time for pruning, and not be cut in the wrong season, and lose half the fairest shoots that would have added to the beauty and strength of the tree. Society is afflicted with a host of such short-sighted gardeners even yet, and the world suffers in consequence.

Matthew Davis laid it all to "Original Sin," and thought of that comfortable self-deceptive commandment which guardians will construe their own way—of the sins of the parents being visited upon the children unto the third and fourth generation. The third and fourth generation of Calvertons would all follow his unfortunate sister to ruin, unless his own exertions to soften the heart of this child were rewarded by a merciful blessing. In her natural buoyancy of spirits, that resisted at times the heavy unequal pressure — in her wild, gay fits, such as all children will exhibit now and then, or they are not half children—in the childish passion and obduracy that followed his efforts to quench the light and keep her always in the sombre twilight of his own thoughts and creed, he could but remember one commandment, and think of the sister who married a scamp, and went wrong, and died in gaol.

" So awfully like her mother ! " he said to his daughter one day when they were sitting up later than Bessy ; " the same odd ways— why, even the same big black eyes, that are all a-fire at times like that coal yonder. We must keep her in, Mary, or she'll throw discredit on all that you and I have done for her."

"She's a child to love, too," said Mary, looking at the fire. Mary was in a softened mood; Bessy had been docile and tractable that day, and evinced not a little affection, and Mary had been less snappish and hard.

"Don't say that too loud—she might hear you!" cried Matthew Davis, glancing nervously towards the door of the little staircase up which Bessy had proceeded a few minutes since. "Don't let her think we are fond enough of her to spoil her, and her blessed soul. I've been inclined to soften once or twice myself lately, she's improved so much, but the responsibility, Mary—the responsibility."

"Ah! yes."

Mary's thin lips compressed, and she was more like her father in the firelight.

"We shall see her a blessing to us some day, perhaps; though we mustn't take credit for good works. How beautifully she sings the hymns, Mary!"

" Not such a bad voice," responds Mary.

" We mustn't say anything about her voice, or it will make her vain," said Matthew, whose voice is of a harsh creation, and reminds one in excited moments of coffee-grinding, " and vanity and vexation of spirit go together. Well, let's have a bit of prayer, and then we'll have a bit of supper, and then I'll just look over this letter of mine again. It's fair news, fair news—sixteen per cent. for a beginning—ah ! "

And he drew a long breath, and rubbed his transparent hand against his side. They had prayers, and a " bit of supper," looking as they disposed of their bread and water like a little boy and girl who had been allowed to sit up late if they kept quiet. With the simplicity of a little boy, Matthew wound up his grace with a " Thank God for a good supper !" and then flitted—for he was a light figure, and was always flitting—to the fire again, before which he stooped and examined a letter, with a portentous red seal like a blister thereon, that he had drawn from the side-pocket of his working jacket.

"Sixteen per cent! If I put a hundred pounds more in it, that will make three hundred pounds — just forty-eight pounds per annum, saying there's no rise—and there's sure to be a rise. Sixteen per cent.—ah-h-h-h! Thank God for a good dividend!"

CHAPTER II.

IS IN REALITY THE BEGINNING.

MR. MATTHEW DAVIS, of Aberogwin, might
have considered himself a charitable man and
a good Christian for offering a shelter to his
sister's child, and taken great credit to his
inner self for the encumbrance. He was not
always backward in impressing this upon
Bessy, when that young lady's tempers were
variable; and Bessy would soften in most
cases, unless there were any harsh addenda
that sent her deeper into the sulks than ever.
But Bessy Calverton was no encumbrance at
twelve years of age; she was no small assis-

tance to Mary Davis, a help at the cottage, and even in the fields. Bessy milked the cow of a morning, and fed the pigs, fowls and ducks. Bessy did the washing of the establishment, in a tub near the stream that wound along the vale, and sang over her work with that sweet musical voice to which Matthew Davis alluded in a preceding chapter. Bessy Calverton walked six or seven miles to fetch candles, soap, *et cœtera*, from an old Welsh woman who kept a little general shop near the turnpike on the Carnarvon road ; she helped with the butter, took her uncle's dinner to the quarries, even went up the mountains after the sheep sometimes, and brought them home out of the snow that threatened them in the winter months better than any shepherd boy in Aberogwin. Bessy could find fish, too, in the lake that lay a mile from her uncle's cottage; and many a trout smoked on the breakfast table, the result of her skill with the angle. She caught so large a trout once that her uncle, in a rash moment of enthusiasm, gave her a penny to buy cakes with ; and although he put it in her money-box afterwards as a better and safer invest-ment, Bessy was so affected by his kindness that she ran at him and kissed him. And Matthew Davis was not fond of kissing or being kissed, although he took her that day round the waist with that strong one arm of his, and lifted her off the ground with it, saying, " Be always a good girl, Bessy." That was a memorable day in Bessy's calen-dar. She was eleven years old then, and began to fancy perhaps her uncle *was* fond of her in his way, and to think she should be always the good girl he recommended—not the hot-tempered, or the over-shrewd child that he objected to, now and then.

In the summer time, with Bessy Calverton twelve years of age, the curtain we have kept down so long rises in earnest. So long an overture we have considered necessary for the purposes of a strange story; will the reader pardon us?—the reader who hates prefatory remarks, and flies, very justly, into a passion when an author bewildered with his space suddenly leaves off his narrative and dribbles out a retrospect of twenty years ago, and the heroine's family-matters and the heroine's grandpapa. Such dry rubbish shot down in the middle of the book, is a bad sign for the author and a tax on the reader. If the first chapter of this story approach in any degree to the rubbish aforesaid, why it is a thing done and ended; and if the reader could have gone on without it, why he is more clever than we are.

Summer time, then. The best though the scarcest of summer times in North Wales; when the sun rises without a cloud in the morning, and the mountains are grey, purple, golden, and then green; when the sky is of a deep blue, and the mountain sheep are in the best of spirits, and even the streams and falls,

though of less volume, ripple away more pleasantly, and seem murmuring of happiness with
the rustling full-leaved trees. On such a
brilliant day in August, when Aberogwin
looked its best—a slice from such an Eden as
our first parents might have revelled in—
Bessy Calverton was kneeling by the side of
the stream half a mile from the cottage, busy
with her washing, and singing in rivalry with
the birds. Mary Davis had a weakness
respecting washing not very uncommon in
Wales—a belief that the water from the stream,
with a good drying after on the furze and
brushwood, was sufficient for all purposes of
cleanliness, and far superior to the steam
and smother of a London laundry. And
certainly the snowy colour of these kerchiefs,
and aprons and collars, was a proof of her
ideas being founded on fact.

Bessy washed and sang, and rinsed the
clothes in the stream, and filled her tub with
fresh water, totally unconscious of a watcher,

travellers being so few and far between Aberogwin way. Stray tourists, when they occasionally tramped through this quiet region, took
the Government road, a quarter of a mile
below the stream, and looked not right or left
in their eagerness to reach Llanberis, or
Beddgelert, or Carnarvon, as the case might
be. But this stranger had been sauntering,
or rather limping, along the side of the stream,
and had for the last hour sat on a bold piece
of rock that had tumbled in earlier times
from the mountain, and watched with some
interest and with no little amusement the
labours of our youthful heroine.

Bessy had sung nothing but chapel hymns,
interspersing them with some extraordinary
variations of her own that were original and
musical, and singing them in a brisk two-
four time, that gave them quite a polka
character. Nearly at the end of her washing
she wound up her last hymn with an extempore lark-like quivering, that tried her voice

and made the mountains ring again, and
elicited a spontaneous " Bravo, Jenny Jones ! "
from her single audience, that startled
Bessy, who nearly tilted her tub into the
stream.

" Steady, Jenny, or you'll make a mess of
your day's work," said he. " I wonder now
if this girl can speak enough English to direct
me the best way to Penberriog," he added,
by way of soliloquy.

Meanwhile, Bessy having recovered her
astonishment, stood by the side of the stream,
and looked across at the speaker. A young
man slightly above the middle height, with a
good-looking face, bright eyes, and chestnut
hair that curled tightly to a well-shaped head.
A young man in a somewhat seedy black
frock-coat, and a waistcoat and trousers that
had been white when he first started on his
journey, but were now travel-stained and
weather-dyed, and ornamented at the knees
with two green patches, which Bessy attri-

buted to saying his prayers on the grass. He wore a rakish-looking felt hat tied with a blue ribbon on his head, and a bundle in an oil-skin wrapper was slung knapsack fashion at his back. At his feet as he sat on the moss-covered boulder lay a walking stick, the substantial handle of which had been cut into a grotesque, grinning Punch's head; and his feet themselves were encased in as disreputable a pair of boots as were ever seen off a White-chapel birdcatcher's—leaky at the sides, and down at the heels, and split up the front, and only half a bootlace between them.

"Is it that way to Penberriog?" he asked, indicating the distant road that wound round the side of the opposite mountains.

"That way," answered Bessy.

"Humph—as uncouth and ill-mannered as most of the aborigines to be met with in these crippling regions," remarked the traveller; "and how far is it, my little Welsh gipsy, to Penberriog?"

" Only a mile-and-a-half—and I'm not a gipsy, nor Welsh."

" The deuce you are not!—what a relief to get rid of the guttural for a moment or two. Only a mile-and-a-half," he repeated, stretching his arms out and yawning; " what a pleasant consolation to a fellow with a sprained ankle, that wrenches his life out at every step he takes. And how am I to reach your side of the brook with my saltatory powers several degrees below zero ? "

" You must go back."

The stranger whistled dolefully.

" Round by the cottage ? " he asked at last.

" Yes—uncle's cottage."

" Does uncle smoke, Jenny ? "

" My name's not Jenny, sir."

" What is it then ? "

" Bessy Calverton."

" Well—does uncle smoke, Bessy ? Say yes, and I'll give you a halfpenny."

" Yes."

The halfpenny was spun at once across the stream, and fell at Bessy's feet.   Bessy picked it up from the grass, and regarded it with some satisfaction previously to depositing it in the pocket of her little checked apron.

" Short reckonings make long friends—uncle smokes—uncle's got tobacco in the house —hallelujah ! "

Bessy stared at this extraordinary summing up—the last word was very familiar to her, although she had never heard it uttered in that free-and-easy tone before.   She had been singing it that morning over her wash by the brook side—she had been taught an English hymn by Mary Davis with a great many " hallelujahs " in it, only yesterday.   Bessy was interested in this new figure in her home landscape—it was something new and attractive.   This young man had not a grave, sour look about the eyes;   his nose was not pinched or his voice hard and inflexible, and he was not chary with his smiles. He must be a very wicked man to smile so much, and look so happy. And wicked men were very good company; she wished there were a few more of them in Aberogwin.

Bessy continued her drying process, and spread the "white things" over the bushes and low stone walls in the vicinity, and then caught up her tub, poised it on her head, and marched briskly towards the cottage, speedily passing the limping stranger on the other side, who laughed pleasantly again, and told her to get uncle's "'bacca" ready. Bessy coloured at the request, paused a moment, then went on at a brisker pace, and was at the cottage door a full ten minutes before her late companion. But then her late companion had taken his time, and sat down again for a minute or two, and stopped to yawn once or twice, and had altogether adopted a most leisurely mode of progression.

"Well, where's uncle Calverton, Bessy?"
he asked of the maiden, at last.

"There is no uncle Calverton here, sir!"
replied a brisk voice behind Bessy, and Mary
Davis's pale face appeared side by side with
that of the bronzed, rosy countenance of her
cousin.

"Ah, I beg your pardon. Good morning
to you, madam—*Bore da*, if that is more suit-
able to time and place and comprehension—
Bore da."

"I speak English, sir," was the grave response.

"Blessings on the English language, that
has struck root in these melancholy regions!"
ejaculated the traveller, as he seated himself
on the seat under the porch, and began fan-
ning himself with his felt hat. "A warm morning, madam?"

"Yes, sir."

"Rather a change for Wales, a warm,
dry morning such as this, I should imagine,"

he remarked ; "last week how it rained, and
how often I caught the shivers in consequence!
Well, this *is* a comfortable prospect," he
added, looking complacently round him—
" something a man can enjoy, and draw into
his lungs, as it were. A pipe and a pair of
slippers, and I might forget the parlour in
Snow-fields, and the churchyard look-out, and
believe myself born for better things. Heigho!
I wonder what half of us *are* born for ? "

It was Mary Davis's turn to regard the
speaker and be puzzled with him, and feel
herself at a loss how to treat this easy gentleman, who was at home on the instant, and
took things so composedly. She did not
feel in one of her cross moods ; the butter had
turned out well that morning, and the pie
she had baked for her father's dinner had the
"loveliest puff crust to it," and the young
man, or gentleman, was a good-looking, good-
tempered man, and it is not the manners or
customs of the Welsh to treat strangers

discourteously. They may now and then
charge you a little too much—witness, ye
gods, that hotel bill of mine, framed and
glazed in my study as a warning against
future improvidence !—but they are a well-
meaning race, and will treat you more civilly
than most people.

"Now, my sweet-singing Bessy," he said,
" where's the tobacco you were to indulge
me with, at this traveller's rest ? "

Bessy coloured, and glanced askance at
Miss Davis, who answered for her—

"This is not an inn, sir."

" A thousand pardons," said the young
man, rising, bowing politely, and seating himself again; "I hope I have not implied that? I
have found amongst the Welsh people so
much hospitality and such little kindnesses
that come from the heart and warm one's
own, that I have grown conceited on the
strength of it, and too presuming. I thought
that Mr. what's-his-name inside here would

not have objected to filling my pipe with tobacco, to cheer me on the Penberroig road."

"My father, Mr. Davis, might not have objected to the gift, sir, had he smoked tobacco, or kept it in the house, neither of which is he in the habit of doing."

"Hollo here!—hollo here, young lady!" cried the stranger, turning to Bessy, "how about the noble coin I spun across the water?"

"What's that?" was the sharp inquiry.

The stranger looked from one cousin to the other, and, objecting to the looks of the elder, said, "Nothing—oh, nothing!"

"Elizabeth" (Bessy was always Elizabeth when Miss Davis was angry) "what's the meaning of this? Have you taken money from this gentleman, or told him a falsehood?"

"I have told no falsehood," said Bessy, reddening more and more; "I never thought about a falsehood."

"It's all right, madam—it's all right," said the easy young man, comfortably arranging his legs upon the seat, and clasping his hands round his knees.

"It's all wrong, sir!" returned Mary Davis, in her severest tone; "and I require an explanation."

"The gentleman told me if I said 'Yes' he'd give me a half-penny, and I did say 'Yes.' I thought nothing of the tobacco."

"Sharp girl this," muttered the traveller.

"And there's your halfpenny—I won't have it—I hate the sight of it. I meant to give it you back again directly I reached home. And you're a tell-tale, and I hate you!"

The half-penny fell smartly on the young man's knees, rolled off, and went under the seat, where all three allowed it to remain, Miss Davis too dignified, Bessy too angry, and the stranger too indolent to touch it. After the explosion, Bessy Calverton bounced into the cottage, slamming the door after her, and Mary Davis, with some little hesitation, said :—

"It was wrong of you to offer the child money, sir. She's not used to money, and it is a great temptation to her. I am very sorry she has afforded in this instance so poor a return for all my teaching."

"I don't think she thought of an untruth, mind you," was the reply ; "I have been considering the matter attentively, and I should put it down more fairly to impulse. Will you kindly allow me a few minutes' reflection upon the matter, under this shady green porch ?—thank you."

He folded his arms after Miss Davis had retired, and cocked his felt hat more over his eyes to keep an intrusive sun-ray therefrom, and fell to considering the matter deeply, and to making points at important parts of the subject by a formal jerk of his head, which increased in intensity, until he jerked his head on to a somewhat narrow chest and slept like a top, deaf to the preaching going on inside. In this position Mary Davis found him an hour afterwards, and hesitated whether she should awaken him ; and finally resolved on returning to the house, and leaving him there ; and in this position Matthew Davis, coming home early that day for a bit of carpentry, at the lattice-work of his porch, discovered the in-truder, and stood staring with as much surprise as if he had been a fossil remain, with something more extraordinary than usual in the conformation.

"I say—you mustn't sleep here," cried Davis, shaking him by the arm at last.

The traveller opened his eyes, and after blinking once or twice—for the sun had stolen full into the porch, and was half-blinding him —looked at the new-comer.

"In nobody's way, governor, I hope?" he asked.

"I don't know that. It's just possible you may be."

"All right, I'll be moving in a minute or two. If I slip off this perch suddenly I shall have the cramp, and if you have ever had the cramp you won't care to be the means of torturing a fellow-creature. May I ask your name?"

"Davis."

"Uncle Davis, for a sixpence!"

Uncle Davis looked surprised, but answered "Yes."

"I have been indulging in a little gossip with your daughter and niece, Mr. Davis," said he, "and glad of any excuse for a rest. For I'm a tourist, who has walked himself out, and—so dead beat, sir! A weak ankle, an indifferent pair of boots, an iron road, and a hot sun on the one hand—on the other, a shady green porch and a not uncomfortable seat. I work hard enough in London, not to enjoy a little rest in glorious old Wales."

"You are from London, then?"

"Yes."

" Which way do you take?"

" Penberriog."

" And your trade?" asked old Davis, carefully putting on his nose a pair of tortoiseshell spectacles, to bring the stranger more clearly before his one eye.

" A carpenter's."

Uncle Davis thought of his lattice porch, his one arm, the clumsy hand he had ever been at carpentry, and considered it a curious coincidence to find a gentleman of that trade at his door.   He had a great belief in calls, and this man might have been led to his house for some mysterious and divine purpose.   He had no faith in the accidents of life—the petty incidents of the day were all wisely ordered, and had each its significance.

" You wouldn't object to a little stroke of work for a moderate price, I suppose?"

" Oh, don't talk of work, old gentleman," said the other ; " I hate work out of season— and in season too, at times—and this is a poor devil's holiday, and there are only fourteen more days to run."

" A long holiday ; I never wasted fourteen days in my life, young man."

" But—"

" One moment—why are you a poor devil ? Do you ever think, young man, of what a devil is, that you treat the word so flippantly ? It's a bad word : your are not justified in making use of it. See here, now."

And the pocket Bible was in Matthew Davis's hands, and the young man, still with his feet on the porch seat, sat and regarded him with an expression of comical horror, and listened to the text that applied to his state in particular, and to the expounding with which it was followed. Matthew Davis became excited, and flung, as was his wont, little bits of Welsh into the argument, and imparted to his remarks the broad Welsh accent, which rendered them entirely incomprehensible. The Welsh interpolations and

the Welsh accent we refrain from persecuting
the reader with—will the reader kindly take
it for granted that both Matthew Davis and
his daughter were true Welsh people, without
having the Queen's English too much cut up?
I do not call to remembrance at the moment
a writer who has attempted successfully to
impart the Welsh twang to his dialogue; and
as I have no confidence in my own powers
that way, I throw myself upon the reader's
charity. If I am not mistaken, I have his
warmest thanks—but authors are mistaken
at times, even in their favourite books!

"Yes, yes, hasty words will come out
head foremost when one don't expect them,"
said the tourist, anxious to stem the torrent,
and fearful of repetition; "and work is good
for the system—I acknowledge it. It puts
fresh muscles into operation, and anything but
the muscles of the legs for a change, say I."

"It's the lattice-work," said Matthew,
pointing above his head.

"Ah! I see—I'll knock that off by way of return for a shelter from the blazing sun. If you don't pay me for it, it wont look so much like work."

"You're very kind," said Matthew, rubbing his one hand against his side after the old fashion, "and it wont take long I think."

"A couple of hours, that's all. Any wood handy?"

"Oh, plenty of wood. And you wont charge anything?—dear me, that's hardly fair. I can't think of your—of your not charging a sixpence or a shilling, to help you on your way, if—"

"I'm not hard up, and I'll have no sixpences or shillings this side of the boundary between Wales and Merry England. If you've any tobac—— any ale, I mean, in the house, why I'll wind up with a glass, and thank you."

"We've buttermilk and—"

"Oh, Lord!"

"Young man, you have walked in unrighteousness many years to be so quick at such expressions," said Matthew, sternly.

"But, my good fellow—buttermilk!"

"I was going to add—and fresh milk. I mentioned buttermilk first, because we never like to waste it."

"I'll put up with spring water till I reach Penberriog," said he with a wry face, as he rose. "Now, where are a hammer, and nails, and a pair of steps. Let us get this little bit of—pleasure over, Mr. Davis."

Mr. Davis flitted with alacrity into the house. This was an agreeable young man— a very handy young man, who had turned up in the nick of time to patch up his lattice, and be rewarded with a glass of spring water. He should have time to return to the quarries, or ride over to Carnarvon bank in a friend's cart from Penberriog, and see if the cheque were paid in yet that he had signed for two hundred pounds' worth

of extra shares in the Black Tor Lead Company. Steps, nails and hammer were
quickly at the disposal of the stranger, and
the rat-tat-tat had begun when dinner was
proceeding inside the cottage. It had
begun in the middle of grace, however, and
Miss Davis had had to ask him to stop for a
moment, which he did, sitting on the top step
and whistling softly to himself.

"This is a queer lot," he muttered,
when permission was finally accorded to
proceed. "I fancy I should catch the
horrors here, and die of it. A dry old
gentleman, who might have asked a fellow
into dinner, considering all circumstances,
that I'm work——no, I wont call *this*
work!"

And he gave a bang to the lattice with
his hammer, that brought the dust and the
Welch earwigs down upon him. Dinner was
half over when Mary Davis, who had been
eyeing her plate with considerable gravity,

suddenly suggested that there seemed enough dinner for four, and perhaps the young man was hungry. Her father looked scared at this uncalled-for observation, twitched his left ear, and considered the plate before him in his turn. There was a little struggle between prudence and hospitality, some critical inspection of the pie—just enough for his supper when he came home in the evening !— and then the better feelings of Matthew Davis gained the mastery.

" Ask him if he'll have any dinner—tell him its pie—perhaps he don't like pie."

Mary Davis went to the door and looked out. The young man was once more sitting on the top step, sucking the end of his hammer, and deep in thought. He started when this little old-fashioned Welsh girl addressed him.

" Will you have a little dinner before beginning work, sir ?—*pie*," she added, remembering her parent's last injunction.

"Thankee, Miss. With your good leave; a man can wo—knock off a little job like this better after dinner. You have given me a start, Miss Davis; for I had just left Wales."

Miss Davis was too matter-of-fact to understand him, and looked her inquiries.

"I had gone back by express to London—the picturesque vicinity of Snowfields, Miss—and was wondering what father and mother, and Hugh and Lucy, and Lucy's sweetheart, were up to at this present moment of time. Perhaps wondering what I am doing, and little thinking I am tittivating an old Methodist gentleman's lattice-work, for the sake of my dinner and a glass of spring water."

He descended the steps, entered the house, and took the chair that had been placed for him, and which faced Bessy Calverton, who had finished her dinner, and was sitting with her hands in her lap, passive and grim.

"Well, Bessy, how are we now?" he asked cheerfully; but there was no cheerful response, or so much as a glance in his direction.

"The gentleman speaks to you, Bessy," said the uncle.

"I'm very well," responded the child, changing colour.

"I'm afraid I unintentionally obtained her a scolding from Miss Davis," said he; "all my fault, and not worth thinking of any more. A quiet child," he remarked, anxious to divert the uncle's attention.

"Yes, quiet, as becomes her years—a steady girl, who, by God's blessing, will do well."

"Amen," whispered Mary.

The stranger fidgeted, and glanced from father to daughter. Were these two odd characters of the genus humbug, he wondered. He was always wondering; but he had not met many people in his life who carried their religion uppermost so plainly; and he was far from a religious man himself.

He hazarded no remark, however; and even allowed Mr. Davis to run over a special grace on his account, without giving an opinion on the subject. He ate his pie, and drank his water, and enjoyed both for a change, and complimented Mary Davis on her pie-crust, which elicited a bow and the first smile he had seen on her prim little face. He asked a great many questions about Wales during his dinner, and if there were any especial objects of interest to be seen in the neighbourhood; for this was his last appearance in the principality, and he should like to see everything, if there were not too much labour attached to it, and his boots held together another fortnight.

Two days at Penberriog to rest his ankle and get his boots half-soled, and then, if the fine weather lasted, he could take advantage of it and enjoy himself.

" You think a great deal of enjoying yourself," said Matthew Davis, drily.

"I have flung myself into dissipation," was the reply. "I have been recommended change of air for an old complaint of mine—a weak chest—and here I am, giving no thought for the morrow, like the—like the lillies, isn't it, who are not able to think, poor things, or perhaps they would? But"—taking note of the contraction of what was once eyebrow before the explosion at the quarries—" the lattice waits without."

He sprang to his feet, and limped at a smart pace to the door, whence he was called back to hear grace by Mr. Davis, who somehow managed to introduce him into the thanksgiving as the stranger within his gates, and trusted that his want of gratitude might be forgiven in his haste to resume an industrious employment.

He was hammering at the lattice at last, and Mr. Davis was at the door observing him. As he stood on the steps, with his coat off, his well-made, if not athletic figure,

evinced no small grace of outline; and the
head flung back to observe better the result
of his work was a well-turned head, that
might have been copied for a Bacchus and not
have disgraced it. Matthew Davis was not
thinking of Bacchus, but of the poor sinner
the stranger was, and the chance that presented itself if he had had but time to sow
some seeds of grace in the nature of this
worker. He gave up the idea, however; it
was late, and he must return to the quarries.
There had been a rumour of some visitors in
the morning, and he scented a half-crown or
two; it was too late for the bank at Carnarvon,
and the sun would be lost behind the high
mountains in a little while.

"I don't think you and I will ever meet
again, young man," he observed. "You will
be gone on your way before I return, I suppose?"

"Oh, yes."

"I thank you for you assistance, sir," he
said formally.

"Don't mention it."

"I have asked my daughter to look you out a small tract I have had by me for some years. A tract that may be a humble instrument to your conversion."

"Is it in Welsh?"

"No, sir;" and the overlooker at the quarries scowled towards the querist, as if doubting his reasons for asking that question. But the carpenter was working busily, and had his mouth full of nails.

"It's a work on regeneration—on the— what's that?—what's that?"

And Matthew Davis was on his knees, groping with his one hand under the porch-seat, and struggling to reach the rejected halfpenny of the morning.

"Who has been flinging money about?" he gasped, when he was on his feet again with the halfpenny in his hand; "who has been mad enough—*fool* enough, I was going to say?—the Lord forgive me!"

"I think I must have dropped it," said the carpenter.

"You deserve to lose it," exclaimed Davis, placing the halfpenny on the top step by the side of the worker's feet. "You don't take care of your pence; you'll never get on in the world, or be a step nearer fortune all your life than you are now. It isn't the value of the money," he added, "but it's a wasteful hand that cast it there—a hand that is its master's enemy. And it would have done good in its way, small as it is. Good day to you."

"Oh! good day," said the other, coolly. He left off tapping at the lattice when Matthew Davis had gone, and sat himself down on his halfpenny and the top step, and looked under the porch after the speaker.

"Well, you're a bit of a character, you are. It's a mercy for you I'm such a good temper, or I might have accidentally dropped the hammer on your head and hurt it. I wonder what his game is?"

And absorbed in the probable nature of Matthew Davis's game, he kept his seat on the top step, and swung his hammer between his finger and thumb, and munched away at two nails in a ruminating, cow-like fashion. The oscillation of the hammer ceased at last, and the nails remained quiescent between his lips, and the thoughts went farther away than his host of the lattice; back once more by express, as he would have termed it, to London—to the cheerful Snowfields, and father, mother, Hugh, Lucy, and Lucy's sweetheart.

CHAPTER III.

"TOADS AND DIAMONDS."

THE young carpenter having been disturbed
in his reverie by the rattling of plates inside
the cottage, had mounted the top step and
resumed his labours ; but the virtue of concentration not being inherent in him, he had
presently sat down on the halfpenny again,
not studying this time, but looking about him
and yawning, and flinging nails at the fowls
that came bobbing and pecking under the
steps.   He was engaged in this amusement
when he became conscious of the door being

ajar and one bright black eye glistening at
him through the crevice. For a few moments
he took no notice of this watchful eye, then
suddenly looking towards it, he said—

"Here—I want you."

The door clapped to, and the eye was lost
to him. He was at work for about the tenth
time when the door softly re-opened, and he
was once more an object of interest. The
child's curiosity amused the carpenter, who
preferred amusement to work at any time,
and who was a lover, as all good-tempered
people are, of childish character. He was
sorry he had hurt this Bessy Calverton's feelings, and that his unlucky halfpenny had
brought upon her a sound scolding; he had
been struck by an amount of shrewdness in
the young lady rather novel in the principality, and he fell into another wondering fit
whether it were possible to draw her out and
obtain her forgiveness. He ceased knocking,
and, without glancing in her direction, said—

"Heigho! I wish I had not offended Bessy Calverton. If I hadn't offended Bessy Calverton, I might have had her helping me with the nails, and holding the hammer for me. Why, I might have told her a fairy tale!"

He knocked two or three nails into the laths, inspected his work, then glanced down again. Bessy had stolen beneath the porch, and was looking up at him with her great black eyes.

"What's a fairy tale?" she asked, in a low breath.

"A beautiful story, all about little girls and fairies, who are no bigger than this hammer, and have wings like butterflies."

"Oh! please tell me!"

And Bessy crossed her hands in her lap, and sat down on the bottom step.

"Well, but you and I are not friends, Bessy. You said you hated me."

"But I won't hate you if you tell me all about the fairies. I hope it's a true story;

for uncle won't let me hear anything that's not true."

"Won't he? Then it's every bit truth, Bessy, so far as I know. It happened a great many years ago, and that's what makes it sound a little strange. Hand up that bit of wood, my little gipsy, and we'll set to work ;— there, the word's out, and it *is* work then! But, Bessy?"

Bessy looked up again.

"I must have another song, hymn—anything you like for *my* story."

"Oh! please make haste!" said Bessy, with a nervous glance towards the cottage from which she had issued. "I'll sing anything afterwards."

"Once upon a time, Bessy Calverton, there was a little girl of twelve years old, with nice black eyes and raven hair; a pretty little girl, whose only fault was that she hated people, and called them naughty names, and tell-tales, and all manner of things."

"Do you mean *me?*" asked Bessy, after a moment's reflection.

"Certainly not, my sharp mountain maiden. Did I not tell you it happened a great many years ago?"

"Ah! so you did."

The lattice work was abandoned again, and the carpenter was sitting on the top step and the halfpenny.

"And she had a sister who was plain and ugly and little, like your"—'uncle' he was going to say, but he recollected himself—"like the top of my walking-stick beside you, and she was always kind and gentle, and lamb-like—but still a little, ugly, cadaverous, crooked-legged angel."

"Angels never have crooked legs, carpenter—it don't say so in the Bible."

"She was only like an angel who *might* have had crooked legs."

"I see, now."

The story-teller continued—went on with

the old story of the toads and the diamonds, enlarging on the extra size of the toads, and the dazzling brilliancy of the diamonds—pointing a moral of civility to seniors whilst he adorned his soul-absorbing tale. Such a tale as Bessy Calverton had never listened to before, told in such a manner as to keep the breath suspended, and the black eyes wide open, and to drown in forgetfulness the mountain scenery, the unfinished lattice, and the stern, little taskmistress in-doors. It was her first initiation into the glowing domains of fairy-land; the land under interdict, and kept ever in the darkness. A story without a text to it, that did not begin artfully like a story, and end with half a page of preaching like the " Sinner's Warning," and the " Downward Path," and other tales that had deceived her so many times and frightened her. This ended happily, and had no talk about repentance, and was altogether bright and dazzling. It opened on a landscape, fair and rose-tinted, and afforded a glimpse of a new world, to which she was a stranger. And the moral sank deep, and the reasoning that lay therein was seized by the child, as the alchemist secures the gold from the dross in the crucible.

"Oh! I wish you lived here always, Mr. Carpenter!" cried Bessy.

"We should be very good friends—you and I, Bessy."

"And I'd never call you names!"

"No, but sing ballads, and put me in mind of a sister of mine I have at home."

"Is she older than I am?"

"A few years, I should say."

"What's her name?"

"Lucy."

"Lucy what?"

"Lucy Speckland."

"Is your name Speckland, then?"

"Yes; Stevie Speckland," said he. "What an inquisitive little maid you are."

"I suppose I am not more inquisitive than

other little girls," said she: "I'm not old-fashioned, am I?"

"Oh! not a bit," was the dry rejoinder.

"I suppose there is not time for another fairy tale, Mr. Speckland?"

"I'm afraid not; but there is a hymn first, at all events."

Bessy began at once. Stevie Speckland had held out a hope of another story, and she dashed into a Welsh hymn, and hurried through the four verses with a rapidity that would have astonished the most go-ahead Methodist of her acquaintance. She certainly astonished Mary Davis, who opened the door and stood on the threshold with an amazed expression of countenance.

"Bessy, what are you doing, child?" cried Mary Davis; "what do you mean by singing a hymn in that manner? Come in-doors, Miss, directly."

The thin, white hand of Mary Davis caught the dress of Bessy, and Bessy flew into the room, and the door closed with a bang between her and Stephen Speckland. Stephen remounted the steps and again attacked the lattice, leaving off, after his old fashion, to think of Bessy, of the fairy tale he had enlarged upon, of Snowfields, of anything that would afford him an excuse to leave off hammering and nailing.

The lattice work was only half-finished, and Stephen was still at his labours, when Matthew Davis came winding up the mountain side towards his cottage.

"You don't seem to have made great progress, young man," said he; "I shall have to finish it myself to-morrow."

"No, you shan't; if I come back from Penberriog to-morrow, I'll keep my word, sir."

"That's right."

"It's a little longer amusement than I bargained for," said Speckland; "I'll go on till sunset, and turn up in the morning."

Stephen Speckland worked a little more

energetically after Matthew Davis's return,
and started for Penberriog at sundown, taking
up his long neglected halfpenny. He kept
his word, somewhat to Mr. Davis's surprise,
and made his appearance in the morning; and
by dint of an extra amount of energy, attributable to sundry pipes of tobacco with which
he fumigated the porch, completed his task by
three in the afternoon. Matthew Davis was
at the quarries all that day, and his daughter
took upon herself to ask Mr. Speckland to
dinner—or rather being a prudish damsel,
who prided herself on deportment, to send his
dinner out by Bessy. Dinner over, and time
before him, and no Bessy appearing to amuse
him, he set to work on an old outhouse door
that had not shut for three years, and had completed that little job just as the brisk trot of
Matthew Davis brought that gentleman to his
home.

The old gentleman was so pleased at the
extra labour of Stephen Speckland, that he

asked him to tea ; and then the Welsh rain coming down by buckets-full, he, after much fighting with his inner self, offered him the use of a spare room, looking out on the porch at which he had laboured for the last two days.

Early in the morning Matthew Davis entered into an elaborate calculation of the repairs required on his premises, and the expense of keeping Mr. Speckland for four days or thereabouts ; and the balance being in his favour, he made his offer of exchange at the breakfast-table.

It was wet weather again, and Speckland had an objection to heavy rains, and preferred being preached at, and making the better acquaintance of Miss Calverton and her matter-of-fact cousin. It was a strange position for him, and there was always something attractive in novelty. He knew the old gentleman wished to make a Methodist of him, and turn him from the error of his ways ; and even a little preaching would be a change, if Mr.

Davis did not pitch it too strong. It would be better resting there and sliding about in Mr. Davis's slippers whilst his boots were being patched up, than shut up in a country inn, with not sufficient cash at his command to be liberal with his orders, and with no parlour customers but Welshmen, who might speak ill of him or swear at him before his face, and he never a bit the wiser. So for four days under the shadow of the roof-tree of Matthew Davis, quarryman or overlooker—a new incident for him, a series of new incidents to the quiet family living in the shadow of the mountain.

Matthew Davis believed not in chance or volition we have seen ; everything marked out and predestined was his creed. And one little incident *may* change a lifetime ; on the instant, or years in the future after the seeds have been sown and supposed to have been lost. Time plodding on for an age perhaps, and then, lo! all change, and figures that might have been more natural in our fevered sleep, stalking into the broad noonday of life, and coming face to face with us.

And so the meeting by Aberogwin stream of Bessy Calverton with Stephen Speckland, of Stephen Speckland with the Welshman and his daughter, evolved in its time more than any of them bargained for.

CHAPTER IV.

STEPHEN SPECKLAND.

STEPHEN SPECKLAND was soon at home with
the Davises. He was a man readily at home
anywhere. His good temper, his quaint
remarks, his willingness to do anything for
anybody, if anybody would give him his own
time to do it in, made him a general favourite—even Matthew Davis began to think
of a son of his who had died when he was a
baby, and to think what a blessing such a
son grown up would have been to his old age.
If he were only a trifle more industrious
Matthew Davis would have made a fair

bargain ; but Stephen was certainly slow over his work, and at the end of four days there was a new cupboard half put up in a recess by the window, and several stairs still out of order between the parlour and the upper story.

Still Matthew Davis was in no hurry to rid himself of the young man ; Mr. Speckland's appetite was not a large one, and his services more than repaid him for the hospitality proffered. There was a chance of reforming him too, breaking him of the bad habit of profane expressions, and teaching him a love for the Bible by reading it at every opportunity—let him stop the week out if it pleased him.

Matthew had become assured of the young man's respectability ; the father and mother of Stephen had been well-to-do shopkeepers once, and Stephen earned a fair amount of money per week when he was pleased to be industrious—he had not introduced a beggar and a scapegrace into his household.

And if Stephen Speckland won upon the good graces of such hard metal as Matthew Davis was composed of, it is not to be wondered at that his efforts to please, his patience under a heavy shower of prayers, and graces, and expositions, interested Mary Davis in his favour, and created a new world in Wales for Bessy Calverton.

The change in Bessy was more apparent; she sang and danced about the house without being checked too readily by Mary; she revelled to her heart's content in fairy tales, which were related to her over the carpentry, or up at the waterfall, whither she once lured him by a recital of its beauties, and heard to its roar all about Blue Beard and the Forty Thieves in return.

" I'm only afraid I˙ shall forget some of them when you go away," she said one day, despairingly; and " We'll see to that, Bessy," was the answer. Bessy kept her own counsel concerning the fairy tales, and Stephen did

not once allude to the subject in the company
of the Davises; therefore Bessy's new world
was all to herself, and she walked happily
therein. Her cousin Mary had no suspicions,
and was not curious concerning the use she
made of her time; she was more gentle with
her, spoke more kindly, the presence of the
stranger seemed to have exerted a salutary
effect on all within that little cottage. There
had been so much of asceticism; each had so
dropped into his or her way of praying and
working, and abjuring every grace and fancy,
that life had become warped, and the change
even of a reprobate's company fell like a
blessing. Mary put it down to novelty;
thought sometimes it might be a little wicked
to feel less cross, less strict in the stranger's
company; to consider his presence almost a
relief there, and to know she would be sorry
when he went away. With the exception of
the quarrymen who came with messages to
the cottage at times, and the few villagers

whom she met on market days, Mary Davis
had had no companionship with the opposite
sex, and this specimen was so good tempered,
so willing to please, so full of anecdote. She
was interested in making him a Methodist
too, for his light vein had jarred on first acquaintance, although she had become used to
it; if he were only religious, he would be her
beau-ideal of a nice young man.

Poor Mary was innocent enough to tell her
father so one evening, when Stephen Speckland had gone down to the road to meet the
carrier's cart, for some mysterious purpose or
other that did not appear; and Matthew
twitched his ear, and looked at the fire, and
then askance out of his one eye at his daughter.
Matthew Davis, we have already observed,
was a suspicious man: one keenly alive to
danger from every imaginable direction. If
his daughter should fall in love with this
young carpenter, who had dropped as if from
the skies amongst them, what a trouble to her

and himself! He had never thought of Mary
possessing a heart, or falling in love before;
she was prim, methodical, pious, and a little
short-tempered; she was above the station of
the peasants and workmen whom she saw,
and was certainly above this Stephen Speckland in position. That young man would
never do for his daughter; he was too careless about money matters, flung pence about
the floor, left his purse—which had four sovereigns and seven shillings in it, for he had
opened it and seen them himself one morning
—on the parlour mantelpiece or the drawers;
and he had a horrid habit of smoking, which
he indulged at the bottom of the garden, or
along the torrent-path, and he had every reason
to believe in his bedroom. An improvident
young man, who, if he married Mary, would
racket away all the money he might be able
to leave her, and bring her to beggary. A
young man he had taken a fancy to himself,
and he was not a man of fancies—conse-

quently, a young man the sooner out of his house the better, so far as his daughter was concerned.

Therefore, at supper-time, when Stephen had returned, Bessy had gone to bed, and Mary was bustling up stairs, Matthew Davis regretted his young friend had not completed all he had promised in the way of carpentry; but he thought he would not keep him a prisoner at the cottage any longer. He knew Mr. Speckland would be glad to start upon his way again.

Stephen, who had begun to drop into the habits of the little family, and who hated to be disturbed too roughly, replied—

" That he was in no hurry, and he should like to finish what he had promised."

Matthew Davis would excuse him, seemed so anxious to excuse him that Stephen coloured, and said, " Very well; he would leave the day after to-morrow."

" Take advantage of the first fine day, if

you have a long walk before you, Mr. Speckland," he observed ; then added, after a
pause—" The wind's in the right quarter for
fair weather to-morrow."

Stephen Speckland did not admire the little
old gentleman's persistence ; he felt that there
was a reason for it, and he jumped at the
wrong one, as most people do when they are
in a hurry to arrive at a conclusion. He
thought Mr. Davis had taken offence at
his dilatoriness, and therefore, fair or foul
weather to-morrow, he would work like a
nigger, finish his task or his amusement, and
be off on his homeward route. He had been
sponging on this Methodist family too long ;
certainly, he had been very comfortable—the
piety of these people had not interfered with
their hospitality—and Methodists were a great
change! He had taken to the girl Bessy ; he
had found attraction in Bessy's cousin, whose
quiet methodical habits he had watched more
closely than she fancied. With such a wife

as Mary Davis, an artisan, one of the " working
classes," might get on in the world ; he was a
fellow who would want some one to take care
of him some day ; he wondered—he was
always wondering !—whether she were engaged to any smart young fellow in the village. Not a pretty girl, but *petite* and
modest, and fifty times more truly religious
than her father, he was inclined to think—
that father who was a bit of a hypocrite, or
he was very much mistaken. But he was
going away now ; and he should not break
his heart, for he had not fallen in love with
anybody, and nobody wasn't going to fall in
love with him. His boots had come home,
resoled and heeled ; and there was a cupboard
that could be finished in a couple of hours,
and a stair or two to patch, and then there
was nothing to stop for !

So the next morning he was the first up in
the house instead of the last, and hammering
away at the cupboard with an energy that

alarmed Mr. Davis, who sprang out of bed and ran to the window, and called out "Who's there!" fully believing something had happened at the quarries, and he had been hastily sent for.

The cupboard was nearly finished by breakfast time, and Matthew Davis sipped his coffee, and speculated as to the object of this sudden fit of energy, and arrived at nearly the truth, and suffered the young man to rise another degree in his estimation, though he was still very glad to see him in a hurry to begone.

" Half an hour after breakfast at the cupboard, and one hour at the stairs, and then my ugly shadow flits away from this peaceful little travellers' rest."

Bessy and Mary looked up at once—Bessy very pale, and Mary, for an instant, with a heightened colour.

" Goings and comings, greetings and goodbyes, are the order of the day, the law of nature, the way of the world. Am I not right, Miss Davis?"

" I did not know you were going away to-day," she said in a low tone.

" A fine day, and one must take advantage of the weather in this mist-ridden country."

" Yes, that's true," she answered.

Mary Davis seemed more thoughtful than usual the remainder of the meal, and even during the long grace that succeeded it, she found, for the first time in her life, that it was a hard struggle to pay proper attention and keep her thoughts from wandering to subjects far different from her father's thanksgiving. When her father wound up by asking a blessing on the stranger's future steps, that he might be spared from danger on the way, and walk uprightly all the rest of his life, Mary reddened a little again, and said *Amen* to it with a lip that faltered. Stephen was not so affected by the prayer, and objected to the introduction of his name therein, and frowned a little as he took up his hammer and turned to the cupboard again. The man *must* be a hypocrite to go on like that, and bang went the hammer against the shelf he was putting up with a suddenness and precision that made father, daughter, and niece jump spasmodically.

" I suppose you will be gone before I return this evening, Mr. Speckland ?" said Davis, when his straw hat was on, and he was ready to depart.

" Sure, sir."

" You'll stop—you'll stop to dinner ?"

" My work will be finished in an hour and a half from this time. I'm used to work in a hurry now and then, when a new piece or pantomime is behind time, for instance."

Stephen Speckland was in an aggravating mood, and threw this new light on his home labours designedly. The old man opened his one eye wider and gasped again.

" Piece or pantomime !" he repeated;

"what do you mean—arn't you a carpenter, after all?"

"Yes—a stage carpenter."

"Good heaven! to think a man connected with plays and play-actors has been under my roof all this time."

" Am I the worse for earning an honest living, old man?" asked Stephen, who seemed inclined to quarrel.

"You are on the way to perdition—can a man touch pitch and not be defiled?"

" Mr. Davis," began Stephen; then he caught sight of Mary's troubled face, and was silent.

" Well, sir—well?"

" I wish you good-bye, sir—that's all."

" What a calling—what a choice for a man who can talk like yourself; and who has, I take it for granted, been tolerably educated."

" My parents fell from their estate before they had much time to educate me. I'm a Bohemian."

" A what!"

" A man of the streets and the world. I taught myself all I know—which is very little. Gathered my scraps of knowledge from any book that came first to hand—I wasn't particular."

" But—"

" But it's too late to argue," he interrupted; " and for once let me call you to order, and remind you of the time we are both wasting. You are excited, and I'm in an ill, unreasonable mood, when advice and religion only aggravate, in lieu of consoling. I should like to part friends with you."

" But—but—but—," spluttered Mr. Davis.

" *But* good morning," said Stephen, emphatically.

Mr. Davis was behind time, and Stephen Speckland was obdurate, and would do nothing but hammer the cupboard. He gave up his last attempt at reformation, and after crying, " Mary, look him up a dozen tracts," flitted along the little footpath that wound to Aberogwin road. Stephen completed the cupboard, and walked silently towards the stairs, taking no notice of Miss Davis standing by the fireplace, or of Bessy stifling her sobs with a mouthful of checked pinafore. After a time the hammer and sawing ceased on the stairs also, and Stephen Speckland made his appearance with his oil-skin knapsack slung round him, and his Punch-headed stick in his hand.

"I'm going now, Miss Davis," he said.

"You are in a great hurry to leave us this morning, Mr. Speckland," she said, quietly.

He might have replied that Mr. Davis was in a great hurry to get rid of him, but he held his peace on that score, simply saying—

"I have been here on false pretences— that of working for my living, and doing no work at all. It was time to put an end to it."

"You must know what is best."

"I shan't forget in a hurry this pretty retreat, hemmed in by the mountains, Miss Davis; it will be something to conjure up in one's mind's eye when the house-roof and chimney-tops are hemming one in."

"I wish we could have made you more happy here, sir."

"Happy? I have been as happy as a king—sermons and all!"

"Our ways are not your ways, I fear."

"We can't be all of one idea in this world, any more than we can be all of one pattern, like a dozen glass tumblers—what's this?"

"The tracts, sir. I—I hope you'll read them."

"I'll add them to an extensive if rather a conglomerated collection of papers, pamphlets, and volumes."

"But you'll read them?"

"Well—yes."

He shook hands with Miss Davis, and fancied that the little thin hand trembled some-

what as it rested in his own. But life is full
of fancies—let him begone!

"Can you spare Bessy to show me the
near way up the mountain—just to put me in
the right track, Miss Davis?"

"Certainly. Bessy, put on your straw-
hat."

Bessy obeyed with alacrity; and whilst she
was preparing for her little journey, Mary
Davis said—

"You have altered your mind, then—you
are not going to Penberriog?"

"No—back again; the short cut over the
mountains in search of a breeze."

"Do you know the way?"

"I have a pocket-compass and an ordnance
map, and fear no man, Miss Davis. So, good-
bye—will you wish me God speed?"

"With all my heart, sir. God speed you!"

He raised his felt hat and went away smiling down the little garden path, Bessy running on by his side, and Mary watching him

from the porch, the repairing of which had been his introduction. The sun was shining, and Mary Davis stood and shaded her eyes with her hands, and watched him and Bessy wind slowly up the mountain side. Why didn't he turn, she wondered—for it was her turn to wonder—and have one more look at the old cottage, if he had been happy therein? —he said he had! So she waited and watched, and he turned at last, and stood looking back towards her. He knew by her white dress still fluttering 'neath the porch that she was standing there. He took off his hat again and waved it in the air ; and she waved her handkerchief back in return, and then went into the house, and closed the door, and, perhaps, shed a silent, incomprehensible tear or two, as she packed away some preserves in the new cupboard that Stephen Speckland had made.

CHAPTER V.

OVER THE MOUNTAINS.

STEPHEN SPECKLAND and Bessy Calverton
went up the mountain, crossed the rustic
bridge flung across the torrent, paused, as we
have seen, to look back at the cottage, turned
the curve of the steep irregular path where
the mountain ascent became more difficult,
and then paused again. They were at a considerable height now, and the roof of the
cottage could just be seen amidst the tree-
tops upon which they looked down.

"So far and no farther, Bessy Calverton."

"But I'd rather go on, please. I'm not tired."

"I can see the track to the summit—half-a-dozen sheep tracks, in fact—and I must not rob Miss Davis too long of her little help-mate. No farther, Bessy; here we say good-bye."

"Oh! I am so sorry you're—you're going away," whimpered Bessy again.

"Thank you, Bessy; when you are a few years older you'll keep such thoughts to yourself; but youth is, what fine speakers call, ingenuous. Well, Bessy, if I am going away, never to see you any more in this life, I must leave the fairy stories behind."

Bessy looked at him inquiringly.

"I commissioned the carrier to buy me a book of fairy-tales at Carnarvon some days since, and I went down the road to meet him yesterday; and here it is, for you to remember Stevie Speckland by, Bessy."

"Oh! Mr. Speckland!" and Bessy laughed

and cried, and trembled with joy at the sight of the gaily-bound volume, with its gilt edges and its glowing pictures inside.

"And are all these fairy tales, sir?"

"Every one of them."

"How kind of you to think of me—to give me such a handsome present. No one ever gave me a present before!"

"This book is only for very idle hours, Bessy, after the work's done, and"—with an expressive grimace that escaped Bessy—"the prayers are over!"

"But uncle," cried the girl with a scared expression, "I—I don't think he will like me to have such a book as this."

"What! will he object to this too—the narrow-minded, narrow-souled Methodist," he added in a lower tone.

"It is not all truth, sir."

"Fancy is good sometimes."

"But uncle don't like fancy—oh, dear!— oh, dear!"

" Don't tell him anything about it, then," was the unwise counsel of Stephen Speckland.

We give ill advice at times, and work evil; we receive bad advice at times, and set it aside, or follow it to our discomfiture; Stephen Speckland was as likely to be in the wrong as any one else. But Stephen Speckland was Bessy Calverton's idol; he had given her more kind words, and told her more pleasant stories, than she had ever heard in her life: his advice must be worth the following, and she was anxious for an excuse to keep that book of golden legends. She said nothing, but put the book in her pocket, and held up her rosy lips to be kissed before Stephen went his way up the mountain.

" Good-bye, Bessy," he said, after he had kissed her; " think of me sometimes in London, where there is no chance of enjoying one's pipe on the green banks, with a waterfall thundering by, and birds singing in one's ear —think of your old playmate a little."

"Good-bye, sir," cried Bessy—"I shall always think of you."

So the man and the child parted, and Bessy sobbed all the way home down the torrent path, to her uncle's cottage. And Stephen Speckland reached the mountain-top, and rested a little there; smoking his pipe and looking down at the peaceful vale and the white thread of silver that wound in its midst, and where he had first met Bessy Calverton. He tried to find the cottage out, but the land was too uneven, and the larches grew high here and there, and shut out the view. There was a fine breeze where he sat, not too cold and cutting a breeze, but one that made it pleasant after the toilsome journey to the summit. He filled a second pipe and smoked that; finally laid on his back in the sun, and gave way to his natural indolence. He had risen early, and worked hard at the cupboard and stairs, and then climbed a tolerably steep mountain—if this were coming out of town

for pleasure, why, the sooner he was back
again the better! What a queer family to
have dropped amidst he thought next—what a
prim little young woman—what an impetuous
child—what a covetous, old, one-handed prig
of a Methodist! What a lovely spot to settle
in if he had money, (his thoughts ran on
next,) with nothing to do but wander in the
vale, or along the brook, or anywhere so it
was not up hill—and fish, and smoke, and lie
on his back as he was lying then, with heaven
looking down upon him. He should like Hugh
and his sister Lucy, and father and mother,
and friends, all enjoying it with him, all on
their backs looking up at the blue sky. That
was the true secret of happiness—to take
things easy and feel the sense of enjoyment
at every pore, and to shake troubles away as
the wind shook the leaves that were good for
nothing off the old trees. That was life—that
was exis——then he dozed and dreamed of
home and of the overlooker's daughter, and

woke up an hour afterwards, shivering with cold, to find the sun looking watery behind a thin veil of misty cloud that had come up he didn't know how. He had left all things bright enough; but all things change, and he must be off on his way ere the rain overtook him and wetted him through.

Stephen Speckland sprang to his feet and stepped out at a brisk pace; it was cold over the mountains now, and he had not improved his condition by sleeping in the open air. He walked himself into a more genial warmth of frame, and maintained the same pace for a couple of hours, till he met with a narrow road that dipped, rose and dipped again, and seemed to have no end. He came to a full stop, consulted his pocket compass and his ordnance map; and whilst thus consulting and studying, became aware of the mist settling down on the hills and enwrapping him as in a thick fog, and stealing its insidious damp through his clothes to his skin.

"Eternally doomed to be out in damp weather and catch cold," he muttered; "the Speckland luck, to choose ever the worst day and the worst opportunity! One might be soon lost on these mountains in a mist like this."

He stopped to fill his pipe for the third time, and make a companion of it; and then stepped out at a pace still more rapid, and ran against another traveller who was advancing in an opposite direction with his head bent downwards, as if butting his way through the mist.

"Hullo!" exclaimed the man.

"Hullo!" echoed Stephen, biting his pipe hard to keep it from slipping down his throat.

"Do you walk along with your eyes shut, that you can't see other people coming?" was the surly query.

"No; do you?"

"I have enough to do to keep the road—I'm no hand on the mountains, in a thick fog like you Welsh goats—I'm an Englishman."

" So am I."

" Misled like myself with the lies of a fine
day, and a path that cannot be missed ? These
Welsh ought to be pitched down some of their
own ugly precipices."

" They might object—good day."

" Stay a moment—I've an empty pipe, and
'bacca's a good friend to the solitary. Haven't
you a screw to spare ?"

" Certainly."

Stephen Speckland felt for a man who was
tobaccoless, and presented his pouch to the
traveller, who filled a horridly dirty short pipe,
and took rather more than half of the Virgi-
nian weed remaining, which he thrust in his
waistcoat pocket for future consumption.

" I'd have taken a little more while I was
about it," said Stephen drily, as the man
unthankfully returned the pouch.

" I took what I pleased, and expected not
a growl from the giver."

"Well, he who gives unthankfully had better not give at all—you're welcome, mate," said Speckland.

"Thank you," growled the man; "I must trouble you for a light now."

Stevie handed him his pipe, and the man placed the bowls together, and puffed and blew at his own whilst Stephen stood and watched him.

A man above the middle height, of burly frame, dressed in seedy black, and standing in enormous boots. A man with a bull neck, and big lumpish features far from prepossessing; a square, massive jaw, dark bloodshot eyes, a dirty wisp of a black moustache straggling anyhow over his upper lip, and ragged, bushy club whiskers that touched his shoulders on each side. A man that the heart would not leap joyfully to meet in a dark lane, or even on a misty day on a mountain road !

Stephen Speckland was not alarmed at the

appearance of this gentleman ; he took things composedly. There might be danger nearer than he thought, but there was little to be obtained by robbing him, even if highway robberies were fashionable in those parts, which they were not.

" You'll know me again ?" said the man, as he returned the pipe to Stephen.

" Very possibly."

" How far do you call it to Aberogwin over this cursed pile of hills."

" There is only one way in this direction, and that would not be pleasant or safe in the mist."

" You mean down the mountain ?"

" Yes."

" I've been down fifty mountains worse than this, and in mists, and fogs, and thunderstorms that would scare the very devil—do you think I care for what is safe or pleasant ?"

" I didn't know you were a Munchausen."

"What's a Munchausen?" asked the man, with a suspicious scowl.

"A great nobleman, who was also a great traveller."

"How many miles is it to Aberogwin?"

"Ten at least."

"And which way?"

"Strike off here from the main path, and keep straight across this table land till you reach the edge of the mountains."

"Well?"

"At the bottom of the mountains you will be one, two, or three miles from Aberogwin, according to your luck."

"Have you come from Aberogwin?"

"Yes."

"Do you know a Matthew Davis thereabouts?"

"There is such a person, I believe," said Stephen, who cared not to be too communicative.

"Very well, that's all I want to know.

You can go, thinking yourself lucky, young shaver, that I haven't trounced you for your off-handedness."

" You might have had some trouble to do that," quietly remarked Stephen, making a somewhat officious display of his thick walking-stick.

" You're a rat, and I'm as strong as a house—if I hugged you in my arms, all your bones would crack like lucifer matches."

" You had better start on your journey, instead of bragging here," observed Stephen ; " the mist is thickening, and your experience in mountains wont serve you much in getting safe down them. I don't wish you any more harm than to get safe down—but I doubt it. Good day to you."

And Stephen Speckland walked on and left the man muttering something in the mist. Here was a new subject for Stephen to think of as he journeyed on; what such a man could want at Aberogwin with Matthew Davis?—some

money business he supposed, or some work to
ask for at the quarries. He paused once as
he thought there might be danger threatening
the cottage, then he laughed at his morbid
thoughts, and went on again. The man was
a bully and a braggart, nothing more; had
possibly been drinking a little too much from
the brandy flask, the metal top of which
he had noticed peeping from his breast-
pocket.

As he continued his way the mist closed
round him with a greater density—rolled past
him in heavy, fleecy clouds, driven by the
wind. Here and there, on lower land, there
came a gap in the mist, which closed in as he
gazed towards it, and left all darker than
before. But he was making a rapid descent
now, and after a time he was quit of the mist,
and could look back at the mountain road
and the sweep of cloud that cut it across and
ended it abruptly in the lowering sky. The
sun had gone now, the rain was falling half a

mile off; he could see the slanting lines from
the black clouds to the overshadowed earth.
On the downward road he could see, too, the
village, and the inn, with a coach before it,
and the travellers cowering together on the
roof in their waterproofs, and with umbrellas
up ; and the coach-horses steaming as though
they had been boiled in a copper and just
taken out. It was striking three from the
church clock in the village he was nearing,
and it was dark between seven and eight in
the evening, now.

"If my mountain friend reaches Aberogwin
to-night, through all this mist and darkness,"
said he, "he has powers of judgment
strangely at variance with his bulldog phy-
siognomy. I would give sixpence to see
him blundering on now !"

Walking into the village at a pace more
leisurely, let us leave Stephen Speckland for
a while. Many chapters hence and farther
away in our story we shall meet him again in

different scenes, with different characters round him. The progress of our narrative takes us back to Matthew Davis's cottage, wherein an imp of mischief is biding its time amongst the gilt-edged leaves of Bessy Calverton's fairy book.

CHAPTER VI.

THE FAIRY BOOK.

IT was five o'clock on the morning of the day following the departure of Stephen Speckland from Aberogwin. The day was still dark and sombre, the mist still hung half down the mountains, and the rain fell at intervals suddenly and fiercely. The lake and stream had swollen in the night, and the fall near the torrent-path was so heavy that Bessy could hear its roaring as she softly descended the stairs at the early hour to which we have alluded.

Bessy Calverton had risen early to have a

long spell at her fairy book, before lighting
the fire for the morning, the usual task that
was allotted her. She was anxious to begin
those stories, the coloured pictures of which
she had gloated over after parting with the
giver. No one was to know a word of her
fairy book, of the priceless treasure that bewildered and charmed her; that she thought
must be true, because it was in such a beautiful book, with gilt edges.

She lighted the fire, gave a hasty dust to
the room—a regular housemaid's dust when
it's her Monday out!—and sat herself on the
rug, to pore over " Beauty and the Beast,"
before her uncle came down, with his tiresome
morning prayers!

And in the whirl of incident throbbing
throughout that story, Bessy forgot time and
place, the rapid ticking of the American clock
in the corner, even the pattering down stairs
of her agile uncle's feet; and that uncle entering the parlour, stood aghast at the

spectacle of the fire out, the kettle cold and unsteaming, and Bessy coiled on the hearth-rug, with the book in her lap, both her hands to her temples, and her black glossy hair ruffled up over her ears.

Matthew Davis advanced on tiptoe towards Bessy, and looked over her shoulder at the book, like the evil genius of all the fairies in Christendom.

Bessy read on, unobservant of a watcher, and oblivious to passing events and the danger threatening her favourite authors, till a long arm was stretched across her shoulder, and a claw-like hand made a dash at the book and secured it.

Bessy gave a scream of affright, and leaped to her feet, then sunk back on a little stool that was in the corner, at the sight of the livid face of her uncle, and the passionate shaking hand that held the book aloft.

"Where—where did this book come from? —this frightful book?" he added, giving a glance at the nature of the contents as he held it above his head.

"Mr.—Mr. Speckland."

"He—he gave you this, and said nothing concerning it to us? Bessy, I don't believe it. You have stolen the money somehow, and bought the book of a pedlar: Bessy, you know you have."

"I know I haven't!" screamed Bessy, springing to her feet, and jumping once or twice with passion. "You have no right to call me a thief! I'm not a thief—I never was!"

"This book——"

"Give it me! It's not yours, uncle—it was given me as a keepsake!" and Bessy made a leap upwards, and would have reached it had not her irritable uncle boxed her ears with it, and nearly stretched her on the red-tiled floor.

"Keep quiet, Bessy; don't add to disobedience a wilful resistance that can do no

good. Light the fire, and let me think of
what is best for you."

Matthew Davis put the fairy-book in his
pocket, sat down at the table, on which no
breakfast things had been laid, and took his
chin in his hand to consult with. Bessy
glanced for a moment at her uncle's pocket
as if strangely inclined to make a second
snatch in that direction; and then, with the
light quenched from her face, and a sombre
shade of sullenness in its place, she knelt
before the fire-grate, and strove to repair the
evil of omission there.

But Bessy was careless that morning, or
the damp weather stood in the way of the
coals lighting, for her efforts were not rewarded by any satisfactory result, and the
grate was still cold and lifeless when Mary
Davis followed her father downstairs as the
American clock was striking six. Mary
Davis had not been down so late as six
o'clock since the winter time; she had been

thinking at her toilet, and the time had slipped away more rapidly than she had imagined, and becoming alarmed at last, she had hastened to take the head of the breakfast table lest her father should be late in proceeding to the quarries. And at the foot of the stairs she stood and held her breath at a stranger picture than she had witnessed for many years in that cottage: the fire unlighted, and the father in a brown study at the neglected breakfast table.

" What's — what's the meaning of this, father ? " she asked, after recovering her breath. " Bessy, what does all this mean ? "

Bessy made no answer, but continued her efforts at the fire-grate, and Mr. Davis finished his train of thought before he looked towards his daughter.

" It means, Mary, that I have been cruelly deceived," he said at last—" deceived in my hopes concerning that child—in her honesty and candour. Do you know anything of that book ? "

He drew the fairy book from his pocket and pushed it across the table to his daughter, who took it up, regarded it with surprise, and shook her head.

" A book of lies, without an object or a purpose even in its lying, brought here by the fiend, or his agent, to shock us and corrupt that girl."

" Bessy, how did you come by it ? "

" I have told my uncle," answered Bessy, sullenly.

" Tell her this minute, minx ! " screamed Davis, who was not choice in his remarks when the victim of excitement.

But Bessy was growing more rebellious every instant under the hard words that were showered thickly on her, and would not answer, and had to be shaken by the shoulder, and would not answer then, but looked up with a dark defiant stubbornness that made the old man flinch a little—it was so like her mother's face, as he had seen it in the latter days at Aberogwin.

"You won't answer, then, Bessy?" he said, more calmly.

"I have told you, and you won't believe me."

"She says Mr. Speckland gave it her—a five-shilling book if it's a penny one—as if Mr. Speckland had money enough to fool away on such a work as this!"

He snatched it from his daughter's hand and banged it on the floor, and Bessy gave a little cry of rage again. As the book fell, it opened at the title-page, across the top of which was scrawled some very bad hand-writing, which the single eye of Matthew Davis was not slow to detect. Once again the book in the overlooker's hand, and the hand-writing under critical inspection—"*Bessy Calverton, the gift of a friend and a wanderer, S. S.*"

" Great heaven! what a man!" exclaimed the uncle; " and I have harboured him in my house, and he has eaten and drunk of my best, and sat at my table, and I have been a father to him. He made six shillings a week difference in my housekeeping, and this is his reward. The serpent was warmed at my hearth, and it has stung me. See the trail that is left to pollute us !"

And smack went the volume on the tiles again, and went sliding towards the door. Every fall of that book, bandied from father to daughter, and pitched mercilessly about, sunk to Bessy's heart. They might think it a bad book—the worst of books—but for the giver's sake they might have been more gentle. Let them call it a bad book if they liked; she would hold to her own opinion, for she had found no harm in it, and she did not believe Stephen Speckland would have given it her, had there been a wrong thought in its pages. An hour ago, in fairy land, she had never been so happy—and now she had never felt so truly wretched. If they took the book away from her she would never forgive them!

Presently the book was in Matthew Davis's hands again, who growing tired of playing at ball with it, dropped it once more to the depths of his pocket. Mary Davis, scared and shocked, went about the housekeeping duties; and Bessy lighted the fire, made the kettle boil, and laid the breakfast things, with a lowering countenance which Matthew Davis watched for some time in silence : he was sorry it expressed no shame, or contrition, or anxiety, only that dogged firmness which was visible on his own at times, but which he did not care to see on anybody else's.

"I hope you are sorry, Bessy," he said at last. "I hope you are going to tell me so before I go away this morning."

" Sorry for what?" was the short answer.

" For keeping such a gift a secret from us ; for reading such a book."

" He told me to say nothing about it; he said reading it would do no harm."

" He taught you to be deceitful!" cried Davis, " and you obeyed him. And oh! my God, bear me witness how I have striven to teach her to be truthful, and she has scorned my efforts !"

Bessy coloured, and bit her lip, and stamped once upon the floor, in her impetuosity; this was false argument, an ungenerous contrast, but she was not old enough to reason with the speaker. She would say no more; she had better keep her tongue still just at present; it was an unruly member, and, despite all effort, only made matters worse.

Breakfast began, and Mr. Davis, who was behind time and would be fined sixpence, was necessarily sharp in his manner. Mary had not much to say for or against; she seldom had in her father's presence. Bessy knew she postponed her scoldings and preachings till her father was out of the way, and poured on

the unhappy recipient a double dose of moral
warning and reproof. From Mary Davis's
silence, Bessy augured no comfort after her
father's departure, although Mary looked more
grave than angry at her across the breakfast
table.

But the father was not to depart without a
greater offence to Bessy Calverton's feelings.
His coffee and bread and butter dispatched,
he pushed his chair aside, went to the
fire, stirred it, patted it on the top with the
shovel, stirred it again, took some pains to
make a red cavernous receptacle. Bessy
guessed what was coming; she had wheeled
round her chair, and stood watching these
preparations with a death-like face, and two
nervous hands upon her knees. And when
her uncle moved his one hand to the breast-
pocket of his jacket, she gave a wild scream,
knocked her chair over, and ran towards
him.

Matthew Davis was always quick in

his movements; he had heard the scream and the fall of the chair, and the book was popped quickly into the fire and held down by the shovel.

"You have no right to do that!—you shan't do that—you cruel, wicked uncle!"

She shook him by the shoulder in her passion, and being a powerful girl for her age, she would have tilted him on his back in her excitement, had he not dropped the shovel and made a clutch at the side of the mantelpiece.

"Bessy," he cried, "do you know what you are doing? Bessy, are you going mad?"

"Give me that book; take the book from the fire. It's you who are the thief, not me!"

The old man reeled against the mantelpiece at these fierce words, and glared at his demented niece. All the passion of her nature, long kept down, had suddenly resisted the constraint of years, the moral but hard pressure which had been day after day exerted to suppress it; an uneven if a powerful pressure, which naturally did harm to some portion of that sensitive organization—a child's mind. Bessy was fairly mad for the time, and deaf to all her good angels. She thought not, saw not, cared not. From her uncle she turned to Mary, who had a hand upon her arm, and struck at it as it lay there; she dashed at the fire, and would have thrust both hands into the flames, to snatch the fairies from their perilous position, had not Mary with a shriek flung her arms round the child's waist and dragged her away. Even then Mary would have found it difficult to restrain her, if her father had not come to the rescue and helped to keep her back.

It was a stormy scene for the quiet little Welsh cottage—a strange contrast to the peace and method that generally reigned therein, and seemed to rule its inmates' lives. Father and daughter struggling with the child they had adopted, the breakfast things disarranged, chairs overturned, the shovel on the hearth-rug, the white jacket of the father torn across the shoulder, the book of fairy-tales blazing in the fire.

Bessy was in the garden at last, with her uncle white with passion under the porch.

"There, don't come in here again—do you hear?—don't come in here again until you are sorry for all your wickedness and passion, and can humbly ask the pardon of those who have protected you so long. An hour or two out there may cool you, perhaps."

Mary passed Bessy's dark straw hat over her uncle's shoulder.

"And here's your hat, you bad one!"

Matthew flung the hat into the garden after her; but Bessy was already out of the garden, and running wildly towards the torrent path.

"She'll catch her death of cold this rimy morning," murmured Mary.

"She'll do no such thing," snapped the father; "she'll run herself out of breath, and then cool down, and be sorry for all she has done. Five years ago she had a fit of the devil—less powerful than this, for the evil which I thought we were conquering, Mary, has grown with her growth, and will require the strongest measures to crush out."

He crushed his own hat that Mary gave him in his hand as he spoke, and stuck it on his head disreputably.

"Send her to the quarries with my dinner as usual, Mary."

"But if she—"

"I tell you," he interrupted, petulantly, "that she'll cool down by then."

He had reached the wicket, and Mary had not left the porch, when he came running back again.

"We've forgotten the prayers—we must not let the devil get the mastery like this, if it— if it costs another sixpence."

Matthew and his daughter returned to the room, and Matthew took his place at the

table and went through an extempore prayer
with less fluency and eloquence than usual.
He was cool and collected when he had
finished, however, and all trace of irritation
had vanished from his face when he was proceeding down the garden path again.

At the gate he stood and looked round him
for a moment, but over the green fields in the
vale, or along the tracks that led upwards to
the mountains on which the mists hung so
low and thick that morning, there was no
trace of Bessy.

" She'll cool down by dinner time," he said
again, as if he needed some such assertion to
re-assure him; and then, at his half walk
half trot, he made quick progress down the
sloping path towards the Aberogwin road.

At the bottom he paused again and looked
round a second time. The mists were heavy
that morning indeed; he could scarcely see
the cottage now, and the ragged fringe
of cloud seemed to touch its very roof.

He had not remembered so dense a mist in the summer months for six years now come the twenty-ninth of August — he was a precise man and great in dates.

"She will come home all the sooner on such a day as this," he thought, or at least he tried to think, as he turned and trotted on his way.

CHAPTER VII.

IN THE MIST.

MEANWHILE Bessy Calverton, fearless of mist and dead to all sense of danger, had run along the upward path—or rather track which her uncle's sheep had worn—and paused not to take breath till she had reached the torrent path, and could hear the thundering of the waterfall in the ravine below. Bessy was in the mist now, and invisible to the watchful eyes that were looking from the road of Aberogwin, and from the window above the lattice porch. She felt not the cold or the dampness of the morning; the fierceness of her passion, the

rapidity with which she had coursed up the
hill, had rendered her hot and panting, and
she was only pausing to take breath and then
proceed again.

She had no settled purpose in view, no intention to escape from the home that had sheltered her childhood; no wish, thought, or will
concerning the future. Her one desire was
for a time to fly as far as possible from her
uncle's house, from that hated room where
the fairy book had been burned, and all the
fancies born of it relentlessly extinguished.
Almost unconsciously she followed the route
that Speckland had taken the preceding day,
as rapidly and excitedly as if she had a
visionary hope of overtaking him, and her
best chance of happiness lay in that hope's
fulfilment.

On went Bessy again up the mountain path,
through the blinding mist, her black hair
dishevelled and hung with beads of wet. Had
she looked behind her now, and seen how she

was cut off from the vale, her uncle's cottage, even the mouth of the ravine where she had paused a little while ago, she might have turned and hurried from the thickening vapour that shut her in and hid Aberogwin from her.

Bessy was well acquainted with the mountain paths, and followed almost unconsciously the surest and safest route to the heights. Had her thoughts been more collected, her sense of caution more developed, she might have hesitated on her upward way, and thus have lost herself for hours, or days, or for ever, according to the duration of the mist in which she was enveloped. Bessy's thoughts were so confused and still so intense beneath her fancied injuries, that the time sped on without her having more than a dreamy consciousness of the dangers she was recklessly confronting. It was not till she stood at last on the top of the mountains—till she had walked some distance across the range, and was conscious that the ground rose no more, that she knew the summit was reached, and became suddenly alive to the perilous nature of her position.

Then her indignation evaporated, and a host of fears took possession of her. Bareheaded and alone on the mountain, in the mist and at such an hour, she began to tremble for her safety. Bessy remembered all at once stories of lives lost by travellers, even by shepherds, on the mountain where the mist had caught them unawares, and bewildered them, and led them to the brink of precipices, down which they had fallen, and at the bottom of which their mangled bodies had been found, when the sun had chased the mists away across the sea. She shivered with fear, and looked wildly round her, and turned to retrace her steps. She must descend at once, and hurry home before her long absence alarmed too much the inhabitants of the cottage; if she slipped and fell—one of her wild thoughts came back, and she hugged it to her breast with something of a morbid satisfaction—why, perhaps uncle and cousin Mary would be sorry that they had burned her fairy book and driven her out of doors!

And perhaps the fairies would protect her going down the mountain, if there were any in Wales, where there were no princes or princesses, or sleeping beauties, only naughty girls like the child in the story Stephen Speckland had told her. And she had a choking and a lump in her throat that might be a toad for what she knew of the matter; under existing circumstances it could not very well be set down for a Koh-i-noor of the first water.

The mist was so thick upon the mountains that Bessy had to grope her way, and the uncertainty as to whether she had turned in the right direction or not was beginning to rob her of the little presence of mind remaining—when a loud halloo sounded from a short distance behind her.

" Stop there—man or devil—stop !"

Bessy nearly fell to the ground with affright. A wicked fairy with a stentorian voice was going to whisk her away for a hundred years or so, and leave all the world —that was her uncle and her cousin—ignorant of her whereabouts. She could hear footsteps rapidly advancing—she cowered down to avoid the spring that would be shortly made on her, and the voice exclaimed :—

" A sheep, by God !"

A heavy hand a moment afterwards was on her shoulder.

" No, a child, by all that's holy—stand up, and speak. Do you know the way about here, or are you another unhappy beggar lost in this accursed fog, and have been out all night blundering to and fro, and getting worse off with every step ?"

"I'm not a beggar, sir—I'm from Aberog-win in the vale."

"And you've lost your way?"

"Just—just for a minute, sir. If you won't frighten me, and don't want to hurt me, I think I might find it again, sir. Please don't lean so heavily upon my shoulder."

"All right—take your time. By —— !" and he gave vent to another oath, "how cold and wet and miserable I am! Hungry and dry, and all the brandy gone, and driven to death's door up here. But take your time—don't lose your wits at seeing me."

And he thrust his hands into his trousers pockets and shivered violently. As he stood there Bessy could hear his teeth rattling like a pair of castanets in a *capriccio* movement. Bessy mustered courage enough to regard the stranger. He was close to her side, and she could see that he was a rather tall, thickset man, with a short neck and a moustache, and great ragged whiskers, and a pair of seven-leagued boots on, by the size of them.

" Well, are you better now ?"

" Yes, sir—thank you."

" And do you think you'll know your way down, my pretty dear ?" he asked, insinuatingly; " do you think it's possible, without breaking both our necks, to find this Aberogwin ? "

" We will try, sir."

" I'd rather go back ten miles on the old road if you could put me in the track. I've been so near pitching head first to perdition once or twice in the dark, that I don't care about risking anything even in the daylight —if this cursed glimmer *is* called daylight in these parts."

" I might lose you across the mountains— if we keep to the edge here we must find the track in a moment, sir."

" Keep to the edge, be damned !" cried the man, leaping away from a more dangerous proximity than he had bargained for; "do you think I'm a goat, or a wild Welsh girl, that you bring me to the brink of perdition so coolly. How desperately ill and weak I am to trust a child like this," he muttered.

Bessy had conquered her nervousness. Assured that he was a human being, and comforted by meeting a companion where she had least expected to find one, her native shrewdness and presence of mind speedily returned.

"Have you seen hereabouts a lump of iron-stone, all jagged and twisted, like a man's head?—Llewellyn's head we call it."

"I've seen nothing, girl."

"And have you been up here all night, sir?" asked Bessy.

"Yes."

"Weren't you frightened when the night came on?"

"Perhaps I was—perhaps I wasn't. What a girl you are to talk, instead of looking about

you for this—what's his name's?—head. I shall
die up here after all, if you don't make haste.
I'm a lump of ice, and all my marrow's frozen
—isn't it enough to kill any man to stand
here all night, afraid to walk about lest he go
clean down some thousand feet to the bottom,
and be picked up smashed and done for?
I'm not so sick of life as that."

A boulder looming through the mist, and
Bessy sprang towards it.

"There's Llewellyn's head, sir!"

"That's a head that deserves to be patted!"
cried the man, recovering a certain portion of
his spirits; "that's a—HULLO! where are
you?"

"Here, sir—follow me, sir—I've found the
track."

"Yes, but I hav'n't; don't be in such blarmed
hurry—don't."

Very carefully and gingerly the man put
one foot before another down the steep
descent—very suddenly he came to a full

stop again, and launched a hundred oaths at Bessy, who had gone on again and left him.

"Can't you keep near me," he growled, "instead of rushing on like that? If you do it again I'll pitch you over the side, and chance breaking my neck my own way. Now then."

Bessy's blood curdled at his threats, and she went on her way more slowly and nervously.

"And what made you come up here this morning?" he asked with some curiosity as he walked close behind his little guide.

"I don't know—I went rushing up and up, and didn't care much where I went to."

"Yes, and you go rushing down and down, and don't care much where we shall both go to, seemingly. Can't you walk slower, or is something the matter with you?"

"Uncle burned my fairy book and turned me wicked, sir," cried Bessy, glad of even such a confidant to unbosom her grief and wrongs to.

"I'll buy you another, if you don't get excited," was the wise observation.

"But uncle Davis won't let me read fairy books; he——"

"Hold hard—uncle Davis!"

His hand gripped the child's shoulder, and he stood a moment and panted for breath, as though suddenly exhausted.

"Arn't you well, sir?"

"First-rate, now. And you've an uncle called Davis, eh?"

"Yes, sir."

"Matthew Davis?"

"Yes."

"By ——," and another oath came ringing forth to affright Bessy; "is this a dream, or have my troubles up here turned my brain? Just tell me your name, and finish it. Bessy?"

"Yes, sir—Bessy."

"Bessy Davis, or——Bessy Calverton?"

"Bessy Calverton."

"How thundering odd!" he exclaimed;

then added, after a pause, " but let us talk of this in a place more safe. We're looking grim death in the face still; and he'll make a grab at us yet if we don't keep our eyes open. Do you turn here?"

" Yes."

" You are quite sure you're right?"

" Quite sure now."

The gentleman slipped suddenly to the left, flung himself to the right to preserve his equilibrium, and drove one leg to the knee into a black spongy morass, where he struggled, and swore, and blasphemed, and where every minute Bessy expected the mountain to fall upon him for his impiety.

" Oh! don't talk like that," she cried at last, wringing her hands, " or we shall never get down safe."

" Don't talk like that?" repeated the man when he was on the path again. " It's enough to make anybody talk, and pretty strongly too. A cursed, slippery, stony, boggy

hole as this is—I shall never get down
—I'm dead beat," and he sat down on
the path, and took off his hat and fanned
himself.

"I'm awfully ill," he groaned; "all
night up there and no brandy to speak of, and
the wind and the cold eating into one's bones.
I'm like a worn-out old cab horse. How
far is it now?"

"Three miles, I should think."

The man groaned, drew the brandy flask
from his pocket, and from sheer rage battered
the wicker side of it against the rock until the
glass broke beneath the attack.

"There!" tossing it down the mountain,
"go your way for a false friend and be damned
to you! I wish I could serve all my false
friends out as easily, and be quit of them.
Oh, my bones!"

"Shall we go on, sir?—or shall I leave
you here and send——"

The man jumped to his feet with alacrity.

"Leave *me* here! You'd better think of such a thing!"

The man did not speak again for some time. He kept his hand on the shoulder of Bessy, of whom he was still distrustful, and groaned and ground his teeth, and walked with difficulty. He was evidently suffering from exhaustion, and the effort to descend was almost beyond his strength, although he taxed it to the utmost, and clung to the child as his only hope of salvation from his peril.

"What's that noise, girl?" he asked, after more than an hour's descent in silence.

"The Aberogwin fall. It falls from the mountain seventy feet, and then runs along the torrent path to the stream."

"Are we likely to fall into it?" he asked, nervously.

"Oh, no, sir."

"It was that cursed water above the fall that I stepped into fifty times last night. Be it cursed for ever and ever!"

" Oh, sir ! "

" Be it—hold hard again ! "

His other hand fell on Bessy's shoulder, and he held her up, and swayed with her once or twice, and then sat down again.

" Let us have another rest. What a baby I am, to want rest while this child here shames me with her strength. Shan't we soon be out of the mist now ? "

" In half an hour, or less, I hope."

" With just a sight of something like earth or heaven, and a man might pluck up courage and make a dash downwards. My soul for a glass of brandy, now—my soul to sixpence that you have brought me the wrong way ? "

" We are safe, sir, now."

" Yes, it looks like it," said the man, ironically ; " it looks—what's that ? Hark ! some one shouting."

Bessy and her companion listened again. There was a faint shout from below, which was repeated a second time, and which was caught up suddenly by the exhausted traveller at Bessy's side, who roared and shouted and yelled with all the power left him.

" I can see a light—two lights!" he cried, springing to his feet again. " Bessy Calverton, we are saved, you and I, from kingdom come. Upon my soul, I'd say my prayers, if I knew any!"

The man sat and answered the shouts, and watched the lights which wound round about the mountain, and seemed to lose considerable time in going backwards and forwards as the track necessitated.

" What a place !" muttered the man, with an impatient stamp of the foot—" what a black, cursed place it is! and what a time they take to reach a man that's famished, frozen, and half dead. If they have only got some brandy for a man who—where the devil have the lights gone ? "

" They have only turned the curve by the dark lake."

" Let us be moving towards them, then ; I'm strong again now, girl. There is hope and good luck coming to meet us, and take us to fire, and food, and brandy. May the man be in Paradise who invented brandy ! Hallo, there ! hallo ! "

The man's spirits had flashed up brighter than they had been hitherto, and he continued his vociferations till the lights advanced nearer and nearer—till three dusky figures, two of them in white blouses and bearing lanterns, and one of them in a jacket torn at the shoulder, turned the curve of the path and were within twenty yards of them.

" Who's there ?—Bessy Calverton ? "

" Yes—Bessy Calverton ! " shouted the man back.

The slightest figure of the three, who had preceded the others, ran towards them, and clasped Bessy with one arm.

" Thank God I've found you, Bessy. How could you be so wild and foolish as to ascend

the mountain in this mist? I had a fear of
it, and I came back again and searched for
you; and the Lord be praised for all his mercies—here you are!"

"And, the Lord be praised, here *you* are,
Matthew Davis. Where's the brandy?"

"Bessy, who's this?"

"Bessy don't know so well as you do, mayhap, if you'll take the trouble to look a little
closer. Where's the brandy?"

One of the quarrymen who had accompanied Davis, and brought brandy with him in
case it were needed, held out a bottle to the
man, and said something in Welsh. The man
snatched at the bottle and drank off the contents, with no regard for her who had brought
him down safe, and was nearly as cold and
exhausted as himself.

"Ha!" with a smack of his lips, "that's
acceptable, but weak. Well, Matthew Davis,
no welcome for so old a friend?"

Matthew Davis took the lantern from the

hands of the man at his side, and held it towards the speaker. The light fell full on the
dark face, the thick sensual features, the burly
form of him who had been benighted.

"Not—not Richard Calverton?" gasped
the old man.

"Ay, Richard Calverton—honest Dick,
as everybody calls him. This is a happy
meeting, Davis!"

Davis made no reply, but put his one arm
round the child, as though he shielded her
from danger by that movement, and walked
with her down the mountain path, the quarrymen and Richard Calverton following slowly
in the rear.

CHAPTER VIII.

" HONEST DICK."

RICHARD CALVERTON followed uncle and niece
to the cottage without intruding his conversation, where it was possibly undesired. Matthew Davis was thoughtfnl, Bessy was silent,
and the two quarrymen spoke nothing but
Welsh: so much the better—Mr. Calverton
was too tired to argue. He had flung a
bomb-shell at the head of Davis by the announcement of his name ; let him recover
that surprise, and harass himself as to the
reasons for his appearance there, until he,

Dick Calverton of honest memory, chose further to enlighten him.

From the mist into the drizzling rain; from the barren rocky earth to close velvety herbage that sprang beneath the foot; from the herbage to the cottage of Matthew Davis, beneath the porch of which pale Mary Davis watched, in much the same place and position as she had watched some hours ago when her father departed for the quarries.

Richard Calverton broke into a staggering kind of trot when he reached the gate of the cottage; started in advance of the party, pushed past Mary Davis, and tumbled himself on to a little hard sofa that was placed beneath the broad fuschia-filled window-recess.

"Don't let anybody speak to me; ask me to eat, or drink, or do anything but sleep, or it'll be the worse for them. Just bear that in mind all of you, for honest Dick is savage when his back's up!"

It is doubtful if any one would have thought of intruding on Richard Calverton, or offering him any particular attention if this injunction had not been delivered, and it is almost certain he was welcome to keep quiet till doomsday. The better for all parties, perhaps, if he could remain in a quiescent state till that indefinite period.

He was asleep in an instant, and snoring with forty horse power. He had fallen asleep on his back, too, and presented about as ugly an appearance in that position as it was possible to imagine. In the light that cast upon him a certain greenish hue as it filtered through the many plants on the inner sill, he was a less attractive object than even in the mist, for there had been no beauties to conceal, and all his indifferent traits of form and feature were now fully developed. To do him justice, it is just possible that Richard Calverton in more becoming attire—say full dressed in a swallow-

tailed coat and white choker—would have
been a few degrees more presentable ; for fine
feathers, as well as fine manners, go a great
way to make a man. Admirable Crichton,
or Sir Charles Grandison, or the hero of that
last novel you and I dozed over, dear reader
—the saints preserve this from a similar indignity !—might have been taken for a suspicious character, after wandering all night on
the mountains, slipping here and there, and
adding layer after layer of mud to his boots
and legs, and getting his hat smashed, and
working the sailor's knot of a handsome
bird's-eye kerchief round to the back of his
neck. In Wales he would have been something
to wonder at ; in London, if he had lingered
too long by the posts at the corners of the
streets, he would have received every attention from Policeman 205, and told to move
on, and got shoved.

So the reader, as well as the Davises and
Bessy Calverton, is seeing Richard Calverton

under great disadvantages—in his Sunday best he might look a different man. Take him for all in all, as he lies there, and the verdict is "A vagabond"—·and a very fair verdict too.

Mary glanced from the broad bull-dog face to the muddy clothes and boots which reposing on her clean chintz covering, revolted her sense of propriety, and then looked at her father for an explanation.

"He's one who has a certain right here," said Matthew Davis, reading her looks aright; "one whom I cannot forbid my house without danger to myself, and perhaps cruel harm to Bessy."

"Has he been here before—he seemed to know the room?"

"Eighteen years ago, when your mother was living, and I had a sister I respected."

"Is he—is he—"

The old man raised a finger and pointed

to Bessy. Mary Davis looked from Bessy to the sleeping man with horror, then crossed to her father, and bent her head close down to his.

" Yes—*her* father ! " whispered Davis.

" Come back ? "

" As if from the grave—as if from some bad world of which you and I know nothing, Mary. The Lord have mercy on all of us ! "

"I—I think I must lie down a little while," murmured Bessy, who had been seeking support against the inner side of the door.

" Take her to her room and see to her," said Matthew Davis ; " she's ill !—Bessy, we won't say anything more about that dreadful book."

" It's not a dreadful book," murmured Bessy.

" Stubborn as a rock," groaned Matthew Davis ; " take her to her room, Mary ; there's

brandy in my cupboard—give her some before she goes to bed."

Mary and Bessy went upstairs ; and
Matthew Davis, giving up all thought of his
superintendency at the quarries that day,
drew a stool before the fire, and sat down
thereon, looking like a very plain little boy
who was stopping from school because he
was poorly and had taken medicine. The
quarrymen had departed ; the American clock
was indicating two ; save the light tread
of Mary's feet above stairs, the only sounds
were the dripping of water from the eaves,
and the noisy snoring of this Richard Calverton. Not only snoring, but snorting, and
gurgling, and choking, and making a hundred
different noises not too pleasant to sit and
listen to. Once or twice Matthew Davis
turned his head, and regarded the sleeper,
with the place where the eyebrows once were
falling over the good and the bad eye, in an
unchristianlike and unmethodistical scowl. In

the sleeper on the sofa he saw his bitterest enemy; the villain who, when he was better looking, and had a claim to a rough kind of handsomeness, had stolen his sister's heart and dragged her down to ruin; the burly ruffian who now came like a blight again within the cottage, as if to work a second mischief greater than the first. This man, a disgrace to civilized life—one who, by a few words, could give his neighbours food to speculate upon for the rest of their lives—a man who, by a breath, might blast his own good name for ever, and blazon out that secret which he had kept so close for many years. He could find it in his heart to curse him sleeping there : to pray he might never wake again, but die with all his sins thick on him, in his brutal ignorance and unconversion.

Matthew Davis was shivering with his cruel thoughts, when Mary silently took her place by his side.

" Bessy is asleep."

" Poor wilful girl.   Fearing what the future
has in store for her, we can but shrink before it, and, and—we may as well say forgiveness for all that has happened this day,
Mary."

" Do you think that Richard Calverton—"

" Hush! don't mention his name ; he might
wake and wish to know what we have to say
against him."

" You will have some dinner, father ?"

Matthew Davis shook his head. He required no dinner ; he only wished to be left
to his reverie before the hollow burning fire.
And Mary kept him company ; for she was
too troubled to think of her own dinner with
the shadow of coming events heavy on the
hearth of Davis.

So the afternoon passed, and the day, that
had had no sun to brighten it, seemed to close
in earlier than usual, and bring the darkness
speedily upon them.   Mary had set the tea-
things by that time, and put some cold meat

on the table, and stolen upstairs to find Bessy
still asleep, and returned again to the fireside
to wait the waking up of Richard Calverton.

It was nine o'clock when he woke up with
a vengeance, and rolled off the sofa on to his
hands and knees, from which he scrambled up
with an oath, lumped down again in a sitting
posture, and stared before him stupidly.

"Thought I was off the mountain, by
Gord!" he exclaimed; "let me see now?
Whereabouts is this?—Matthew Davis's cottage, and the Methodist imp himself croning
there by the chimney corner, and keeping
all the warmth from a man who's dying of
cold. Davis," he bawled, "where's the girl?"

"Asleep—don't make such a noise."

"Oh! asleep is she; well, how long are
we to sit in the dark and catch the horrors?"

"We seldom have more light here than the
fire affords," said Mary.

"Oh, are *you* there? Miss Methodist Davis,
I suppose?—proud of the introduction the

old gentleman hasn't been polite enough to make," said he. " Well, let us have a light for a change."

Matthew nodded to his daughter, and a light was soon on the table, and brightening the scene. Calverton sat and watched the operations till the light more clearly brought into relief the cold meat, when he made a plunge towards it, seized the knife and fork, and commenced a ravenous attack.

" No—beer, brandy, rum, gin, anything but slosh," he muttered, as Mary placed a cup of tea at his side, "it's just like you country set of people; so temperate!"

" Will you say grace, father?"

Matthew Davis rose and delivered his grace at the usual length, whilst Richard Calverton gobbled his bread and meat, rolling his eyes now and then from father to daughter, but not breaking on their prayers with his remarks.

The grace, earnestly delivered as it was, seemed to check one or two speeches that hovered on his thick lips, and he ate his food with a wry face or two, but made no comment. Let the old chap pray; it didn't hurt him, and perhaps such cant pleased such kinds of critters!

When Richard Calverton had finished all the meat in the dish, to the silent dismay of Matthew Davis, he said,

"We may as well commence business at once, Davis. I suppose it's not very hard to guess why I have come here?"

"I am a bad hand at guessing."

"I've come for the girl."

Davis groaned, and Davis's daughter tightened her lips and looked with alarm at the speaker.

"It has been very kind of you to take care of her so long, whilst I was abroad trying for a fortune that I never got. I'm obliged to you, and there's an end of it; but I want the girl—she'll be of use, and I've come two hundred odd miles to fetch her."

"If you, her father, have any consideration for the girl—one honest wish to save her soul from being utterly cast away—you will let her stay with us. I ask you, Richard Calverton, for your own sake, as well as mine and hers, to leave her to our care."

"If you were to talk to me till morning— if you were to preach at me, and pitch all your bible nonsense at me, and go down on your knees both of you, and kiss these dirty paws of mine, I'd have the girl away. I'm her father, and the law's on my side. Odd and sing'lar to have the law to back Dick Calverton; but there it is plain, and—my daughter's wanted!"

The dirty paw to which he had alluded fell with a heavy bang upon the tea-board, and startled the hearts for a moment into the throats of his listeners. Fiercely resolute in his determination, they knew there was no power on their side to balk him in his will, and that all effort to dissuade him would be useless. They sat and listened patiently.

" Just look here. I'm a father, with a father's feelings ; there's comfort for a man in his declining years from that child, and that child I must have. I'm in business now, and any girl of her age is handy in a business. Every help saves money—and you know what saving money is, old Davis?"

" Poor girl—poor girl!"

" What is she a poor girl for? Am I such a reprobate and ruffian and Blue Beard? Ain't I honest Dick?" he added, with a grin.

" You say so."

" It's my natural title—it was given me years ago by grateful friends. There's no one can point to a spot upon me and say that's a black spot—a gaol spot that won't burn out or wash clean, do what you will. In all my life I've never seen the inside of a prison, felt the touch of a policeman on my arm, or the click of a handcuff on my wrists. I've been the luckiest—the honestest fellow down White-

chapel. There's not a soul alive can say
Dick Calverton did this or that, and had six
months or years for it! What does such a
man as you, whose sister died in gaol, mean
by calling out 'poor girl?' Do you taunt a
man for marrying in a doubtful family?"

"Stop there!" cried Davis, leaping to his
feet, and leaning across the table with his
clenched hand extended; "stop there, Calverton!"

The man laughed scornfully.

"Well, I don't want to rile you and make
things more uncomfortable than they really
are. Bottle up that pucker, and tell me if
you can raise a hand to balk an honest man's
intention?"

"I am powerless to stop you—you are her
father—more's the pity!"

"Then to-morrow I'll call for her," said
he rising and shaking himself like a dog.
"I needn't fear you'll spirit her away with
actions for damages before that one eye of

yourn. You wouldn't care to fork out your money for that purpose perhaps, or get locked up like—like many an unfortunate person has before you!" he added, after a pause.

" Are you going to Penberriog to-night?" asked Matthew Davis, nervously.

Objectionable visitor as this ruffian might be at the cottage, the prudent man, jealous of his good name, would have preferred him in his house, oaths and all, to his getting drunk in the parlour of the " Llewellyn Arms," and blurting out his relationship with that reck-lessness that seemed to care for nothing, and stand for nothing in his way, relating in his cups the cruel story of a family's dishonour to the wondering customers that might be there. Possibly evoking a quarrel by his personalities, and fighting the matter out in the peaceful streets, where there were fifteen hundred quarrymen and two policemen. Richard Calverton was a shrewd man—the reader may possibly think so, to have pre-

served his honesty intact for so many years—
he read all that was passing in the mind of
Matthew Davis.

"Trust me with my tongue, old fellow,"
he answered; "I'll do you no harm; no
oyster shall be closer in his shell than Richard
Calverton in his. The healthy constitution
with which Providence has blest me, has
enabled me to shake off the ill effects of
mountain air and late hours, and no brandy—
I can march on to Penberriog manfully, and
walk off the effects of that weak tea of yours.
Ugh!" and he shuddered visibly at the re-
collection.

Calverton took his shabby hat from the
sofa, and stuck it in true Whitechapel fashion
over his eyes, giving himself rather more of a
hang-dog appearance than ever.

"'To-morrow, and to-morrow, and to-
morrow,' as I heard a fellow say once at the
play, and then I come here with the early
lark for Bessy. With your good leave, I'll

just see if she's asleep. A father's feelings—
a father's feelings, Miss Davis!" he said, as she
sprang up, and seemed for a moment to have
an intention of intercepting his progress.

If she had had such an intention she abandoned it, and allowed him to proceed heavily
to the upper story, his clumsy feet kicking each
stair as he ascended it. But Bessy Calverton
slept soundly—worn out with fatigue, there
were no noises round her that had power to
waken her. Mary Davis held the light above
her head, as Calverton went to the bedside,
and looked down upon his daughter.

If there were any parental feelings existent
in that broad breast, passing under that
knotted lumpy forehead, he kept them buried
deep and gave no sign. He might have been
looking at a statue, or at uncle Davis's bible,
for all the interest evinced in his bloodshot
eyes.

" She's a good-looking lass," he remarked;
" a girl with pluck in her too, or she would

have never come up the mountain in that cursed mist. What's that on the mantelpiece, governor?"

His wandering glance had alighted on the brandy bottle which Matthew had ordered to be brought out for Bessy.

"A mixture," was the evasive answer of Matthew Davis; for brandy was dear in Wales, and one had to go a mile and a half to procure it.

"I hate mixtures, especially country ones!"

"It's good for a cold," said Davis, with an artful pretence of pressing the matter on Mr. Calverton's attention.

"Keep it," growled Calverton, as he turned to descend; "I'll find something better for a cold than that stuff in Penberriog—something that will work out this infernal screwing at my joints. I haven't quite got rid of it, after all."

"As you please," said Matthew, repressing

a grim twitch, as he followed him down stairs. In all his trouble at the man's appearance, and the object for which his black shadow had fallen across his path, he could not help chuckling inwardly at saving his brandy and stealing a march on honest Richard Calverton.

Honest Dick was under the porch at last, straightening his limbs a little, and giving vent to one or two groans, and a light sprinkling of oaths.

"Not ship-shape yet. What a black night for honest men like me to be abroad."

"Do you know the way?"

"Matthew Davis, I never forget. Up the mountains, where I had never been before, I lost my way—down the mountain here to Penberriog is an old road, known to me in the courting days, when you and I had a little quarrel. I never forget my quarrels any more than my roads—I've a lumber-room of old grievances here," tapping his forehead. "Good night."

"If there's a score marked up here against any one," tapping his forehead again, "I work it off—I take my own good time, but—Matthew Davis"—and the hand went from his forehead to the old man's arm—"I never forget!"

Davis shivered under the man's touch, and drew back a step.

"You understand—good night to you."

"Good night."

The door closed, and Richard Calverton, like one familiar with his way, went along the garden, and down the path to the Aberogwin road. He talked to himself as he walked onwards, stumbling now and then over the loose stones that lay in his path, and anathematizing them for getting there. He never forgot—he had said, and to hear the deep intensity of hate with which he had spoken, Matthew Davis could not doubt it. Was there no other object save paining that old man, who had been the guardian of his child for many years, that brought him two hundred miles from home?

CHAPTER IX.

PARTINGS.

THERE was no help for it. Bessy Calverton
must leave the peaceful retreat of Aberogwin;
there was no power to keep her there. Matthew Davis felt that all the efforts of eight
years would be dashed down in as many
weeks, by him who had suddenly stalked as
from the grave with his indisputable claims.
It was not even possible to delay the giving
up of the child for a week or two, without
delay bringing an action and costs. And
actions and costs were things that Matthew
Davis particularly objected to.

Bessy Calverton woke early the next morning to find some one kneeling at the side of her bed. She reached out a hand and placed it on the light braids of Mary Davis.

" Is that you, Mary ?"

" Yes—it is I, dear. How long have you been awake ?"

" Only a minute. I suppose you are very angry with me still ?"

" No—no, not angry."

" But you think it *was* very wicked to read that fairy book ! Why should you know so much better than Mr. Speckland what is good for people ?"

" The reading might not have been a very great crime, although unprofitable and wasteful reading which distracts the mind from higher thoughts. I—I don't think it was so very wrong, and perhaps father was a little hard, Bessy. But then, dear, you were so secret over it—kept the book from all your best friends."

"You would have taken it away from me —and it was a gift that I was to be careful over, and to prize. And he burnt it—oh! Mary, he burnt it and had no mercy!"

The child sat up in bed, with her old excited face; but Mary flung her arms round her, and caught her to her breast.

"You must not feel anger in your heart against him now, Bessy. You must set all that aside, as he has done, for the few hours more in which you have to stay with us. For you are going away, my dear—you are going away!"

Bessy raised her dark wondering eyes and looked at Mary's face. It was so new and agitated a face, and it had always been so grave and quiet, and she spoke in so kind a tone, too—she who did not always speak kindly, but snapped her up and scolded.

"Going away!"

Bessy thought it was all through the fairy book, till the sudden remembrance of the man she had encountered in the mist awakened a new fear.

"That man, Mary?—I heard him say his name was Calverton. Who can it be that has a name like mine?"

"Your father."

Bessy looked bewildered, then buried her head in Mary's bosom again, and trembled very much. She had heard so little of her father, only a few pressing questions at an age more early had elicited the fact from her uncle that her father was abroad and likely to remain there; and the sterner truth, that it was better for her in this world and the next. And now the father had stalked into the waking life, and she had seen him, and cowered before him, and heard strange awful words escape his lips. She forgot all about her fairy book then, and, clinging closer to Mary, cried—

"Oh, don't let him take me away!—ask uncle not to let him!"

"My dear Bessy, there is no help for us. He *is* your father, and we have no right to hold you back when he asserts a claim; and —and—dear, he may be a better father than you fancy. You must try to love him and obey him, and he will love you again, I think —I hope! Why, he must love you even now, Bessy, or he wouldn't have come so far to fetch you home."

"I don't want him to love me!" cried Bessy, energetically.

"I woke early this morning before the light, to pack away a few things of yours in a bundle, which is on the drawers there, dear. There's a little book, too—a present of mine, and a substitute for the fairies. You must promise me to read it very often."

Bessy promised.

"In the midst of evil and temptation fly to it, and find your comfort. When the evil spirits whisper in your ear, clasp it to your heart and fear not; open its pages and read therein the lesson of endurance, firmness, faith. Oh! Bessy, I have often tired you with my preachings, but they *were* all for your good! You will remember this last little sermon of mine, for your cousin's sake, won't you?"

"I will never forget you, Mary."

Mary felt what power of affection was evinced by the pressure of those young arms; felt at that moment what love she had kept back by her austere manners, and where the secret to the child's best feelings lay. Give her the eight years over again, and that child to work with, and she would not think her love a weakness, or the child's impulsive nature something to be ever checked.

"Yours will be a different world now—a crowded world, with many faces round you and not many friends; for friends of the true stamp are very scarce, my dear. You will fight your way and pray to your God, and in the little house upon the mountain side there shall be prayers rising up to heaven for you whilst I live!"

Mary struggled with her firmness, but her voice broke and became harsh, and the tears welled over. She was but a young woman, whose feelings had been walled in and subdued by asceticism; but there are times when the heart must open, and the feelings must rise and leap the stone boundary of prejudice —and this was one. Mary had known no real grief since her mother died, and had had little to sway her emotions and disturb her. Shut in the cottage with a hard and callous father, and seeing but in him and the Methodist preacher, who banged the bible every Sunday with his double fist, and bellowed out his prayers, a model to be copied, she had progressed in her sombre way, and gradually ossified.

Bessy was heart-broken now. She had been in doubt all her life if there were anybody to love her, and now her discovery was made in the last hours of separation—if separation it were to be; she would see her father, and tell him how happy she was, and how hard it would be to leave her uncle's home. It was a new Bessy Calverton at the breakfast-table; she walked straight to her uncle and kissed him, and said she was sorry for all that had happened yesterday; and Matthew rested his hand on her head, and prayed to God to bless her in her darker pilgrimage.

The breakfast table was not cleared when the latch clicked, and Richard Calverton appeared in the parlour.

" Good morning to you all. Well, Bessy, haven't you a kiss for your poor father? "

Bessy went timidly towards him, and raised her face, and he made a great display of his affection by a noisy kiss that frightened her. He rested his heavy hand upon her shoulder, and shook her in his boisterous humour.

"A plucky girl, who saved my life, and deserves the best of everything in this world, and she shall have it. Silks and satins and jewels, and a fine house to live in some day, and a—and a library of fairy books all with coloured pictures ! "

"The voice of the tempter," groaned Matthew.

"The voice of an affectionate father, old dead-and-alive ! " cried Calverton—" of one who will take care of her, and bring her up a credit to him. There, Bessy, go and put your bonnet on."

"If you please, I should like to say a few words to you in the garden."

"Hallo ! who's put you up to that fly ? "

"What fly, sir ? "

"Who's been giving you a lesson to learn so early in the morning, to get over honest Dick ? Ah ! " with a conceited roll of his head, "it *must* be early in the morning,

Bessy, to get over your innocent father. Come, put your bonnet on, and let me see if you know your lesson perfect."

Bessy Calverton seized her straw hat, followed her father into the garden, and closed the parlour-door behind her. Her father walked direct to the wicket, where he waited for her.

"Now, of course you don't want to leave dear uncle and dear Mary—and they've been very good to you, and you're a comfort to them, and you'll never be happy anywhere else—and all that palaver. That's it, ain't it?"

"Yes, yes, sir—but—"

"But it's no good talking, Bessy. I'm like that cursed big mountain there, hard and stony, and no words sink into me. I've made my mind up, girl," he said, "and when that's once made up, perhaps a thunderbolt might change it—nothing softer. I daresay they've been pitching it strong enough against me—don't believe 'em. You'll be happy enough—there's nothing in the whole wide world to keep a girl like you from being happy. Lots of company, singing, evening parties, cakes, ginger beer, and brandy balls. And dolls!" he said, suddenly adding that last important item to his list of temptations.

But Bessy was disconsolate, and the voice of this black-whiskered tempter charmed not.

"You've had pretty teaching, Bessy, to be dragged up in this bearish fashion. By George! it's not honest teaching that sets a child against her father. Don't you want to love your father—to see your mother—"

"My mother!" screamed Bessy.

"Ah, your new mother, who'll be a comfort to you—and your real elder sister, that's been crying to see you—oh! ever so long."

"But have I really an elder sister, sir?"

"You have—four years older than yourself—such a pretty sister, and her name's

Charlotte.   We shall be the playfullest
family in Whitechapel.   Bessy and Lotty,
and Dicky—I'm Dicky ! "

There did not seem much play in him, and the
child felt greater terror the more she considered her new life.   For it was a strange
life, and full of wonders.   A new mother,
and a sister that she had never seen—she
prayed they might be better than this father !
She was turning to go back and tell Mary
she had failed in her efforts, when her father
caught her by the arm.

" Where are you going ? "

" To Mary."

" Never no more.   Nor to uncle, nor to
anybody.   You are going back to London
with me, and they shan't put any more last
words into your head and make you quite
undutiful.   You've got your hat on—I'll buy
you a shawl at Penberriog—there's a car I've
hired at the bottom of the hill, waiting to
take us on—and you'll come on now ! "

"Oh! no, no!" screamed Bessy, making an effort to wrench her arm from her father; "not now. I must see and speak with them again—you must let me go!"

"Not if I know it."

"There's my bundle—and they haven't bidden me good-bye."

"We wont have their bundle, and their good-byes may be damned."

"But I will not go away like this!" screamed Bessy; and as her father gave her a jerk by the arm, she clung to the gate and resisted his attempts to move her.

Uncle and cousin from the window saw the struggle, and hastened down the garden path to end it. Old Matthew Davis, fairly roused, spoke forth his mind boldly, and cowed by his torrent of words the bully who stood facing him.

"Like Richard Calverton to the last, and unlike all other men, I believe, that were ever made in God's image. Cruel, ungrate-

ful, selfish, and despicable, with not one
common thought of gratitude or word of
thanks for the many years that I have kept
your child from harm, and striven to make
her good, and teach her right.   An unchristian coward, with power only to work
evil, and sparing not that power on your innocent child.   The vengeance of your God
will follow that brutal effort to drag her
down to ruin—mark me!"

"Complimentary," growled Calverton, "if
I could understand it."

"Will you not let the child say good-bye
to us?" asked Mary; "receive the little
things we have packed up for her?"

"There, go and say good-bye, and make
your best bow—and look sharp about it,"
said he, thrusting his hands in his trousers
pockets, and sauntering a few paces down
the path.

Bessy ran to her cousin and clasped her
round the neck.   She did not say "good-

bye," her heart was too full for words. From her cousin to her uncle, and then back to her cousin again, whose heart she had that morning only begun to read aright. Mary thrust the bundle in her arms, and whispered another blessing over her, and then let her go —never to return!

From that time never to return. The path that seemed so straight—winding ever by the purple mountains and the rushing stream, or under the grassy slope from which the larches sprang so green and straight and pointed heavenwards—turned sharply, suddenly from that quiet home, and wound along the deeper, steeper way, the end of which was lost in the surging crowd of troubled human life. Such sudden changes happen to more homes than Matthew Davis's—to more lives than Bessy Calverton's: the sunshine on the rest of many wayfarers for a little while, and the blue sky shadowless above them—and then the sudden blight across the landscape, and the tiny figures dotting it—units in the great mysterious sum God works by myriads —sinking here and there, or struggling upwards still to the brighter light and the better times that have been swept away from them.

CHAPTER X.

THE HOMEWARD JOURNEY.

THE horse and car that waited in the Aberogwin road for Richard Calverton and daughter
was now rattling on its way, making the distance greater every moment between it and
the little cottage Bessy had called home.
Richard Calverton sat with his hands in his
pockets, in a corner of the open car, his back
screwed round as much as possible against
the back of the driver, for comfort's sake and
ease. He had nothing more to say to Bessy,
even had she been conversationally inclined;
it was a brisk morning for August, and never

having properly regained the circulation of
his blood, he was soon blue with cold, and
inclined to recommence the castanet movement to which Bessy had first listened in the
mist.

Bessy was not disposed for dialogue ; having
recovered the first outburst of passionate grief
which had followed her departure from the
cottage, she sat silent and stolid, nursing the
bundle to which her father had offered no
further objection to her taking away. " He
was independent of all Methodists," he had
said, with the old important roll of his head,
as Bessy had mounted the car ; " he had laid
by a little money, and had opened a good
business, and he could buy his daughter all
she wanted to wear, without coming to Wales
for charity. Let her keep the bundle if she
liked though—she would find he wasn't a
hard father."

On rattled the car, through Penberriog, a
large silent village, at that hour with only

children playing about the roads—past the Penberriog quarries, which accounted for the village silence, and where a thousand odd men were working up the mountain's face, and the picks and hammers went on unceasingly, and the sharp peculiar crack were followed by the puff of curling smoke and the rattling down of slates. Along the mountain road, through more silent villages, with an old woman in a hat perhaps coming to the door to see them pass, and pausing only at the inns, where Richard Calverton filled his brandy-flask, and bought biscuits now and then for Bessy. In a town at last, where Bessy remembered to have enjoyed one grand holiday, when she went marketing with Mary three years since —a large town, with a narrow main street of shops, that sloped down almost to the edge of the bay, in which were ships and boats at anchor, and beyond which shimmered and tossed the sea in the light of that morning's sun.

Here Richard Calverton dismissed the car,
and walked up and down the street till a
stage coach was drawn from the yard, and
four horses were harnessed to the shafts, and
travellers arrived and made a fuss about their
luggage and the best places, and wrangled
with the guard concerning them. At the
back of this coach Richard Calverton and
Bessy took their seats; and then they were
dashing out of the town and through the
country again; and the sea went further and
further back, and got mixed up with the sky-
line and lost; and then they were nearing the
mountains again and skirting their base, and
dashing through more deserted villages. A
long, long ride that Bessy grew tired of, and
Calverton slept throughout, with his head on
his broad chest, his hands still in his pockets,
and his outstretched legs taking up more
than a fair and legal share of room. Some
of the passengers were interested in Bessy
and her father, others interested in nothing

but their books of reference and the time of
day, and the proper adjustment of their
rugs about their knees. Those interested
in Bessy offered her their guide-books to look
at the pictures, and asked her a few questions,
to which she responded timidly and with
nervous glances at her sleeping sire. Finally
another town, with no sea to boast of, but a
large railway station, where men and women
were hurrying to and fro, and railway porters
were wheeling heavy trucks of luggage, and
all was hideous confusion to poor Bessy.

In the third-class compartment of a railway
carriage at last—dark, stifling, and cavernous
as third classes are—thanks to the people
who never ride in them!—where there was
little room, and a host of heterogeneous company: seedy tourists, who had done their
North Wales excursion cheap; careful old
gentlemen, who had money to spare, but did
not lavish it on railway accommodation;
Welsh labourers making for other towns, or

seeking new fortunes in the London about
which they had heard so much; men, women,
and children—heaps of children! A terrible and
weary journey, with her father smoking all the
way in defiance of the bye-laws, was this to
Bessy Calverton, in which the biscuits were
found necessary, and even a sip at the burning
brandy from her father's flask; a journey
which lasted till ten o'clock at night, clattering, shrieking, and clattering from one
station to another, through towns and cities,
and long sweeps of country, and more tunnels,
towns, and cities—dragging its freight of
human souls from daylight into darkness—
from the Welsh town bright in the sunlight,
to the crowded, noisy, shouting terminus in
Euston Square, where the lights were flaring,
and a hundred people bawling orders, recommending cabs, waiting to carry parcels, looking
out for pocket-handkerchiefs, or ostentatiously
displayed gold chains, or even a stray port-
manteau from the luggage heaped upon the
pavement.

A thin, tall individual with a cap and torn peak, and a corkscrew twist to his hair on either side, suddenly appeared before the weary travellers.

" What, Joe?"

" What, governor?"

" All right at home?"

" All right and square."

" And business brisk?"

" Brisk as ever," was the reply; " got the kid I see."

" I believe you."

This brief dialogue over, father and daughter, accompanied by Joe, walked out of the station into the street, where an omnibus was hailed, and where another journey—the last—was commenced.

Commenced and finished, and Bessy so exhausted now, that she slept and nodded along the streets, and had to be pulled up with a jerk now and then to keep her from sudden plunges into the roadway. From a broad thoroughfare, where the shutters were closing on the shop goods, and only the gin vaults were ablaze with gas, and alive with drinkers, who quarrelled and blasphemed, and rolled in and out the easy-swinging doors, to a maze of dark and dirty streets, where the ways grew narrow and more narrow; and Joe walked in the muddy road, and whistled softly to himself.

Another halting-place at the corner of a street; a house ill lighted, and with a noisy lot of brawlers round the doors; through these people and the shop into a back parlour, smelling strongly of spirits, and lighted by a fish-tail burner, the glass around it shattered and jagged at the top.

Bessy opened her eyes to look vacantly round her, grow more conscious, and begin shuddering. There was a shabbily dressed man with a large nose sleeping by the fire, and a woman of thirty-four, or thereabouts, looking at her across the table; there was a

girl with her bonnet awry, and her cheeks
rouged, bending over her with more interest;
there was a mangy, carroty dog growling at
her ankles, and inclined to resent an unwarrantable intrusion; there was Joe helping her
father out of his great-coat, and the rattle-
rattle of an imbecile piano somewhere at the
back.

"Oh! dear, is this home?" sighed Bessy.

"Yes, home," said Calverton—"isn't it
good enough?"

CHAPTER XI.

HOME!

BESSY remembered no more till the following morning. The big-nosed man by the fire, the woman by the table, the girl in the tawdry finery at her side, her amiable father and Joe, all became indistinct and lost, and she woke up in the morning to find herself in a little triangular shaped room, with a triangular shaped ceiling, that was six feet from the floor near the door, and three feet and a half near the window.

A poorly furnished room, with an uncarpeted floor; a rickety chest of drawers that had lost one of its front legs, and was leaning forwards gracefully; two cane-bottomed chairs, one of which supported an ewer and basin— the ewer handleless and spoutless. There was a looking-glass nailed against the wall, or rather a little dab of silvered glass framed with red lath—a toilet article to be bought in Whitechapel any Saturday night from a heap of miscellaneous material on a truck, where "everything was on the board for a penny!" Altogether, not a cheerful room to open one's eyes in for the first time, if accustomed to anything better, brighter, or more clean.

Bessy woke up with a start, for two feverish hands were on her temples.

"Oh, dear! did you touch me?"

"I was putting your head into bed again," said the girl she had seen last night, somewhat abruptly; "you were hanging it over the side, and trying to hurt yourself."

"I have been rather restless in my sleep, I think," said Bessy, rubbing her eyes. "I have had such bad dreams! Are you Lotty?"

" Yes; who told you so ? "

" Father told me I had a sister called Lotty."

" All the worse for you that you have," was the short reply.

" Why ? "

" Don't be curious," said the girl, petulantly. " Are you going to get up, or to lie here ? "

" I'll get up if you please," answered Bessy. " What time is it ? "

" Past ten."

" Ten ! " exclaimed Bessy. " Oh, dear, I was never up so late in my life."

Bessy began hurriedly dressing herself, regarding her new sister during the operation; and her sister sat on the disengaged chair regarding Bessy in her turn. Bessy thought it very strange to have a sister so old as that, and to see her then for the first time in her

life—for last night belonged to dream-land,
and the figures therein were misty children,
that she could scarcely recall. And this was
her new sister; a hollow-cheeked, sunken-
eyed sister, who was handsome still, but about
whose handsomeness there was something
ghastly. It was a waxen face; now last night's
rouge had been smeared from it, and the dark
hair—dark as Bessy's — was pushed behind
her ears in a wild, Chinese sort of style,
that gave her a desolate appearance. Bessy
fancied she could trace in the young woman's
features some traits here and there of her
own : the shape of the little straight nose, the
colour of the eyes, the turn of the chin, were
possibly like hers, although the face was altogether strange and weird—a face that time
in a bad humour had withered early, and
scored prematurely with lines.

"Well, Bessy, you won't forget me in a
hurry again," said Lotty, after she had borne
this scrutiny several minutes.

"I am thinking how strange it was not to have seen you before; to have had a sister all these years whom I never spoke to— never saw; who never once wrote to me in Wales. No one even told me I had a sister until yesterday."

"Oh!" said the girl, with affected unconcern.

"It won't make it so lonely here," said Bessy, with a shiver, "to see you now and then; to have you coming up into this dreary room when you have time, to keep me company and talk to me. Perhaps I shall not be so very miserable when you begin to love me."

Lotty moved uneasily in her chair, and her fingers twitched nervously at a faded pink silk bow at her throat. Bessy fancied, too, that she was breathing hard, as though she had been running. A curious sister this, who did not care to reciprocate her sentiments, or waste too many words on any topic.

"I thought my heart was broken yesterday, Lotty."

"Did you?" was the hoarse response.

"To leave uncle and Mary, who had both been kind and good to me so long—I wasn't grateful, I know it now!—and to come into a place like this, where there were strangers, who might be hard and cruel to me. A wicked place too, London, isn't it?"

"Wicked?" with a short laugh—"I believe you!"

"And so I thought my heart was broken, as I said," continued Bessy; "but now I fancy I may become used to it in time, if father will not be too cross with me, and my new mother will be kind and bear with me; and if you my elder sister will teach me what to do to please you all, and will love me in time like Mary did— like sisters should!"

Bessy in her simple earnestness had stolen to her sister's side, and passed her arm round Lotty's neck—and Lotty had started up with a cry and shaken her off.

"That'll do, girl!—dont come near me yet—
I'm not used to your new-fashioned ways. Go
on dressing, and don't make a fool of yourself
—and me."

Bessy felt her heart sink. Disappointed in her
father, and now in her sister, who thrust back
the affection she desired to lavish somewhere.
Her uncle and cousin in Wales had never
cared to be told of her love for them, and had
kept her affection under pressure; and here,
in her new world, it was the same, even worse!
Bessy had fancied it would have been different
with a sister—why, in a little religious book
she had left behind there was a woodcut of
two sisters who had their cheeks resting fondly
against each other, and she felt that sisters
should be affectionate and loving.

But this sister had shaken her arm from her
neck, turned away to the window, drawn
up the blind, and taken her place thereat with
her back towards her—a position that she
maintained till Bessy was dressed. Bessy

looked towards her wistfully, and wondered what there was to interest her from the window, where only the murky house-tops were distinguishable.

"Are you ready?" she asked at last, turning round.

"Not quite ready. I—have *you* been crying?" asked Bessy, whose sharp eyes detected some difference in the face since it had been turned away from her.

"Crying!" cried the woman scornfully, "what do you think Lotty Calverton has to cry for! She was past crying, and crying for, years ago; nothing ever affects or troubles her. She's hard and rough and wicked—don't go near her, she's dangerous!"

"I suppose you take after father, then?" suggested Bessy, after some deliberation.

Lotty laughed, in that short wild manner, to which Bessy was growing accustomed, and replied—

"Yes, a father's girl! Don't I look like him?—haven't I his amiable expression on this old woman's face of mine? Yes, like our dear, Christian, pious father!"

She struck her hand heavily on the door-handle as she spoke, and Bessy jumped again.

"What did they bring you here for, and shut away every chance of doing good, or living honest?—what did *you* come for?—who cared for you or wanted you?" she cried fiercely. "When you saw that father—what he was like—what he was sure to prove like—why didn't you pitch yourself from the highest place you could find, and save your wretched little self from the clutches of the devil?"

"Oh! Lotty, what do you mean?"

The girl paused, muttered "Nothing!" and then asked abruptly, "What Betty was waiting for now

"I was looking for my bundle," said Bessy.

"In the bottom drawer—what do you want with it?"

"There's my bible there—a present from cousin Mary—I—I always have to read it before I come down stairs."

The girl laughed again.

"You are a funny sister—we're not used to all this goodness at the 'El-Dorado.'"

"Where's that?"

"Here—this is the 'El-Dorado'—a famous place for famous company."

Bessy had found her bundle and the bible within it—a new little bible with gilt edges, and on the fly-leaf of which was written, "A present from Mary to her dear cousin Bessy. A gift to her in this life, the patient study of which will prepare her for the next."

"If father is waiting breakfast, I will only just say my prayers and—"

"Stay as long as you like—don't mind us," said her sister, hastily stepping on the landing, and closing the door behind her.

Bessy obeyed her instructions, and half-an-hour afterwards she was timidly making her way down the narrow and dark staircase, the stairs of which were broken in many places, and the number of banisters to hold by not extensive. She reached the parlour safely, however, where her father, Lotty and the woman she had seen last night, awaited her. A dirty tablecloth and some odds and ends of breakfast things were on the table, but Mr. Calverton had finished his breakfast long since, and was standing with his back to the fire smoking vigorously.

"This won't do, Bess," he said roughly as she entered; "you'll have to turn out earlier and make yourself more useful, girl, to please me—or our wheels won't run together very nicely. We've finished breakfast long ago."

"Your father's such an early riser," said the woman, laughing.

"That's what you call fun, I take it," said Calverton.

"Take it how you like," responded the woman, far from civilly.

" I'll take a little thing off here, and have it at your head in a minute," growled Calverton, his hand moving towards some china ornaments on the mantel-piece.

Mrs. Calverton made no answer, but began cutting some thick slices of bread and butter. Mrs. Calverton was a wise woman, and evidently knew where to stop.

" You'll have to get up early and help Lotty," said her father, again addressing Bessy.

" I am a very early riser, generally," was his daughter's reply.

" Glad to hear it."

Mr. Calverton having smoked his pipe, retired from the parlour into the bar of the small public-house, of which he was proprietor, leaving his daughter with Lotty and his wife. When the door had closed behind him, the mother-in-law put a large red hand on each of Bessy's shoulders, and drew her towards the light that struggled through a dirty window at the back of the room.

" So you're Bessy Calverton ?"

" Yes, ma'am."

" You don't remember me ?"

" No, ma'am."

" Look again."

Bessy looked attentively at the woman who addressed her. A tall woman of five or six and thirty, with a face that was strange to Bessy—a dirty face, too, over which some filaments of coarse hair hung loosely, having straggled there from the general body behind her ears, where it had been thrust last night, in Lotty Calverton's fashion, and left there for ease and elegance when she rose that morning. A bold face, though much lined— a face that had possibly been a brazen, good-looking face in the early days before she married honest Dick. No, Bessy did not remember seeing her before.

" Well, it's no wonder. You were a young one then, and I've altered mightily. I was your earliest pal at Brixbank, where your mother died."

"At Brixbank—"

"Prison," added the woman; "there's no use in making bones about it. Prison it was, my little gaol-bird. And if you don't recollect it, it'll do you good to freshen your memory a little. Ha, ha, ha!" with a wild shriek, "wont it?

"How will it do me good?" asked the inquiring Bessy.

"Keep you from being proud and stuck-up, and thinking yourself better than anybody else. I've been a gaol-bird myself, and see how humble *I* am!"

Bessy thought she should not take very readily to this new mother of hers. But the new mother was of variable moods, and first appearances in her instance were likely to be deceptive.

"Humble as the 'arth, and trodden under foot as much, ever since the awful time when my character was lost, and everything went wrong, and from prison to the streets, and

from the streets to prison, it was always—
what's the use of keeping back from you
what everybody knows, and taunts me with.
Crushed from fifteen years of age—crushed
now!"

The woman sniffed violently, and made extensive use of a ragged cotton pocket handkerchief, and rolled her head from side to side,
and moaned.

Bessy regarded her with more interest, but
Lotty tilted her chair on the back two legs,
and sat with her head against the wall, callous
and indifferent. As Bessy passed her mother-
in-law to take her seat at the table, she caught
Bessy in her arms and kissed her, and said
she'd be a mother to her; and Bessy thought
her breath reminded her of the brandy she
had sipped yesterday from her father's flask.

She left the room a few moments afterwards, and Lotty's chair lumped on its two
front legs as the parlour door closed.

"Don't mind her, Bessy—it's all gin!"

" What is ?"

" All that gammon about her feelings, and her being crushed, and such foolery. She'll be laughing her head half off in another minute—and that'll be gin too !"

" I—I hope she will be kind to me."

" Did you come here for kindness ?" asked the girl; " oh ! then—don't you wish you may get it; and if wishing's good for anything—why, I'll wish it, and much good may it do you—there !"

" Thank you."

" I don't want your thanks," she grumbled; " eat your breakfast, and be quiet, do."

" What makes you cross, Lotty ?" asked Bessy; " arn't they kind to *you ?*"

" Am I complaining ?"

" No; but you talk strangely—don't look happy."

" You're a child, and mustn't judge by looks. Looks about here—Whitechapel-way —are deceptive, Bessy Calverton. That woman there, you appear to take to, will deceive you with the rest."

" You don't love her, then ?"

" What a fuss about love you are always making," she exclaimed. " There's no love in this place—don't expect it. And, for God's sake, don't love her whose not one mind half an hour together, and is always drunk or maudlin ! If it hadn't been for her marrying my father, you would never have been brought here. She knew you were born in prison, and sent to Wales. He was in Australia, and neither knew nor cared. Why don't you eat your breakfast ?"

Bessy did as directed, and her sister sat and watched her with as strange an interest as if she were some scarce animal recently imported into the country. It was an ample breakfast, but Bessy did not do justice to it, her heart being full and heavy. It was a breakfast on a grand scale, compared to the simple fare at uncle Davis's, but Bessy did not enjoy it half so much. There were coffee and bread and butter, and half a herring, and some treacle in a cracked saucer, but all these White-chapel delicacies had no charms for the child —this little Welsh flower so suddenly trans-planted to an uncongenial soil. It is the nature of plants to droop a little after change of air and scene—some recover and grow all the braver, others droop and die!

" How old are you ?" asked Lotty, at last.

" Twelve. Are you many years older than I, Lotty ?"

" What a girl for questions you are," said Lotty. " Are Welsh people always so curious and prying, and unsatisfied ? How old am I —guess ?"

" I don't think you're so old as cousin Mary—she's twenty-five next Michaelmas. I should think," with another glance at Lotty, " you're not more than twenty-two."

The girl laughed. It was the same old scornful laugh, but of longer duration, and, perhaps, this time with a slight mournful ring in it.

" See how soon we grow old in a place like this, Bessy," she cried ; " get crow's feet, and wrinkles, and red eyes—I'm seventeen ! "

Bessy returned the cup to her saucer in her astonishment.

" But then I've seen life, and worked hard, and been treated badly, and kept late hours, and drank a great deal. We're all such drinkers here—and you'll drink in time, so don't be scared, unless—unless—"

She quitted her chair, cast a hasty glance over the parlour blind into the bar, and then came close to Bessy's side.

" Unless you run for it ! You'll save body and soul by running away from here, and ruin both by staying. Isn't there a friend— a single friend, who can hide you from this den, and all the fiends that make it so like hell ? "

" You are hurting me ! " exclaimed Bessy,

as her sister's hand griped her arm unnecessarily hard.

"Not one friend?" she repeated, as her grasp relaxed.

"Not one."

"Lord have mercy on us both—how like we are! Why you and I *are* sisters; arn't we?"

"Yes— and you will love me in time, and show me where the dangers are, and keep me from them all you can!" implored Bessy; "if you don't learn to love me a little, no one will perhaps here."

"But you won't learn to love *me*—me, a castaway!" cried she, holding her at arm's length; "you can't do it. It's against nature—law—your bible, for what I know, for I never opened one."

"Oh!"

"And you can't love me?"

"Yes I can—and will!"

Lotty caught her sister to her breast a

moment, thrust her as impetuously away, called herself a fool, a stupid fool, a blind, drivelling fool whose brain was going, and then darted from the room, and left Bessy to finish her breakfast by herself, with the carroty dog at her feet, whining and worrying for some fragments of the feast, and tattooing incessantly with the stump of a tail which had been bitten short in the days of his puppyhood.

Bessy was afraid she had offended Lotty in some way, still more afraid that the life stretching beyond would be toilsome, unloving, and full of shadows. Life in Wales had been dull and monotonous, hard and toilsome too, and brightened but by little evidence of affection ; but in this place, and with these strange people who claimed relationship, what fate awaited her ; and what dangers, of which she had been warned, were lurking in the distance?

The father brought his burly frame into

the room once more to give her some insight into her duties—brought another pipe-full of tobacco in with him, and nearly stifled her with its smoke, as she sat and listened to him.

" You'll have your work to do, and make yourself a handy girl—you'll have to see nothing, and talk of nothing, and keep your eyes and mouth shut. We kill curious people here ! "

And his fierce black eyes seemed as full of fire as the bowl of his clay pipe.

Bessy felt her old shivering fits return.

" You're a mighty sight too inquisitive at present—cut it. You're a little hasty, too, in your way, and inclined to go against the grain, I fancy—cut it, or we shan't agree. You'll have to work in peace and quietness—get up early, and put the bar to rights with Lotty, and serve customers with Lotty, and attend to people in the concert-room with Lotty in the evening, and sing a song now and then to please the company if you have a voice—and go round for orders with Joe, perhaps, and, in fact, make yourself generally useful. Be obedient, and quick, and serviceable, and we shall cotton together comfort'bly—run on your own road, and bring your creaky wheels against mine going t'other way, and, thunder of heaven, there'll be a split between us pretty soon!"

"But—"

"But you'll keep silent and say nothing. I've given my orders, and I don't want to have them talked over, as if you had a soul of your own—which you haven't—which you never will have here. You mustn't come any of Lotty's airs with me—she's a bad one."

Oh, dear! Lotty a bad one too. Bessy's heart felt heavier than ever.

Richard Calverton was about to add a few little supplementary remarks, when the big-nosed man of yesternight came skulking into the room. He neither walked, nor marched, nor ran, nor came slowly, but absolutely skulked, trailing after him a long great-coat, made for a larger man than himself about the beginning of the present century. He came skulking, then, into the room, and put his hat on the breakfast table, and unwound from his head a silk handkerchief that he had worn under his hat, and left a few stubbly grey hairs in an upright bristly condition by way of a ragged fringe to his dirty baldness. Having disencumbered himself of his head-gear, he took off his greatcoat, and presented to Bessy's eyes an attenuated figure clothed in a suit of black, that was three parts threadbare and one part shiny—consequently, altogether shabby.

"Any letters, Richard?" he asked, submissively.

"Seven."

"Seven, now? Well, that's not so bad. I suppose now, Richard, you wouldn't call it bad for one post?"

"You'd better make a change if you want to board and lodge here any longer," was the rough reply. "A man with brains like yours —an elder brother and the genius of the Calvertons—ought to have gumption enough to turn more honest pennies."

"Richard's right," he muttered confidentially to himself.

"Well—any news?"

"Not any."

"Charles Edwin Calverton, you're a humbug!"

"Eh?"

"A sneaking, two-faced, no-rent-paying, cringing old humbug! You're trying your old game—keeping all your honest pennies to yourself, and forgetting what a heap you owe me."

"I was going to say——"

"You were going to say nothing, if I hadn't found you out. What do you mean by putting me in the papers, you old rascal, without my leave and consent? And how did you manage it, and how much did you get for it?"

"Very little, Richard," with a sigh; "nothing, in fact, worth mentioning. I thought it was a pity to lose a chance, and I know the papers like such things at times. So I wrote out your accident in the mist at Aberogwin just as you told us yesterday, and coloured it a little, and called late at the newspaper offices, where they cut down the paragraph, and gave me one shilling and sixpence for it, the few who cared to have it at all."

"Will you square a week's rent, or go?"

"I'll square, Richard, if you wish it. I'm very short of money, but I'll square."

Some money passed from the elder to the younger brother, and some letters from the younger to the elder.

"There, Charles Edwin—and now try your hand at something else."

"Do you think 'Nervousness of Twenty

Years' Standing' going down in the market?"

"I should go back to Destiny."

"I thought of trying characters by hand-writing again, and making it six postages in-instead of twelve; but your superior judg-ment———"

Richard Calverton did not wait for the remainder of the compliment, but went out of the parlour and banged the door behind him. Charles Edwin drew his chair nearer the table, put on a pair of green glasses, which made him look more hideous than ever, and pro-ceeded to read the answers to an advertise-ment of his, recommending an especial cure for aggravated "Nervous Disorders of Twenty Years' Standing," or any number of years, he was not particular, so that he obtained his postage stamps. He glanced once over the top of his second letter at Bessy, and asked "how the little dear was this morning?" but made no comment when she had responded, but grew absorbed in business and dead to

passing things. Bessy thought of the bad
ogre she had read of in Stephen Speckland's
fairy book, and was glad to sidle from her
chair and leave the student alone at the
breakfast table, with his elbow abstractedly
in the butter plate, and make for her room,
where she might cry over the present, and
pray for a better future.

But she had scarcely reached the door of
her room when her father's deep voice, ringing like the bay of a hound up that narrow
staircase, called her down to some light
household work, which consisted of scrubbing
sundry pewter pots with sand. So the day
went on, and Bessy remembered that the
dinner was delayed by three gentlemen, about
as seedy as Charles Edwin, who called to see
her father, and were asked into the parlour
and locked in, and who issued forth one by one
half-an-hour afterwards, and went different
ways, after looking cautiously round them.
And then the night stole on, the awful noisy

beer-swiling, gin-drinking night, when a large room at the back was filled with half-tipsy men and women—men like her father in their manners, and all of whom swore as volubly, and whose ages varied from the sharp-faced cunning-looking youth with his cap on one side to men as old and drivelling as Charles Edwin; and women—some bold bad-looking women, whose very looks iced Bessy's blood, and the tones of whose voice made her put her fingers in her ears, and rush away till brought back by her father. Children of night, and heirs to the devil's black legacy, let us leave Bessy the scared witness of their revelry, their efforts to seek forgetfulness in the coarse brutal excitement which the " El-Dorado " of Richard Calverton afforded—a strange house, at which the law winked for the sake of quietness, and which a few easy moralists, who had never stepped across its threshold, thought necessary for the amusement of those "working-classes" who never patronized it. For these were the classes that worked at nothing but evil, and were even in their idleness planning further mischief—a vile black refuse from society, which dens like the "El-Dorado" gather together at times to drink, gamble, fight, swear away each other's souls. A deadly crew, whose sense of right was drowned in Lethe years ago, but whose capacity for wrong remained awfully immense.

And Bessy watched and wondered, and prayed against the dangers that even she could see around her. Poor prison-flower— thrown back amidst the reckless crowd from which she had risen—will use become second nature with this child too, or will the guardian angels of such children keep her still within the shadow of their wings?—angels who might be born of the earnest prayers whispered by the Methodist girl amongst the Aberogwin mountains.

END OF THE FIRST PART.

PART THE SECOND.

"AMONGST THIEVES."

CHAPTER I.

"THE EL-DORADO."

IT is considered smart writing in these latter days to sneer at copy-book morality, to turn a happy period with a jest at the old aphorisms which we wrote in our finest text, and with tongues on our chest. And yet there was wholesome doctrine in those old-fashioned head-lines, and children of a larger growth might have studied them with advantage. And possibly they have done good in their time, and checked more than once the rash word and the false step—who knows? Then, if they were trite, how true they were!

And if three-fourths of them were from Solomon, what did we boys know about Solomon, or care either? And, alas! how many of those wise, good observations, for our daily guidance, did we take to heart then?

In the-copy book that Mary Davis bought for Bessy Calverton were scored those head-lines to which allusion has been made. Every fortnight or so had Bessy written, as we in our time have written, the very true remark of the Apostle, that "Evil communications corrupt good manners." Bessy and her obsti-nate quill pen had spluttered over that maxim a dozen times at least, thinking more of the general effect than the moral to be deduced from the maxim, and spelling in absent moments "communications" with a "k" or two, as we may have spelt it in "the merry, merry days," &c.

Bessy thought more of her copy-book warning, when she had settled down at the

" El-Dorado," and become habituated, if not
resigned to the strange, dark life in which her
own now moved. It might have had some
little effect on her thoughts, natheless the
evil communications that preyed upon "the
good manners," and worked a certain amount
of mischief. Take the plant from the light
and pure air to the cellar-depths, and the
change will destroy ; thrust that plant of
human life, the child, whose nurturing requires
more care, into the midst of temptation, and
the darkness that enwraps it will kill much of
good, must destroy much of principle, by the
awful law governing things evil.

Bessy Calverton, we have already endea-
voured to show our readers, was not a model
heroine; she had had her fits of passion,
her childish obduracy in the Aberogwin cottage,
where only obedience was expected to things
just and honest. And when obedience was
expected in her father's house, where there
was no justice, honesty existent, and where

the iron will forced that obedience and made
it a matter of rule, was it to be wondered
that the feelings became blunted, and the
sense of right and wrong of a necessity confused? Still, there were fair precepts, the
result of careful teaching, living in the heart
of Bessy, struggling in the darkness for the
light, only yearning for one single ray to
grow towards it and put forth green young
shoots. It was in the hands of time, or in
the greater Hand that ruleth time, to send
that ray; or, for some wise purpose, keep it
ever hidden. And Bessy struggled on amidst
the blight, and lived and thought of Mary Davis
for four years and a half. A long period to live,
and a strange place to fight the battle of life in,
and still be on defence, if weakened by the
coward blows that rained on every side. Four
years and a half, and Bessy Calverton was no
longer a child, but on the verge of womanhood—with the thoughtful, set expression of a
woman on her features. It was a place in

which to age, and Bessy could not dwell
therein without growing old in thought,
and womanly. There was nothing near
her to sustain her childish thoughts; there
were no children like herself to keep her company, and no honest hearts to take an interest
in her innocence. Dark, mysterious, stern life
went on here, day by day, and Bessy drew
breath in its midst, and lost her child's looks
with the roses that the mountain air had
planted on her cheeks.

In our last chapter we sketched faintly the
duties of Bessy Calverton for one day; make
it more arduous, take from it more kind
words, set about it more grim faces, cast round
it a seething, restless crowd of beings losing
fast all claim upon humanity, and that has
been our heroine's life since we left her last in
Choke Street, Whitechapel, at the sign of the
"El-Dorado." Her father's "humour" was now
less apparent, and his stern commands more
frequent; her mother-in-law's idiosyncrasies

were governed by the quantum of gin imbibed during the day, and consequently as variable as Lotty Calverton had prophesied; and Lotty, loving Bessy after a fashion and in her own way, did not make Bessy's life more happy by her strange capriciousness. For Lotty's nature was a jealous one; and her younger sister must evince no affection for another, show any sense of gratitude for kind words from any one but herself, or Lotty was as sullen as the rest.

And yet Bessy Calverton had exercised no small amount of good over Lotty; she had not known her in the early times before the father belonged to dream-land, and could not guess how her presence there had awakened some fitful flashes of the better nature. Lotty had been selfish, wilful, and stubborn; passed step by step from bad to worse; hearing no prayers, knowing no good advisers; and left to proceed her own way, so that she stood not too much in the way of her father. And the sudden appearance of Bessy at her side, flung young and guileless in the midst of that world that had been her own ruin, brought into life all that sympathy for those in moral danger which exists in most women, however reckless—one gift of the Creator's not wholly cast aside. And Lotty to a certain extent was Bessy's guardian; in her amiable moods a fair adviser. She did not seek to direct her sister's life, or even to encourage those thoughts which had struck her as so new and strange on their first meeting; but if any direct temptation stood in the way, or Bessy had resolved on some rash step, that could but have ended in casting darker shadows on her path, Lotty was there to teach her prudence.

Charles Edwin Calverton possibly possessed the most equable temperament in this small household. At the expiration of the period that has passed between our first and second book, he was almost as great a stranger to his niece. Always busy; presenting always the same bland smile, and giving utterance to the same mild remarks on things in general ; agreeing with brother Richard just as often ; to each member of the family as constantly obsequious, he was the same seedily-attired, cringing, skulking, big-nosed individual with whom Bessy had made acquaintance four years and a half ago.

He was also a man there was not much chance of making out—he kept so quiet, took such little interest in things passing around him, and applied himself so diligently to his own *ad captandum* schemes for drawing fees from credulous members of the British public. He was a man who traded in public weakness, and the brains within his dirty bald head were always busy on some plan to bring postage stamps in his direction. Bessy only once remembered his becoming egotistical, and affording, or pretending, to afford some little clue to his character; and that was one gin-drinking night, when some stroke of luck, in an unseen

direction, had rendered Richard Calverton
generous enough to stand glasses round. The
Calvertons were a boasting family; we have
seen that Richard Calverton had placed to
his credit the fact of possessing a name which
no judge's decision had tarnished; and
Charles Edwin went further on the occasion
mentioned, and called heaven to witness that
he had never merited durance vile in all his life.

"Say I live by my wits, my dears," he
said, paternally, that night, "and that I appeal to human weakness, and human weakness
answers—that is the fault of those who respond, surely. I am an honest man, and
shall turn into my grave as into my bed, and
be comfortably tucked up, without a fear. I
work hard for my living. I believe I teach a
lesson to general society, and make many a
simple youth and maiden better and more
wise."

"Ain't other people as honest as yourself?"
growled his brother.

"Ay, ay—I don't say anything against other people, Richard. I wouldn't in my self-defence cast a slur on any member of my family, or anybody's family, for all the world. That is my little opinion, and there is an end of it. Any letters for the Derby prophet by this post, Richard?"

"Yes, but you'd better leave them till the morning."

"Wherefore, brother?"

"Because you're too drunk to answer them —that's wherefore."

"I think, Richard, your remarks are incorrect."

"You generally are wise enough to keep a quiet tongue, and you are either drunk, or getting too old and talkative for this house."

"You're hard upon me, Richard."

Richard continued hard and the very reverse of fraternal, till Charles Edwin took up his chamber candlestick and skulked up

to bed under a volley of abuse. Richard
Calverton had taken his brother's remarks as
an indirect allusion to himself, and a man
vain of the sobriquet of "Honest Dick"
might have been inclined to think the postage-
stamp hunter's self-congratulations had left
the rest of his family somewhat low down in
the scale. And was not that unjust? In
Bessy's grim novitiate had she witnessed anything unfair or dishonest going on at the "El-
Dorado"? Could she not have laid a hand
upon her heart and said solemnly, "I have seen
nothing,"—and would not every word have
been pure gospel truth? What if there were
many meetings in the back parlour at unseasonable and uncertain hours?—that the faces
were ever changing, and high words went on
at times, and money chinked, and sundry
articles were handed to and fro, and some
mysterious work that required a furnace and
an iron ladle took place occasionally in the
wash-house in the rear of the premises—was

there anything in all that prejudicial to the fair fame of Richard Calverton? Bessy knew it was called " Calverton's School " — and though many who attended it were big men who ought to have known their letters better, yet others were only youths, and a few quite little boys, who wore their hair in " number sixes " at the temples, when law had left them hair sufficient for such ornamentation.

Bessy Calverton had had at first a dreamy consciousness of something wrong, and had given voice to her fears to Lotty, and been rewarded for her pains by that young lady's unpleasant little laugh.

" What business is it of yours?" Lotty had said; " you must learn to keep your curiosity back, and not ask these dangerous questions. I am four years older than you and have never asked them—it don't matter to me and you, we're not expected to go to school ourselves, and all's right enough, I daresay. Right or wrong, keep quiet, Bessy, and see nothing."

Bessy took Lotty's advice; she was glad
to have some little doubts of her father's
dishonesty, and if to see more was to scare
her with her consciousness of crime, why let
the screen remain between herself and the
cruel knowledge. A man is always innocent
till he is found guilty, and if the policemen
were suddenly dropping in at times with kind
inquiries and search warrants, why nothing
was ever discovered, and unjust is the mind
that refuses to the accused the grand benefit
of the doubt! The "El-Dorado" might be
"marked," and convenient as a house of call
for doubtful characters, and allowed to exist by
the police as a handy means of dropping on
those characters when necessary—but the
landlord was an industrious man, who meant
well. If Fate had pitched him in a poor
neighbourhood, lay the blame on Fate and
not on this man, who worked hard for his
family, and was content with "just an honest
crust." So Richard Calverton argued at

times, when galled too much by frequent
" droppings in," or by the police-inspector's
knowing wink, and his " Take care, old fellow,
or we shall have you some day!"—and so the
old fellow did take care, and kept his eyes
open, and thrived.   He had a golden dream,
too, like other men or dreamers, had honest
Dick—a vision of retiring from business, and
keeping a pony trap, and in his last days
turning out a SWELL! His ambition was
laudable, and not too wild; he was a man of
the world, who could even pick out in the best
society one or two swells who had once been
in *his* line of business.

Although many good resolutions abided with
Bessy Calverton still, yet there were many she
had lost, and a few which necessity had compelled
her to give up. She had expected all the praying
and preaching which she had been a witness
to at uncle Davis's would cease at the " El-
Dorado," but she had anticipated leave of
absence, on Sundays at least, to seek some

little Methodist chapel—or some church, if Methodist chapels were unattainable—within a stone's throw of her home. But her father would have none of what he called psalm-smiting dodges—and Bessy was useful of a Sunday as well as another day; and the " El-Dorado" opened on Sundays at one, and did business on the sly before one by a back entrance that opened on Jingle's Court.

" You'll stop at home and earn your salt, Bess Calverton — we don't want people's piety standing in the way of people's profit. You've had praying enough in Wales to last for fifty lives—you've got it all over young, like the whooping-cough, so consider yourself lucky."

Bessy had no power to resist, and contented herself with the bible that Mary Davis had slipped in her bundle. Bessy read her bible for the first year pretty regularly, and then her work became more arduous; she went to bed late and rose more early, and

her eyes were heavy with sleep after the
concert-room was closed, and she was shut
in her little top room. She was glad to rest,
and postpone her old practice for a day
or two, then a week, then altogether.
Mary Davis had begged her not to forget
that practice, but Bessy thought a little indignantly that Mary Davis had forgotten *her*
entirely, and could not care much what she
persevered in or resigned for ever. From
Mary Davis she had not received a single
letter since their separation; and she had
written five or six letters herself, giving Mary
her address, and telling her the sad news that
she was far from happy; and to all epistles
never a word in return came to Bessy's hands.
So Bessy gave up writing at last, and kept
her news to herself, and, as we have implied,
grew indifferent to many things that in old
times would have touched her heart. And
Bessy once accustomed to this life was not
wholly unhappy—there was less restraint on

her actions than at Aberogwin; if she ran not counter to her father's wishes, she might follow her own without fear of a check. Bessy's greatest trial, greatest effort at opposition occurred when she was fourteen years of age, and her father, who had discovered that she possessed a tolerable voice, had wished her to exercise it for the benefit of the company who patronized the "El-Dorado." This "El-Dorado" music-room was one of Richard Calverton's chief sources of profit we may premise—formed also a fair excuse for meeting many friends and members of the school, whose constant appearance there might have made matters look a little doubtful. Sailors from Ratcliffe Highway visited the "El-Dorado"—got robbed there sometimes—men, women and children, a few of them honest, but inclined to idleness, made a dash at the amusement gratuitously offered by a liberal landlord. Calverton supported a comic singer and his wife; Lotty sang at times, and now it was Bessy's turn, and Bessy shrank from the ordeal, and resisted.

" I'll give you a week," shouted her father, after a stormy discussion—" one week, to get rid of that infernal temper, and then we'll come to strong measures—just bear that in mind— strong, red-hot measures, that won't suit you."

Lotty was witness to this threat, and turned pale ; the mother-in-law, who had drunk less gin than usual, thought Bessy wanted some of the nonsense shaken out of her.

" Give in, you young fool," was the strong, if uncomplimentary remark of Lotty; " he'll beat you almost to death, as he did me once —as I have never forgotten or forgiven, and then you'll care for nothing."

" But to sing, Lotty, on that platform, with all those people staring."

" Better there than in the front of it, with the people making love to you, and you en- couraging them to drink and give their orders faster. That's awful work! Give in !"

So Bessy gave in, and made her first appearance in public, and was vociferously applauded. She made a second and third, and sang better each time, and drew crowded houses to the "El-Dorado," the patrons of which began to *encore* her, and to rather daze her with her triumphs. Then the comic singer's wife gave her some little insight into music, by the aid of the cracked instrument called by politeness a piano, that appertained to the establishment, and taught her her notes; and fresh triumphs excited Bessy, and made singing, even at the " El-Dorado," a pleasant change after her day's work. So for two years and a-half singing at this place, bewildered by her success, becoming habituated to strange society, low words, coarse oaths, yet preserving in the midst of them some of the old pure thoughts that had had their birth in Wales, Bessy Calverton glided on to womanhood. And at this stage of her career, and in the midst of danger, we take up her history.

CHAPTER II.

CLOSE on the new year in Choke Street,
Whitechapel. Another merry Christmas
passed on its way, and those who have had
the means or heart to enjoy themselves
therein slowly sobering down. There has
been little merriment in Choke Street; little
chance for its denizens to make high holiday
with meat at tenpence a pound and bread on
the rise, and the frost that set in early in
December still nipping the life-blood from the
fireless poor. No fair revelry in Choke
Street, and in the courts and alleys adjacent

—honest people besieging workhouse doors, or begging in the broad thoroughfares, where the gas could show their famine-stricken faces, and touch the hearts of the few with money in their pockets. A bitter winter, with trade at wholesale houses slack, and therefore affording little employment for those dependent on them—for those strug-gling to live in the cellars and garrets of such neighbourhoods as Choke Street. Men and women out of work, hanging at the corners of the streets, and grumbling at the fate that had so far reduced them ; men growing desperate, and stopping those more honest in the dark by-ways ; and women still more desperate than that, plunging to the lower depths from which salvation was a miracle. Honest life shimmered but faintly in these dusky streets, and wrestled against temptation—here and there, thank God, re-sisting to the last—and prayed for better times in the rooms where looms stood still, and tools lay rusting idly. And amidst it all, the habitually reckless and dishonest lived and waxed fat—offering a terrible temptation to those who had walked uprightly; small shopkeepers in Choke Street ran into debt, and fell back in their rent, and had the broker's men upon them, and greedy hands upon the goods that constituted home; whilst such places as the " El-Dorado " were as extensively patronized, and sold as great a quantity of adulterated liquors, as if Whitechapel were the land of plenty. Well, there were plenty of drinkers in Whitechapel; and poverty makes men drink at times, and in Richard Calverton's vitriolic mixtures there was soon forgetfulness. Another glass there, landlord—score it up at fifty per cent. upon the slate that hangs behind the door; and then who thinks of the wife shivering at home, and the hungry children crying out for bread !

Richard Calverton, therefore, did not feel

the ill effects of the sharp season in Choke
Street. Christmas was a busy time at the
" El-Dorado," and the Christmas guests who
frequented the music-hall were numerous, if
not select. All Christmas week the large
room at the back was crowded with its usual
audience, who encored Bessy Calverton, and
encored the comic singer's wife, and encored
the comic singer whose songs, if not always
the most select, were full of points, and
vociferously applauded, and brought the
blushes yet to Bessy's cheeks. And Bessy did
not hear the worst of them ; in the small
hours of the morning, when Bessy was asleep,
and the audience were more thin, but more
furious and drunk, the wretched mountebank
gave loose to all the ribaldry and obscenity
that men more depraved than he had written,
and the devil's children clapped their hands
the louder, and drank, and swore and made
Pandemonium envious. And the stray policeman on the Choke Street beat passed the

house and uttered no complaint, and stopped
to gossip with honest Dick, if he were loung-
ing at the doors, and even to drink a glass of
spirits with him, after a careful glance to right
and left.   Honest Dick was very generous
with the regular policeman—and the path of
virtue was not included in the beat of Choke
Street policemen in general.

It was New Year's Eve at "El-Dorado"; the
clock behind the bar—which was always half
an hour slow, and told lies like most in that
establishment — was   striking   nine ;   they
were becoming busy in the concert-room;
Joe was attending to the customers, Bessy
was singing her first song, Lotty was amongst
the audience, and Richard Calverton wandered
up and down, with his pipe in his mouth, and
saw that everybody behaved themselves and
drank reasonably fast.   Richard Calverton
had kept school that afternoon, and had been
evidently pleased with the progress of his
pupils, for he was in a fair and smiling humour ;

and his scholars were in the concert-room, spending their pocket-money in a handsome manner.

Richard Calverton was paying great attention to Bessy's singing that evening—speculating in his mind whether, with that voice, more might not be made of her in some way; and failed to notice the arrival of a new comer, who slipped into a vacant seat near the door, and took his place amidst a crowded audience. The new arrival was a very tall, thin man in black vestments, a white neck-cloth, and large cotton gloves, which were frayed at the finger-ends, and allowed the fingers to appear. A pinched face, that might have represented forty, fifty, or even sixty years, it was so deeply lined and full of thought; and yet with eyes that might have been a child's, they were so bright and earnest. The stranger might have received more attention from the audience on a night less busy; but this was a full house,

and the customers of Richard Calverton had
found some difficulty in obtaining a good
place, and there were more new faces than
one in the concert-room. Richard Calverton,
who had a habit of examining the countenance
of each member of his large and happy
family, might have detected the stranger,
and felt nervous on the subject, had not
his back been turned to the low entrance
door. The new comer stooped a little as
he sat—was evidently inclined to give way
in the back when seated on a form with
no support in the rear. He was of an inquiring turn of mind, too ; for though he leaned
his forehead on his head as though a little
weary, he peered very cautiously from under
that hand at the general company. A boy of
fifteen who was seated on the same form with
him, and had been arguing some important
topic with a man some twenty years his senior,
glanced at him for a moment, and then resumed his conversation ; and Lotty Calver-

ton, who sat behind him, was still wondering what the presence of *that man, of all others*, might indicate, and whether curiosity alone had brought him to the " El-Dorado." If curiosity, it was a morbid feeling that gave him pain and rendered him uneasy ; for he stifled a half groan once with his handkerchief, and fidgeted somewhat uneasily on the form, and nervously played with a pewter teaspoon that lay handy to his fingers. If curiosity, it was an act that had some daring in it ; for curious people were sometimes taken for spies at the " El-Dorado," and served out accordingly. Many men constitutionally brave, and knowing this harmonic establishment only by repute, would have thought twice before venturing therein ; but this man, curious or nervous, betrayed at least no outward fear of his company. And yet the oaths that rang in his ears were new to him, and the ribald speeches fell like ice-bolts on his heart, and the crime-shadowed faces hovering about him told of the danger that a moment's want of self-possession might incur.

Joe, the barman, waiter, boots and nondescript, whose business it was to see everybody with full glasses, caught sight of this gentleman at last, and after critically inspecting him with his head on one side, asked—

" Any orders ? "

" A glass of gin and water, Joe."

Joe looked harder than ever at the stranger. He was no longer suspicious, only puzzled to guess where he had seen the gentleman who called him by his Christian name like his friends and acquaintances of the " El-Dorado." He supposed he was a friend of the governor's —a sham parson on some quiet lay or other: all right—it was his business to be " mum ! " And the stranger, who had his wits about him, and had heard Joe's Christian appellative from other lips, stirred absently at his gin and water, and then pushed it a little aside, untouched.   The comic singer had by this time made his appearance, and after being received with much hammering of mugs on the beer-stained tables, launched into some coarse doggerel, which the audience drank in greedily—for thieves are fond of comic songs, and require relaxation as well as honest folk. The company becoming absorbed in the legend, the stranger half rose, and took a careful survey of the inmates of the room. Lotty touched his arm, and whispered hurriedly, "Sit down!" and he resumed his seat at the warning, and steadily regarded Lotty. They were grave earnest eyes, at which Lotty Calverton shrank a little, although she put on her boldest look to meet them.

"You don't remember me?" she asked in a low tone.

"God bless me!" with a scared look at the rouged cheeks, "No."

"So much the better, Mr. Parslow. I didn't think you would. Ah! you may look till doomsday," she added, with that unpleasant short laugh of hers.

"I don't generally forget faces, and yet yours is entirely new to me, my poor girl. Stay, now—let me think."

A finger of one of his shabby gloves was put to his forehead, when Lotty said—

"Don't think—don't try to think! All the better for me if I'm never remembered, for you were an enemy—that's all."

Mr. Parslow regarded her in a bewildered manner, whilst Lotty, who was interested in the stranger's presence, and had all a woman's curiosity to learn the reason for it, said—

"There is no good to be discovered here. You'll be doing better and feeling safer if you go home at once."

"Do you think so?" was the quiet rejoinder.

"You're one of those men who are always trying to do good, arn't you?" was the abrupt query.

"I have made the attempt once or twice—succeeding now and then, and failing very often," replied Mr. Parslow; "why do you ask me that question?"

"Because if that's your game here, sir— end it. It'll never come to anything with us—we're too bad, too hard, and have been too long here. Take my advice and go."

"You are very kind—but I do not think there is any danger here, however much the strangeness of the scene may inconvenience— startle me."

"You may be insulted."

"My poor child, I am used to it."

"You may—"

"Pray understand me, I have no wish to stay here. I am not foolish enough to suppose that in this place, and at this time, there is a chance of doing good. With that object I am not here."

"What then?"

"You will excuse me, but you are a stranger to me—perhaps the very last that I should— stay—stay—I know you now, my poor weak suffering woman!"

"Don't talk so loud! No, no—you can't —it's impossible—it is five years ago."

"Five years to-morrow—New-year's night."

"Ah,—yes!"

Lotty for a moment hung her head and then tossed it back defiantly.

"Well, you see you were in the wrong, and had better let me gone my way. All your preaching was foolery and lies—see what I am still, what I said I ever should be."

"But you didn't follow my advice."

"And never shall!" with that laugh again which changed the colour of her listener.

It was a strange muttered dialogue in that crowded room, and amidst that wild assemblage, the stern reality of life playing its part amidst the coarse abandonment that these wretched outcasts called amusement. The singer had by this time concluded, and in the hubbub that followed the termination of the song, Lotty could converse with less restraint.

"Tell me what you want here? I may help you."

"But you say I am your enemy."

"No matter."

"Will you come to St. Owen's, and let me reason with you?"

"No."

"Well then—I think for all that, I'll trust you. I am tired of this awful scene, and shall be glad to escape. Which is Richard Calverton?"

"You don't want to harm him?"

"No."

"And you haven't come to reform him?"

"No."

"He is behind us, standing by the door—the stout man with the short pipe."

"And which is his daughter?"

The girl looked so surprised that he added,

"Surely he has a daughter—Elizabeth, I think her name is."

"And you don't mean *her* harm?"

"God forbid."

"She was singing when you entered."

"Oh! dear, so bad as that! And that was Bessy Calverton—how sorry I am!"

"What do you know of Bessy Calverton?" cried Lotty, sharply.

"Very little. But I wish to see her—I bring her a message from a friend."

"Is it important?—will it do her any good?"

"I think so."

"Sit quiet, and drink your gin and water; I'll try if I can manage it."

Mr. Parslow took the first part of her advice, but left the gin and water untasted before him. Once he looked round to see if Lotty were still there, and saw her picking at the fringe of her shawl, and deep in calculation; but the second time he turned his grave face in her direction she had vanished, and a black muzzled individual in a fur cap was in her place. Mr. Parslow was conscious of the room becoming still more full, and people pressing on him as he sat, and Richard Calverton's deep voice issuing directions for his visitors' accommodation, and the talking, laughing, ribald jesting gathering strength, and making the night hideous. He sat and shuddered, and his face took perhaps a deeper shade, but there were interest and sympathy on his expressive features still; it was a deep thoughtful countenance, that seemed to say, " In what manner and by what means would it be possible to save these people ?"—a question that was difficult to solve. Through his mind at that moment passed many schemes that in his enthusiasm he might consider practical, with time and opportunity given him to act, but the fallacy of which a moment's sober practice would have warned him. Given an army of such men as Mr. Parslow to act upon such brute beasts as these, and what result would follow ?

Bessy came forward to sing again, and he watched her with great interest, taking note of every action, every look, to which she had been trained, and wondering if any trait of character were developed thereby. A song that was rapturously applauded, followed by a desire of those nearest the door to push closer to the platform, and of those near the platform to push out at the door and go home, or seek a little fresh air in the streets, previous to plunging back to more harmony and gin. In the midst of this bustle Mr. Parslow was touched upon the arm, and the voice of his late companion whispered in his ear— "Follow me!"

Mr. Parslow rose and struggled through the crowd towards the door, where Lotty Calverton awaited him.

"You'll find her in the parlour."

"Does she know—"

"She knows nothing. I have not had time to speak to her."

"Is she alone?"

"There's her mother-in-law with her—you

needn't mind *her;* she's too drunk to understand much to-night, even if you meant harm —which you don't?" with an eager glance towards him.

" Do you think it is likely?" asked the tall man, eyeing her closely.

" No—not now," was the reply, after meeting the glance and averting her own; " but we don't expect much good here—and harm turns up so naturally ! "

Mr. Parslow would have answered, but she dragged him by the arm through a little side-door, into the parlour, where Bessy was standing by the mantelpiece, and the mother-in-law dozing in Calverton's arm-chair.   Both looked up as the door opened.

" A gentleman that wants to speak to Bessy."

Bessy looked towards the tall stranger with surprise; Mrs. Calverton sat and stared, and tried to remember in what world of dizziness she was at that moment located.

"A gentleman that wants to speak to me!" repeated Bessy.

This was something new and strange, and could but perplex her. She turned to Lotty for an explanation, but Lotty had retired and closed the door upon them. She regarded her intruder with some interest.

"Miss Calverton, I believe?" was the first question.

"Bessy Calverton—yes, sir."

"I am the bearer of a message from Aberogwin—a Welsh village, that I think you have some knowledge of."

Bessy felt her heart leap within her, and the colour mount to her face. From Aberogwin!—after so many years, so long a life away from them, to think of her at last!

"Yes, sir—I remember Aberogwin?"

Mr. Parslow detected a faltering in the voice, as the memories conjured up by the name passed swiftly across Bessy Calverton's mind. What a different scene to this, and what a difference in her!

" You were brought up there, my child?—had friends there, four or five years since?"

Bessy, with her dark, wondering eyes upon the messenger, again replied in the affirmative.

" I have to deliver you the love of Mary Davis, and to ask, in her name, if she be quite forgotten?"

Bessy coloured and hung down her head. Then her quick spirit a minute afterwards flashed up at the implied reproach.

" Tell Mary Davis *I* have a right to ask that question, although I thank her, late as it be in the day, for her new interest. Give her my love, sir, and tell her I am well."

" And have not forgotten her?"

" If it will please her—you may say so."

There was the abruptness of the elder sister in the answer, and its tones seemed to startle Mr. Parslow.

" They at Aberogwin were anxious to learn

if you were changed much—if the new life
had done much—pardon me, if I pain you,
my child—to spoil you?"

" You must judge for yourself!" and
Bessy regarded him with a somewhat defiant
air.

" Thank you," he said, after a moment's
contemplation of her; " I *have* judged."

" Ah! that's short and sweet," remarked
the mother-in-law, breaking in for the first
time on the conversation; " it's easy for the
gentleman to see how you've improved, Bessy,
since you gave up that outlandish, heathenish—
hic— place in Wales."

" I think there is some one at the bar,"
said Bessy shortly, and Mrs. Calverton, just
sober enough for business, rose and made
towards the door. As the door closed Bessy
came nearer to the gentleman, and regarded
him steadily.

" You have judged—well?"

" Do you ask for the result?"

" Yes—and as quick as you can, sir—you mustn't stay here."

" I must write to Mary Davis the natural, but not very cheering, news that you have altered. Leaving your quiet religious home in Wales, and exchanging the companions there for the strange people I find you amongst here, must have worked the usual change. In no good society, surrounded by temptation, we must fall away from right. But—" with a sudden dash into the subject as though it had warmed him, " you are very young, and were, if all accounts be true, so different—it cannot be too late to make one struggle for that right, before it sinks utterly away. In the midst of temptation one can fight against the Evil one, and conquer him, with God's help—there is no estate so low, but an honest will, an earnest prayer will raise you from its depths. And Mary Davis prays it may—that if you have forgotten her, and all the good lessons conned over in times past, you will at least not forget your Saviour."

"There is little chance of thinking of Him here, sir," was the moody answer.

"Then the heart yearns not for him, or it would make the effort," he cried; "Bessy Calverton, as God's messenger more than your cousin's, I ask you not to pass Him by—I implore you, for your soul's sake, to make one stand upon the downward road?"

"Are you a minister?"

"I am."

"Pray leave this house then—you are very kind to think of me, and wish me well, but—pray go now, sir."

"Can I see your father?"

"Not for the world."

"Will you come to St. Owen's, and—"

"I will make no promise. I have made so many promises in my time, and broken them all, that I will make no more. Leave me to think of your words."

" But will you think of them ? "

" Yes—I'll try, if you will only leave me."

"God shield you, my child, then," and Mr. Parslow went out of the room with a sigh. He had done his duty, what he considered his best, but his experience of life assured him how little the chances were in his favour of any permanent good arising therefrom. He saw that he had moved her ; that in this Bessy Calverton he had been asked to seek out there were all the materials that might be worked to a good purpose— affection, impulse, youth, and some fragments yet of early training ; but that there was also a restlessness, an impatience, which, surrounded by the elements of discord, would sweep her away from better thoughts—perhaps submerge them for ever. In such a life—worse even than Mary Davis had feared—what could be expected from one who was not armed at all points to resist ?

He went out at the door by which the mother-in-law had passed, and that maudlin female raised the top of the counter, and pushed back a door that went on hinges, and allowed egress to the front of the shop.

"You're the parson, ain't you?" she asked —"the man at St. Owen's?"

"Yes."

"Ah! then don't come preaching here; my husband won't like it—nobody'll like it much, and you will only come to harm. We're of No Church here, and allus shall be. I might a' been a good woman once myself, sir, and gone to church—and I stopped away, and came to this. The Lord be merciful to me, but I'm a whopping sinner!"

"Ask the child to come to me next Sunday after service, if you have any wish to serve her."

"She's like my own flesh and blood, sir," and Mrs. Calverton began to cry over the pewter-covered counter.

Mr. Parslow was a fair judge of the real from the sham, and sham sentiment with him was a little worse than bravado. He turned towards the door, and met Lotty on its threshold.

"Take care of Bessy; ask Bessy to read the bible Mary Davis gave her," said he.

"Oh! I've heard enough of Mary Davis in my time, and am sick of that name," was the jealous answer.

Mr. Parslow would have replied, when a sudden turmoil woke up in the concert-room, and voices shouted in their highest keys, and women screamed, and tables he could hear went banging over with a crash.

"God bless me! what's that?"

"Only a fight!" was the cool response. "They'll get it over in a minute, or have it out in the street. Stand aside—here they come!"

The door of the concert-room swung open, and two men in their shirt-sleeves came tumbling out, and hitting fiercely at each other, with a mob of excited faces following them, and a hundred voices bellowing at once. Mr. Parslow was merged in the stream before he could escape, and carried away by it to the middle of the road, and hemmed in for some minutes, despite his desperate struggles to get free. He was standing on the pavement at last, and the dense mass was swaying backwards and forwards in the roadway, as the central combatants fell to right and left, and dodged each other's double fists. He turned away and walked down the street, trailing a thin walking-cane absently along the narrow pavement. At a few streets distant from the " El-Dorado " he stopped suddenly, and clapped his hands to his breast pocket, to his waistcoat pockets, his trousers pocket, his coat tails, and then remained motionless and breathed hard.

It must have been a heavy loss to have scared him so; for he remained several mi-

nutes in that thoughtful posture, changing it
at last to feel carefully in all his pockets
again. A steel watch-chain was dangling
from his waistcoat pocket; it had been cut
and the watch whisked off, but the loss of
that did not appear to sensibly affect him. It
was the loss of that which had been in the
breast pocket of his coat—he had buttoned
his coat carefully when entering the "El-
Dorado"—that for a moment unnerved him.
He took off his hat, and let the freezing night
air blow on his damp forehead; then he felt
in his pockets for his handkerchief to pass
across his face, but that had vanished also
like a dream.

"Justly served, to venture there with the
money," he gasped forth at last— "justly
served! My own old foolish, wicked over-
confidence."

He was still standing in the street when a
policeman came slowly in his direction, and
flashed his bull's-eye lantern on him. He

seemed well known in that neighbourhood,
for the man touched his hat.

" Anything wrong, Mr. Parslow ? "

" I've been robbed of my pocket-book and
my watch."

" About here ? "

" Near the ' El-Dorado ' public-house."

" Ah !—that's a bad look-out."

" Don't—don't you think there's the slightest chance of finding them again ?" he asked
with nervous eagerness.

" Not the slightest, sir," was the reply ;
" still you'd better come round to the in-
spector, who'll book your statement, and make
inquiries. The watch may be stopped at a
pawnbroker's."

" It's not worth five shillings," said Mr.
Parslow, with a sigh ; " but it went very
well at times—a little fast, that's all."

It suggested itself to Mr. Parslow that it
had gone fast enough at last, but he did not
give utterance to the thought, though a slight

twitch at the corners of his mouth showed a certain appreciation of humour under difficulties.

Mr. Parslow did not proceed to the police-station as directed ; he had his own suspicions of who had taken his money, and though he tried to shake away the thought, it would arise in spite of him.

" I'm very sorry to think so," he murmured, as he retraced his steps to the " El-Dorado," with the visionary hope of finding the pocket-book lying somewhere by the way ; " I'm not a suspicious man—and I *did* think better of her than that. But I was so careful in that crowd, I remember. Still, Jacob, we won't be too hard in our thoughts, because we have lost all our money."

Presently he was before the " El-Dorado" again ; it was late in the night, and the man who had served him with the gin and water at an earlier hour was putting up the shutters. There was music in the concert-room, and all the revellers had not gone home yet; but the street was deserted, and the light in the bar was turned low, and the crowd, and pocket-book, and watch of a little while since had gone and left no trace.

Once he stepped into the roadway, as if to enter the "El-Dorado;" then he paused and turned back again, and went off in an op-posite direction. As he moved away, there was a shout of laughter from the inner room that seemed rejoicing in his loss and mocking his discomfiture; and at the corner of the next street a peal of church bells suddenly rang out, and roused the echoes, and made him jump a little.

"Ah! the old year dies," he thought, "and I had forgotten the old year, and the advent of the new one, in my trouble. By rights, the little church should have been opened to-night, and I in my pulpit instead of these benighted streets. Should the ill success of the last new-year's eve have deterred me this? Haven't I acted wrongly and been justly chastised for it; and is not this a judgment? A strange beginning," he murmured aloud, " with a troubled conscience and no money."

He certainly had a quiet sense of humour at the bottom of these morbid thoughts; for he said a moment afterwards, " Well, Jacob, my good man, a happy new year to you!"

CHAPTER III.

THE POCKET-BOOK.

"I HAVE to deliver you the love of Mary Davis, and to ask, in her name, if she be quite forgotten?"

The words were ringing in the ears of Bessy Calverton when she was in her room that night, and the key was turned against the troubled world in which she lived. The "El-Dorado" had nearly completed its night's business; the comic singer had delivered his last song, and gone home with his wife; only a few of the worst and vilest still remained to talk over a little matter or two with honest Dick.

Bessy had been in her room an hour, but still sat at the bed's foot, in her merino dress, and with her hands clutching her elbows, thinking of the strange messenger, and his stranger message. She had recovered her indignation at such a message from one whom she fancied had neglected her, and was battling with many a thought, and a few suspicions. She had not bestowed much reflection on her changed life lately; she had been borne passively, helplessly, onwards with the black, turbid stream; she had grown resigned to her new life, and acclimatized. She did not know how much she had changed until she went back in thought to the Aberogwin mountains, and remembered what her life was there; she did not know all the thoughts that had grown with her, and were hemming her in, until Mary's message fell like a light amidst the darkness.

"The love of Mary Davis!" It sounded sweet and comforting to her now—the love of the cousin, still true to her, still remembering her—praying for her, she believed, as she had not prayed for herself lately. " The love ! "— to her who had almost forgotten what love was.

No, Mary Davis should not be forgotten again. A hundred obstacles might prevent Mary from writing ; and perhaps her own let- ters had not reached Mary, or Mary's replies had been kept back from her. Why had she ever doubted Mary, remembering what she was ?—harsh and severe at times, but always truthful, and knowing no change.

Bessy was tired ; the candle had been burn- ing an hour ; it was two in the morning at least, and bitterly cold. Just for once, for cousin Mary's sake, she would read her little bible in remembrance. A fair return for all the unjust thoughts that had possessed her. Bessy had forgotten it was the New Year—and how strangely, for her, she was keeping it when she trimmed her candle and opened the only book of God in the "El-Dorado." As she opened it she thought of the minister's words, and Whom he had told her to remember; and she was thinking still with the open book in her lap, when a low tapping at the door diverted her attention. Bessy softly inquired who knocked, and Lotty's voice exclaimed, "Let me in—I must speak to you a moment!"

Bessy opened the door, and Lotty, with her dress huddled round her, and her hair in all the wild disorder of a Pythoness, came into the room, and locked herself in with her sister.

"I saw the light under the door half-an-hour ago, and did not think of coming to you—I have leaped out of bed with the thought though, and here I am!"

"What's the matter?"

"Nervousness—superstition—foolery is the matter, Bess. What book's that?"

"The bible."

"That I was to ask you to read—Mary Davis's?"

"It is Mary Davis's bible—yes."

"You think more of her than me—your own sister!"

"Have I thought much of her lately, Lotty?"

"Well, no—nor of me either—though that's my fault. Bessy, put the bible away—I want to talk to you."

Bessy complied.

"And put out the light, or Dick Calverton coming up the stairs presently will scent mischief, and be in upon us."

Bessy saw the force of this remark, and extinguished the light also.

Lotty curled herself on the bed, and wrapped the patch-work quilt round her naked feet, and shivered.

"How cold it is to-night!"

"Why didn't you stay in bed till the morning, Lotty?"

"All my good resolutions would have flown away by the morning—they always do."

"Have good resolutions brought you hither, sister?—oh! I am so glad!"

"They've nothing to do with you—what have you got to be glad about?"

"Tell me what you came for?"

"Tell me first what you think of that parson?"

"A good man, Lotty—one who wishes to do good."

"There's no telling one of 'em," said Lotty; "sometimes I fancy he can't be one of the canting, sneaking hypocrites they say all parsons are—at other times I have my doubts that he's no better than the rest. It's so precious odd—it's so awfully odd, to hear a man about here, for no rhyme or reason, begging you to think of yourself and God Almighty! It don't seem natural in Choke Street."

"We are not used to such kind friends, at all events," said Bessy, a little bitterly.

" If he earned a penny by it, one might see through him—but there's no guessing at him, and it makes me wild. Bessy, do you know that fellow, five years ago, saved my life."

" Saved your life ! "

" I was tired of it—I had been made a wretch of and betrayed—I had been struck and kicked, and ill-treated at home; and I found myself on a lonely bridge at midnight, and saw the water rushing through the arches, and —and I was desperate ! "

" And that man—Lotty, that man ? "

" He must have read my motive in my face, as I sat shivering in the dark recess. He stopped and spoke to me, and made me nervous and timid, and drew tears—such a fool as I was to sit and listen and believe in him ! Wasn't he my enemy to turn me back upon such a cursed road as this."

" No, no."

" If it had been a sin to drown myself, it would have been one more sin, and so an

end to me. But to live and sin on, and
perhaps drown myself at last—and where's
the good he did me five years since?"

"And have you not seen him since that
night?"

"Yes, but he hasn't seen me. I have
passed him at all hours and seasons, wandering and prowling about the streets. I
have met him in all the courts and alleys.
He's a parson, and keeps a little church
about half-a-mile away, and makes a bad
business of it, for he's as poor as Job. He's a
good man, and he can't get on better than us
bad ones. Where's the heaven looking down
on that, now?"

"Hush!"

"Hush!" repeated Lotty; "what is it has
turned you so squeamish all of a sudden, that
I should hush? Is it that fellow, or Mary
Davis's bible? I'd give something to see
this Mary Davis, mind you."

"Never mind Mary Davis now; tell me

what you came so late for, Lotty—for I'm very tired."

"That man was robbed going away from here."

Bessy, who had been seated on a chair by the bedside leaped to her feet with a little scream.

"Don't make that row, or I won't tell you another word."

"R—r—robbed!" gasped Bessy.

"Perhaps it served him right for coming where he wasn't asked, or wasn't wanted. What could he expect to find at the 'El-Dorado,' or what good did he think to work with his fine messages from that mincing, Methodist cat you think so much of. Shall we say it served him right?"

"No—I will not say it," said Bessy, firmly.

"Well, we'll say it didn't—that he's no hypocrite, and that he's a very poor man, and such a loss will beggar him. There's the pocket-book—what's to be done with it?"

Bessy could hear something impetuously slapped on her bed in the darkness, and she cried—

"Who took it? How did you come by it?"

"There was a fight downstairs as usual, and the parson and I were carried away by the crowd. His pocket-book was stolen, and passed from hand to hand to mine—his watch went another way, and won't be heard of any more. I've nothing to do with that. In the morning some one may ask me for this pocket-book; what shall be said about it, Bess Calverton, of Choke Street?"

"Who passed it to you?"

"I don't know nor care—there's the book."

"Will you give it in my hands, and let me take the blame?"

"Not any blame—I'm not such a coward as all that."

"Don't you think it right to return it to Mr. Parslow in the morning?"

"Who'd take it to him? Do you think I can go out of my way to St. Owen's church, and be aggravated by his preaching and worrying?"

"Let me take it."

"And he will set you against me, and tell you what a bad one I am!"

"No, he will not do that, Lotty."

"Hide it then out of my way—here's the book—hide it, for God's sake, and don't tell where you've put it, lest I should come back before the morning and run away with it again! There are thirty pounds in it; and if I had thirty pounds, I could go abroad and be quit of all this. Catch, there!"

She could see her sister's figure in relief against the window, and the pocket-book whirled accurately into Bessy Calverton's lap.

"They'll ask me what I did with the book —leave that to me. They won't think or

dream of you in the matter, and you can
take it back to Mr. Parslow. Have you got
it there safe?"

"Yes."

Lotty heaved a sigh of relief, and struggled off the bed, and huddled her things
more closely round her.

"And there's an end of it, and the
preacher can think himself lucky. Tell him
so, Bessy; and tell him, if he thinks he did
me any favour on that night he met me
facing death, that I am quits with him now
on that score. Good night!"

"Stay and sleep to-night with me."

"No—better away—better alone! Go
away early in the morning, and never let me
hear a word of that accursed pocket-book
again. It's a fine thing to be rid of temptation, the bible says, Bess."

"Yes."

"I don't feel much the better for it yet—
perhaps it will come right in the long run.

There's only one fine thing hanging to all this, that I can see."

"What is that?"

"The fine passion Dick Calverton will be in when no pocket-book turns up. That's one grudge less I owe him."

"Oh! don't talk like that."

"Don't be afraid," her short laugh sounding strange and unearthly in that darkened room; "I'm all talk—nothing more. Hide that pocket-book, Bessy."

She unlocked the door, and disappeared as abruptly as she had entered; and Bessy, with a more nervous feeling than she had experienced for four years and a-half, closed and locked the door after her retreating footsteps. Bessy's first impulse was to relight the candle and see if the money in the pocket-book were safe; and then the warning she had received from Lotty concerning her father recurred to her, and she contented herself with drawing up the window blind. Facing the "El-Dorado," on the opposite side of the way, was a gas lamp, which threw within the room a feeble glimmer, sufficient for Bessy's strong sight to make out the pocket-book's contents. It was an old roan pocket-book, with a steel cut clasp that opened with difficulty, and with a suddenness that spilt one or two papers on the floor, which Bessy picked up again and restored; a bulky pocket-book, with a dozen receptacles, all brimming with papers, letters, memoranda, and with one especial pocket secured by a second strap, which Bessy unfastened, and brought six five-pound notes to light in consequence. Bessy Calverton, we have seen, was of an inquiring disposition, and her fine feelings had not been developed during her sojourn in Choke Street. Having secured the money again in the inner pocket, she without a thought as to the unwarrantable intrusion on the confidence of Mr. Parslow, stood close against the window straining her eyes to make out one paper

after another, in her eagerness to discover
the name of Mary Davis. But the hand-
writing was crude and angular, and the
remarks on the papers were in lead-pencil,
and difficult to decipher by that miserable
glimmer across the road.

Bessy fastened the pocket-book in despair, and went to bed with it under her
pillow, and could not sleep for thinking of
it, and of some method to escape early in
the morning to St. Owen's and restore it to
its rightful owner. There was a church
clock striking four when she fell asleep at
last, and dreamed that sister Lotty was
stealing into the room with naked feet, and
groping in the shadows for the money.

CHAPTER IV.

THE BETTER SELF.

THE Reverend Jacob Parslow rented apartments—sitting and bedroom, with attendance—in a slim eight-roomed house near the little church of St. Owen's, of which he was incumbent. A slip of a white house in a shabby-genteel row of houses, all of the same colour and size, and christened St. Owen's Terrace. Everything seemed squeezed together and suffering from pressure in this parish, where space was valuable and rents were dear. The church itself, with its eyelet-holes of window each side of the door, and with its door

open on the empty white-washed church,
looked like an edifice taken by the throat and
gasping for breath behind its iron railings.
For St. Owen's church was small to match the
neighbourhood; had been built by subscrip-
tion, and after much hard fighting, and
was a poor specimen of contract work —
steepleless, and devoid of ornament, and re-
sembling more a stable or a free school. An
unendowed church, in which the pews were
the only income that kept Mr. Parslow on his
legs, and where the pew renters were needy
shopkeepers in the aggregate, who went back
in their rents, or were overtaken by insol-
vency and paid nothing in the pound. A
church that brought in something less than a
hundred and fifty pounds per annum, and possessed no patrons, and wherein Jacob Parslow
did all the work, and flinched not at his
arduous duties, and kept a brave heart in the
midst of a crowd where hearts were failing
every day.

It is to be easily imagined that the Reverend Jacob Parslow found it hard to live with many claims upon his purse, and found it still more hard to put up with the loss of thirty pounds, which at one fell swoop was borne away from him.

Still, the next morning, whilst detailing the loss of his treasure to his landlady, who stood worrying the door handle, and listening with a horrified countenance, he appeared to have surmounted his first feelings of despair, and prepared himself to face the worst. He was breakfasting somewhat late, although he had risen early, and gone deeply into an elaborate calculation concerning the ways and means to meet those demands upon his purse which no loss of his could stave off for a day. And he made the sum come pretty near the mark—just a five pound note out, for which fortune might provide in some way, and if not, which, tightening the screw a little more, he might wring out. There were too

many books on the shelf opposite, and he
knew them half by heart; he would sell some
of them to-morrow. There were some Dres-
den China ornaments that had been his mother's mother's; but he required necessaries of
life, not ornaments, and the heirlooms to which
he had clung to the last must go the way of
many heirlooms before them. Then he could
dispense with the thick pair of boots he had
resolved upon yesterday, and have his own
half-soled again, or patched up in some way
that would keep the wet out till the streets in
his parish were dry with summer dust. It
was bracing dry weather now, and might
not rain anything to speak of till the next
quarter, when he should have cash in hand.
And that New-year's dinner he had thought of
giving the poor weaver's wife and children—
why, with a sigh, he must dispense with that,
and they would never be a bit the wiser, not
having known of his good intentions towards
them. And, last of all, there *was* a pawn-

broker's in the parish—there were a hundred and fifty, perhaps ; he had not counted them, but golden balls were as plentiful as oranges, and he should have no difficulty in pledging a few things if he *were* run very close.

" So, Mrs. Elsley, there's nothing for me to grow grey over "—(he was grey already) —" a worldly loss which there was no preventing must not be made a grief of. And I haven't time to grieve in this busy little district."

" 'Tis enough to make you ill, sir," remarked the landlady.

" Oh, I haven't time to be ill, my dear madam," said he, quite cheerfully. " If I have not put money by to meet a loss like this, so much the greater shame to an early improvidence that made me poor before my time. I think, Mrs. Elsley, we'll have a plain dinner to-day — something light and inexpensive, which I will leave to your good taste."

Mrs. Elsley bore away the breakfast things

and Mr. Parslow, with the aid of a lead
pencil and the back of Mary Davis's letter,
which he had had in his waistcoat pocket,
dashed amongst the figures again, and tried
to work his intricate sum into an impossible
quotient. Given the residue of his pew rents
and what x or unknown quantity could be
deduced therefrom to keep him out of debt
till Lady-day. He was not quite certain,
but it was somewhere in the figures, and he
had been a bad hand at figures all his life—a
fifth-form dunce, who had only brightened up
in composition, and escaped the thunders of
the forum. He would give up figures and
scratch off some notes for next Sunday's sermon—notes on the beginning of another year,
and how it behoved all to commence it with
cheerfulness, and faith and resignation. There
were some happy hits to be made in that
sermon, and it really seemed as he sketched
it out to make him better. Why, it even
made him warmer; he would let the fire out,

and save some of the coals till night set in, and that cruel frost which *would* never go away came sliding in underneath the door, and through the gaps in the window frames, not one of which fitted properly in the terrace of St. Owen's.

A gentle tap at the door.

" Come in."

" What is it, Mrs. Elsley ?" he inquired, with an effort at peevishness that was a miserable failure; " you really must remember that I have two more sermons to write, and to-day's Saturday."

" Well, I don't think it will be so unlucky a day as Friday, sir."

" I—I don't understand you," and Mr. Parslow looked up with a heightened colour; " it won't—it isn't—"

" It's a young woman wishes to see you from the Hellaboravo."

" Bless my soul—bless my soul now," and Mr Parslow ran his fingers through his scanty hair, and ruffled it up the wrong way in his excitement. A young woman from the " El-Dorado "—one he had misjudged, too, in his secret heart. God forgive his erring judgment on his fellow-creatures—it was very wrong of him!

When Bessy Calverton was shown into his room, he rose up like a true gentleman as he was, and placed a chair for her, and stood twirling his pencil in his hands till she was seated. Then he took the one remaining chair in his room, and looked at her so steadfastly, that Bessy turned scarlet beneath his gaze.

" Well, Miss Elizabeth Calverton, I need not say I am very glad to see you. And I need not say I hope you have brought me very pleasant news."

" I hope so, sir."

Bessy drew from the bosom of her dress the pocket-book, which the reverend gentleman received. It was doubtful whose hand shook the most during the exchange.

" Pleasant to get back money one has despaired of—still more so, my dear child, to witness this fresh evidence of an honest heart struggling in the midst of temptation, and coming off triumphant. The fear of losing six valuable bits of tissue paper is well recompensed by such evidence of honesty before me."

" Will you look at the money, sir ?"

" Not now."

" There is still a watch missing, I hear— and, and—I am sorry to say there is no hope of that."

" Pray do not trouble yourself about it— a plated thing, that continually required winding up, and would not have fetched me five shillings at the hammer. The poor thief who despoiled me yesternight has made a bad harvest this time. You are very sad, my child!" he added in a graver tone; " you do not bring the gift to me unwillingly ? "

" I would have come through fire to bring it you ! "

"I am glad to hear you speak so bravely—thank you, my girl!—this is a cheerful, heart-exhilarating day!" and he rubbed one hand rapidly against the other, as a witness to his blissful state of feelings.

Bessy rose.

"Pray don't go yet—I wish to ask you so many questions about your father and yourself—whether something cannot be done to place you in a different sphere, and give you some better, higher chance of living? Surely you are not content with your position—life—friends?"

"There is no help for me!" murmured our heroine.

"Then we must make help!" he cried, warmly; "father and child are tender relations, that should not be meddled with, unless there are grave and holy reasons that require foreign interference. And I have a reason here!"

"You must leave me to myself, sir; and I

must trust in the God I have been forgetting lately. Will you tell Mary Davis, when you see her, that four years and a half have not wholly made me bad. That by a struggle —and I *will* struggle!—I may date something nigh to an awakening from her last kind message. And, will you also say, I have not forgotten her, although not a line of hers has reached me since I left Aberogwin."

" I will gladly communicate all this to Miss Davis," he replied. " I have not the pleasure of knowing that lady personally."

" Indeed, sir !" exclaimed Bessy.

" Miss Davis discovered my name in the Post-Office Directory, I believe, and wrote earnestly requesting me to make some inquiry concerning you. She stated her story, and her concern for you, briefly and simply, and begged me to take the case in hand and com‧municate the result to her. I shall have pleasant news to send to Wales."

" Tell her, sir, that I will write soon."

" Certainly—certainly."

" There is one thing more I should like to say before I go, sir," said Bessy, reluctantly.

" What is that ?"

" That my sister Lotty, her you spoke to last night, is not so bad as you may think, sir. That it was Lotty's first suggestion to restore the money which the men robbed you of—and that but for Lotty I should have known nothing of the theft."

The Reverend Jacob Parslow's countenance beamed again. Human nature was looking up so in Whitechapel !

" Really, now—really !" And then that countenance changed suddenly again, and he turned hastily to the window, and looked across at another row of houses as huddled together as the row in which he dwelt.

" And that poor girl is your sister ?" he asked, in a voice that faltered a little.

" Yes, sir—my elder sister."

" And you are living in the same world,

exposed to the same elements of evil, left
with as little moral guidance, and with as few
true friends. We must stop it, by God's
help !"

He struck his hand upon the window sill,
and then began an impatient tramp up and
down the room.

" We cannot afford to let this one sheep
wander from the track, and be for ever lost.
A thousand fathers like your own must not
hinder us in our good work. We have fought
our way through harder obstacles than this,
and are living now to tell of them."

" Better leave me to myself, sir," answered
Bessy. " I am hemmed in, and there is no
escape for me."

" If you remain there, you are lost !" he
cried, excitedly.

" I will do my best, thinking of such holy
lives as yours."

" But when your courage sinks, or the
danger comes more near, or these new resolves

grow old, and are things of the past to be set aside— what then ?"

"I can but do my best," repeated Bessy. "When the dangers press on me too heavily, I may grow firm and fly them ; and, some day, if I am very weak of heart, of faith, I will remember the good man living here, sir."

"Well, I must think—and so must you, my child. For a little while, I need not fear you —or my knowledge of human nature, what it can bear and resist, is scantier than my vanity assures me. For a time, good bye to you. The blessing of a better life be resting on you soon !"

Bessy placed her hand timidly in that of the minister's which was extended towards her, and then went away with a heart more light than she had felt for many a day. What a change, and in how short a time—how few the incidents to give her strength, and restore her once again to something of her better self!

That little cottage up the mountain side did not seem lying so far back in the past now— she could hear the voice of Mary Davis, and see her figure underneath the porch, and the dash of the waterfall beyond was in her ears, and murmured of new hopes.

And whilst thus hurrying on, and speculating in the distant dream-land, a slipshod, toothless old man came face to face with her, and leered up at her from beneath the greasy brim of his hat.

"Good morning to you, Bessy; your father thought I should find you somewhere here!"

And dream-land vanished in the instant, and left the grim reality; and the cutting north-east wind that was rioting in Whitechapel that day seemed to rush at her heart, and pierce her with its fangs.

END OF THE FIRST VOLUME.

R. BORN, PRINTER, GLOUCESTER STREET, REGENT'S PARK.

NO CHURCH.

BY

THE AUTHOR OF

"HIGH CHURCH."

> " And as we fall by various ways, and sink
>   One deeper than another, self condemned
>   Through manifold degrees of guilt and shame;
>   So manifold and various are the ways
>   Of restoration, fashioned to the steps
>   Of all infirmity, and tending all
>   To the same point, attainable by all—
>   Peace in ourselves, and union with our God."
>   WORDSWORTH.

IN THREE VOLUMES.

VOL. II.

LONDON:

HURST AND BLACKETT, PUBLISHERS,
SUCCESSORS TO HENRY COLBURN,
13, GREAT MARLBOROUGH STREET.
1861.

The right of Translation is reserved.

LONDON :
PRINTED BY R. BORN, GLOUCESTER STREET,
REGENT'S PARK.

PART THE SECOND.

(CONTINUED.)

"AMONGST THIEVES."

N O   C H U R C H.

CHAPTER V.

A FAMILY FRACAS.

CHARLES EDWIN CALVERTON shambled along by
Bessy's side, and made no further comment on
his meeting with our heroine. Keeping his
eyes bent downwards he appeared to take no
notice of Bessy's agitation, Bessy's curiosity
and fear. Having fulfilled the mission of his
brother, he had subsided into his usual
skulking self, and for all that he betrayed to
the contrary might be thinking as he walked
of some pet scheme—perhaps "luxuriant

B 2

hair and whiskers "—to bring the postage-stamps as thick as snow-flakes on him.

Bessy glanced towards him once or twice as if for explanation, but he kept one shoulder to the wall, and crept along with his face averted from her.

When they were but three streets removed from Choke Street her uncle for the second time looked at her under cover of his shabby, napless hat.

"Ain't you afraid of going home?" he asked in a hasty whisper.

"I—I don't know. What have I to be afraid of?"

"You see it's all known—and your father, though I say it as shouldn't,"—he looked very hurriedly round him lest honest Dick should be at his elbow—"is not the most amiable, or the most considerate, when things run a little contrary."

"I have done no wrong."

"I don't know what you've done, Bessy—

it's no business of mine, and, for the love of heaven, don't implicate an innocent man, who's trodden under foot too much already. But, Bessy," looking round a second time, " take my advice and let things go their own way with your father. Right or wrong, there's only harm follows interference. Hear, see, and say nothing—it's the wisest."

This was a new phase of Charles Edwin's character, and Bessy regarded him with surprise. Her uncle had not condescended to address so many words to her during all her sojourn at the " El-Dorado ;" and as for offering her advice on any point, Bessy would as soon have expected advice from the comic singer, or Joe the barman. It was the old advice that Lotty in other words had bestowed upon her before, and Bessy shuddered, for it implied a giant's power, and a tyrannical giant's use thereof in honest Dick.

Charles Edwin delivered his warning in his usual feeble whine—something like a professional beggar who trails along at your side and details his imaginary griefs—and made the pavement at his feet more the object addressed, than Bessy Calverton.

"I shouldn't have got on with him for so many years, if I hadn't truckled to him, and shut my eyes, and minded my own business. He's too big and strong to live with and not allow him his own way. You ought to have known all that by this time, Bessy. I've given in, and been ground down and spat upon—and I can live with him, and work for my bread in quietness."

Had Bessy been looking at him then, she might have noticed a peculiar change in the expression of Charles Edwin's countenance; a more hardened, and less senile expression, that gave him a look of the brother whom he feared. But Bessy was thinking of her own future, and as the voice of the speaker changed not, she failed to observe the bushy grey eyebrows contract, and the little grey eyes beneath them gather something of fire.

"I do not fear," said Bessy.

"Lotty tried the obstinate once, and much good it has done her," added he.

"Poor Lotty!"

"And if you'll take an old man's advice, you'll give in. It's easy policy, and wants no studying. I say it's wisest—and I know it's best. Ugh! how abominably cold!"

And he turned up the greasy collar of his great-coat above his ears, and thrust both hands to the bottom of his trousers pockets and skulked along more than ever.

"I'm not afraid of the hard words he may give me for to-day's action," said Bessy at last; "it's my first attempt at anything like right since I left Wales, and I feel all the better for it."

"Right," sneered the old man.

"Have I acted wrong?"

"Oh, no! All this is very good and praiseworthy of you, Bessy Calverton, but it

won't pay in Choke Street. I may admire
your conduct in my own way, for I'm a hard-
working, honest fellow myself; but I can't
think it judicious, and—and it *has* been very
badly managed. You're not sorry for what
you have done?"

" No."

A third hasty glance right and left before
he addressed the pavement again.

" You'll tell him so?"

" If he ask me."

"That's what we call 'pluck;' but it's no
use, Bessy, unless——"

" Unless?" repeated Bessy, as he increased
his pace, and seemed afraid of his subject.

But Charles Edwin did not answer until
they were within a few paces of the corner of
Choke Street. And then, before that corner
was reached, he took his right hand from his
pocket, and made a hasty snatch at her shawl
and drew her back.

" Unless you've pluck enough to end it all
—at once!"

"What do you mean?" gasped Bessy, for Charles Edwin was then looking at her for the first time, and it was so white and agitated a face, that it did not resemble her uncle's in the least.

"You're one more of us going to the bad, unless you end it all at once!" he cried, with strange excitement — "unless you've pluck enough to run! Anywhere—with anybody; you can't be worse off, and there's a chance of being better! Why don't you end it all at once?"

"Run away?"

"There's nothing to stop for but ruin at the 'El-Dorado!'" he continued, in the same strange excited tones; "and we haven't turned the corner yet—we're not in sight, and no one knows I have found you! I'll tell him I have never met you, and, with all his cleverness, he won't be a bit the wiser. Run, my girl, and be one Calverton the less!"

For a moment Bessy felt inclined to follow his advice ; then thoughts of abandoning Lotty without a word of farewell, and the fear of flinging herself in the midst of the great London wilderness, without a friend to help her, save Mr. Parslow, perhaps—and he was already suspected by her father—deterred her, and made her resolve to follow in the old track, whilst strength was left her to combat the evil round her. No, she would not fly !

Charles Edwin relapsed into his old habits — even regarded Bessy with some nervous fear.

" Well, well—you are right enough, Bessy. Perhaps I was only trying you—having a little bit of fun, just to keep myself warm this cold morning. You—you need not say anything about it to your father ? "

" I will not speak of it. You meant it for my good, I think, but I can't run away yet ; I—I am too weak."

" Only a joke of mine; don't think of it any more, my dear. Just done to try you, for —he, he! — I shouldn't have let you go! But still, you may as well not — not mention it to Richard."

Bessy repeated her promise, and he muttered something about Richard not always being able to appreciate a bit of fun.

Silent the rest of the way home, uncle and niece, each following an especial train of thought, and inclined not to rise from the depths again. Along that narrow, poverty-haunted street, where honest life was frost-nipped, and only evil seemed to flourish, to the establishment of Richard Calverton, licensed victualler. Half-a-dozen doors from those respectable wine and spirit vaults Bessy could hear the elevated voice of her father, and it reminded her of the muttering amongst the mountains before the storm used to break with all its force over Aberogwin. Richard Calverton had not reconciled himself to his

losses or wrongs yet awhile, and the voice of
the disconsolate welled into Choke Street.
Bessy glanced at Charles Edwin again, but
that gentleman had his hands in his pockets,
and his eyes directed downwards, and his
teeth were rattling with cold ; he had forgotten his advice, or his attempt at a little bit of
fun to wile away the time.

Silently, but with a rapidly beating heart,
Bessy, anxious to meet the worst and end
suspense, passed rapidly through the shop
into the back parlour, and made her appearance in the midst of her family.

There is a peculiar statistical state called
" sixes and sevens," to which most families
are   subject   at   times — and   which   this
especial day in particular had descended on
the house of Calverton.   And Richard Calverton at " sixes and sevens " with himself
and the world was not a pleasant object to
look at.   As Bessy entered he was standing
in the middle of the room, from which the

table had been thrust and overturned, hurling
denunciations on everything and everybody,
and swearing with that easy volubility for
which he was particularly distinguished.

Lotty and Mrs. Calverton were witnesses
to this heated harangue; the former standing
by the fireside, with one elbow on the mantelpiece, her chin clutched in her thin hand and
her dark and sullen countenance turned to
her father—the latter sitting all of a heap in
a corner, nursing her knees, rocking herself
to and fro, and moaning miserably.

" So you have caught her !" he cried ; and
then turning to Lotty, and shaking his fist
close to her face, he shouted :—

" Now, you lying Jezebel, what can you
say now — what more lies have you handy
to humbug me with ?   Shall I send you down
again for this ?"

Lotty did not flinch ; and the steady con-
centrated doggedness in her eyes seemed
to arrest the blow, for Calverton after a

moment's hesitation turned away with a growl and walked to Bessy.

"You're the worst of them—what have you got to say? he cried in the same elevated tones.

"I wouldn't speak so loud, Richard," suggested his brother, meekly, "I heard you half way down the street."

"Mind your own business, and don't tell me what to do—I'm no fool."

Richard Calverton nevertheless took the hint and lowered his voice, while his brother stooped, set the table on its legs, wheeled it into the opposite corner to that wherein Mrs. Calverton was deposited, sat down before it, drew a handfull of letters from his pockets, and was instantly deep in their contents, and deaf to all the turmoil seething around him. Charles Edwin seemed to have the enviable art of disassociating himself from passing things, and wrapping himself completely in his own estimable thoughts. He worked away busily, making notes on the backs of his letters with the stump of an old pencil, and steadfastly minding his own business, as fraternally recommended.

"What have you got to say?" repeated Calverton, giving a shake to Bessy's shoulder to facilitate her powers of speech; "you've done all the mischief—can't you find a tongue to prate of it?"

There were some forcible adjectives sprinkled about this speech, that the reader will kindly take for granted.

"I have done no mischief," said Bessy; "I have returned the pocket-book to the gentleman who lost it last night—was there any harm in that?"

Calverton wheeled round to Lotty again, and showered fresh oaths in her direction, and struck the mantel-piece with his clenched hand, and finally thrust her from her position several paces across the room.

"For two pins I'd smash the life out of

you, you young she-devil!" he cried, "and put an end to you and all your thundering lies at once. Didn't you tell me a moment since that Bess knew nothing of it—that her going out this morning had nothing to do with the pocket-book—that you didn't know where she'd gone, and didn't care? By all that's holy, it's enough to make me kick you!"

"Kick away—you're brute enough!" was the rejoinder.

"Mind you, I'll tame you yet," he hissed; "you're not iron, and I am. You'll come to grief before the day is out, or my name's anything but Calverton."

"And I've done my best to bring 'em all up dootiful, and be a mother to them, and make 'em love you!" croned Mrs. Calverton.

"Shut up, there, will you!"

And honest Dick took from the mantel-shelf a stone-china ornament, that possibly weighed a pound and three quarters, and looked menacingly in the direction of his helpmate. Mrs. Calverton shut her eyes, and re-commenced her rocking and moaning.

"Was there any harm in that?" said Calverton, mimicking Bessy's voice but indifferently well; "thunder me, there was harm, and you'll know it too. It might not have been his pocket-book. I might have wanted to give it back myself—it wasn't your place to interfere. Now, look here, girl—a clean breast of all this affair will be the best for you. How did you come by it? I know all about it—but how did you come by it?"

Bessy did not answer. He might know all the story, but its recital might still further implicate Lotty, and bring upon her a fresh outburst of paternal wrath!

Calverton replaced the ornament on the mantel-piece with a smart crack, and grasped Bessy's arm till she winced again.

"How did two papers bearing Parslow's name come on the floor of your room this morning?"

Bessy remembered on the instant the fluttering of papers to the ground yesternight, and the hasty gathering of them in the dark.

"I opened the pocket-book, and some of the papers fell out. I told you that I had the pocket-book, and took it back to Mr. Parslow."

"And Lotty gave it you?"

"I will not answer," was Bessy's firm reply.

The hand on Bessy's arm was like a vice —and the face that looked in Bessy's like a demon's.

"I must break you in, before you grow as bad as all the rest," he hissed. "You turn against me too, and seek to blacken my name, and call attention to this house!—YOU take upon yourself to act, without my wish or my consent! You come out with your

old Methodist ways, and try to balk *me*—
—ME, who never was balked yet! Curse
you all, I'll put an end to it!"

He thrust her from him as he had thrust
Lotty, and Mrs. Calverton, at an earlier
stage of the proceedings, and Bessy gave
a cry of pain. Still, she felt stronger to
resist now; stronger in herself and her good
intentions. The old impetuosity—that old
spirit that had carried her to the mountain
top in a time of danger, flashed out at this
indignity, and she cried passionately—

"You may curse me if you like—you
have already cursed me by the life you
make me lead, and by all the evil thoughts
that come to such a life. I have a right
to act honestly yet—and it was right and
honest to return that book to him who had
been robbed. You are my father, and yet
you blame me for it! Oh! my God!"

"We shall understand each other better
by-and-bye," said he. "You are getting too

old and knowing for me. What you have
done to-day might have transported me, and
devil a bit would you or anyone else have
cared for that. How much was in the
pocket-book ? "

" Thirty pounds."

" You'll have to earn it in some way or
other, for I must make it up, or the whole
school will be upon me. I never was over-
reached in my life yet, and it isn't Bess Calverton that's going to steal a march on me.
You'll have to earn it—I'm not particular how."

" I've had enough of this ! " cried Lotty,
suddenly breaking in upon the dialogue—
" don't pitch your spite on her—I did it
all ! I'll tell all you want to know. The
pocket-book was passed to me, and I gave it
to Bessy, and asked her to take it back—
there, that's all ! Score the thirty pounds
against me, and do your worst—if the worst
hasn't happened to me years ago ! " and here
she burst into her short discordant laugh.

" Don't come interfering with me," said Calverton. " I've heard so many lies to-day, that I can't tell which is truth and which isn't. At present, I don't care. There's thirty pounds owing to the school, and money's scarce. Bessy will begin working to-night; there's a new song for her."

Charles Edwin's pencil ceased to work for a moment, and Lotty's face flushed a deep crimson.

" Not *that* song ? "

" We're getting too dull at the ' El-Dorado,' and want freshening up. Bessy's a lively girl, and must take the comic line."

" I'll sing it."

" You've no voice, you young screech-owl ! "

" Give it to Jones's wife."

" Jones's wife is a fool, and won't trouble me much longer. Bessy shall sing it; it's not wanted till one o'clock in the morning, so there's time enough to learn it. We don't want any squeamish nonsense here. You can keep to your room and practise it all day; if you do it well, perhaps we'll call it a pound off the thirty — and *do* it well you must! Will you go upstairs now? — you're much better out of the way at present."

Bessy silently complied; she would be glad to be quit of the noise and confusion, and shut herself in her room, and think. Her father had not betrayed so much violence and rage as she had anticipated; but there was something in his looks, his voice, his meaning words, that smote her with a greater horror. Something dreadful and undefinable hung over her; she felt she was entering on a new life, darker, and full of greater danger; but she felt also that her strength to resist had increased, and remembering the promise she had made the incumbent of St. Owen's, she could believe her better thoughts would keep her harmless.

She was aroused from these thoughts by

her mother-in-law's appearance in the room.

"Here's the song, Bessy," said she, entering with rather an unsteady movement—"and you'll be a good girl, and a blessing to both of us, and learn it."

"Put it on the drawers."

"You mustn't rile your poor father too much. He works hard, and has much to put up with. We must humour him."

Mrs. Calverton was inclined just then to bepraise her husband—possibly for the rule governing "contraries;" for honest Dick had pinched her, and shaken her, and thrown her into a corner that morning, for allowing Bessy to talk with Mr. Parslow yesterday.

"He has been a good husband to me. He was sweet on me afore your poor mother died, and she was jealous—he, he!—and if he's rough at times, why, it's human nature. So, don't mind his being a little rough with you, Bessy; it soon blows over, and he means nothing."

"What is the song about?" asked Bessy.

"Oh, a fancy song that they've got at the 'Crown' beer-shop, and which they don't sing nicely, though it draws the custom away. Your father thought you could do it better, for you're good-looking, and can sing well. There's Calverton calling."

The mother-in-law hurried downstairs, and Bessy, after five minutes reflection, seemed to have resolved to make the best of her position, and struggle on for a little while longer. She rose and went to the drawers, from which she took a dirty sheet of paper, on which some verses and music were scrawled in ink; and then, as she unfolded the manuscript, it was snatched suddenly from her—as her fairy book was snatched in times past by Uncle Davis—and torn into strips and scattered on the floor, by the nervous shaking hands of sister Lotty.

CHAPTER VI.

RESOLUTIONS.

BESSY CALVERTON stood and regarded her sister Lotty with amazement. Accustomed to her exhibitions of anger, jealous fretfulness and captiousness, she had not hitherto been a witness to a display of passion that changed her very looks, and affrighted Bessy with the change. No madwoman leaping into the room and giving vent to all that frenzy actuated her could have more seriously disturbed Bessy at that moment.

" Lotty, dear, what is the matter ?"

" The matter is, that you mustn't learn

that song, or sing that song, whatever comes
of it. That this is my old, old life, step by
step—and I say it shall not be! There shall
be one at least without the black mark on
us—I have tried to shut my eyes and close
my heart against you—but I can't! That
song I have torn because it is not fit for you to
read—not that it is wholly vile, but that it is
one step away from modesty, and honesty,
and all that's good, and is shameful for a girl
like you to sing."

"Can it be helped?"

"Yes."

"Is this your old advice; to succumb to
everything—to blindly obey all cruel orders
given me?"

"Oh! you taunt me with that, do you?
Well, I deserve it. Shut that door and lock
it again."

Bessy complied, saying—

"Does father know you are here?"

"Yes, I have been sent to see how you

take to the song, and to tell you from him
that it must be sung, and there is no escape.
With all his cleverness and cunning, he
is no judge of human nature — he does
not understand me, you, anybody in this
house—he'll come to grief some day ! "

" But what is to be done, Lotty ? " asked
Bessy, with a piteous look at the strips of
the song scattered about the carpetless
floor.

" I'll tell you in a minute—wait a bit,"
said she, gulping; " then I shall be cooler,
and speak better."

Lotty walked about the room several minutes, and Bessy stood by the drawers and
watched her.

" It's only fever heat now, and I can
speak," said she, pausing at last. " Just
listen, and don't interrupt. You were right a
moment ago to taunt me—"

" I did not mean it ; I—"

" Do let me speak," cried Lotty peevishly ;

" I don't want any excuses—I hate them. I can't tell what has happened to me—I'm going mad or foolish, or something—I wasn't like this before you came. Did you bring a curse with you, I wonder ? "

Bessy would have answered, but Lotty's look warned her to keep silence

Lotty was strangely excited, and her thin hands kept clenching and unclenching with a nervousness that was new to her.

" Before you came, I cared for nothing—I had been taught to care for nothing, and I learned my lesson well. When you were here I thought, what is the girl to me that I should trouble my head about her—let her go her own way and leave me mine ! You bothered me, and I sought to *stash* it somehow. But, Bessy, soul and body couldn't stand the wear and tear of that—for you were my sister, and you didn't think of me, or talk to me like anybody else. You asked my help at times, and took to me—to one who had never had a dog to love her from the day she was born! Well, I fought hard to keep you back, but you would come between my bad thoughts and myself—you would make me think, and I tried so hard not! Then I grew selfish and jealous at last, and thought again, 'Let her stop—I love her in my own odd way, and she makes home bearable to me—let her stop, and fall away, and go wrong like myself. I shan't be so much alone!'"

"Oh! Lotty."

"What—you will keep talking!" cried the excitable Lotty. "How can you talk and listen too—with me so much to say, and so little time to say it in? I thought all that, and fifty times more than that, till to-day; and now to-day has changed me, God knows for better or worse—I think it must be for the better, though I shall die when you leave here."

"Leave here!"

"I have thought it all over, and go away

you must. Whatever happens, get away from this house. You can't do harm by leaving such a place as this; you must escape some wrong or injury, if you run into the very jaws of death. So, Bessy, you and I will say good-bye to-night—and, please God, never meet again!"

"Don't say that, Lotty—let me rather stop here, and brave life out with you."

"And such a life!" said Lotty, with a shudder. "No!"

"But where am I to go?—what can I do?"

"I have been thinking of it all, and planning it all in my own way. The thoughts I have had are enough to drive one mad," she cried, clutching her temples between her hands. "They come so fast, and burn so here! Now, listen to all that I have been thinking of, and then say yes or no to it— only remember, Bessy, to say no, is to make you a wretched outcast like myself. I see it now."

Lotty took a fresh breath, and resumed.

"Watch your opportunity to-night and escape. Here's money—don't begin to plague me with questions about that, or I shall hate you—it is honest money. Run for it, then, and wait in Monument Yard till some one comes to help you."

"But if no one come."

"Mr. Parslow will. Between this time and that you must write to him, telling him that for your soul's sake you have fled hence and need a guide to place you in some poor, honest home. Mention the place of meeting, and he will come to help you, I am certain."

"But the letter, Lotty?"

"Will reach him. Write it and give it to me, and have no fear."

Bessy wrung her hands. It was a great step in life, and she was young and naturally fearful of its consequences. In the dark sinful home there was some love to lose by going away, although she knew the dangers were advancing rapidly, and her own father was her greatest enemy. If it had not been for Lotty she would have been glad to escape and seek a better life in an atmosphere more pure; but to face the world alone, and confront it with her girlish strength—she so weak!

"Oh, Lotty! do say you will go away with me!"

"And mar your life—and bring you a share of all the suspicion and disgrace that will cling to me, wherever I go—not so bad as that, mind—not so bad as that, after all these awful years! You and I are better apart—you cannot brighten my life, and I can but blacken yours. Now, write your letter; and watch your opportunity, and when the night gets dark, and you hear me coughing at the bottom of the stairs, come down cautiously, and run for it."

"But I must see you again, Lotty."

"Well, at some time or other—we'll say

that. I'll try and believe that I am going to meet you some day. But you mustn't think of me too much, or mention me to any one, or ever write to me at this place—better think me dead, and try to believe it."

"No—I must see you sometimes, or I will stop here," said Bessy firmly.

"Well, leave time and place to me—Mr. Parslow will let me know where you are, and some day I'll find courage to see you, if you will only wait and be patient. You feel now how much for the best it is that you should go."

"Yes—it is best."

"You must leave me something as a keep-sake."

"Anything, dear Lotty, anything."

Bessy flung herself into Lotty's arms; and Lotty, to whom any evidence of affection had always seemed distasteful, suffered the arms of her younger sister to encircle her neck.

"This is precious odd and babyish!" she

muttered—"but it can't last much longer, Bessy. What a fool I am—what an old blind beetle-headed fool!"

And Lotty turned away her head, to hide all evidence of her woman's weakness from her sister, and struggle with some heavy sobs, that would find utterance in spite of her.

"Oh! I won't go!" cried Bessy.

"May I drop down dead if you don't!" cried Lotty vehemently, as she broke away from her—"may the house tumble on you—may the curse of her who wants to do what is right fall on you for balking her. You will go, for the sake of everything that's holy—you can't stop for the sake of all that's hellish, and cruel, and false!"

"What will he say and do to you?"

"He may not suspect me—he knows I am a selfish woman, and would rather have you here. If he does kick or strike me, I can get over it in a day or two, or run away too, my own way. If you think of me again, I shall say something awful!"

And her face darkened, and it was the face of Lotty Calverton that Bessy had seen downstairs that morning when she first entered, to confront the storm that threatened her.

"Well, well—I must go. God will watch over me, and you. I am going to pray again, and try so hard to be good."

"Arn't you curious to know what present I want?"

Bessy answered in the affirmative.

"It's the bible of that Methodist girl—ah! you won't part with that, even for my sake—and I ask for nothing else!"

"Yes, Lotty, if you wish it—I will part with it gladly. I am so pleased to hear you speak of my bible, and—"

"Stop that, Bessy," said her sister hastily; "I don't want credit for good works—I hate good works, you know."

" No—no."

"I tell you I do—and I ought to know best," was the peevish response. "Do you think if I hankered so much for a bible I couldn't buy one at an old book-stall. It's Mary Davis's bible I want—for *that's* always putting you in mind of her you think more of than your own flesh and blood. When it's gone you'll think of me more often, and less of her, perhaps!"

"She was very good to me, Lotty."

"So would others have been in her place, and not have made half the fuss about it," was the reply. "Say no more about her, for it always upsets me half the week. You'll let me have the bible?"

"Promise me to read it, then—if only once a-week, on Sunday mornings—if only once a month—make some promise?"

"How precious good you've turned all of a sudden again! Is it that old pauper of a parson?"

"He has reminded me of much that I was

learning to forget—he is a good man, Lotty —you know that."

"I don't want to hear him praised," was the curt reply of this strange woman ; "and I want to be off downstairs. Perhaps I will read it—there ! "

She unlocked the door, returned, and said in a low tone :—

"You'll hear a cough outside in half-an-hour's time—slip the letter underneath the door then, but don't come out or open it. Clear away these torn pieces of paper. Get ready your things—the fewer the better— and be prepared at dark, or any time after dark, for a fit of coughing at the bottom of the stairs ? Do you understand all this ? "

"Yes."

"I shall see you again, so don't make any noise now. Get ready and don't change your mind. Think of all this over again, and you'll feel the stronger for it. There's one lie more to tell—for this is a house

where lies thrive gloriously—one can't live
here and not lie. The song is being learned,
remember. Good-bye."

Lotty was gone; and Bessy, after writing
her hurried earnest letter, was left to think
of it again, as her sister had recommended. And she *did* feel the stronger for
reflection; and from the depths of the shadows around her the fair hope of a better life
began to start therefrom, and make her heart
more light. She would miss Lotty very much,
but they might meet under fairer auspices;
and there might come a time, with God's
help, when she might be of service to her,
and save her in *her* turn, however much
Lotty might disbelieve it. She would build
on that hope; for it would give her courage
to breast the waves that rose so high now,
and hid the land of promise. Of her father
she thought only with a shudder; he had
been so hard and stern and dead to love,
that only fear of him was then apparent, and

love for him had never been encouraged by
one smile. He had not been a father to
her, or treated her like a daughter ; in his
cruel selfishness, his love of gain, his want of
feeling, honour, common decency, she could
but estimate him at that moment as the great
enemy of her young life. She must escape—
it would be happiness to escape ; new dangers,
mysterious and unknown, were threatening
her on all sides. In the mists upon the
mountain she had met her father for the
first time—in the mists more dense around
her present life let her part from him for
ever, and pray to God to guard her in her
wanderings. Half-an-hour afterwards, Lotty's
cough sounded outside, and the letter was
slipped beneath the door with a trembling
hand. It was the first step in the resolu-
tion that seemed to grow more strong with
her, true to her sister's prophecy.

It was striking two downstairs when Mrs.
Calverton made her appearance with Bessy's

dinner. Mrs. Calverton walked with a trifle more difficulty than at the period of her first visit, and the current of her thoughts had undergone a change. She came in sullen and lumpish, and pushed the plate towards Bessy, in a by no means courteous manner.

"Here's your dinner. Your father thinks you'd better not come down, as he *must* swear if he sees you. Not that that matters much to anybody, but he don't easily forget the loss of thirty pounds, and perhaps one row the less saves trouble. Stay up here and learn your song, and leave the old dog growling!"

Mrs. Calverton trundled out of the room again, after two ineffectual attempts to neatly clear the door, and Bessy felt relieved in mind when her mother-in-law reached safely the bottom of the stairs. Bessy's heart was too full for dinner, and she put her plate outside the door again, where the dog, who had worried her heels five years ago, paid his respects, and neatly polished it off. The afternoon crept on, and Bessy's heart beat nervously as the grey clouds that had been looming overhead all day took deeper shading as the light died out, and the gas-lamps began to flicker in the street.

Presently, she heard heavy feet ascending the stairs, and a wild sense of terror caused her to rush to the door and lock herself in again. She could not face her father; his very looks would ice her heart, and perhaps let her own secret escape by some word or look that fright might scare from her.

" Hollo, here! open the door. No nonsense with me!" and the heavy fist of honest Dick arose the echoes of the " El-Dorado," and nearly split the panels in.

" What do you want with me?" asked Bessy, pale with fright.

" Have you learned that song? Are you going to be obedient, and sing it?"

Bessy thought of Lotty's words, " that to
live in such a place one must lie ;" but she
struggled against the untruth which rose to
her lips.

" I don't know it yet—you must give me
time," was the answer.

" Well, don't play tricks with me, for
you're not out of my black book ; and if you
add another score to it—thunder of heaven !
it'll be next door to grim death ! "

" Will you let me learn my song in peace ?"
asked Bessy.

" Well, learn away, and be dutiful for once.
You'll be wanted in the concert-room at eight,
remember, for the other song ; so, sharp's the
word."

He struck his hand against the panel of the
door once more, and it sounded to Bessy as
though he smote upon her heart. She gave
a sigh of relief when his heavy feet lumbered
down the stairs, and she was alone in the
twilight with her many thoughts. Could she

escape? Was there a chance of it? Had
Lotty sent the letter to Mr. Parslow?—and
would he meet her, help her, indicate the way
to the bright new life, from which to look
back on this would be looking on a hideous
dream? She prepared a little bundle of
clothes, put on her cloak and hood, and then
knelt down at the bedside, and prayed as she
had not prayed since she was a little girl, and
lived at Aberogwin. In the midst of her
prayer she thought of Mary Davis, and wished
that her flight were back to the peaceful
Welsh home, and that her father knew nothing
of its inhabitants. It struck six, and she
was praying still for help on the unknown
road before her.

Night at last, and Bessy watchful at the
half-open door, listening breathlessly, and
hearing nothing but the beat, beat, of her
own heart. If Lotty should fail in her project
after all, and her father's suspicions, perhaps
of treachery, keep him watchful, what was to

become of her, with her song unknown, and the terrible threat of that father hanging over her? She must escape, and seek a new friend in the ranks of the untried; she felt it was her only chance now, as she stood in her dark room and listened. She had to cower back and softly close her door, as Charles Edwin Calverton came shuffling up the stairs. He might be her friend; she believed in her heart that he wished her well, but she could not trust in him. The old man reached the top of the stairs, and Bessy could hear him stop outside her door, and listen and breathe hard through the keyhole. After a moment's pause he tapped softly.

"Who's there?" asked Bessy.

"Only me. Are you in the dark?"

"Yes."

"You won't say anything about this morning?"

"No."

A long pause; then he said with a jerk—

" Make a run for it as soon as you can. Make a—"

He shuffled away hastily, and went into his own room. The voice of Richard Calverton below had scared him in the middle of his warnings.

Seven o'clock, and no signal yet. Bessy felt her heart sinking. The visitors were dropping in to the concert-room, and her father's voice seemed never for an instant to die away in the lower regions, but to haunt them like an evil presence.

Near upon half-past seven she was sure, when the signal came at length, and Lotty coughed violently below. Bessy caught up her bundle and stole rapidly, silently down the stairs, and met Lotty in the dark, well-like receptacle below, where the two doors opened, one to the parlour, the other to the bar.

" Don't make a noise, Bessy—don't say a word. There's a ' school' to-night in the parlour for a minute or two, and father's locked in with his friends. That drunken cat" (meaning her mother-in-law, the reader will bear in mind) "has just gone into the concert-room, and the field is clear. Stoop down as you pass the parlour window—and creep silently to the door by the counter, and then—away like the wind! Are you ready now?—what are you trembling at, girl?"

"Good-bye, dear Lotty—come to me soon. The good God watch over you!"

"Too late for that—I'm lost!"

"It is not too late to repentance, Lotty."

"Don't preach, but go. Where's Mary Davis's bible?"

"Upstairs in the drawers."

"Then go now—put your arms round my neck for a moment, and let me feel your face against my own. This is a hard—harder —parting than ever a wretch like me bargained for in *her* life. Go, I say!"

And Lotty stamped her foot impatiently. Bessy released her hold, uttered a second blessing, opened the door by the bar, and crouched down so that her figure might not be level with the parlour window as she glided past. Lotty's face watched her round the door, and Lotty's white lips, perhaps, prayed for her safety to that God of whom she thought so little, and in whose mercy she believed not. Safe round the bar, and slowly making her way along the outer side of the counter—alive to the slightest noise that might give warning of the dangers in the way of her escape.

Bessy was gathering her dress round her, and preparing to rise to her feet, when a click of the latch of the door leading to the music-room struck her motionless. The mother-in-law appeared upon the threshold.

" Mother ! " cried Lotty, " what's the matter with the clock—who has stopped it ? "

" Stopped it ! " repeated Mrs. Calverton,

turning round quickly, and looking towards the time-piece over the parlour door. It was Bessy's last chance; she rose silently, and crossed the shop, looked for a moment at her mother-in-law, still standing and stupidly regarding the clock of the " El-Dorado," at Lotty's face ghastly white with fright, at the lighted room beyond the parlour blind, where thieves and vagabonds wrangled over their spoil, and wished each other dead for grasping at the lion's share; and then she was in the street, where a hurrying crowd of snow-flakes welcomed her to her new world— a cold and cheerless welcome, typical of the greeting such wanderers as Bessy Calverton meet with from a world that knows no mercy, but is hard, and stern, and unbelieving !

END OF THE SECOND PART.

PART THE THIRD.

THE NEW LIFE.

E

CHAPTER I.

A NEW LIFE WITH THE NEW YEAR.

ON the new road in life which circumstances had mapped out for Bessy Calverton hurried our heroine, fearful only of pursuit and capture. Once free from the " El-Dorado," she seemed, even in the midst of the whirling wind and snow, to breathe a purer atmosphere, and with every step away from the haunt of drunkeness and crime to feel more like the Bessy Calverton of old. She could have already rejoiced at her escape had it not been for the white, haggard face she had seen last in her direction, and that had

E 2

looked towards her so full of sorrow and
regret. Bessy knew a little of London now :
she had been on messages for her father occasionally ; she had been out once or twice
with her mother-in-law and Lotty, and there
was no difficulty in discovering the Whitechapel Road, and the Minories, and Fen-
church Street, and the broad thoroughfare
leading to London Bridge. The snow was
falling heavily, and Bessy had to pause
every now and then and shake it from her
mantle, and the top of the little bundle that
she clutched to her breast. It was a New
Year's night in which there was matter for
satisfaction to more than her ; the snow gave
promise of a change in the weather, of times
a trifle more warm—perhaps of cessation to
the bitter frost that had struck at life and
hope in many homes. People in the streets
were trusting that ; shivering women bent on
scanty marketing expeditions met and talked
of it ; outcasts huddled under the great wall

and round the doors of Whitechapel union
seemed hopeful of it, and the frosted policeman stopped to express the same opinion
with the tradesman under shelter of the snow-
laden shop-blind. Bessy did not feel much
change in the weather herself; she was not
warmly clad, and, despite the pace at which
she walked, the fear of a hand upon her
shoulder, and a voice calling her to stop,
kept her heart cold with suspense. The
streets were full of people that night; and
those who had money to spend were seeking
the best market and the cheapest wares. In
that neighbourhood there were signs of the
hard season everywhere : in the scantier show
of goods in every window; in the famine
prices; in the high figures on the baker's
tickets; in the paucity of goods on coster-
mongers' barrows—in the majority of lookers-
on to buyers—in the multiplicity of beggars
in the streets—in the claims that real charity
made over sham at every dozen yards—in

the jostling crowd of Barmecides feasting on
steam from cook-shop areas, and on sights of
joints through cook-shop windows. Steeped
to the lips in poverty and want as was
this neighbourhood, Bessy thought it was a
happier world to live in than her own, and
that amidst it all there were fewer dark faces,
evil words and looks. She sighed for no
more higher, better life, than amongst the
struggling poor around her; and she caught
herself looking more than once into the faces
of those who streamed rapidly past, and
wondering which looked kindest, and which
might take most readily to her.

From the poor neighbourhood to the less
busy but more grand; past larger houses, wholesale firms and city tradesfolk, who closed early
and barred out the frost, and were not much
affected by the mercury at zero—in Grace-
church Street at last, and inquiring her way
for Monument Yard, with a more hopeful
heart. So far on her way, and untracked yet
—there must be hope for her!

Bessy reached Monument Yard in safety, and very dark and still it was round the base of the monument even at that early hour. The city life and turmoil at a few yards distant, seemed as far removed from it as from the period which that stone column was raised to commemorate. The snow had drifted there, and only a straggler now and then shivered past on the other side of the way, in the direction of Lower Thames Street. All was silent, and Bessy looked nervously over her shoulder once or twice for those pursuers who might be stealing along in the shadow of the houses, ready to clutch her, and bear her back to Choke Street. She gathered courage as the time went on against that fear, although the new distrust of her letter having failed in its mission began to oppress her with a greater sense of doubt. And yet Mr. Parslow was a minister of the Gospel, a good and humane man; she was not distrustful of him in her heart. If the letter had reached his hands, and he were well, Mr. Parslow would surely appear there to befriend her—her child's knowledge of human nature assured her of that truth.

And the child's estimate of Mr. Parslow's character—true and genuine, and one that a child might read—was not a false one ; for the clocks were chiming the half hour past eight in a variety of tones, when a tall figure advanced at a brisk pace towards her, and Bessy recognized the friend whom she had seen that morning.

Mr. Parslow was still great-coatless, but the rough nature of the night had brought forth a white worsted comforter, and an umbrella of a seedy green silk—cullender pattern. Mr. Parslow was evidently of a careful turn of mind, for the bottoms of his black trousers were tucked half-way up his legs, allowing a liberal display of Wellington boots.

"My poor girl, have you been waiting long ?" he asked anxiously, as he came up.

"Not more than half an hour, sir."

"This is clean against the laws of one's country," he said, looking round him cautiously: "aiding and abetting a child in rebellion against her own father. Upon my word, Jacob," said he, adopting his usual habit of apostrophizing himself, "you are improving in your moral character. But they have treated you badly, Miss Calverton."

"My sister Lotty thought every day brought a new and greater danger to me," she replied.

"And sister Lotty's experience has been hard and cruel. God bless my soul, it is pleasant to see the better nature flashing up in her, resisting wrong, and arming in the cause of right. It shows what might be done by time and perseverance in the most benighted places. But let us be moving, Miss Calverton."

"Will you call me Bessy, sir—it sounds more like a friend."

" To be sure. Bessy Calverton," he said ;
" a fair name, to which, by God's help, we will
add a fair life—eh ?"

" By God's help, sir."

" And our own—we must not sit down
with folded arms, and wait for blessings.
This is a world of workers, Bessy."

" I'm not afraid of honest work, sir."

" That's well said. This way !"

" Over London Bridge, sir?"

" Ay—we must put the broad, muddy old
Thames between ourselves and the ' El-
Dorado.' Upon my word," said he, endea-
vouring to give a light tone to the conversation, for the sake of raising Bessy's spirits,
" I shall begin to appreciate the burglarious
and pocket-picking professions in my neighbourhood presently. There is something very
exciting in going dead against the laws, and
walking about with your head over your
shoulder, in momentary expectation of a set
of knuckles in the back of your neck—ex-

tremely exciting and rather pleasant. Am I giving you a fair share of the umbrella, Bessy Calverton?"

"Thank you—yes."

"You had better let me carry that bundle, and take my arm. It's extremely slippery, and you don't seem to get on very well."

"But—but—sir—"

"But, Bessy Calverton, I'm a horridly obstinate man," said he, seizing the bundle, and tucking it under his arm—"a man of fierce passions, who, once crossed, might fly into a frightful temper and commit himself. Take my arm."

Bessy timidly complied, and the Reverend Jacob Parslow marched along more sturdily. As they proceeded over London Bridge he asked a great many questions concerning her home and parents, of the cause that had led to Bessy's sudden determination to escape, of the life more early in the Welsh village, that seemed to lie back so many years from the present time.

"Well," said he, when he had elicited those particulars necessary to arrive at the true history of his companion, " conscience bears me out in my resolves, rash as I have been. I am inclined to act on the moment, shut my eyes and dash forwards; and now and then, as a matter of course, I bring my head with a smart rap against a wall. But there is something more than chance in all this; you cross my path, arouse my sympathies; you appeal for help against those deadly ills besetting all lives as crossed and chequered as your own. I should not be a minister of God, a faithful servant of my Master, were I to resist that appeal, and leave you surrounded by temptation. The rule that makes such interference as mine, in most respects sinful and inexcusable, cannot apply here. In the dark side of human nature there are exceptions to all rules, and the best way to act is prompted by our hearts. You do not regret this step, my child?"

" No, sir."

" You will not be afraid of working for your bread—working hard, perhaps—with a Christian woman, whose life may teach a better moral, afford a brighter example, than you have witnessed lately ?"

" I shall be glad, sir—not afraid."

" My experience lies not with rich people; I have no connexion with them. If I knocked at the door of a great house in the western part of this metropolis, the hall porter would slam the door in my face, and tell me there was nothing to give away—not even gentle words. I have been puzzling my head a great deal about you this afternoon; you have spoiled one of my best sermons by interfering with the heads, and the summing up in conclusion is no summing up at all. I have been thinking what is best for you, and I have fixed on an elderly lady for your companion, one who attends my church occasionally in fine weather; a very dear old friend of mine."

"You are very good to take all this trouble on my account, sir," said Bessy. "How am I ever to repay you!"

"By letting me see with every visit that I have not been deceived in my estimate of character. I expect," he added, as his hand fell kindly on hers an instant, "great things here; you must not disappoint me!"

"Trust me, sir!" cried Bessy.

"Now, do you know anything of Snow-fields?"

"Snowfields, sir!" exclaimed Bessy. "I —I once knew a gentleman who lived in Snowfields. Yes, I am sure it was Snowfields; for I thought then it was singular to have snow-fields in London, and told him so; and he said it was black snow—very thick and nasty."

"What gentleman was that?" asked Mr. Parslow, with some interest.

"A Mr. Speckland, who called once at my uncle's house in Aberogwin."

Mr. Parslow came to a full stop, and looked over Bessy's bundle at the white pavement.

"Dear me, now, that's strange!—that's exceedingly strange! Perhaps I have done wrong, after all."

"In what way, Mr. Parslow?" asked Bessy, alarmed.

"The Specklands are not a church-going people, and are neighbours of my friend's. Respectable and hard-working people, but neither God-fearing nor God-loving. I am almost sorry you are acquainted with them."

"I only remember one Mr. Speckland, sir —and I do not think he will remember me, now. But he was a good young man, sir— very kind to me."

"Stephen, or Hugh Speckland?"

"Stephen."

"I know him," said Mr. Parslow drily; "but—sufficient for the day is the evil thereof, and I shall leave you in safe hands.

A good young man in his way, Bessy—but one of the great No Church class, to fight against which is up-hill work."

He spoke warmly, as though he had been lately fighting up-hill himself against the class he spoke of; and then he turned out of the noisy Borough, where they then were, into the narrow streets leading to Bermondsey, Snow-fields, and parts adjacent.

The life changed suddenly as they entered those streets—in an instant it was Choke Street again, and there were Choke Street shops, and Choke Street faces round them. A neighbourhood as poor—full of as squalid people, with courts and alleys branching right and left, and whispering of evil haunts, and where poverty in their midst might still be struggling to keep honest, or losing faith with every hour, as the waves brought a hope to their feet, or dashed it away.

The similitude struck Bessy.

"This is like home, sir," said she.

Mr. Parslow fancied he heard a half sigh escape from Bessy's lips, and he looked askance at her.

"Let us hope that that which constitutes home will not be missing here, Bessy. From the new home is to date the new life—don't forget that. See here," he added, with a flash of his old humour, "Snowfields it is, and no mistake."

He stamped the new pair of boots, he had speculated in that morning on recovering his money, briskly on the pavement, and shook the snow therefrom, and then turned into streets more narrow still, some of which were crossed by railway arches, looking dark and cavernous that wintry night. At a few yards from one of these arches that spanned the roadway, Mr. Parslow stopped before a small house, and returned the bundle to Bessy.

"I think this will be home," said he, as he applied his hand to the knocker, and raised the echoes of the street with his fantasia.

"Does the lady know I am coming?"

"Not yet."

"But if she should object, sir,—if I cannot work to please her—if—"

"My dear girl, how many more ifs! Like the rest of the world, Bessy Calverton, worrying yourself to death with unreal speculations on impossible futures."

The door opened, and an old woman, almost as tall as Mr. Parslow, stood in the entry and held a flickering light towards the street.

"My eyes ain't good—but that's surely my young master?"

"Young master it is, and isn't," said Mr. Parslow. "Here, Mrs. Wessinger, I have brought you a New Year's gift."

"You're always kind—why, Lord bless us, it's a young woman."

"Lord bless us all this New Year's night— Amen."

"Amen, sir,—and come in."

Mrs. Wessinger led the way along the

narrow passage to the back parlour, where a scanty fire was burning, and where a pile of work, in the shape of women's boots and shoes, was heaped upon the table.

" Glad to see you have plenty of work, Mrs. Wessinger."

" Yes, more lucky than most of my neighbours, Mr. Parslow—I'm thankful for it, as in duty bound."

Mrs. Wessinger had a brisk manner of speaking, that was not unmusical when one became used to it ; and was a tall, white-faced woman, with high cheek bones, whose appearance on close inspection was possibly not exhilarating. A woman whose rapidity of movement reminded Bessy of her uncle Davis, for she had stirred the fire, taken a chair, put on her spectacles, filled her lap with shoes, and was hard at work at shoe-binding before either of her visitors had sat down.

" You'll excuse me getting on, master," said she ; " but there's a Sunday's dinner to earn, and it's past nine now. You never like to see folk idle. I was never idle in dear old Hampshire, was I ? "

" No, no, Mrs. Wessinger—ever industrious and cheerful—a pattern to all house-keepers."

" You are very kind to say so, sir. Take off your mantle, child," with a momentary glance at Bessy, " the snow begins to thaw in this warm room."

Accustomed to the reeking air of the " El-Dorado," the warmth of the room had not particularly struck Bessy.

" And you, sir, have your feet wet as usual. There are the old slippers upstairs that I always keep for you—I'll fetch them in a minute, if you'll excuse the light."

" No—no—I'm well shod to-night, thank you. Don't go—I shall leave you in a minute or two, when I have explained my errand. I have my overwork at home, too."

" Always busy, sir."

" And yet always behindhand, so don't compliment me, Mrs. Wessinger. What a woman you are for compliments, Mrs. W.; why, you spoilt me with them when I was a boy."

" No, sir !" said the woman, with a pleasant smile and shake of the head, that quite changed her expression of countenance.

" Well, well, this is not business, and I am coming one day next week to argue the matter thoroughly. Now, Mrs. Wessinger, old friend, companion, playfellow, I am going to test your interest in me to the utmost."

" I shan't flinch."

" Here is a poor girl without a friend, in a world of temptation—young and pret—and so on," he corrected ; " who has a story to tell you, which will touch your heart, I think. Will you take my word that she needs some firm and steady friend, and give her the shelter of your roof a little while, and help her in your way ? "

"Take your bonnet off, Miss, and put your bundle down. This is the best home I can offer you—you're welcome!"

"Oh! madam!" cried Bessy, moved by this spontaneity.

"I know nothing of you," and the grey eyes looked searchingly at Bessy, whilst the hand worked on like a mechanical power distinct in itself. "I have known many young women in my time, and been deceived in a great many, and find they do not take to old and ugly people like me. But you come here with the best of references—and as I said before, are welcome. What is your name?"

"Bessy Calverton."

The woman dropped her needle, picked it up hastily again, and recommenced her work.

"I had a daughter Bessy once, who died about your age, and nearly broke her mother's heart—you remember her, Mr. Parslow?" ·

" Well."

" As innocent as heaven all her life—is there truth in that old saying, that the good die first, do you think, Mr. Parslow? I'm no scholar."

" Good, bad, and indifferent all die at their proper time, Mrs. Wessinger," he said, in half-reproof; "there is no rule for it— only a line of Wordsworth's poetry."

" Ah! I don't read poetry ; it never agreed with me."

" You must teach Bessy shoe-binding, Mrs. Wessinger, and make her a help to you. Whatever time you may lose in teaching, I—"

" Don't say any more, please, Mr. Parslow —but leave Bessy with me. She and I will get on very well together, I daresay. If she is handy with her needle she can earn her living perhaps."

" I have not done much needlework since I left Wales. But I was considered handy then.

" Will you begin now ?"

" Certainly."

And Bessy, anxious to make herself useful,
was soon at the table watching the movements of Mrs. Wessinger, and receiving
her first lesson in shoe-binding. Mr. Parslow rubbed his hands slowly up and down his
knees, and watched the progress of the
lesson.

" She'll be of use to you, I see, Mrs.
Wessinger," said he, rising ; " well, I
leave her in good hands. Don't turn
so pale—we haven't been friends so long
that you cannot afford to miss me."

" You have been so kind—you are my
only friend !" cried Bessy ; " how can I ever
thank you !"

" Pooh, pooh—nothing to thank me for,"
said Mr. Parslow ; " didn't you rescue me
from next door to beggary this morning, and
are not my thirty pounds very cheaply
earned. Don't say anything more about it,

Bessy Calverton—and pray don't publish my small services to the world, or you'll go back to Choke Street, and the Reverend Jacob Parslow may find himself in the House of Correction—ah, well, I was very fond of change once!"

"You will let sister Lotty know where I am, sir?"

"Hum — if she come and ask your address. Under other circumstances some risk might be attached to it. Good-bye, Bessy Calverton—in the new life, I shall mark progression."

"Yes, sir."

"Frankly spoken. And the new life begins well on the threshold of the new year, with the new and better friends, and the great God watching over all. Courage, my poor girl—and faith!"

He shook her by both hands, and murmured something to himself, at which Bessy bowed her head a little and looked down.

She felt it was a short prayer for her safety and protection by the light upon his face, although he uttered never a word that she could hear. Mrs. Wessinger followed him into the passage, and the parlour door being left open Bessy could hear the name of Speckland mentioned once or twice.

"I promised to look up that young infidel every time I set foot in Snowfields; is he at home, do you think?"

"Always at home, for the matter of that, Mr. Parslow."

"I will just look in, though I will not be betrayed into argument at this hour of the night, and with a sermon and a-half to write when I reach home."

"He is harder and more obstinate every day. I wouldn't waste my time, sir. You might convince a brick wall before Hugh Speckland."

"Well, we're friends—I'll say good evening to him."

" Oh, sir—I know what that means."

Mr. Parslow laughed pleasantly, then he spoke in a lower tone, concerning herself, Bessy was assured; and after a moment or two the door closed, and Mrs. Wessinger came into the room like a small steam-engine, and was in her chair and hard at work on the instant.

" Now, tell me the story of your troubles, Bessy; and don't mind me counting my stitches whilst you talk—it's a habit I have."

Bessy related as briefly as possible the beginning of her real troubles, which dated from the arrival of her father in Wales. She spoke simply and earnestly of her trials and temptations since that period, ending with her flight that day from the objectionable quarter of the " El-Dorado." The story affected Mrs. Wessinger; like Mr. Parslow, she was one to take an interest in the struggle of the oppressed for light amidst the darkness, and she listened attentively, and once gave a hasty wipe to her eyes with the back of her left hand, the right being ever stitch, stitch, stitch, with a monotonous regularity that nothing seemed to affect. More and more the impression deepened on Bessy that that right hand was possessed of powers of volition distinct in itself, and was not swayed by any of those emotions that affected the rest of her frame. It was the hard-working hand, that had its task before it, and would not be distracted, and might be made of wood or iron, or be a cousin-german to that "steam arm" concerning which the comic singer at the "El-Dorado" had sung now and then, backed by a grand chorus from the audience, and a violent hammering of beer mugs.

"You're better away, girl," said Mrs. Wessinger. "It was a blessed thought of yours to think of Mr. Parslow, who's a blessed man if ever there was one. I hope it won't come true that saying I spoke of, that the good die first, or there'll be mourning in Whitechapel."

"He is not ill?" asked Bessy, alarmed.

"No, but he works too much, and fags too much, and has no one to help him," said Mrs. Wessinger. "He is one of those good men who work hard for little pay, and less thanks, and nothing but death will tire him out. Do you see how old he's looking, and he not forty yet?"

"Not forty?"

"Ah! you may well look surprised, my child. Not forty. I held him in my arms a baby down in Hampshire. His father was a rich man then, and he was a little bit free with his money, but open as the day, and frank, and good. But the father was a spend-thrift, and gambled in mines, and went to ruin, and shot himself in his room one day; and Jacob Parslow took a turn and went serious, and studied for the Church, and showed in his poverty and trouble what we don't all show—Christian fortitude."

"A great gift!" murmured Bessy.

"Ah! pity it isn't catching, like the measles, or that opposite affair, which we can all show—the grumbles. But you don't work?"

"I am not quite used to it yet."

"Well, it's rather hard work for young fingers as a beginning; but I have had it to do for many years now. I was brought up to shoe-binding in Southampton; and I took to it again when affairs went wrong with my husband, and he was rui—never mind; that's a story that's neither here nor there. Let us talk of Mr. Parslow again. I told you he was the best of men, I think?"

Bessy answered in the affirmative, and Mrs. Wessinger continued her untiring theme, until the candle burned low, and the hours glided away, and the work was finished.

"Will you wait here till I return, Bessy?"

"Oh! you must let me go with you," said Bessy, starting up; "I shouldn't like to be left here all alone yet."

"But you must be tired?"

"No, Mrs. Wessinger."

"Put on your bonnet and come marketing with me, then, if you're not afraid of the snow."

Bessy complied, and went out marketing with Mrs. Wessinger. Mrs. Wessinger took her work home to a wholesale bootmaker's in Bermondsey, received some more work, which Bessy carried for her in her apron, and then did her marketing in the same brisk, business-like manner as she had done her work at home. Estimable pattern for ladies who go out "shopping" was this brisk old lady of sixty-seven—one who could compute time and understand its value; one who only asked to see goods that she wanted, and knew to a fraction when she was overcharged, and when she had obtained a bargain; a woman who slaved hard for her bread, and earned little money; and yet had nothing to complain of—possibly a contented woman.

Going back with the snow to Mrs. Wessinger's home, they made a straight cut through two streets more narrow than the rest, and came out amongst more railway arches. It was striking eleven as they passed a house adjacent to one of the arches, the parlour window of which was low, and lighted by a fish-tail burner.

Some one was standing by the door smoking his after-supper pipe sedately.

" That's a nice thing for a weak chest such a night as this," said she, pausing for an instant.

" Ah, don't scold me, nurse Wessinger," was the good-tempered answer, " I have been so hard worked to-day."

" Man was meant for work."

" Well, I'm not grumbling—a happy new year to you, Mrs. Wessinger ! "

"Thankee—and the same to you," was the brisk response.

"We've had your pet parson here to-night again. He and Hugh have been at it, hammer and tongs, for a good hour."

"And Hugh as aggravating and pig-headed as ever, Stephen—I know."

"Ask him."

Stephen pointed to the parlour-window, and Mrs. Wessinger passed on, and Bessy had not the courage or the heart to greet her old friend then. And yet her heart leaped to-wards him as to one link of the better times; and as she glanced at him, she thought how years had altered him and aged him, as well as the Mr. Parslow of whom Mrs. Wessinger had spoken. But it was the old good-tempered friendly voice that had made the Welsh home a different place, and it was pleasant to hear it at that time. Mrs. Wessinger stood looking through the parlour-window, with Bessy by her side. The blind was only half drawn before the window, and allowed an observer to see a dark-haired stern-looking man poring over his work. He was quick to detect a figure at the window; for he looked up as if to frown away the inquisitive eyes upon his labour. Bessy saw some likeness to Stephen Speckland in the face, but the face was more lined, and the frown upon it was not agreeable to meet. It disappeared, however, as he became aware of Mrs. Wessinger's presence, and he gave a half nod, the eighth of a smile—certainly not more —and then bent more studiously over his task.

" A happy new year to you, Mr. Hugh— a better one than the last in all respects ! " called Mrs. Wessinger."

" Thank you," sounded the deep voice from within.

"I hope you haven't offended Mr. Parslow," said she, at the top of her voice, through the window; " I'll forgive anything but that."

Hugh did not answer, but he frowned again, although this time at his work.

"A bad temper—a hard man," said Mrs. Wessinger, moving on again—"I suppose Stephen's the best of a bad bunch of them."

"Bad?"

"Well, after a fashion. What Mr. Parslow calls the No Church class—always a bad lot, my dear."

Through a maze of little streets to more railway arches, and Mrs. Wessinger's house, the owner thereof opening the door with her latch key, and admitting Bessy.

A series of rapid movements, consisting of laying down her purchases, jumping out of her grey plaid shawl and coal scuttle bonnet, lighting her candle, stirring the fire, and then the wonderful hand working again with all its old energy. "Half-an-hour to twelve and twopence to be earned; that's for the lame man who goes to church every Sunday—for the twopence Stephen Speckland says, but I know better than that! Now, Bessy, open that cupboard and get out the supper things, and then we'll talk, and work, and have our supper, and finish the week out."

Mrs. Wessinger managed to eat her supper and work meanwhile till a church clock struck twelve almost immediately behind them, as if it were in the yard, and then the work ceased, and the arm was still.

" One day gone of the new year, my child," said she; " so the time slips away, and scrambles us along with it. This day twelve-month past, and you didn't think of sitting here."

" No, ma'am."

" And this day twelvemonth to come, and we may wonder at new changes—ay, this day week even, for the matter of that. We're soon topsy-turvy in this blessed world."

It is a world of change, and new phases happen every day. To Bessy Calverton, late of Choke Street, the days before another change were few. There are lives that, year after year, appear to know no alteration, plodding in the mill-horse round of every day, with nothing new or strange to startle; but there are others smitten by a restless fever, and destined to meet new faces, fight new battles at every turn of the shadowy road ending in six feet of earth.

CHAPTER II.

THE OLD FRIEND.

THE manners and customs of Mrs. Wessinger strongly reminded Bessy Calverton of the old Welsh life. Her Welsh life "with a difference;" for Mrs. Wessinger, though a stanch church-goer, and a persistent reader of her bible, was not hard and inflexible over it, but had ever the cheery word, and the quick, almost spasmodic smile, which softened so strangely her pale face.

Mr. Parslow had chosen well in selecting Mrs. Wessinger for the guardian, adviser, teacher, of this nature run wild : every action

of the old lady formed so strange a contrast
to all that Bessy had lived amongst for the
last five years. Here was poverty that complained not; that took the ills that flesh is
heir to with philosophic composure; that
worked hard, day and night, for a living, and
repined not; that amidst the privations and
trials of such a life as hers, found ever something to be grateful for, and repaid it by a
simple, earnest devotion, that was touching.
One week of Bessy Calverton's novitiate
brought back many of the old thoughts,
accustomed her to her new life, and warmed
her heart to her companion. It was a dull,
quiet life, that might have been more lively
with advantage, Bessy thought; but still there
was little time for anything save work; and
Mrs. Wessinger, who was a sharp woman as
well as a pious one, kept Bessy's attention
directed to her needle. During the week we
mention Bessy kept silent respecting her
former acquaintance with Stephen Speckland;

the Specklands, she fancied, were not favourites of Mrs. Wessinger, and she was anxious to win upon the old lady's heart all she could, and not intrude unpleasant thoughts to distract her. Bessy's nature was a loving one ; but adverse circumstances all her life had kept her affection thrust upon herself. It had been as much a weakness to evince affection in Aberogwin as in Choke Street, Whitechapel ; and kind words were strange to Bessy. She took readily to Mrs. Wessinger in consequence, although it was more that lady's manner than her words that evinced a growing love for her.

Bessy Calverton saw nothing of Mr. Parslow that week ; pressure on his time kept him away from the little house in Snowfields. On the following Saturday he wrote a line, asking "if all were well," which Mrs. Wessinger answered, and Bessy added a postcript.

Mrs. Wessinger only rented one room in the house in Snowfields—that little back parlour

to which Bessy was introduced by Mr. Parslow. It served her for kitchen, bed-room,
parlour and all, and was of limited space, and
but scantily furnished; the sofa under the
window serving duty as a bedstead for two
about midnight. That little house of four
rooms contained several families beside Mrs.
Wessinger and Bessy—they economize space
Snowfields way. Bessy could never comprehend where all the people came from of a
morning, or went to of a night, there was
such an incessant tramping up and down the
stairs, and the faces she met in the passages
seemed always new to her. They were rough
men and women some of them—their voices
and manners reminded her of her father more
than once—and they were fighting hard to
live at that time. Work was scarce with the
majority of the lodgers, and the agent who
called for the weekly rents was always at
high words, and threatening summonses and
seizures. Health was not strong in that

house either, and Bessy remarked that the
children who were taken ill, or the women
who failed to keep well, or even the husband,
who grew despairing and talked recklessly of
getting money somehow, all wanted Mrs.
Wessinger immediately. She was the good
genius of that house, and ever ready to obey
the summons for her assistance and advice;
she was a woman who by some happy con-
trivance found a bright side to everything—
had a way of nursing, talking, consoling, so
peculiarly her own, that even her enemies
gave way, and asked for her in their time of
trouble. For Mrs. Wessinger had her enemies, and her little tiffs and grievances with
fellow-lodgers—was a woman who spoke her
mind when anything struck her as unjust or
wrong, and knew how to take her own part
against an imposition. But she was always
ready to help, if her humble assistance were
required in any way—as we shall presently
see—and friend or enemy made no differ-

ence in the alacrity with which she caught up her lap-ful of boots, and hurried upstairs, or over the way, or next door, stitching all the way in much such a manner as Bessy remembered the industrious housewives of Wales knitted along the mountain roads on market-days. And the Mrs. Wessingers are not few and far between amongst the " working-classes," concerning whose true natures, habits, sympathies, most of us are still in the dark. We crush them with abuse, or we raise from them some impossible hero, with more virtues and accomplishments than Crichton, and make him the foreground figure in a novel, and there is no real life in either.

It was Monday of the new week—Bessy's second week in Snowfields—and Mrs. Wessinger and our heroine were busy shoebinding in the back-parlour we have mentioned once or twice. The frost had set in again, and Bessy and Mrs. Wessinger had drawn the little table that they had between them closer to the fire, and Bessy was thinking of Lotty over her work, and hoping at some early day to see her. She had disguised nothing from Mrs. Wessinger, who had heard Lotty's story, and was quick enough to guess, by a deeper shade of Bessy's countenance, when she was thinking of her and her past home.

"You're thinking of that sister of yours, Bessy," said she, looking up. "Haven't I told you, over and over again, that thinking don't do a bit of good, and that we must wait for certainties before we grow doleful. No news is the best of news, you know, my dear."

"Perhaps she'll call on Mr. Parslow this week."

"It's very likely."

Bessy was buoying herself up with that possibility, and stitching away more busily, when a peculiar knock assured Mrs. Wessinger that the ground-floor-back was wanted. It is remarkable what variations a knocker is capable of in a poor neighbourhood, and how a double or a treble knock, a flourish with the knocker or the solemnest of dabs, is significant of the first, second, or parlour floors required, as the case may be. Mrs. Wessinger was wanted, and Bessy tripped with alacrity to the door to answer the summons. Bessy gave a start when she had opened the door and recognized the gentleman who knocked — no less a welcome face and old friend than Stephen Speckland. Bessy blushed as Mr. Speckland looked at her; but that gentleman, dreaming not of a face that he had met in Wales starting up in London streets, addressed her with some formality.

" I beg your pardon, Miss," said he, " I wanted Mrs. Wessinger."

" She is in the parlour, Mr. Speckland."

Stephen looked quickly at her again as she stepped back to allow him ingress; but even the mention of his name did not suggest who this young woman was. Bessy thought it was strange, as she shut the door and followed him, forgetting for the moment that five years had intervened between the present time and their last meeting, and that she was a child at Aberogwin.

"Here—nurse Wessinger to the rescue! The old lady's got the horrors again."

"Does she want to see me?" was Mrs. Wessinger's inquiry.

"Yes; and she's very sorry about that last little dispute, and thinks she was in the wrong now."

"Ah, that's very natural," was the dry rejoinder.

"And Mrs. Wessinger will come to Seymour Street in the course of the evening, and do her best, for the old lady's sake?"

"You ought to know Mrs. Wessinger by this time."

"For a good, motherly soul, that's always at hand in a storm," cried Stephen; "to be sure."

It was the frank cheerful manner of old times — the Aberogwin times — and Bessy wished that he had remembered her.

"Bessy, you will wait here till I return, dear?"

"Yes, Mrs. Wessinger."

Stephen Speckland, who had taken Bessy's seat, and Bessy's thread, and was twisting the latter round his fingers, gave a quick glance towards our heroine again. His brown eyes opened as he gazed, and he rose *à la* Macbeth at the ghost of Banquo, and pushed back the chair and cried—

"Is it Bessy?—the Bessy of North Wales? It is, by Jove!"

Bessy blushed, and coloured, and laughed, and he came towards her and held out his hand.

"We parted good friends, you and I. I hope you haven't forgotten me, Bessy—Miss Calverton, I should say."

"I remembered you at once, Mr. Speckland."

"And the old lattice porch, and the half-penny that you hated me for giving you, and the fairy tales, and the fairy book, and the Welsh songs with such a lot of g's in them? Ah! that was a holiday!"

"And the torrent path, and the toads and diamonds story, Mr. Speckland, and the last walk up the mountain side before you said 'good-bye!'" cried Bessy Calverton, with sparkling eyes.

"Ah! it's a dream now!" cried Speckland, "and you and I are in Snowfields. What a waking, eh, Bes—Miss Calverton? And how you have altered, and what a precious time it was ago!"

"Hoighty-toighty!" exclaimed Mrs. Wessinger, "this is very strange to me, remember. What does it all mean, Stephen Speckland?"

"That Miss Calverton lived at Aberogwin five years since, and I was wandering there on a constitutional tour, and spent a few days in her uncle's cottage. She was a little girl then, and rather fond of fairy tales."

Bessy was embarrassed, and felt that she was no longer the little girl who had made a hero of this wanderer. But she felt very happy amidst her confusion, for it was pleasant to be remembered by this light-hearted man.

" Old friends turn up strangely enough at times," commented Mrs. Wessinger; "it's a pity, perhaps, that you *have* come to light again, considering all things."

" And what a hair-brained, rackety, un-principled, good-for-nothing fellow I am, please add, Mrs. W."

" I see you treasure up my opinion of you, Stephen."

" I'm fond of criticism, even an old—"
" woman's," he was going to say, but he corrected himself, and added—" friend's ! "

" Have you been quite well since you were in Wales ?" asked Bessy.

" My old complaint—a weak chest, I think

they call it—I call it no chest at all—only an apology. And uncle Davis and Miss Mary— I hope they are both well? I can see them now, as plain as possible!"

And the mental vision appeared to give Mr. Speckland pleasure, for he rubbed his hands together, and laughed.

"I left Wales two days after your departure, and have not seen them since," said Bessy, with a sigh.

"Why—how's that?"

"I think, Bessy, you had better keep your story to yourself," said Mrs. Wessinger, whose right hand had been vigorously working all this time; "and I think, Mr. Speckland, that this is really not a mite of business of yours."

"Spoken like an oracle, nurse Wessinger," said he; "you'll come and cheer up the old lady—I may tell her that?"

"Arn't your spirits good enough?"

"Oh! she's used to me—and your ways are not my ways."

" So much the better for me."

" Well," with a careless toss of his head, " I own it."

" More shame for you."

" And I own that, too."

" Ah! we shall never quarrel," said Mrs. Wessinger, trying hard to repress a smile.

" And Miss Bessy will, perhaps, come with you and see Lucy and brother Hugh, and father. They have often heard me speak of my Welsh trip—it did good to the whole family, that little journey—Hugh says to this day it saved my life."

" Bessy can do as she likes," said Mrs. Wessinger, with a significant glance that said, " Say no." But Bessy was young, and in doubt as to the true meaning of Mrs. Wessinger's glances, and anxious to see the Speckland family, of whom she had thought so much, and said " yes," with so much alacrity, that she blushed afterwards at her precipitation. She must try and remember that she was seventeen years of age, and not the little girl Stephen Speckland was so friendly with.

Stephen Speckland departed on the strength of this promise, and Mrs. Wessinger surveyed Bessy through her spectacles.

"I shall never take to people who keep things back," she said.

"You did not speak kindly of them a week ago, dear Mrs. Wessinger," cried Bessy, her great eyes filling with tears, "and I thought at that time I would not mention that I had ever met with Mr. Speckland."

"I'm a hard old woman sometimes," said Mrs. Wessinger.

"You don't think you will ever have cause to speak hardly, think hardly, of me?"

"I think not—I hope not, my child."

"I will stay at home here, if you think it right."

"My child, you have made a promise, and must keep it. Besides you wish to go—and there is no harm likely to befall you—far from it."

" You don't like the Specklands ? "

"That's a hard question to answer ; some I may like, some I may object to. They are an honest, hard-working family, and have met with many misfortunes in their time, seen much illness, and borne their trials well. But it is not a house where much is thought of Him who sent those trials to them."

" But Lucy Speckland ? "

" Lucy is about the best—but she's in the midst of evil example, and don't find her way to church very often. Before my little difference with Mrs. Speckland I used to call for her and take her with me ; I think I was wrong to leave that practice off, for the sake of my own silly quarrels, and she so helpless."

" Helpless ! " repeated Bessy.

" Yes—poor girl—she's blind ! "

Mrs. Wessinger's cross mood melted perceptibly away. The thought of Lucy Speckland's infirmity softened her heart to the family in general.

" They're a poor set of castle-builders," said she, "and there's only one matter-of-fact member of the family. It's a pity he's so bad-tempered and obstinate, for he works the hardest, and keeps the lot of 'em together, I'm inclined to think. But let us be going, Bessy —there's little occasion for me to speak of their good and evil qualities when you are to see them all directly."

Mrs. Wessinger gathered her boots together, stitching meanwhile, after her usual habit ; and without going through the ceremony of any further equipment than a bonnet stuck extinguisher fashion on the top of her mob cap, prepared to sally forth to the relief of the lady attacked with " the horrors "—whatever that particular complaint might happen to be. Bessy, with her bonnet adjusted more decorously, took up her work also, and prepared to follow Mrs. Wessinger.

Mrs. Wessinger, after managing to open the door without much disarrangement to her stitches, paused and looked back at Bessy.

" Let us see now. That mad-cap fellow Stephen is at home all day hulking about, no doubt. I wouldn't talk more about Wales with him than I could help."

" Why not? " asked the surprised Bessy.

" I've an odd reason for it," said she, gruffly, " don't ask me."

" Very well," said Bessy, with a half sigh, as she followed Mrs. Wessinger, thinking she was odd in her manner as well as her reasons sometimes.

CHAPTER III.

THE SPECKLANDS.

THE Specklands were at home in full force when Mrs. Wessinger and Bessy entered the front parlour, through the window of which they had peered on the evening of Bessy's first arrival in Snowfields.

Stephen, who had been seated at a little table near the fire opposite his father, rose to do the honours of reception.

" An old friend and a new one, " he said, by way of introduction. "Mrs. Wessinger and Miss Calverton. You have all heard me speak of Bessy Calverton I met with once in Wales."

" You've talked enough of Wales for a dozen," said the father; "find a chair for Miss Calverton—glad to see you both," he added, with a patronizing air; "we're at cards rather early in the morning, Stevie and I, Mrs. Wessinger."

" So I see."

" I'm an old man, who requires amusing—even the doctor bears me out in that—and Stevie has nothing particular to do till the evening at the theatre. He's an awful cribbage player, though; Hugh beats him hollow."

Hugh muttered something in reply to this over his work, which was on a kind of bench near the window, to catch all the light that the railway arch had left him. As Bessy glanced towards the figure on the high stool, who sat with his back towards her, she thought he might have been polite enough to have acknowledged their arrival by a nod, even if he were pressed for time and had so much to

do. Bessy had not observed, in the confusion
of entering, that he *had* looked round, given
a quick jerk of his head towards them, by way
of salutation, and turned to his bench again,
before Bessy, at least, had been aware of his
presence.

Bessy had leisure to take stock of the room
and its inmates whilst Mrs. Wessinger and
Mrs. Speckland were "making it up" in a
corner. It was a long, low room, which had
been once front and back parlour, with a
partition between; but Hugh had wanted
space to breathe in, he said, and Stevie had
knocked away the partition and made one
room of it, and not a very spacious room,
after all. Bessy remarked that there were a
great many shelves about, with tools, and
blocks of wood, and parcels thereon; that the
furniture was scanty, and the boards neither
carpeted nor clean; and perhaps the only
member of the Speckland family clean at that
moment was the blind girl sitting by her

mother's side on a rickety old sofa near the
window at the back—a smaller window
than that at which Hugh Speckland sat, and
which, for some reason or other, had been
painted white, and might have looked like
ground glass to a person of a sanguine turn
of mind.

Lucy Speckland was a pale-faced young
woman, not unlike her brother Stephen in her
looks ; and Lucy Speckland's mother was a
tall, cross-looking old woman, with a mad,
miserable face, strongly indicative of the
complaint under which she was labouring.
Perhaps her son Hugh took after *her*, thought
Bessy. As for Mr. Speckland, senior—tall
and thin, too, like the rest of them—if he
took after anybody, it was Charles Edward
Calverton, of Choke Street, Whitechapel ; for
he was almost as shabby, and presented as
old and time-battered an appearance. His
voice was stronger and more harsh, however,
and he carried his head uprightly, and with

some haughtiness, which her uncle had never done in his life. He was a man who evidently required a great deal of attention and amusing; for Stephen had not said half a dozen words when he touched him on the arm and pointed to the pack of cards.

"Lucy can talk to Miss Calverton," he said, "and make her welcome. It isn't often I have a chance of a game at cribbage, the Lord knows, or that there is any one good-tempered enough in the way—not meaning you, you're always good-tempered—to play me a game, and keep my brain from brooding over my misfortunes. And the doctor said I was to be amused as much as possible."

Hugh gave a slight shrug to his shoulders, and continued his work.

"Mr. Hugh is like me," said Mrs. Wessinger, whose needle was rapidly flying over her shoes; "not too much time to spare at this hour of the morning. The will, but not the way."

" Not even the will just now," was the dry answer.

" Except it's a will of your own," said Mrs. Speckland, with some avidity. "I lay my horrors all to you."

" How's that?" and the stern face of Hugh Speckland looked towards his mother for the first time.

" Blocking the light out with your beastly paint here," said she, giving a jerk of her head in the direction of the window near which she sat, "and keeping it all to yourself *there*."

" The churchyard and its dreary graves drove me mad every time I looked towards it," was the reply, " and no one complained till it was finished. Then—everybody complained! It shall be altered to-morrow."

" I don't want it altered."

" It shall be altered, I say," repeated Hugh Speckland, as he turned to his labour, and seemed to work extra hard, to make up for the time he had lost.

"That's how he goes on, Mrs. Wessinger, and I so miserable. Sixty-nine years old, and no one to comfort me. Mrs. Wessinger, I'm going to church regularly after this—every Sunday morning, mind. It's time I turned over a new leaf."

"Well, it *is* almost time," said Mrs. Wessinger in reply.

"I want a little comfortable talk with you, Mrs. Wessinger—I've something on my mind —will you come up-stairs, please, and cheer me up a bit?"

Mrs. Speckland rose and marched from the room, followed by Mrs. Wessinger, who whispered something to Lucy as she passed her. Lucy Speckland was by Bessy's side a moment afterwards. She laid her hand on Bessy's, and then touched the work in her lap.

"You are busy—shall I disturb you by talking to you?"

"Oh, no."

"Mrs. Wessinger tells me she works better when she has some one to gossip with. Hugh can't bear anybody to speak to him, or interrupt him. Do you know you are like an old friend to me—I have heard so much about you."

"Indeed!"

"Before I was blind, Stevie used to make me jealous of you by telling me how pretty you were—and how nicely you could sing, and what a difference there was between you and me. There's a great difference now," she added with a sigh.

"Have you been blind long?" asked Bessy.

"Two years now—my sight completely worn out, they tell me," said Lucy in reply; "but I'm not broken-hearted—even to the darkness that never grows less I have become accustomed. Perhaps," she added, after a pause, "if there were not a hope left me yet in the future, I might feel more despairing."

Stephen looked towards her over his cards.

"Oh! here comes the story of that sweet-heart of yours. I wonder you have not more maidenly reserve."

"But Bessy Calverton is an old friend," said Lucy, "and I am proud of Harry. I call Harry a hero."

"But Harry is in Canada, and some of the 'coloured gals' will pick him up now, and put Lucy Speckland's nose out of joint."

"I don't fear them—white or coloured."

"But—"

"Why don't you play?" snapped the querulous father; "what a lad you are to wander, and forget, and keep people waiting. I never was properly amused. Don't you see I have pegged three holes."

"So you have—twenty-seven, that makes three holes again by running cards."

"No—I played the eight between."

"That makes no difference."

"But it does—you can't take them."

"Very well," was the easy response, "I

don't want them—play again, old gentleman."

" But you see you can't take them?" said the father, who was very particular, not to say disagreeable, over his cribbage.

" Oh, all right."

" But it isn't all right, if you think you can take them, or that I want to cheat you of three holes.   Hugh."

Hugh looked round after a little inward struggle with his complacency.

" Come and look at these cards, and satisfy Stevie he can't take three holes—he won't believe me."

Hugh ran his left hand through a mass of black curly hair, gave a hearty tug, too, in fact, and then plunged off his high stool, and came with three or four rapid steps to the little table by the fireside.

" Now then—what is it?"

" Stephen makes fifteen two, and I make three holes by running cards, and then he blunders down another six, and calls that

three holes.   He can't play any more than a
baby."

"Hasn't he been a baby all his life?" and
the hand of Hugh shook his brother by the
shoulder.

Bessy, glancing askance at Hugh Speckland, thought he did not look so very cross
and ill-tempered then.   And as he stood by
his father's side surveying the game, Bessy
had an opportunity of observing him more
closely.   He was the tallest of a tall family,
notwithstanding that he stooped a little, the
result of close application to his work.   It
was a face with some hard deep lines upon
it—a swarthy face, expressive of a will of his
own, and a power in himself to carry that
will out, that nothing could stop.   Bessy
had fancied he was old as well as cross-
looking until then, but as he stood there he
did not seem more than thirty years of age,
which was his right age we may add, within
a month.

" A spoilt baby too."

" True enough," answered Hugh.

" And haven't you been a man all your life, Hugh ? — strong and determined, and keeping us all properly in harness? And if it hadn't been for——"

" That'll do ! " was the quick interruption, and Hugh was stern and grim again.

" When you have both done chattering, perhaps I shall know if Stevie was wrong in wanting to peg three holes ? " said the father.

" He was wrong—it's plain enough."

" Perhaps you'll believe Hugh, though you wouldn't me."

Hugh seemed annoyed at his father's persistence, and bit his lip, and let his bushy black eyebrows lower a little over his eyes, till he caught Stephen's comical look of resignation, and half smiled again. From Stevie he glanced to Lucy, and from Lucy to Bessy Calverton, whose face—it being in his way

just then—he condescended to regard attentively.

"Miss Calverton is from Wales, I think?"
he said at last.

"Yes, sir."

"Do you know the bridge at Aberglaslyn
pass?"

"I have crossed it once or twice with
uncle."

"Is this like it?"

He walked to the window, and returned
with a woodcut that he placed in Bessy's hand.
One glance, and Bessy was in Wales again.
The mountain stream was winding through
the pass; the bridge was spanning it; the
grand old mountains rose on either side;—
it was home again, with home scenes round
her.

Bessy's eyes sparkled, and her impulsive
nature led her to drop her work, and clap
her hands, with the sketch between them.

"It's dear old Wales again!"

"I finished engraving it on wood yesterday. I don't much like the execution of it, Stevie," he added, turning to his brother.

"Oh! you're never satisfied."

"I suppose the drawing is the best part of it, and that's not my work. This Aberglaslyn," he added, as he received the sketch from Bessy's hands, "must be a fair resting-place?"

"Go and see it," said Stevie, shortly.

"I!" with a scornful laugh.

"Are you never to have a holiday, but slave, slave all your life at that infernal wood-engraving and etching?" said Stevie, warmly; "are you so much stronger than the rest of us, that you can afford to shorten your life by this hard work?"

"Old reasoning, that I am tired of by this time," said Hugh; "I'm well enough."

"Well enough—yes," said the father; "Hugh can't neglect his business, and leave us here, and no one to take care of us."

"Am I no one?" cried Stephen.

"Didn't Hugh call you a baby just now—and you are not such a manager as Hugh, after all."

"Who said I was, old gentleman? I'll back Hugh—"

"I wish you'd back your game more closely, and not talk so much!"

Hugh Speckland returned to his bench, leaving his sister and Bessy to continue their conversation, and his father and Stevie to the enjoyment of their fifth game at cribbage.

"Are you not curious about my Harry?" asked Lucy, after a time; "I tell every friend about him—and you are going to be a friend of mine."

"Am I?" said Bessy, with a bright smile.

"I think our talking disturbs father and Hugh—do you mind bringing your work to the sofa?"

Bessy did not mind, and presently she and

Lucy Speckland were on the sofa, which
Lucy's mother and Mrs. Wessinger had vacated. Lucy, full of her subject, began at
once.

" Harry is an old friend of brother Hugh's
—he and Hugh went to the same school
together—worked at the same business as
apprentices. Harry gave up the engraving,
and went to Canada, first falling in love with
me, like a silly fellow as he was."

" But—"

" But I was not blind then, and had roses
on my cheeks. My sight had been always
weak certainly, but I was not prepared
for such an affliction coming quickly and
suddenly upon me—the result of overwork.
I gave up then, and tried to break my heart
by thinking of Harry in Canada, and how I
could never go to him and be his wife as I
had promised, when in the new land he had a
house to ask me to some day. Hugh wrote
to Harry, telling him that, and Harry's

answer—oh, my dear old Harry's answer—
can you guess it?"

"I think so."

"He would not take my word to give him
up, he wrote me in reply; he would still
work for me, wait for me, look forward to the
day when he could recross the seas to take
me back to his new home. And he keeps
me to my old promise—as if I wanted in my
heart to be kept, Bessy!—and once a month
his letter comes to me with the great news
that he is in full work, and putting a little
money by."

Bessy felt the tears swimming in her eyes;
this was a story that beat all the fairy tales.
The first love story that she had heard in
her life; the first time that she had heard of
love in any way or shape. And she was at
an age to appreciate such a story; to feel
that if she were the blind girl how she could
sit down content with the eternal darkness
that stretched before her, blest by an affection
so disinterested and so pure.

"So some day I shall be one the less off brother Hugh's hands. Hugh, who works hard for all of us, and says so little, and is always wrapt in business, and will know no holiday. Sometimes I remind him of my anxiety to do too much—but his poor, blind sister teaches no moral to him."

"But is there any occasion for such constant work?" asked Bessy.

"Hugh says so—I don't know. Stevie tells him he is very obstinate, but Hugh is not to be turned from his projects by anything that Stevie says. And Hugh is always so dull and grave, and says so little to make home what it ought to be—if it were not for Stevie, I don't know what we should do," she added.

"Is he always so good tempered?"

"Always the same," said the enthusiastic Lucy, with whom Stevie was evidently the favourite; "nothing disturbs him, and no disappointment affects his spirits in the least.

And he does not earn half the money, enjoy half the good health of brother Hugh. Sometimes I think," in a whisper, "that he is more ill than we believe; he has so bad a cough at times, and his hand feels more thin and cold every time I touch it. Do you think him much changed?"

"He is looking older," was the reply, "but not changed a great deal."

"Listeners never hear good of themselves," said the voice of Stephen Speckland at their side—"looking older! I give you my word, Miss Calverton, I am growing younger every day. What has Lucy been talking about, Miss Calverton, to make you look so alarmed?"

"About you and brother Hugh, to be sure."

"And that wonderful hero, Harry, of course?"

"Of course," replied Lucy.

"Well, it is my turn to talk now.

I want to know all about Wales and the Welsh folk I left behind there, and to catechize Miss Calverton, and see if she's well up in fairy lore. Father's asleep, and there's a chance of shaking ' fifteen two ' off a fellow's brain. Heigho!" with a yawn, " I wish he did not want quite so much amusing."

Bessy glanced towards the father of the family. He had fallen asleep in the elbow chair, with his head on his chest, and his hands in his pockets, and presented not a very amiable expression of countenance in that somnolent position.

" Still, one good turn deserves another, and when the poor old chap could afford it, he gave *us* a turn—Hugh a good education, and me just half a one, owing to bankruptcy. We wanted education, and now he wants amusement—it's all square enough."

" There's a knock at the door," said Hugh, without looking round—" three talkers and one worker—is the worker to answer the summons ? "

" Shame on the talkers, Hugh, if that were the rule."

Stephen was on his feet, when Hugh leaped from his stool with a bound that upset it, and woke up his father.

" The wind's in the east— I forgot. Keep back, Stevie."

" Upon my honour, this is making a baby of me."

" Keep back ! " with a stamp of his foot— " haven't I said it ? "

And Hugh Speckland opened the door, and fiercely snapped the little boy who stood on the top step, and was at that particular moment essaying to repeat the summons with the end of an umbrella.

" Are you in such a desperate hurry, stupid, that you can't wait a moment ? "

" Please, sir, I was told to be in a hurry, and not wait an instant until I had found Mrs. Wessinger, and given her this note ; and Mrs. Wessinger, they thought, was at this house. It's a message from Mr. Parslow."

"Are you to wait for an answer?"

"Yes, sir."

"Come inside, then."

The boy stepped inside at this abrupt request, and Hugh went upstairs three steps at a time, and delivered the note to Mrs. Wessinger. He had returned, picked up his stool, remounted it, and re-commenced his engravings, when Mrs. Wessinger came hastily downstairs, and entered the room. The startled look upon her face, and the hand not at its work of shoe-binding, were sufficient to apprise Bessy of something new and strange —something that she felt affected her.

"Oh, my dear Mrs. Wessinger, has anything happened?"

"A letter from Mr. Parslow," she gasped; "he thinks they have found you out!"

CHAPTER IV.

ANOTHER CHANGE.

Bessy sank back on the sofa from which she had sprung at the entrance of Mrs. Wessinger, and turned deathly pale. Mrs. Wessinger dropped her lapful of boots, and ran to her.

" Mr. Parslow only *thinks* so, Bessy, mind," she cried. " Here, read the letter, dear, and judge for yourself."

Bessy recovered from her first shock, took the letter, and read as follows :—

" Dear Mrs. Wessinger,·—Remove Bessy immediately from your house. I was followed yesterday to the corner of your street, where

I branched off, having my suspicions. Those suspicions have been confirmed this morning by a letter fron Bessy's sister. Ask Mr. Hugh Speckland's advice; tell him the whole story. He's a sensible man, if a little obstinate now and then. Let me know what he advises by the bearer.

" Yours, in haste,

" JACOB PARSLOW."

"What is to be done, Mrs. Wessinger?" asked Bessy. "Oh! I can never return to the 'El-Dorado' now!"

Mrs. Wessinger picked up her boots again, placed them in her lap, and looked from Hugh Speckland—who, recovering the first surprise of Mrs. Wessinger's announcement, had philosophically continued his engraving—to the aroused father in his elbow-chair, and from the father to Stephen, and back to Hugh again.

"Is it a secret?" asked Lucy Speckland,

whose hand had stolen to the trembling hand of Bessy's.

"It's nothing but what I can trust you with, if Bessy likes," was the answer. "I am asked to tell all to Mr. Speckland."

"And Hugh can give us his advice on the subject," cried Stephen. "I'll back Hugh Speckland's advice against the world!"

"When will you ever understand that Hugh Speckland is busy?" was the testy answer.

"But here's danger threatening a friend," said Stephen.

"Danger?" repeated Hugh.

"I believe so, judging by these two scared faces."

"Don't say I'm scared, Stephen," said Mrs. Wessinger, who prided herself upon her self-possession; "there's nothing in the whole world of which I am afraid. But this child here," and she began the shoe-binding again suddenly, "is seeking to escape bad company

—has got a bad father, in whose hands and under whose roof she is not safe."

Hugh Speckland left his seat and joined the group, with his dark face full of interest.

"Let us see how the matter stands. Who tell's this story?"

Bessy looked her appeal at Mrs. Wessinger, who immediately began. She was not always a woman of few words, but she was a considerate woman, and saw that the recital of Bessy's trials and troubles was painful, though necessary. Briefly, but forcibly, in her own homely English, she communicated the leading features in Bessy's story, warming with the recital, and carrying away more than one of her auditors, deepening the look of interest on Hugh Speckland's face, and rousing from his characteristic coolness the phlegmatic Stephen.

"And there's my dear young master's letter," she added, thrusting the letter into Hugh's hands; "he can trust in you, knowing there's common sense in you, if not much reverence. I may have my own ideas on the subject as to what is best for Bessy Calverton, but Mr. Parslow solicits your advice."

" The strangest part of the letter to me," remarked Hugh, after a careless glance at its contents, " the advice of a man who is a dreamer and a visionary, and whose word or honour is hardly believed in."

" He never said that !" cried Stephen.

" He implied as much; but that isn't the subject. My advice is, let Bessy Calverton stay here for a week or two."

" Stay here !" exclaimed Mrs. Wessinger. " Good gracious ! "

" If your house be not marked, your street is. If this man be anxious to get his daughter back into his clutches, there will be spies near you ere long, and then Miss Calverton's security is worth *that !* " and he snapped his fingers.

" But—stay here ! "

"If you have friends in whom you can trust more, take her away," said Hugh, coolly; "I look on it as a matter of precaution."

"You are very kind to offer her a shelter," said Mrs. Wessinger, thoughtfully; "and I am a woman of no friends. And Bessy will be no expense to you, for she can earn her own living now, and is handy with her needle—and—what does Bessy say?"

"That grateful as I am for Mr. Speckland's kind offer, I think I had better return to the 'El-Dorado,' than be an encumbrance to him here. I am a stranger to Mr. Speckland, and I would rather go back."

"But I won't have it!" cried Stephen Speckland, indignantly starting to his feet. "I know the 'El-Dorado,' in Whitechapel by report, and—I won't have it! There isn't a Speckland here will have it—I know!"

"Perhaps if I were to return to Mrs. Wessinger's, and take my chance," suggested Bessy.

"No," said Hugh, decisively.

"Perhaps if—" began Speckland, senior, from the elbow-chair, when Hugh held up his hand and said—

"Don't let us have too many opinions—we can't follow them, and they only bewilder us. Miss Calverton"—turning to Bessy, and speaking with less abruptness —" you are welcome here, and are safe here—will you take my advice, and stay until some opportunity presents itself of acting better. You are under no obligation to us, remember."

"How is that?" And the eager look with which Bessy looked up told it was only a sense of obligation that kept her reluctant to accept his proffered shelter.

"My brother sometimes tells us a story that warms our hearts to the kind Welsh," said he, and Bessy understood him and felt grateful. She could not help turning away her head and shedding a few tears, however; it seemed a hard fate to be passed from one shelter to another in this strange manner, and have no just claim to the mercy that kept her from the world.

"Well, I suppose it is best," said Mrs. Wessinger, with a sigh. "Mr. Parslow, perhaps, thinks so, and it is not for an ignorant old woman like me to set my opinion against his. Time at the present moment is everything; and—Hugh Speckland's offer is at least a handsome one. I'm going to shake hands with you, young man."

"Thank you," said Hugh, with an odd smile.

"You mayn't think much of the honour," said she, sticking her needle in the bosom of her dress; "but it takes time to shake hands, and loses stitches, and puts one out a bit. There, sir."

Hugh Speckland and Mrs. Wessinger shook hands with some formality. "I shall think better of you, Mr. Hugh, from this day. I knew you were an industrious man, and a thoughtful man, but I thought you were a hard one, too, and no Christian."

"What do you call a Christian?"

"I'm not going to argue with you—I have only to thank you, now, for myself, and for Bessy here, who is too much flurried to say much at present. But if she stays till Sunday, I shall fetch her regularly to church, and—"

"But supposing your house be watched," said Lucy.

"Mr. Parslow did not call there in order to prevent that," said Mrs. Wessinger; "and every one who lives in Snowfields can't be watched, my dear. I shall call on Sunday, unless I have my own suspicions; and if anything should detain me, I hope I can trust you, Bessy,—with yourself?"

"You may trust me, Mrs. Wessinger."

"They're no church people here—but you mustn't mind their bad example. Set them a better one, my child, and shame them into reverence. But I'm not going yet, and I have a message to send back to Mr. Parslow."

Mrs. Wessinger left the room, and Hugh, after muttering " What a strange woman this is !" walked to his bench, and, to all intents and purposes, had soon forgotten Bessy Calverton's troubles. He had given his advice, like a man of business, and evinced but little excitement in the matter. He was not so impressionable a man as his brother, who had began to walk about the room, and talk loudly.

" And that man who stole my tobacco on the mountains was the man who took you away ?" he said turning to Bessy; "heavens ! what a life for you, after that quiet little Welsh home—what a father ! "

" He *is* my father," said Bessy timidly.

" Oh ! I beg your pardon—I'm rather hasty at times," was the reply ; " but your wrongs have upset me for the present. Here, I'll have a game at cribbage."

And he dashed at the pack of cards, and woke up his father, who was dozing again, by slapping his hand on the little table that stood between them.

So it was arranged that Bessy Calverton's new home should be in Seymour Street, in the midst of friends, all of whom, with one exception, she had but seen for the first time that morning. It was a strange life of change —from the present what was to evolve, and whither would it tend? Was she ever to be settled again, and, looking round at the friends at her side, say, "This is my home, and I am content with it!"

Bessy was a girl of spirit, and had resolved to be only indebted to the Specklands for the simple shelter of their roof. She had her sister's money still untouched, and when she could not earn sufficient money to pay for her board and lodging she would make up the deficiency with that. She was anxious to satisfactorily arrange that matter, before considering herself settled in her new home. Her quick perception saw that Hugh Speckland wasgeneral manager to the establishment; that his will was law, and no one opposed it; and she thought that that matter had better be arranged at the first convenient opportunity; and for that opportunity she waited anxiously.

Mrs. Wessinger left Bessy in her new home at an early hour, Mrs. Speckland having suddenly rallied, and got the better of her horrors. So much better, that she had objected to Mrs. Wessinger "preaching," as she called it, and thought she needn't have been quite so personal, or taken such a mean advantage of her nerves. But Mrs. Wessinger's mind was too much occupied in parting with Bessy to be affected by Mrs. Speckland's ingratitude, and many were the injunctions which she bestowed upon her young *protégée* before separation.

"Keep a stout heart, Bessy, and go to church regularly, and read your bible when-

ever you have a chance—and take the shoes
home yourself—you know the house—and
work with diligence—and don't forget me, and
—God bless you, my dear!"

A hasty kiss followed this benediction, and
then Mrs. Wessinger was gone, and Bessy was
alone with her new friends.

Mrs. Speckland revived in spirits very
rapidly after the departure of her friend; Mrs.
Wessinger had cheered her up so much by
presenting the bright side to everything concerning which she had mourned, that this
eccentric lady might now be considered over
proof. Mrs. Speckland's "horrors" had been
engendered by manifold causes; by an idea
that her son Stephen's cough was wearing him
to the grave, that her son Hugh was working
himself to death, that she and her husband
were clogs on the efforts of their children to
live, that Harry would never keep his word,
and Lucy break her heart in consequence;
finally, that she was very wicked in herself, and

ought to think of another world more
often—a fact that there was no disputing.
And when these "horrors" came on, Mrs.
Speckland was a nuisance to herself and
family, shedding a torrent of tears one minute,
and indulging in invectives and personalities
the most bitter in another. And Mrs. Wessinger had roused her from this last nervous
attack, spoken of the hope there was for
Stephen if he only took care, and the necessity there was for Hugh to work hard till the
reputation he was earning as an engraver
brought him greater profits, quoted Lucy's
own confidence in that hero across the seas,
and wound up by agreeing with her on the
other world subject, and reading a few chapters of consolation to the old lady from a small
volume she invariably carried in her stocking-
shaped pocket.

Having recovered from her horrors, Mrs.
Speckland was a good-tempered, garrulous
woman enough, whose main use in that house-

hold, when Stephen was absent, was to amuse
Mr. Speckland, from eight a.m. till midnight.   After an early tea Stevie rose to
depart, and received some fifty directions from
his mother about his great-coat, and the scarf
round his neck, and the proper method of
counteracting the effects of the night-air,
when he left the theatre at a later hour.

"You won't be very late," said Speckland,
senior, "or get talking with half-a-dozen
people when the work is over, and then come
crawling in at one in the morning, waking
everybody up in the house?"

"Everybody" meant Mr. Speckland senior
in particular, though he did not intend to
convey that meaning just then.

"I shall be home early to-night.   There's
not much work, now the pantomime runs
easy."

"How does it take?"

"Not very well, I fear—there's a great
deal of paper in the house already."

Bessy wondered what that had to do with the question, until the father's next inquiry solved it.

" Plenty of orders then ? "

" Oh ! yes."

" You might as well have brought home one or two," said the father; " it's precious odd you can think of everybody but a poor old fellow like me, who finds it so hard to be amused."

" But you can't go by yourself."

" Your mother likes a good play—don't you, Sarah ? "

" Well, it does me a heap of good some- times—after one of my ' horrors,' espe- cially."

" Here are half a dozen orders, if they're worth anything," and Stephen fluttered them down amongst the tea-things.

" God bless my soul, what forgetfulness ! " exclaimed the old man, stamping both feet feebly in his passion ; " and you going away and saying nothing about them, and leaving me here with no chance of amusement till bed-time. Mrs. Speckland, we'll go to the 'Royal Albert Theatre' this evening—you and I. Perhaps the pantomime will cheer us up a bit."

" Perhaps Miss Calverton will come with us?" suggested Mrs. Speckland, who had heard Bessy's story from Mrs. Wessinger, and was good-tempered enough in her way to feel for our heroine's position.

Hugh Speckland certainly worked with his ears open, despite his apparent concentration of ideas, for he answered for Bessy Calverton at once.

" No."

" Why not ? " asked the father, impatiently.

" Too many people—some one might recognize her."

" I have no wish to go," said Bessy ; " I would rather not go, thank you."

Bessy thought of Mrs. Wessinger's dismay at receiving such news as her departure to the theatre with Mr. and Mrs. Speckland.

"Miss Calverton's better at home," said Stephen, "and Hugh's always in the right. Well, good evening for the present. I see a beetle-browed manager looking a week's warning at me for being behind time!"

And Stephen Speckland hurried away. It was too early for the old people to start for the theatre, despite Mr. Speckland's slow rate of progression. Besides, there were a few toilet arrangements to make on the part of Mrs. Speckland, although Mr. Speckland did not feel inclined to dress for the pit, and even refused to have his face washed.

"Just get your bonnet on, Sarah, and don't worry me," was his testy remark; "it's particularly hard I am to be so constantly interfered with. What a blank this place is," he said with a half groan, "now that boy's gone! Sometimes I wish he wouldn't stay at home of a day—it's so miserable after he's left."

Something bumped heavily on the bench at which Hugh sat.

" What's that ? " cried the father.

" Nothing," answered the deep voice of his elder son in reply.

" So miserable," repeated the old man, " with no one to amuse a man. I dreamt of the country again last night, Hugh," he called out.

" Indeed ! "

" Thought of a cottage, and pigs, and ducks, and fowls to feed and rear, and the old lady and I jogging along so comfortably ! "

" Do you think you would be happy a day in it ? " was the question.

" Hasn't it been the dream of my life— wasn't it my dream before the business went to the dogs, and didn't the doctor say last week that a little place in the country would be the making of me ? "

" That doctor's a fool ! " cried Hugh.

" How's that, now ? "

" Isn't a man a fool to recommend a little place in the country to a family in our position—to talk of it at all, and we struggling hard to keep a roof over our heads? Why don't he recommend us port wine for our health, and champagne suppers as a specific for such false dreams as you had last night ; and a carriage and four to take the air in, when the weather permits. The man's a fool ! "

" Don't see it," responded the father, who was of an argumentative turn of mind, and who so seldom lured his son into conversation that he was glad to seize the advantage of his communicativeness on any subject whatever ; " a place in the country might be the making of me just the same, although I haven't a chance of one—unless it's my own native workhouse. I believe the parish will pass you to that, if it's particularly recommended, and backed by a medical certificate. And that'll be the end of it, Hugh, and we shan't be a burden to you—your mother and I— after that."

" Stuff!"

"And that doctor can't be a fool; for he goes to the root of all complaints—he reads us all like a book. ' Speckland,' he said to me only last week, 'you want amusing, old gentleman; keep your mind employed, and you'll run on for years.' And isn't he clever with Stevie ?"

" I doubt it sometimes."

" Yes, I know that; for you flung away a guinea on a greedy physician who told you just the same thing."

" Well—well," and Hugh Speckland's feet beat a nervous tattoo on the lower rail of his stool.

"I—I hope Mr. Stephen is not ill ?" cried Bessy, to whom this talk of doctors and physicians was alarming.

" A weak chest, that's all," said the father;
" where he got it from, I don't know. I
haven't a weak chest!"

" And he has been so much better the last
two months," said Lucy.

" Growing out of it," affirmed Mrs. Speckland.

" Time he did, at twenty-eight years of
age," was the satirical comment of her husband;
" and time you had a bonnet on, if you think
of taking care of me to-night. Some of
these nights, mind you," said Mr. Speckland,
a fresh grievance suddenly beaming on his
mind, " the couple of us will be jammed to
death in the crowd at the doors; and all
through the want of a strong arm to take
care of us."

" You don't expect me to go ?" said Hugh,
shortly.

" Well, not in a general way, of course; but
when you're not busy—"

" I'm always busy."

"But sometimes people are not in a hurry for their work, and—"

"But I am always in a hurry to finish it, lest new work should come in and hamper me; and—I hate theatres, and all belonging to them."

"Even stage-carpenters?" asked Lucy, drily.

"No, no—I forgot myself. Stage carpenters excepted—eh, girl?"

And he looked round at his sister with one of his rare smiles. How much he was like his brother when he smiled, Bessy thought once more.

Mrs. Speckland's bonnet was on at last, and Mrs. Speckland ready to escort her lord and husband to the "Theatre Royal Albert," whither at last they betook their way, as feeble a couple as ever ventured forth pleasure-taking. Hugh thought so too; for as they passed the window he flung the graver into a little tray at his side, exclaiming—

"I must stop this! They're not fit to go

alone—they're too old, and weak and helpless. There must be madness in our family,
I verily believe!"

"Oh! Hugh!" cried Lucy.

"Stevie was mad to give them the orders,
and they're mad to go, and I'm the most mad
fool of all not to put a stop to it. Is it to be
expected that I am to accompany them, and
lose four hours' work, and be wearied to death
by a wretched company of mountebanks.
Haven't I been once or twice?"

"Yes, and always began quarrelling, Hugh,
with some one," said Lucy.

"Only once, girl, and then the old man
was the prime mover of mischief. He was in
the right; for he wanted the man's hat off in
front of him; and the man was obstinate, and
half drunk, and wanted it on."

"And you knocked it off."

"Ay, and his head, too, nearly."

And with a grim smile at the reminiscence
he turned to his work again.

Lucy Speckland and Bessy Calverton were thus left to their own resources for the rest of the evening; Hugh spoke no more, but went fathoms deep into his work, and lost all consciousness of things passing around him until a later hour arrived, and a new intruder stepped between him and his labours.

Bessy and her new friends made great progress in each other's affections that long evening together; they had much to discuss, and seventeen and twenty-one are soon friends and confidants. Bessy worked busily with her needle, and talked of her Welsh life, and the blind girl sat by her side and listened with rapt attention.

Bessy abjured her life in Choke Street now; it was a bad dream, from which she trusted she had for ever awakened. Gone for ever the dark faces, the cruel life, the cruel thoughts belonging thereto, and now the light streaming in upon her, even amidst the

honest poverty in which her present lot was
cast. If her father and mother-in-law were
only parts of that dream, and not such tan-
gible realities—if only sister Lotty were a
figure in the waking world, and beside her!
With sister Lotty near her, away from evil
companionship, her bitter thoughts, and
her reckless attempts to seek forgetfulness, what might be done to lead her on
a fairer road?

The night wore on; the blind girl talked
of the hero of *her* life, and the hopes that lay
beyond them, and kept her heart so light.
And Bessy, listening, thought of the words of
Mrs. Wessinger some time ago, and fancied
there was no small truth in them, and that
some of the family at least were castle-
builders on a grand scale.

Glancing towards the silent industrious
figure under the gas jet by the window, she
wondered if he were a castle-builder too, or
content with that wearying unflinching labour

that kept him spell-bound, and dead to the outer world in which other castle-builders lived. If he were working alone for the roof above his head, as he termed it, for a home for father, mother, sister, his life was the hardest and most dark. Such a life might account for the irritability which he had already evinced half-a-dozen times.

It was striking eleven, and Lucy was speculating whether Stephen would return at once, or wait for his parents, when a hasty, impetuous knock announced the absent members of the family, or some unlooked-for visitor.

Hugh was leaving his work reluctantly when Bessy set down her own and hurried to the door. She was a quick girl, and had already seen that few things disturbed Mr. Speckland more than interruption at his engraving. He bestowed a grateful glance in her direction, and said half-apologetically,

"I am on a very delicate piece of shading just at present," and remounted his stool, and had forgotten the knock and the visitor, before that visitor had entered the room. He was soon brought to a knowledge of the new arrival however by the brisk —

"Good evening, Mr. Speckland; I trust you are in a more amiable mood than you were on Saturday?"

Hugh looked up quickly and confronted Mr. Parslow, who was regarding him through an enormous pair of green spectacles.

"Good evening," he replied; "I did not expect to see you at so late an hour."

"We cannot choose our own time, if we have our work to do."

"Will that truth excuse me?" asked Hugh, as he turned to his engraving.

"Ah! you're a quick rascal," said the clergyman; "but you stand excused, sir, after I have thanked you for your advice concerning Bessy Calverton—and for your kind offer to shelter her. You have heard her story, Mr. Hugh?"

"Yes—a sad one."

"By God's blessing, I will make a change in it," he said, warmly; "I am only waiting my time to place her in a better position, and I feel assured she will not be long an inconvenience to you here."

"I have not hinted that Miss Calverton is likely to be an inconvenience."

"No, and she shall not—neither an inconvenience, nor an expense, rest assured, Mr. Hugh."

"I require no assurance,," was the short answer.

"I knew I could trust you," said Mr. Parslow; "with all your odd bad habits, I felt there was true metal in you—didn't I say so, on that Saturday?"

"You said a great many things that I didn't pay attention to."

"Ah! and you say a great many things that you don't mean, and are only uttered for aggravation's sake," was Mr. Parslow's meek reply. "I shall see you going to church, and reading your bible some day yet."

Hugh shrugged his shoulders.

"And you have evinced a great deal of forethought in—"

"And you not any, Mr. Parslow," interrupted Hugh.

"How, sir?"

"Your house is watched, yourself an object of suspicion, that poor girl's safety in danger, and yet you come here and brave all."

"Jumping at conclusions after your old fashion," said Mr. Parslow. "Do you think I should have taken all those precautions this morning, to imperil them to-night? No, sir; Jacob Parslow knows better than that."

"You are here," said Hugh, briefly.

"Exactly so. How I came, is quite another question. After the receipt of Mrs. Wessinger's message this morning, I was a little uneasy about you, Bessy," laying his hand on the dark braids of hair of Bessy Calverton, who stood by his side, anxious to speak. "I had a host of instructions for your future course, and saw no way to communicate them save by a long letter or a personal interview. The interview being best, here I am."

"Are you certain that you have reached here without discovery?"

"Quite certain. The only thing that troubles me, is the mean advantage I have taken of my position as incumbent of St. Owen's, and the still more disrespectful manner in which I have treated the church. I have made the church the means of baffling a young vagabond of sixteen, and I'm not happy in my conscience. Are you paying attention, Mr. Speckland?"

"Yes, sir," was the response.

"I must premise that the young vagabond aforesaid has been watching my house for the last three days, dogging my steps in every

direction in a manner rather irritating. A
bright thought occurred to me after the
receipt of Mrs. Wessinger's message. St.
Owen's church has a back and a front entrance, and the back opens on Weston Street,
which there is no reaching except over
the side-gate of the church, or round Harper
Street, which is five hundred yards off. Suddenly remembering this, I took down my
pass-key, went to St. Owen's, entered the
church, ran in a very unseemly and indecorous
manner down the middle aisle, slipped out at
the vestry door into Weston Street, and stole
a march on that young Jack Sheppard, who is
kicking his heels outside the church now, for
what I know of the matter. Perhaps," he
added doubtfully, " I haven't acted quite
right in making the church an instrument for
dodging a disreputable character; but there
was a good end in view, and that's everything."

" You will not always own that," said Hugh.

"Well, well, not everything; but there's a great deal in having a good end in view," said the incumbent of St. Owen's. "Thank you, Mr. Speckland, I consider myself reproved. *I* don't fly into a towering passion and look daggers under reproof!"

"Nor I, if the reproof be just."

"But you can't say—"

"Mr. Parslow," said Hugh, letting his hand fall heavily on the bench, "I said last Saturday night week, when you tormented me about my moral state for a full hour at least, that I would be drawn into no further arguments with you, if you lived till doomsday. I will keep my word—I will have no more of it! We are both of excitable temperaments, and not polite in our remarks when we grow warm in our reasoning. I shall respect your motives more, you will respect mine more—when you are aware of them — if we defer further discussion till that indefinite date of which I spoke."

"But, my dear sir, I am not compelled to agree to all your proposals—and discussion *is* good for you. If I can once convince you—"

"I ask your silence, sir." And Hugh glared fiercely at the clergyman.

"I give in to-night, because I am not here on my old mission," said Mr. Parslow; "and because through this ingenious disguise," removing his green glasses as he spoke, "and with that expression on your countenance, you look absolutely hideous. I am here to give you a little advice, my child," turning to Bessy, "instead of Mr. Speckland. Will it harm her, do you think, Mr. Hugh?"

"No."

"She may have hidden motives, also, for a course of action very different to that which I shall earnestly advise her to follow," said Mr. Parslow.

"I shall not answer," and Hugh began to grind his teeth, and apply himself diligently to his wood-engraving.

"Very good, sir; time is precious, and it is now—" he put his hand to his waistcoat pocket to draw out the old silver watch that had vanished at the "El-Dorado"—"it is now—half-past eleven, I should think. I can't say for certain, not having my watch with me just at this moment."

He looked at Bessy and laughed, but Bessy did not appreciate the humour of the observation, and his own face shadowed an instant afterwards, for a sinful act was never a jest with him.

"Come, Bessy, let us get over our little gossip as soon as possible," and he led her gently to a seat by the fireside, seated himself beside her, and absently took the poker from the fender and began stirring the fire. Lucy Speckland had risen on hearing his approach, but he begged her to be seated; he had no secrets to communicate, and he would be very sorry to drive her away. But Lucy pleaded a few words with brother Hugh, and

went to his side ; and Hugh spoke to her once
or twice in a tone more different, and less harsh,
than perhaps he adopted to any other member of his family. For she was the betrothed
of his friend, as well as a sister grievously
afflicted.

" Bessy," began Mr. Parslow, in a lower
tone, " I have been thinking a great deal of
this new life of yours to-day ; puzzling my
head as to what was best for you. Has Mrs.
Wessinger, may I ask, given you any good
advice to-day ? "

" Yes, sir."

" A worthy woman ! Why should I have
doubted her good offices ? " he said.

After another stir of the fire, he continued—

" My first impression, Bessy Calverton,
was, that this house in particular was unfit
for you as a dwelling-place—that the example
to be met herein might affect the good thoughts
which have lately, by God's grace, found root

within your heart. These Specklands are of the No Church class, and No Church stands on the devil's own ground, and is full of pitfalls. Still—still, I have great faith in you."

" Thank you, sir, thank you !" said Bessy; " you shall never have cause to regret it. With every day I value more your great kindness and charity towards me ! "

" My profession teaches me charity to the stranger—don't flatter, me, Bessy Calverton, or engender pride in my own feeble efforts to do good," said he, hastily. " What I am desirous of saying is, that here in this family you can offer some little return to the Father of all kindness and charity, and for whose mercies you confess yourself grateful."

" Pray tell me how, sir ? "

" I have been for two years interested in this family," said Mr. Parslow, in a tone still lower; " more particularly interested in that eccentric, bad-tempered, good-hearted fellow under the gas-burner there. There are fair traits of character in each of the members of this family, I honestly believe. The Speck-lands are well-meaning and considerate; they are attached to one another. With such ma-terial to work upon, if I only lived more near, I believe much good might be effected. Now, Bessy Calverton, will you assist me in this work, in your own way?"

"And that way, sir?"

"By example. Under any condition, and against all adverse circumstances, show them an exemplary religious life is yours, and that it is the best and happiest. Evince to them your faith in God by following his laws, and walking uprightly in his ways. I ask you, Bessy, to work earnestly for this end; it will be a noble task for you, and it may work more than either of us dream. It may be a blessed hour that sets you in this benighted house."

"Oh, sir! can I ever do good? It seems

M 2

so strange that it should ever be in *my* power."

" Why not ? " he asked, enthusiastically, —" it is an easy task if the heart be in the right place. A word, a look, one simple action, may work good to twenty lives. This is an experiment of mine—there may be only a few weeks in which to work it out— you will be zealous ? "

" But, sir, there is one thing that troubles me. I must work for my own living; I must not be dependent on these kind friends here."

" Certainly not—if even our kind friends could afford it, which I doubt," he returned; " you are earning money, I hear ? "

" Yes, sir."

" And if I—that is—"

" Will you leave me entirely to my own resources for the present, sir, and wait for me to ask help? I have some little money of my sister's."

" Pardon me—but honest money, I hope."

" Yes, sir, honest money."

Mr. Parslow, after thoughtfully regarding the fire a moment, said—

" Well, be it so. Will you arrange that little matter with Mr. Speckland, or shall I ? "

" I would prefer it ? "

" That's well," said Mr. Parslow, rising— " that shows self-confidence, and makes me proud of my little pupil. I have great faith in you, Bessy."

" Thank you," responded our grateful heroine.

" But remember, Bessy, life is full of trials, and there are stumbling-blocks at every turn of our road. We must not give up, or grow dispirited, because our efforts prove weak, and our best intentions betray us. In this family you may be encountering your greatest temptations against right yourself ; for there is no absolute wrong to startle you,

and the easy life of these people may get the
better of your promise to me."

"Never, sir, never!" And Bessy's cheeks
flushed, and her eyes sparkled.

"Well, we leave it for time. In a little
while I shall see you again; my spies will
grow tired of watching me, and there will be
more ways of getting quit of them than by
the indecorous plan I adopted this evening.
So good-bye to you, and God bless you!"

"You have not told me anything of my
sister, sir."

"I have not seen her, Bessy. Only received the hasty note of warning this morning.
I am inclined to think that she is also watched;
but I must find an opportunity of ascertain-
ing that. Trust to me, Bessy."

Bessy trusted him with all her heart—for
she had already learned to reverence him as
the good genius of her life. Mr. Parslow
went away after a few more observations
addressed to the hard worker at the bench,

who responded in monosyllables, and only answered heartily to the "Good evening" with which he at last addressed him.

And Bessy drew her chair closer to the fire, and sat and thought of all that might lie before her in the life beyond, and if it were possible good could come of it. She thought so then, and the thought dimmed her eyes, and made her chest heave. And the Specklands —father, mother, and Stephen — returning from the theatre at an hour more late, found her still thinking, dreaming—possibly as great a castle-builder as any in that humble home.

CHAPTER V.

A TRANSITION STATE.

BESSY CALVERTON was downstairs at an early hour the following morning. The daybreak had not brightened Seymour Street when she entered the parlour of the Specklands, and found the gas burning, and Hugh in his old position on the high stool, just as the family had left him yesternight.

"Oh! dear," cried Bessy with a start, "have you been up all night, Mr. Speckland?"

"Not I," was the answer.

Bessy had been anxious to have a little

explanation with Mr. Speckland concerning "money-matters" that morning, and had risen more early than usual for that purpose; but Mr. Speckland was in the room before her, and so busily at work, that Bessy felt nervous in intruding on his studies. She had already seen enough of Hugh Speckland to feel assured that he resented, almost as an insult, any attempt to distract him from his engraving; and she therefore sat herself before the fireless grate, awaiting a more favourable opportunity.

Having risen before daylight, she had had no opportunity of reading her little bible that morning, and that was her first duty now; she had promised Mrs. Wessinger—she had promised Mr. Parslow. Bessy began to read, and Hugh Speckland to fidget over his work, and grow less intent upon it. Anything new or strange evidently disturbed Hugh Speckland; and the appearance of this intruder, at an hour when he expected the room to him-

self, harassed and annoyed him. He looked
round at last.

"Can you see to read there?" he asked
abruptly.

"Thank you—yes."

"Why don't you light the fire?"

"I am not cold, thank you," replied Bessy.

Bessy had finished her chapter, closed her
book, and found the engraver still regarding
her.

"You are a student, I see. May I ask
what book that is?"

"The bible, sir."

"Oh!"

Hugh began to work with increased
rapidity at this answer. To read the bible
in the house of Speckland was more new and
strange than to break upon his studies at an
early hour. He did not know whether there
was a bible in the house; he believed his
sister had had one once, before her blindness
rendered its perusal an impossibility.

The daybreak was stealing in the room now; the shadow of the railway arch across the road became less dark. Life sprang up in the streets outside; those happy enough to have work before them were already on their way to business; those with no work at their fingers' ends were out in search of it; and men women and children with no bread to eat, were hastening to secure the best place at the workhouse gates, or seeking broader thorough-fares to beg a stranger's help. Bessy fancied the room was soon lighter' than usual, and a hasty glance towards the opposite window accounted for it, and reminded her of a little dispute between Hugh and his mother yester-day. The obnoxious paint had been removed, and the churchyard beyond the low wall at the back was looking in upon them again, with all that strength of ugliness for which a London churchyard is remarkable. Hugh had said it should be altered in the morning, and pressure of business had not rendered him neglectful of his promise. It was certainly a dreary look out, Bessy thought, and Hugh had shown himself a man of judgment in excluding such a prospect from his family.

"I wish you would light that fire," said Hugh tetchily, for the second time; "we're not so hard up for coals, but that we cannot afford to burn them half-an-hour more early sometimes."

"Will you let me speak to you for a few moments?" asked Bessy timidly.

Hugh could not refrain from smiling.

"That's a pitiful face, Miss Calverton. Are you afraid of me?"

"Lucy says—that is I hear—" and Bessy stopped again.

"Lucy says," repeated he; "well, what does Lucy say?"

"That you don't like to be interrupted at your work—that it makes you—cross in fact."

"Who is not cross, when a foolish or an absurd question comes between a man and his ideas—when all the petty annoyances of housekeeping are thrust between him and the thoughts that bring him bread? Lucy is quite right."

"Yours must be a very dull life, Mr. Speckland."

"Why so?"

"It seems a life all to yourself," said she; "wrapped up in your work, you appear to forget home and those that belong to it—oh! I hope I have not offended you."

Hugh had pushed his work from him in earnest, and had turned for a moment of a scarlet hue.

"Meaning that I am a selfish man?"

"No—not selfish."

"A life all to myself, you say—forgetting home and home faces. Well, you are only one more."

"One more," repeated Bessy.

"One more who don't understand me. Once or twice I have tried to explain, and have been flattered by my listeners' attention and acquiescence, and then all the old jealousy, sense of wrong—almost distrust! I work hard for those who are not able to work for themselves, and the result is, Miss Calverton, a life to myself. But that is not selfishness."

" No, sir—I did not mean selfishness. You are the last who—"

" Ah! don't flatter me—I like hard words best—I am more used to them! Call me selfish—perhaps you are right. Call me bad-tempered and obstinate—well, there's not a doubt on that point—I perfectly agree with you."

He drew the block on which he was engraving nearer to him as he spoke, and Bessy said, quickly—

" But I haven't spoken yet of myself, sir."

" Is it the question of *yourself* that has induced you to beard in his den such a very fierce lion ? "

" Of my position here—of the expenses, and my share in them."

" Don't worry me with money affairs—I have quite enough of that topic at all hours of the day."

" But I do not wish to be an encumbrance to you, Mr. Speckland—of course I shall not think of that. I have money by me."

" Keep it if you're wise."

" And I hope to earn a little money by shoe-binding, which, added—"

" Your family was kind to my brother in Wales—I will not—"

" But, sir—"

" I *will not!*" shouted Hugh, with a vehemence that made Bessy's heart leap into her throat; " and my will is law here, Miss Calverton must understand. When I am losing money, instead of saving it—when I feel your presence here an expense to me, it will be time enough to talk of this matter. At the end of a week, a month, when there has been an opportunity of testing how much you have cost me. But not now."

He shook his head and looked very firm. And that shake, *à la Burleigh*, and that significant look closing all argument, had invariably ended the question with all of his family, who had ventured at any time to oppose him. But we have seen once or twice in the course of this narrative that Bessy Calverton had a will of her own, as well as Mr. Speckland, and let it master her sense of discretion occasionally. And Mr. Speckland's *brusque* manner was new to Bessy, and rendered her indignant, and forgetful in the heat of the moment of the right course to pursue. An instant afterwards, and she was putting on her bonnet, and tying the strings with a nervous, agitated hand. Hugh looked up from his work again. He had thought the question settled, and that his strong " I WILL!" had ended all resistance. Father, mother, sister, brother had never opposed him further than that; and yet this girl seemed more inclined to resist his authority than the rest. And he had meant it for· her good, too—confound it!

" Where are you going? "

" Back to Mrs. Wessinger's—I'll not stop here."

" Your father will find you there."

" It can't be helped now."

Bessy had caught up her lapful of boots from the sofa, and was making towards the passage, when Hugh came after her and seized her by the wrist.

" Just come back, Miss Calverton."

" Let go my wrist, sir; you have no right to hurt me."

" I beg your pardon; I did not know I was hurting you," and he relinquished his hold as he spoke; " but you must not leave this house."

He was standing between her and the door, looking more determined than ever, until the indignation visible on Bessy's face softened his own stern looks and made him smile. He even laughed at last—the first time for many a day—and the laugh was frank and pleasant, and like his brother Stephen's.

"I see we shall take time to understand each other, Miss Calverton," said he; "our faults and failings, virtues and weaknesses, are not to be comprehended in a single day. I am in the wrong, and you are right to reprove me. I grant your own way, Miss Calverton, and for the better understanding of each other, suppose I accept for board and lodging the same sum as Mrs. Wessinger has been accustomed to receive from you?"

"Very well, sir," said Bessy, cooling down; "then I'll stay a little while."

"Only a little while!"

"I don't think I shall be very happy here," said she, "or make any one happy."

"Perhaps this is not a happy home," said he, his face shadowing again; "there are

such here and there, and where the fault lies
it is difficult to guess. Call this an unhappy
home, and set it down to Hugh Speckland's
fault, and you stand on the borders of the
truth. I have owned I am a bad temper—
naturally a villanous temper—that constant
work, want of society—nay, want of change,
perhaps—have narrowed still more, and made
a nuisance to my relatives as well as myself.
Well, bad habits grow upon one."

" You should try to shake them off, sir."

" I haven't the time, child. It is a great
effort, and requires so much labour. Can
you ever remember, Miss Calverton, tying a
stone round the neck of a prejudice, or a
weakness, or a distorted idea, and sinking it
deep in the great sea for ever ?"

" Yes—thanks to the good man who called
here last night."

" A good man ! Oh ! another impossibility,
in which I have no faith. Do you mean Mr.
Parslow ?"

" Yes."

" And he talked you out of your old bad habits ?"

" I think so—I hope so."

" Was a habit of rushing at conclusions one of them ?   Putting on your bonnet at a hasty word, taking offence thereat, and flying for your life to the street door ?   Ah ! that *was* a bad habit—thanks to the Fates, we are rid of it altogether !"

" I'm not surprised that this is an unhappy home, sir !" cried Bessy, stung by his satire.

It was his turn to wince, as though a hot iron had seared him.   He had asked her to consider him as the cause of that unhappiness ; but still the re-assertion pained him more than he would have cared to acknowledge to this girl of seventeen.   He was still standing by the door, regarding Bessy with a strange expression, when Stephen Speckland came two steps at a time down the stairs—a rate of progression rather new and alarming for him.

" What's the matter?" asked Hugh.

" What's the matter here, you mean?" said he, laughingly; "is it a fit of indignation, or a game at romps?"

" Romps, you ass!" exclaimed Hugh, stamping his foot on the floor at the idea.

" Well, there is no saying what new character you may appear in at last, with that secret of yours that you keep so comfortably locked up in yourself. This is a transition state."

"So much the better, then."

" Ah! so much the better. Good morning, Miss Calverton. Are you going out?"

"She was going home a minute or two since. I was too hasty with her, and spoke harshly. There, Miss Calverton—see what a penitent I am."

" And the penitent is forgiven?" said Stephen, looking anxiously from one to the other.

"Yes," said Bessy, "if there's anything to forgive."

Hugh bowed his head, as if in thanks for the free pardon accorded for all his offences; and then, snatching a cap from a row of pegs in the passage, opened the door, shut it after him, and started down the street at a rapid pace.

"That's a bad sign," said Stephen; "he hasn't gone off into one of those tantrums for eight months now. He'll take a long walk, and perhaps not be back till late to-night."

"I'm sorry, if it be my fault."

"Well, it's nobody's fault, I imagine," said Stephen; "and the walk will do him good, for it's a very long while since he has had one. What has it been all about, Miss Calverton?"

When they had entered the parlour, Bessy very briefly related the particulars of the dispute she had had with Hugh; and Stephen listened and stared at the window, which now commanded such a fine view of the neighbouring churchyard.

"Hugh certainly likes his own way," said Stephen, "and gets it pretty often, considering what a world of contradiction and aggravation it is. But I came down in a hurry to light the fire, lest——"

Bessy waited for the completion of the sentence ; and Stephen, after a moment, added—

"Lest Hugh should find it cold this winter morning, and lose time over his work ; or Lucy should go groping about in the dark, and hit herself between the eyes with the mantelpiece — she's not quite so handy as most blind people I have heard of, poor girl. But, talking of Hugh," he said, applying a match to the fire, "I should like you to know a little more of that good fellow—the best of fellows, or I'm a Dutchman, Miss Calverton !"

And he struck his knee smartly with his hand.

"What a pity that he is so very hasty ?"

"There is not a more thoughtful or consi-

derate man under the sun, despite his hasti-
ness," said Stephen, when the coals were
burning up. "I could talk by the hour
together of honest, old, hardworking Hugh.
If I only had half his energy—half his
thoughts—I should be twice a better hand at
helping him to keep this roof above our
heads. Irritable as he is, Miss Calverton,
he's a man that never complains because the
lion's share of work, the lion's share of money,
is expected from him. He is full of little
kindnesses, that are only spoiled by his rough
way of making them ; he—he's a trump, in
fact, Miss Bessy ! "

It was pleasant to see this man warming
at the recapitulation of his brother's merits,
striving to the utmost of his power to turn
the bright side of his brother's character to
this young girl, inclined perhaps to take a
false estimate from the weak points it had
lately exhibited; if in his eagerness he
possibly overcoloured the merits of Hugh

Speckland, some of the brightness he would have cast around his brother fell to his own share, and showed what a good-hearted fellow he was.

" Why, you must know, Miss Calverton," he continued, seeing Bessy still a patient listener, " I should never have had the pleasure of your acquaintance if it had not been for Hugh. I was recommended change of air at that time, and the finances were not in first-rate condition, until Hugh proved there were eight pounds more than we could possibly get rid of; and sure enough in our little joint-stock cash-box there appeared an extra eight pounds that I could not account for then, and that I only discovered afterwards was drawn from Hugh's savings' bank account—in fact, was all the account he had at the Finsbury bank, and had taken seven months to save. That's Hugh Speckland."

" A good brother," answered Bessy, with the tears in her eyes.

"He never knew what a holiday was himself, but he gave me one out of his own hard earnings. Ah! and that was a holiday—mountains, and valleys, and waterfalls! I must have been born with a soul for the beautiful, only necessity wouldn't allow it fair play. Well, mother, how are the horrors this morning?"

"Don't laugh at me, Stephen," said Mrs. Speckland, who appeared at this moment; "you, who are always laughing at everything, should spare your poor mother's infirmities. Where is Hugh?"

"Gone in search of a bloater for breakfast, after polishing the back parlour window, according to orders. See how bright and cheerful we look this morning!"

"Ah! I was in a bad temper with myself and the world," sighed the mother, "and did not know what I was saying. And he painted the glass over because he thought the funerals were bad for my spirits—I wish he had your easy temper, Stephen."

"Much good would it do you, mother."

"You're looking pale this morning, Stevie ·—are you quite well?"

"To be sure—always well."

"Don't it strike you, Miss Calverton, that my dear son here is looking pale?"

Stephen laughed as Bessy's dark eyes were critically turned towards him—but it *did* strike her, nevertheless, that there was a pale haggard expression on his face, now the mother had mentioned it. Still she kept her opinion to herself, for the mother's. sake—oh! these mothers are always so over-anxious and fidgety!

Mrs. Speckland began to busy about the room, to put the kettle on the fire, and rake out the lower bars for a nice clean place for the imaginary bloater which her eldest son had started in search of. Bessy volunteered her assistance, which was accepted, and presently Lucy came slowly downstairs, and finally Mr. Speckland, senior, rather worse in

temper for last night's amusement and late
hours. It was singular how quickly the
absent member was missed, despite the
silent position he invariably maintained at
the bench by the window; the blind sister's
first question was, " Where's Hugh ? " as if
a voice had whispered of his absence in her
ear ; and the testy father put the same ques·
tion before he had shambled into the easy
chair, and taken up the best place at the fireside, to the exclusion of three-fourths of the
warmth from the rest of his family. Stephen
had the same answer concerning the delicacy
for the early meal, interspersed with a few
remarks on the scarcity of fish in frosty
seasons of the year, and the probability of
Hugh having crossed to Billingsgate in search
of bloaters—for that Hugh, if he once took it
into his head to have a thing, he *would*
have it, as they all knew !

Hugh must have gone further than Billingsgate on the errand attributed to him by

his brother, for the morning and afternoon passed, and the high stool still remained vacated, and the wood block untouched, and those who called to see him on business—there were one or two—were asked to call again by the blind sister, Stephen's business having taken him early to the theatre that day. Bessy continued very thoughtful over her work, perplexing herself with reflections concerning Hugh Speckland, and fearing that her own hasty remarks had helped to disturb him. She had expressed her conviction that it was no matter of surprise that his home was unhappy, and he had immediately taken offence at the assertion, despite the little regard he had had for the feelings of others. She could scarcely believe that the few words she had spoken would have sent Hugh wandering motiveless about the streets ; and yet the observations of his father later in the day appeared to confirm her own doubts.

"One of his fire-away fits," observed

Speckland, senior, who was hard up for
amusement, and sat twirling one thumb over
the other, and watching Bessy at the shoe-
binding, till his fixed intensity of gaze
made her nervous and prick her finger—
"taken the huff, and lost a day's work. If
he wanted to lose a day's work, why didn't
he stay at home and play cribbage with his
poor father?   That boy has no thought."

"Perhaps he has met a friend," suggested
Lucy.

"He hasn't any—he offends them all,"
said the father—"where he got such a villanous temper from, the Lord knows—always
nagging and finding fault, or wanting things
that don't belong to him. I wish I was out
of it, in that little cottage in the country that
the doctor recommended me, because he
knew I should never have a chance of getting
it, just like all the doctors—rabbit them!"

He took a fancy to talk of the country to
Bessy; she had lived in the country many

years, and must have seen a great many cottages that would just have suited him. He would just tell her the identical cottage he should have liked, and the identical-sized pigs and cows and ducks. Lord, how they would have amused him, if fate had not been so precious hard upon a man! When he was in business for himself, ten years ago, he put by money for a cottage for himself and the old lady when they should grow old; and then came difficulties, and money-drawing, and bankruptcy, and old age spent in a wretched dirty little hole in Seymour Street!—look at it!

And all this mourning for the unattainable and unalterable fidgeted Bessy ; the old man talked so much of his misfortunes, and the pity to which he was entitled in consequence. Bessy was glad when he changed the topic to Stephen Speckland, even though he contrasted him with his elder brother, and thought Stephen better tempered, more clever, and *amusing*. He could not understand a man working himself to death one day, and then sulking his time away or losing another in search of a bloater for breakfast—he thought that extremely selfish and ridiculous, and perhaps it was true enough, or Stephen would not have said it so seriously!

The object of these remarks made his appearance about seven in the evening, walked straight to his bench by the window, covered it with papers which he drew from his coat pocket, and then settled himself on his stool, as though there had been nothing remarkable in his absence. He had begun work when his father called out—

"You have been a long while gone, Hugh!"

"I have had a great many places to call at."

"Oh! I thought—"

"And I have come back with plenty of orders. Something to be grateful for at a time like this, when work is scarce, and half Seymour Street starving."

"Ah!—yes. Stevie won't be back till very late—there's a new piece out at the 'Royal Albert,' Hugh."

"Is there?" was the absent answer.

"I shall miss my game at cribbage—and it's like a composing draught to me, Hugh. I suppose," turning to Bessy, "you don't play cribbage, Miss Calverton?"

"No, sir."

"I must teach you the game when—you are a little less busy," he added, with a wistful glance at the shoebinding.

"Mother plays it very decently," remarked Hugh.

"Very indecently I call it, unless your ideas of a decent player are different to mine."

"Perhaps they are."

"I call a person who counts fifteen two with a nine and seven, far from a decent player, and your mother always does it."

"I can't count the pips very fast," apologized Mrs. Speckland.

" I never said you could, Mrs. Speckland,"
was the bitter reply.

" I'll play you a game at nine—if you'll
only keep quiet," cried Hugh, in desperation.

" You'll forget all about it."

" Is it a habit of mine ? "

" Well," said the father, after a moment's
reflection, " perhaps it isn't."

He would allow so much as that to a son
who was to play him cribbage at nine o'clock,
but he allowed it with a bad grace, Bessy
thought, although Hugh continued his work
and made no comment. And as the little
clock in the corner struck nine, Hugh was
off his stool and crossing the room to his
father's table.

The cribbage continued till eleven—would
have continued till a later hour, if Hugh had
not suggested it expedient for his father's
health to retire to rest at an hour more early
than that of the preceding evening; and his
father very unwillingly complied, and thought

it was like Hugh—glad to cut his amusement as short as possible—he didn't play cribbage with him very often, goodness knows! But he did not think of resisting Hugh's wishes. Bessy saw that Hugh expected obedience, and she wondered how she could have so boldly confronted him herself after so firm an assertion of his will that particular morning. Bessy was proceeding to her own room, after a "Good night, Mr. Speckland," which he had returned, when he called her back as she reached the stairs. Bessy returned.

"Did you want me, Mr. Speckland?"

"You were right, Miss Calverton, this morning, and I was wrong, that's all."

"I—I am afraid I offended you very much this morning," said Bessy, after a little hesitation.

"You set me thinking, that's all. I see now, this is a strange, unhappy home, although there is little opportunity of my making it more cheerful without losing time that is of value to me. Still, I might be a little different, less snappish possibly, more like that warm-hearted brother of mine. Do you remember that last remark of Stevie's, before I—I took a walk to collect my ideas, as well as my orders?"

Bessy did not remember at the moment.

"He said mine was a transition state. Try and believe that, Miss Calverton, and make allowance for me. My brother went nearer the truth than he believed. Do you understand what he means?"

"To be sure, sir," said Bessy, a little indignantly.

"Understand, also, that in the light words of that brother there are home-truths sometimes; and I think—I hope—there's truth in that last shrewd observation of his. Why shouldn't this be a transition state? I hope for something better, brighter than this present life of mine. I don't call this life—only the approach to it!"

He took his square, well-cut chin in his hand, and looked intently into the street beyond the window, as though the life he spoke of were somewhere out there in the darkness; and Bessy went away to her room without his heeding her departure.

Stealing into the room five minutes afterwards, to take upstairs some work that she had forgotten — work that she intended to prosecute in her room to-morrow early instead of intruding on Mr. Speckland—she found him still looking at the life lying beyond, and so absorbed in the prospect that he was unaware of her re-entrance or exit. And that life, whatever it might be, did not seem to brighten his face very much, Bessy thought, or alter in any degree the stern expression of his countenance.

194

CHAPTER VI.

THE GOOD EXAMPLE.

Bessy Calverton soon became accustomed to life in Seymour Street, to the new home which a threatened trouble had made for her. Not only accustomed, but happy also; for there was much to reconcile her to this new home, despite the singular temper of Mr. Hugh Speckland. Those round her were nearer her own age—had not lost the thoughts, wishes of youth—were not always interposing between her and her day dreams, the cold practical truths in which no day dreams could live. Mrs. Wessinger had said the Specklands were a castle-building family, but the blood runs cold within our veins when we give up castle-building for ever. The Specklands were a warm-hearted race; even the old gentleman, with his mania for amusement, his querulousness and infirmities, was not bad at the heart, but keenly alive to the dangers of the over-work that made Hugh so pale, or the cold easterly winds that set Stephen coughing. Bessy even began to fancy that there were times when his desire for amusement was a trifle feigned, in order that Hugh should abandon his engraving, and Stephen should not venture into the night air. Not that Mr. Speckland, senior, was anything but a disagreeable man for all that—blind to many of his son's virtues, and forgetful of time and place and person fifty times a day, and always hard to please.

Still, Bessy Calverton was happy, despite the bad tempers of the old gentleman, and the periodical attacks of horrors on the part of his wife, who found her sins too heavy for her at times, and thought the world coming to an end, and occasionally succumbing to these ideas, would cry and wring her hands, and ask for that dear good soul, Mrs. Wessinger. Mrs. Wessinger always appeared at the summons, and consoled the nervous old lady, and was glad of an excuse to see more often the girl who reminded her of the Bessy she had lost once, and perhaps had never ceased to mourn for.

Mrs. Wessinger had no cause to mourn over the moral decadence of Bessy Calverton, in the midst of a family whose religious notions and duties were lax. Bessy had not forgotten her promises to those who had befriended her in her hour of greatest need; and, possibly, some part of her happiness was attributable to the progress she was making by the very force of her example. For, if evil communications corrupt good manners, as we, backed by our old copybooks, have attempted some chapters antecedent to prove; so the good example ever before us sets our brain pondering on the goodness and fitness of things, and the little effort it would take to make ourselves better Christians and men.

The reader will not understand from this attempt at a moral reflection, that Bessy's habit of reading her bible regularly, going to church in all weathers at regular periods, had reformed the whole family of the Specklands—families don't reform quite so suddenly, and there are stubborn natures that think giving way, even to a good habit, a weakness to be rigorously suppressed. But Bessy, mindful of Mr. Parslow's wishes, looking upon obeying them as some little return—however little—for all his past kindness, kept strong in her first resolves to begin here the new and better life; and the force of her example brought Lucy to her way of thinking, did some good to Mr. Speckland, perhaps made those sterner members of the family reflect a little more—

for they were thoughtful at times, and respected her motives at least. And Bessy was happy not only in witnessing some little change round her, but in having for companions, as we have said, those nearer her own age. So six weeks passed, and each week Bessy had contrived to earn, thanks to Mary Davis's early tuition in the matter of needlework, an amount of money sufficient, with a very little addition from Lotty's gift, to defray the expenses of her board and lodging. The sense of her independence in that respect made her heart light, and some portion of the old colour she had had in Wales return to her cheek. She knew how happy she was now, by the feeling of horror that she experienced in looking back at that " El-Dorado " life to which five years' hard training had habituated her—by the wild desire that kept her brain busy on impossible schemes, to save Lotty even yet from the wrong, and the shame, and the ruin which had sprung

thence to mar her life, and cast her to a lower
depth, concerning which Bessy Calverton
mercifully knew nothing. Once during those
six weeks she received a few hasty lines
from her sister—significant of little but that
she knew where Bessy was, and that those
around her were in ignorance, and adjuring
her to keep quiet, and not venture out much in
the day-time yet awhile; and concluding with
a wish not to seek to know anything concerning herself. " Leave me to my own
time," were her last words; and Bessy sighed
as she thought she had no power to do
otherwise.

Bessy had not forgotten Mary Davis in
those six weeks; she had written a long
letter to her at Aberogwin, thanking her for
that undying interest that had induced
her to correspond with Mr. Parslow, and
detailing the new life begun in Seymour Street,
and the new hopes arising therefrom.
And Mary Davis had answered, and prayed

God to strengthen Bessy in her good intentions, adding the sad news that her father, who desired his kind love to his niece, was far from well, and that his failing health troubled her a great deal. Still she trusted in the better times, and hoped to shortly send the better news.

Bessy had become quite one of the family with the Specklands, at the expiration of those six weeks; one to be loved and made much of, like that great spoilt child, Stephen. Bessy was ever ready to oblige, to lend a helping hand in any direction; and such natures are sure to take with people who want obliging and helping rather more often than ill-tempered people would care about. Then it was discovered that Bessy Calverton had a sweet voice of her own, and that voice was induced, after a week or two, to enliven the dull hours of the Specklands, and amuse the old gentleman in particular with some of the Welsh ditties, and those sentimental songs

with which, in the early days of the " El-
Dorado," Bessy had been accustomed to en-
tertain her father's guests. And it was a
sweet voice, if not of any great power ; and
Hugh Speckland fell into a bad habit of
leaving off his work whilst she sang, and thus
losing a portion of that valuable time which
he appeared to estimate so highly. Still he
made little comment on her singing— he
was not fond of paying compliments—and, at
the conclusion of her ballads, engraved with an
extra vigour, that possibly made up for lost
time. Stephen Speckland enjoyed these little
musical evenings most of all, perhaps, for he
was ill with one of his old attacks, early in
the fourth week of Bessy's sojourn there, and
hardly strong again at the expiration of the
sixth. Bessy had an opportunity of judging
how weak he was, and what a hollow
cough he had during the time he lay on the
old sofa under the back parlour window. His
spirits seldom seemed to fail him, however ;

and in the midst of that illness that kept him weak and from adding money to the common fund, he had ever the light answer and the frank, open smile, and was the one least solicitous concerning his health. Bessy's songs came in handy at this juncture; and he maintained that it was Bessy's Welsh airs that had set him on his feet again in "Auld Lang Syne," when he was seeking health and strength amongst the Aberogwin mountains.

Stephen Speckland was fond of talking of Wales during the time that his ill-health kept him at home; it appeared to have been the one holiday of his life, and reminiscences of it made his cheeks flush and his eyes sparkle. And it was pleasant for Bessy to talk of her Welsh home, of the few days he spent there, of the old fairy tales, and the sad end to the fairy volume which he had bestowed upon her as a parting gift. Then there was consider- able argument as to the merits and demerits of Mr. Davis, and Bessy found herself warmly

defending her uncle against Stephen Speckland, and becoming excited in his defence,
till the laugh of the invalid assured her that
he had been prosecuting his opinions in order
to rouse her indignation.

"You're only talking like this to aggravate
me," she would say at last.

"Guilty, Bessy," he responded; "but,
like my old father, I'm a little inconsiderate
in my search for amusement. And it's so odd
to hear you defending the grim little man
from whom you ran away in the mist."

"I've grown wiser and better, I hope."

"Ay, and pr——, and all manner of
things," said Stephen; "but the old gentleman's looking wistfully towards me, and I'm
not too ill to be unamusing, I suppose."

"Shall I play your father a game at cribbage?" asked Bessy; "I think I understand
the game now."

"No—you are one of the workers, and I
one of the drones, Bessy."

It was always Bessy now : the formal Miss Bessy, the still more formal Miss Calverton, had been set aside during those six weeks, and Bessy was called by her own familiar name. She was a girl who took readily to real friends—and it was like home now, that little house in Seymour Street. Stephen and Lucy might have been her brother and sister all her life, they were so kind and friendly ; and the father and mother were almost equally considerate. Only that cross brother Hugh called her Miss Calverton still, and occasionally, in softer moments, Miss Bessy ; but even Hugh Speckland was as kind to her as to the rest of his family, sometimes, she fancied, seemed to pay some little attention to what she said and did, and was not always cross when necessity compelled her to intrude upon his working hours. But perhaps this was fancy—she could scarcely tell, his manner was so equable and hard.

Until Stephen's illness took a turn, and the

doctor was out of the house again, Hugh was a different being as regarded his brother Stephen. Bessy could see that he was anxious concerning his brother; that he lost time in talking to him, and still greater time with the doctor in the passage, and the parlour door closed against the conference. Hugh did not seem to consider time or money in matters of illness; he was crotchety and difficult to satisfy, and brought more than one doctor into the parlour to see Stephen — doctors who were always friends of his, he said, and were not going to charge much. And no one but the doctors and Hugh Speckland knew what was wrapped up in the little piece of paper that passed from the latter to the former after each interview.

"Don't you think I'm in safe hands, Hugh," said Stephen, "that you bring these fresh faces to see a fellow who has only a bad cough?"

" I was always hard to please—and a dozen opinions are better than one."

"Why do you always hold so fast to your own, then," said Stephen, with a laugh.

" Perhaps because I am conceited enough to think no one knows better, Stevie—but you can't aggravate me to-day."

" Why not ?"

" The last—friend of mine, gives me good news."

" Did you expect bad ?"

" God forbid," was the exclamation; "but these doctors evade the plain yes or no, as if you and I were children, Stevie."

" And this last doctor ?" said the brother, with a little natural anxiety.

" Says there is nothing to fear—that your constitution may be somewhat weak, but that with common precaution we shall make an old man of you."

" And the other doctors ? "

"Oh! the others wanted to look wise and say nothing."

"Well, there's good news at last, then."

"Don't you think so?" with a quick glance towards Stevie.

"To be sure—who says a word against it? You're not of a sanguine temperament like the rest of us—and if you believe all's well, we haven't anything to say to the contrary. Besides, am I not as strong as a house again!"

It was strange that during the next few hours the brothers appeared to change characters—Hugh to be talkative and good-tempered, and Stephen silent and meditative. Only for the first few hours, and then pressure of work brought Hugh to his senses, and he turned to his never-ending occupation, whilst Stephen assumed his old character, as though it had been a cloak that he had laid aside for a moment.

Stephen Speckland resumed work at the

end of the six weeks, and the house was less
cheerful in his absence. Mr. Speckland,
senior, more at a loss for amusement, began
to grumble again, and to talk of the change
of air that the doctors had once recommended
him; and Bessy thought it *was* strange
how different Stephen's absence made the
place and everybody in it. Why, she felt
different herself; and when a slack night at
the theatre brought him home at an early
hour, her spirits were only second to his own.
And she was interested in Stephen for another
reason; she fancied she could detect in him
at times flashes of a new thoughtfulness, that
she took for an awakening to a better idea of
life and its duties; he stayed at home of a
Sunday, and once Bessy caught him with her
bible in his hands. Certainly the Sundays
were not like summer Sundays, when monster
excursion trains offered temptation to the
workers for a plunge into fresh air, hill, dale,
cornfield, and sea-beach; and the bible had

only been open at the fly-leaf, where she had very neatly written " Bessy Calverton." But there was a change, and, oh! if only she were to be the means of making a better Christian of Stephen Speckland. Bessy had grown enthusiastic over her work lately; she had seen progress, and that progress encouraged her. The satisfaction of doing good worked a great change in herself, made her more gentle and amiable, almost rendered her a heroine. She had found her vocation, and, with all the sanguineness natural to her character, she set to work earnestly to effect greater changes than the mere aspect of things warranted. And Bessy was a castle-builder, too—as we shall see at a future stage of our history.

Bessy made a great attempt in the right direction at last—one Sunday morning when the bells were ringing for church. Bessy was ready for departure, and had entered the parlour to wait for Lucy. The usual Sunday scene was enacting in that parlour: Hugh

Speckland engraving with the same persistence and intense application that had no respect for particular days; Mrs. Speckland making preparations for the cooking of the Sunday's joint, and Stephen on his back on the ancient sofa, reading a penny journal, and intensely interested in the double murder in which the leading tale just at present luxuriated. The father of the family was still in bed—he never rose till twelve of a Sunday—and possibly dreaming of a country house, and lots of amusement.

Hugh glanced from his work as Bessy entered, and said, by way of general information—

"It is raining."

"I'm not afraid of the rain, Mr. Speckland."

"And there is not a respectable umbrella in the house," said Stephen.

"My cloak is warm and thick, and will keep out a great deal of the wet."

"Perseverance, thy name is — woman!" said Stephen.

Stephen laughed pleasantly as he made the remark; but Bessy felt there was a degree of bitterness in the words, and was quick to resent it.

"And infidelity, thy name is—man!" cried Bessy — "irreverence and ingratitude, too! I can see all that now. Look at you—look at Mr. Hugh!"

"What have I done?" said Hugh Speckland, and there was a more humorous expression on his face than was usually exhibited when his attention was distracted.

"You are always working; you don't think that Sunday is a day of rest—a day on which to be grateful, at least, for all the mercies of the past week, if you haven't had time to be grateful before."

"You mean a day to put away work, and go to church or chapel?"

"Certainly I do."

"But I should have to work harder than ever the rest of the week. Am I not slave enough to my labours, Miss Bessy?"

"Well, you had better work more hard—than work now."

"I have tried the day-of-rest principle," he said, "and it don't answer. I have my theories, you have yours. For mercy's sake, don't follow too closely on Mr. Parslow's steps, and become argumentative. Freedom of opinion is a blessed law in this country."

"I am not clever enough to argue," said Bessy, with a sigh that made Hugh Speckland smile, despite his attempt to hide any signs thereof; "I only know what is right and wrong."

"A deep knowledge, which is beyond me! Right and wrong seem so inextricably woven together, and the false approaches so near to the truth, that the truth baffles me, and the lies ever deceive. But you are an enthusiast; how long will it last?—how long *has* it lasted?"

Bessy remembered her life in Choke Street, at the "El-Dorado," and her face flushed. Perhaps she was premature in her attempts at conversion—she, a "church goer" of six weeks! Still, this was a new life; the dark life following the days of old amongst the Welsh mountains was gone for ever. She felt, with a kindling of that enthusiasm at which Hugh Speckland scoffed, that there was no power on earth to make her pass back to it again. She was sanguine and over-confident; and a greater trial to her faith than the "El-Dorado" was rapidly approaching. The shadow was in that room, at that time—and Bessy knew not of its presence.

"I don't say you are in the wrong, Miss Calverton," said Hugh, seeing her colour change; "neither that your fervour is evanescent. But I am a man of the world, and have seen many converts. The man that lives next door took the pledge last year, and is now a drunkard and a beast; the churchman swears to thirty-nine articles, and then goes over to Rome."

"Exceptions to the rule, Hugh," cried Stephen from the sofa; "an unfair argument, and I call you to order."

"Stephen the righteous to the rescue!"

And with this home-thrust Hugh turned to his work.

"Stephen the anything but the righteous, Hugh," answered the brother; "but I can't see races and classes gibbeted for the weakness of stray members. That's not free-thinking, but the very reverse."

"Possibly—possibly; don't harass."

"You object to churches and churchmen—"

"Stop there!" cried Hugh turning round again—"I object to nothing of the kind, and it is you who sweep down upon me with a general condemnation. I was told once to judge for myself, and see what good it would do me—and I was weak enough to follow Parslow's advice."

"Mr. Parslow!" cried Bessy.

"Well—yes," said Hugh with a slight gnash of his teeth at having betrayed himself; "but don't tell the reverend gentleman so, or he'll go mad with conceit. He succeeded some two years since in talking me into a resolve to try religion as a friend, and a comforter; and I was more hot-headed at that time, and made a dash for it. I went to church, and saw a half-minister half-priest, who played with his religion, and flaunted in my eyes his flowers, lace, velvets, and other trumpery, and intoned a something that might have been cursing or praying for what a listener could comprehend, and ducked himself to the East and made crosses—and that was a religion I was to seek, and find good in! A fancy, sponge-cake religion, that only fools and women would run after—people fond of singing and show, and setting that before God's word."

"But Mr. Parslow does not set singing and show before God's word; he—"

"I am only giving you my experience," interrupted Hugh; "I did not care to face Mr. Parslow, and acknowledge that his reasoning had moved me. I tried the Dissenters after this High Church frippery, but they did not please me with their arguments, and I was forced to retreat and find comfort in my own way again."

And his hand fell heavily upon the table.

"And your own thoughts will never bring you comfort, Mr. Hugh."

"Are you sure of that?" was the question.

"Quite sure."

"You are a philosopher—and philosophy forgets the last bell is ringing for church, and that Lucy has been waiting and wondering at the door these last three minutes."

"Oh! dear," cried Bessy, and in another moment she and Lucy were out of the house. Bessy had some difficulty in keeping Hugh from her thoughts that morning—another side to his character had presented itself, that was strange

and new.   He had acknowledged that her own
good friend and generous helper had had
power to turn him a little from his course;
he was not so hard and inflexible as she had
hitherto believed.   Time might work wonders
even with him, and the opportunity to live
better might come again, with God's will, and
in His mercy.   If he had only met with some
simple earnest divine in the time when his
better nature awoke for an instant, and made
one step towards the right.

Returning home from church that morning
her thoughts wandered to Hugh's brother—
that friend of hers whom she had known
longer, and could never look upon as a stranger
—him she was thinking of perhaps a little too
often in the depths of that heart, the workings
of which she had not learned to comprehend.

If Hugh had been moved, would it require
such a great effort, such an intensity of purpose,
to work a change in a nature more easy, and
a temper more ductile and variable?   She was

little more than seventeen years of age, but Mr. Parslow had said that the humblest instrument might work illimitable good—and if she could only see Stephen reading his bible, and accompanying her and her sister to church before she left Seymour Street for ever! And Bessy's conviction that her sojourn at Seymour Street would not be of long duration, spurred her to fresh efforts that very afternoon.

"Won't you put that book down and read a better one, for once?" asked Bessy, as Stephen lay on his back on the sofa, poring over a well-thumbed volume.

"What do you call a better one?" asked Stephen, languidly.

"The bible."

Stephen looked up surprised.

"I say, Bessy Calverton, what is the matter with you to-day?" he asked, "that you charge us poor Specklands, right and left, and will have no mercy on our sins?"

"I want to see a change here."

"Hasn't it been a change for the better ever since Mrs. Wessinger brought you in the midst of us?"

Bessy coloured at the hearty manner with which he spoke, but she responded—

"But I want to see a great change before I go."

"Go!" he exclaimed, sitting bolt upright; "go where?"

Bessy told him of her conviction that she should not remain long in Seymour Street; spoke also, in the fullness of her heart, of all that Mr. Parslow had said to her in that house some weeks ago.

"And I don't see that you have any excuse to lie here all Sunday, and never think what day it is."

"But I do know what day it is, Bessy," he answered; "a comfortable, easy day, with the blessed consciousness of no work at the theatre of an evening. I can shut my eyes, and fancy myself in Wales by a stretch of my vivid imagination, more especially now the voice of Bessy Calverton rings in my ears."

" You haven't even Hugh's poor excuse of overwork."

" Do you want to see me at church, with my hair very straight, and my eyes very much turned up ? "

" I should like to see you at church now and then."

" How comforting it is to have some one interested in your welfare—your moral welfare, too !"

" You are laughing at me !" cried Bessy, indignantly.

" I beg your pardon—don't be cross. I can't bear to see——*anybody* out of temper. It unsettles me."

Before Bessy could reply, he added quickly—

" Do you really want me to go to church ? Will it give you any satisfaction ?"

" Yes."

" I'll go this evening !"

Stephen Speckland kept his word, and went to church with Bessy, his sister and mother. He dozed once or twice during the service, and yawned at the curate's sermon, which was certainly an indifferent composition, and indifferently delivered. But he made no complaint; he had volunteered to accompany Bessy of his own free will, and it was pleasant coming home to have Bessy's hand upon his arm, whilst his mother and sister went on in advance. He did not know what made it so pleasant; he did not seek to know. He had found it also very pleasant lately to have Bessy an inmate of his house; to watch, more often than any one knew save himself, her figure flitting about the room, or in graceful repose over the eternal shoe-binding. Pleasant to hear her sing, and talk of old Wales, it had been for the last three weeks especially; but coming home from church with her, something more softly exciting and bewildering than he could exactly account for. Perhaps church was doing him good in some secret way; he would accompany Bessy next Sunday again, and Hugh might wonder at the alteration as much as he liked.

So Bessy Calverton, seeing with every day some change in those around her; finding means to amuse the old gentleman, keep the horrors from the old lady; discovering much to love and admire in Lucy Speckland's trusting nature; looking on Stephen and Hugh as brothers, whose merits improved upon acquaintance—was, as we have already affirmed, happy and content. She had worked some little good during her sojourn there; she would hope and pray for more. That last Sunday had seen Stephen Speckland make one step in the right direction; and from the first step what might not evolve? It is the first effort to move that is difficult and hard to conquer; and after that there is much to hope for. And Bessy, seeing Mrs. Wessinger late that Sunday night, communicated to that amiable old lady the result of her own efforts, and startled her not a little by informing her that Stephen Speckland, after a little struggle, had been to church that very evening.

" I have much hope of doing good here now, dear Mrs. Wessinger," said Bessy ; " and Mr. Parslow and you both thought I might."

" Don't be over-sanguine, my child ; that is as bad as want of confidence."

" But to think of Stephen going to church with me !" cried Bessy ; " surely that proves that he is not the thoughtless, wild young man you once warned me of."

" Ah ! I don't know exactly what it proves, at present."

And Mrs. Wessinger went home in a reflective mood.

CHAPTER VII.

A RISE IN LIFE.

BESSY, hopeful and impetuous, continued her efforts to make a convert of Stephen Speckland, and was rewarded by Stephen's regular attendance at church. She fancied she could detect a great change in Stephen during the progress of the fortnight following his first appearance in a place of worship; he was less volatile in his manner and flippant in his remarks, and was never from home save when necessity took him to his work at the theatre. Once or twice he relapsed into a thoughtful mood, from which, by a vigorous effort of his own, he would manage to escape, and bring out the cards and cribbage board for his father's amusement; but he played his game worse than ever, and met with the reproofs of his sire, and subjected himself to odious comparisons between himself and brother Hugh.   More than once, Bessy looking up from her work, met his thoughtful gaze directed towards her over the cards he held in his hand, and was conscious of colouring and feeling nervous and fidgety in consequence.

And yet there was a secret sense of happiness in the midst of it all, that she strove to combat against as though it were wrong. Bessy was young, and had read little in novels of the one great subject that makes novels attractive, and novel readers of the feminine gender precocious.   Her mind was disturbed, and a new world of thoughts, wishes, desires, was opening its golden gates to her.   Her heart, she knew, was in the work of Stephen

Speckland's conversion, but at that time she knew little more save that his voice suddenly near her began to make that heart beat; and that in his frankness, and utter disregard of self, there was the same attraction as had drawn her to him in the times when she was younger. She felt he was a very dear brother of hers—that he was not stern and strange like Hugh, with whom it would take a lifetime to become familiar. Bessy lost her work next week, and Mrs. Wessinger also found less employment for her industrious arm. The times that had been hard became harder still to the poor, and the iron frost seemed as if it would never go away. Bessy was troubled at being out of work, knowing Lotty's little gift would perceptibly diminish, now the expenses of board and lodging were to be deducted in full from it; and if work came not, what was to become of her in the dim future lying beyond? Bessy thought so much of this, that her abstraction was remarked, and very singularly, as she thought, by no less a person than Hugh, who, as a rule, appeared to pay little heed to anything save his own wood-engraving.

"You are thoughtful, Miss Calverton. May I ask if any bad news has disturbed you?"

"No, Mr. Hugh," said Bessy; "but I feel conscious of shortly being an idler here, doing nothing for my support. That must not be."

"Surely you are not going to fret because that wretched shoebinding trade runs slack?"

"Is there anything for which to be joyful?" asked Bessy.

"Yes!"

Bessy regarded him curiously; but he was very busy with his engraving, and frowning desperately at it.

"What is there to be joyful for?" asked Bessy.

"I may tell you some day."

"But—"

Hugh snapped her up in much such a manner as he had snapped her in the earlier days of their acquaintance.

" But I am busy now; you must not stand at my elbow and interrupt me in my work. I never allow it."

Bessy turned away quickly at the remonstrance, and felt half inclined to remind Mr. Speckland that he had begun the conversation which he was now so anxious to put an end to. What a bad-tempered man he was, to be sure! If she lived till doomsday in Seymour Street she should never like him much; he marred all approach to liking by a sudden churlishness, that sent the affections flying back to their shelter. She wondered what manner of man he would be with less work on his hands; whether he would be more like Stephen Speckland, of whom she thought so much, and tried so hard to keep from thinking; for Stephen did his best to make home happy, at least.

Stephen made home happy in earnest one evening by bringing home the good news of a rise in life for him.

" Old Simmonds has opened his eyes to my virtues and accomplishments at last. The first carpenter has resigned, and Stephen Speckland is to reign in his stead, at a salary of fifty shillings a week. Who is the first to wish me joy ? "

Hugh left his high stool to shake his brother by the hand.

" I, who have prophesied so long that you would never rise higher than thirty shillings a week, ought to be the first to congratulate you on your success."

" Thank you," said Stephen, as they shook hands heartily.

"And don't lose it again with that horrid habit of putting things off till the morrow," added Hugh.

" Oh, I have done with procrastination, and idling away time, and letting fellows

less swift of foot, and with less brains, perhaps—for I am a *leetle* conceited—get before
me in the race. In the new life, I am going
to turn over such a large new leaf!"

"So you always say," remarked Lucy.

"And so I say again for the twentieth
time, and mean for the first," said Stephen.
"Fifty shillings are something in these days,
and must not be treated with undue indifference. A really new leaf — for there is so
much to spur me on, and give me strength
to work upwards. What are you looking at,
Hugh?" he asked, as his pale face reddened
a little beneath Hugh's fixed intensity of
gaze.

"What new incentive to exertion lies before
you, Stevie?"

"Perhaps it is a secret; and if you have
your secret, Hugh, you must put up with
mine."

"I don't blame you," was the response, as
the speaker turned again to his work.

"Perhaps Stephen is thinking of a wife, now," commented Lucy, archly.

Stephen laughed very heartily at this, and, after a habit of his, brought a hand smartly down on his knee.

"Stephen Speckland a married man!" he cried; "that's a fancy picture indeed, Lucy. Who'd marry a hare-brained fellow like me, keep me and my house in order, and make me a loving wife? Who'd chance life with a man whose health is precarious, whose ideas are wandering, and whose capabilities of making a woman happy are extremely doubtful?"

Bessy looked up at this moment, and met his gaze directed towards her. It was very unaccountable, but she started and turned her face quickly away, and felt her heart leaping strangely in her bosom. Very strange and incomprehensible behaviour of hers, which she trusted Stephen had not remarked; and yet he had looked somewhat meaningly in her direction, or she was full of fancies that even-

ing. Yes, she must be full of fancies, for she
had never thought of marrying or giving in
marriage before, and Stephen's remarks perplexed her. She wished she was in her own
room, to think of all this—to seek in some
manner to account for Stephen's manner, and
her own agitation. She was glad when
Hugh's voice — the hard, unsympathizing
voice of a man of the world—broke a silence
that was at least painful to her.

"What are fifty shillings a week with a
wife?"

"Working men marry on half, and less than
half, Hugh."

"More fools they."

"Well, perhaps so, although working men
have no appearances to keep up, and the
working man's wife sits not idle, but works
too. But with fifty shillings a week, Hugh—
why, it's a good round sum to begin housekeeping with, and—but you were always a
cynic, and I won't argue with you! And

who says I'm thinking of marriage?—what folly! And," he added, hurriedly, "who's going to wish me joy of my great rise in life besides Hugh? Father, mother, Lucy and Bessy—all silent!"

Thus appealed to, the congratulations began to pour in from the remaining members of his family, and Bessy ended them by timidly wishing him joy herself. Fifty shillings a week was a great rise in life to him, although the father grumbled a little over it, and thought it might as well have been sixty. Still the work was lighter, there was more supervision and less manual labour, and consequently more opportunity to amuse his poor old father when he was that way inclined—which wasn't often, unfortunately.

The evening wound up with quite a celebration of the event; and even Hugh was persuaded to abandon his work early, and take a seat by the fire, and join the general festivities, heightened as they were by gin and water, and a plate of mixed biscuits. One of the happiest evenings Bessy Calverton had spent in Seymour Street; the Speckland family circled round the fire, and all talk of work and the past wherein they were better off, dropped for the time. There was singing too; and after Bessy's song Stephen sang, and then Lucy, and then Hugh was called upon, and Bessy felt quite alarmed at the liberty taken with that grave figure, who sat with his arms folded regarding the firelight.

"Catch Hugh singing!" exclaimed the father, with a short grunt; "catch him amusing anybody, more than he can help."

"But this is a special occasion," said Stephen; "and Hugh always comes out on special occasions, and does his best. Am I not right, Hugh?"

"Where's your precedent?"

"When Lucy's sweetheart went away to Canada, didn't he spend the last evening here, and wasn't Hugh Speckland the gayest of us all?"

"A different occasion altogether, when the spirits required raising. A miserable occasion, and a friend about to leave us for ever."

"To begin a new life, for the better, Hugh—like myself."

"Yes, but he was going away, and you were all dull and low-spirited; to-night you can get on without me."

"And Hugh has such a first-rate voice, Bessy," said Stephen; "come, try your power of persuasion on this flinty-hearted being."

"Oh! he will not mind what I say," was Bessy's reply.

Hugh made an uneasy movement in his chair, frowned, and then laughed lightly.

"What a demoniac I must be," he said; "even Miss Calverton looks upon me with fear, and is afraid of my snapping her head off. Haven't I said half a hundred times it is only stepping between me and my work that makes me irritable; and now the work's on the shelf, and the worker sits here at his ease."

" That is as much as to say you are in a good temper, Mr. Hugh," said Bessy.

" Try me."

" Well, then—I will ask you, as a favour, to sing."

Hugh Speckland began at once an old English ditty in a deep bass voice of some power; he sang with feeling and expression, and the song being a plaintive one, brought the tears into Bessy's eyes. She had not imagined until then that there was any poetry in Hugh's nature, and had expected some national song with a defiance to invaders and Frenchmen. But this was a song of the affections, and sang by one who could possibly feel deeply. She might never understand him, but she would be glad when Hugh had less work to do, and earned higher prices.

Yes, it was a happy evening, and some

portion of the happiness seemed to remain
with Bessy after it belonged to the past, and
Hugh sat so sternly at his post that she
could scarcely imagine he had ever softened
so much as to sing a sentimental love ditty.
Did Bessy Calverton know what made her
feel more happy after that night; why her
step was lighter, and the shadow of the "El-
Dorado" still further removed from the present? In the solitude of her own chamber,
over the little work that she obtained at
times, did she breathe the suspicion to herself, and think how strange it had all come
round at last? Could she have believed it in
the far-off time, amongst the mountains, when
Stephen Speckland watched her kneeling by
the Aberogwin stream—did she believe it
even now? She would not have owned it
even to herself; she was content with the
uncertainty, and afraid of each step that
brought her nearer to the truth ; for she was
very young, and there *was* happiness in doubt.

She knew that there was an alteration in Stephen Speckland, and she treasured the remembrance of the strange look he gave her when they were talking of his marriage? But he might not have her in his thoughts —was it likely? There might be a young lady somewhere who loved him, as that generous nature deserved to be loved, and she would not be very much surprised if that suspicion should prove to be correct, one fair day in the future. He was different in his manner towards her, but so was his brother Hugh for that matter; and it might be easily accounted for, by the better knowledge of each other they were gaining every day. They were no longer strangers, and a little difference might be naturally expected. But then—ah then!—this secret hero of Bessy Calverton's life—he had been always her hero—went to church every Sunday with her, and looked at her very thoughtfully when he fancied she was too absorbed in her work to observe him, and seemed to manœuvre a little to obtain a seat by her side when he was at home of an evening. And Bessy, looking at herself in the glass, thought she *had* seen uglier faces once or twice in her life; and perhaps there would not be anything extremely extraordinary in a foreman of stage carpenters, with the munificent salary of fifty shillings a-week, falling in love with her some long, long day hence. Bessy could fancy love a plant of slow growth in Seymour Street, forgetting that it is not the solace of a life amongst that mysterious race, ycleped the "working-classes." Time is valuable Snowfields way, and love-making must be knocked off in some spare moment, when business is slack, and a fair face has time to distract.

Bessy, we re-assert, would not have acknowledged those thoughts, or considered for an instant that Stephen Speckland was falling in love with her—no, not even when that night came which was to be ever remembered, which was to rise before her, and be spoken of in a time of future trial.

It was late in the evening, and Bessy, Lucy and Hugh were the only occupants of the sitting-room, Hugh apart from the ladies as a matter of course, at the old post and the old labour. Mr. and Mrs. Speckland had been upstairs an hour, and Bessy and Lucy were left to sit before the fire and talk of Lucy's Harry. Lucy was more than commonly loquacious concerning her Harry that night—full of his virtues and accomplishments, and anxious that Bessy should read, for the twentieth time or thereabouts, a letter from that faithful lover, that had that morning reached Seymour Street. A letter more full of love than ever, spanning over every doubt with a greater and stronger arch of hope.

"You are sitting up late to-night," remarked Hugh; "cannot the next reading of that letter take place to-morrow?"

" But Stephen has not seen the letter yet."

" Leave it on the mantelpiece for him."

Lucy did not see the advantage to be gained by that advice; night or day she never intended to part with that last, loving, hopeful letter—and to leave it on the mantelpiece, with a brother absent in mind and absorbed in his work, was to make a pipe-light of it perhaps before the sun rose. For Hugh Speckland always smoked one pipe a day— in the very early morning, before he went weary to his room. She would sit up for Stevie, and Bessy would perhaps keep her company—and Bessy, strange to say, had not the slightest objection !

Stephen came home a few moments after- wards, and the letter was placed in his hands when he was leaning against the mantelpiece, and looking down at the raven braids of Bessy.

"What's this ? — another love-letter of Lucy's !" cried Stephen ; "what a lucky girl you are !"

Lucy gave a little sigh—an acquiescent sigh, that had no sorrow in it.

Having read the letter carefully, Stephen returned it to his sister, and looked down thoughtfully at the black hair and the straight parting again.

" That Harry's a trump—eh, Hugh ?"

" One in a thousand," remarked Hugh.

" I don't see that," said Stephen, quickly ; " he was engaged to Lucy before he went away ; he hasn't a right to change. The man who would change because sorrow and afflic-tion have attacked his sweetheart in his ab-sence, deserves to be kicked."

" Possibly."

" And I should like the kicking of him," added Stephen.

" Very likely," said Hugh ; " still, Harry's one in a thousand, and men do change as the world goes round—and women too, for that matter. What are the chances against Lucy ever crossing the seas even now ?"

" Well, we will not make Lucy miserable by recounting them."

" It is good policy to be prepared for the worst."

" Are you ?" asked Stephen.

" Always."

" But you hope for the best too, Hugh ?"

" Sometimes."

And the head bent lower, and the figure that sat with its back towards them denoted an anxiety to be troubled no further with the subject.

" Well, it's good policy ; but I never think of the worst—I catch it by the throat and stifle it, Hugh."

Hugh did not reply.

" And Lucy stifles it too."

" And lives on in a hope that makes the darkness around her more light," added Lucy ; " she has faith in her Harry—and castle-building is a happy employment, let Mrs. Wessinger say what she will."

" You take after me, Lucy," said Stephen; " oh! the rare castles I have built, and the rare castles that have fallen, and not buried my heart in the ruins."

" Yours is a light nature, that finds a loop-hole to escape before the great fall comes," said Hugh.

" I don't know that."

" There is not a disappointment in the world that you would not shake off in a week."

" Yes, there's one," was the quick answer.

" Indeed," said Lucy; " will you inform your patient listeners what that may be."

" Not yet!"

" But when shall we know? " asked Lucy, with all a young woman's persistence. " You have made me and Bessy very inquisitive."

" Bessy don't say so," said Stephen, regarding the parting again.

" Perhaps I am a little curious," said Bessy, looking up archly.

" Well, you'll know in good time, perhaps ;"
and Stephen looked at her so earnestly, so
mournfully, that Bessy felt her heart throbbing, as though it were in some manner connected with his secret. His words had been
uttered lightly enough, as if to deceive the
blind sister and the unobservant brother ; but
the looks were for Bessy alone, and, perhaps,
were speaking the most truthfully.

And when Lucy had left the fireside, and
taken the liberty of intruding on Hugh's
studies, and recommending him to leave off
work for that evening, Stephen's words were
stranger still, and Bessy's heart no calmer in
consequence.

" ' Not a disappointment in the world that I
could not shake off in a week,' " said he,
quoting Hugh's words in a lower tone. " Do
you believe that, Bessy ? "

" No, nor I do not think Hugh believes it
either."

" He did not give much thought to the

nature of some disappointments," said he ; "but then I *am* a frivolous fellow, and Hugh is a great judge of character. Still, I think there is a hope that comes once to every man's life, and to see *that* blown away by an adverse wind is to find one's ideas in the dust, and all the despairing ones uppermost. Well, that's the fortune of war, more often than not. Will you wish better luck to my hope, Bessy Calverton ? "

She hesitated. There could be no harm in wishing it, however ; and she did not guess at his one ambition—she had no right. Yes, she trusted his hope would not fail him—or, failing him, would be as lightly surmounted as his brother had prophesied.

" And you hope it will *not* fail me, Bessy ?"

" Yes," answered Bessy, looking down and evading his glance; "there is no harm in hoping that, I suppose ? "

" You don't know what you are wishing," he said, in a lower tone still; " oh, Bessy ! if you only knew—if I——"

He stopped, and was silent so long that Bessy, who had shrunk away from him, tortured by wild doubts, and yet experiencing throughout a strange thrill of happiness, found courage to look up and meet those eyes again —more mournfully expressive than ever in that moment.

He changed colour then, and said, rather hurriedly—

"Don't think of anything I have been saying to-night, Bessy. It's all folly—nonsense — perhaps madness. I'm a frivolous fellow, and don't know my own mind yet. There may come a day when I can speak of it more—when——"

Stephen paused once more, and Bessy instinctively followed his glance, and looked towards the window. Hugh was still talking with his sister Lucy, but he had turned half round on his high stool, and was watching them intently, with a deeper frown and a darker shade upon his face than she had seen hitherto.

" Are you going to keep up all night there, you two ? " he asked sharply.

" Not quite," was the laconic answer of his brother.

" Is there a secret, concerning which Lucy and I are to be kept in the dark, that you whisper so low ? "

" I have nothing to whisper about, Hugh," replied Stephen. " Good night to you, old fellow."

" Good night," was the response ; and deep, and almost morose, it sounded after the hearty adieu of the younger brother.

" And a better temper to you in the morning," added Stephen. " I may as well wish you that before I go."

" Thank you."

Stephen had reached the door, when he turned back and went to Hugh.

" Is anything wrong ?" he asked, in a tone that was intended to escape Bessy's ears.

" Nothing that I know of."

"You are different to-night, Hugh, or my eyes deceive me."

"Your eyes deceive you."

" On your word ?"

" On my word—sceptic."

And the brow relaxed, and the shadows vanished, and the two brothers looked with a half-laughing face at each other. Bessy thought how like they were at that moment!

And Bessy had much to dwell upon that night; and there were many sleepless hours spent in her humble bed before she closed her eyes, and thought no more of all that had happened to perplex her.

And how much more was there to perplex her on the following night when Stephen came home again and spoke a few words to her in the dark passage. She had opened the door for him that night, and his first words were, "Is that you, Bessy ?"

When she had responded in the affirmative, she felt his hand gripping her by the wrist.

"Bessy, I was talking of a hope last night —it was the folly and madness that I spoke of also. It's gone."

"What is gone?" gasped Bessy.

"Nothing that affects you, mind," he said quickly, "nothing from which I shall not recover in a week, as Hugh said. I mention this to you in particular, Bessy Calverton, because the subject may be unintentionally revived, and to speak of it may give me a little pain, just at present. That's all. You must be on my side; and if Hugh or Lucy speak of my hopes," with a short hard laugh, that reminded Bessy of her sister Lotty, "turn the conversation, if I am pressed too hard. May I ask so much?"

"Yes—but—"

"But say no more about it, Bessy. It was only one hope, and now it's gone. And I am not broken-hearted, girl—what a prophet that brother of mine is!"

CHAPTER VIII.

ANOTHER WARNING.

BESSY did not know what to make of this extraordinary phase of Stephen Speckland's character. It troubled her; it even made her sad. He had lost the great hope of which he had recently spoken so sanguinely; and she, infected with the same castle-building fever, had had a dreamy consciousness of being connected with it. Ah! what dreamers we are all. Here was Bessy Calverton still in ignorance of Stephen Speckland's secret, and Stephen talking of the one hope shattered at his feet.

And in that dark entry, on the night mentioned at the close of our last chapter, he only spoke of it to Bessy, and seemed the same light-hearted fellow she had ever known as he stepped into the midst of the familiar life of home. Hugh was right, thought Lucy, there was not a disappointment in the world that Stephen could not shake off in a week! Who would have thought save Bessy, to whom a glimpse behind the curtain had been vouchsafed, that the great fall had come, judging by his easy, off-hand manner, and the little change that followed his hasty confession. For there was a little change that Bessy's watchful eyes could detect; a greater anxiety to amuse his father when at home, and a habit of leaving home more often, under the plea of business at the theatre—only a plea *that*, Bessy felt assured. Then he was a trifle more reserved towards her, and called her Bessy less often, and seldom looked at her now, not even when he might think her too

busy to observe him. Still it was only Bessy
who could mark a change—to the family he
was not different, and no one detected the
false ring in the jest, and the effort to
sustain the old smiles. And perhaps the jest
came as readily and in the smile there was no
deception after the week that Hugh had given
him had passed; for Bessy saw that he was
resigned, or determined, and, in either case,
possibly content. Somehow she felt very
miserable herself—as if some light had been
shut from her path, and some wild, dreamy
hope from her heart; she did not know what
—she would not know! If she had been a
castle-builder herself, almost unconsciously
rearing up some fabric which a breath was to
dispel, why let the ruins fall round her, and
no one be the wiser — she would not be
the wiser herself, for she confessed nothing,
even in her secret chamber, with the door
locked against the world.

She had been taught a lesson perhaps on

the folly of dreaming, and was none the worse for that task which is set us all in our turn.

Bessy would have liked to know, however, what that one disappointment was of Stephen Speckland's; it did not affect her in any way —but she was curious, and his manner gave no clue to the mystery. Why had he spoken so earnestly to her—was it only because she was younger and impressionable, and might feel for him more?—would certainly not laugh at him for betraying something like senti-ment.

But all this was vain speculation; why should she disturb herself concerning that which troubled Stephen Speckland so little? Let time pass on its way and bring peace to her—and in the practical world before her let idealism die. She had no right to appear concerned or grow pale, or become thoughtful—so Bessy worked busily at shoebinding when there was employment of that kind in her way, and

chatted and smiled again, and forgot not the
good example, in which Mr. Parslow encouraged her— even though Stephen suddenly
gave way and went not to church with her,
but stopped at home and talked worldly
matters with Hugh.

It was one Sunday night, nearly a fortnight after Stephen's eccentric behaviour,
when a turn was given in a new direction to
Bessy Calverton's thoughts. The frost had
broken up by that time, and poverty was
a degree or two removed from starvation,
and did not die of cold and hunger in the
public streets. Bessy, Mrs. Speckland, and
Lucy had returned home to Seymour Street
with Mrs. Wessinger, whom they had met at
church; and Mrs. Wessinger having no work
on hand, was inclined to saw the air with her
prayer-book whilst haranguing Hugh on the
evil of his ways—Hugh engraving his hardest
meanwhile.

" You'll never come to good, Hugh Speck-

land—I've said it a hundred times before.
And all the extra money you may earn by
such ungodly labour will turn out wrong, depend upon it."

"Turn to dry leaves and grasses like magic
money!" said Stephen; "serve him right."

"I'll chance the transformation," remarked
Hugh.

"You chance more than that, young man."

"My good lady, you must spare me a sermon this evening," said Hugh, rising. "I
have done work—I have done more than work
to-night, and to-night ends a long struggle.
This should be a memorable day, God willing!
I'm going for a walk."

"Alone?" asked his brother.

"Yes. I am a savage bear, you know, and
only fit for my own companionship. Good-
night, Mrs. Wessinger."

And Hugh had hurried away before that
well-meaning old lady could repeat his adieu.

"Driven him clean out of the house,

ma'am!" was the comment of the father; "and Sunday evening is the only time when he is a little bit amusing."

"A walk will do him good, Mr. Speckland," said Mrs. Wessinger in reply; "he's looking ill enough."

"Eh—what?"

"He's looking ill enough," reiterated Mrs. Wessinger; "and if some of you don't interfere and stop his games early and late over those stupid blocks of wood, he will fall into a bad way."

"Good Lord, Mrs. Wessinger, you're enough to bring on my horrors!" cried the alarmed mother.

"He works too hard; stop it."

"Stop Hugh working!" exclaimed more than one who knew the hopeless nature of the task.

"I would hide the blocks, and stop it that way," said Mrs. Wessinger.

"But you work as hard," said Stephen.

"No, I don't; and if I did, it agrees with me, for I can think peacefully over mine. But when a man works hard and thinks hard, too—thinks clean contrary to his work, and don't think comfortably—he must give way at one time or another."

"What did he mean by ending a long struggle?" asked Lucy; "he spoke differently—more hopefully, I fancied."

"Ah! you're full of fancies," was the father's response. "You need not worry yourself about what Hugh said. I've known him sit and mutter over his work for hours together, and make my back creep to hear him. It's a struggle that only concerns himself—for he thinks of no one else, I wager."

"Wrong," said Stephen, quickly.

"I say, right!"

"Wrong!" repeated Stephen more determinedly, and the voice was so like Hugh's in its depth and intensity, that it produced the same effect, and quelled dissentient voices. And in the pause that succeeded, a single knock without announced a visitor. Bessy was quick to respond that evening; she had been sitting near the door, and before Stephen or Mrs. Speckland could rise, she was at the street door, regarding doubtfully, and with some nervous excitement, a woman whose face was thickly veiled. The woman remained so motionless that Bessy asked at last her business, and then the word " Bessy ! " hastily escaped her.

Bessy sprang into the street and clasped her arms round her.

" Lotty !—it's Lotty come to see me, at last ! "

" Hush !—don't make such a noise, girl ! " she cried. " Put on your bonnet, and come a little way with me."

" Will you not come in ? "

" No, no—not in there; I'm not fit for any honest home. I can talk better to you alone. I have much to say."

Bessy returned to the room, communicated in a few hasty words the startling intelligence of her sister's arrival, listened to a warning "to be careful, my dear—to be very careful, and make haste back," from Mrs. Wessinger, and to a question, "Is it quite safe?" from Stephen, and then rejoined Lotty, who passed her arm through hers and hurried her down the street.

"I didn't think to trouble you yet awhile, girl," said Lotty; "but there's danger abroad, and there are hints dropped at the 'El-Dorado' of a clue to your whereabouts. You must find another home, or the black hound will have you."

"Hush, Lotty!"

"Ah! it was always 'hush, Lotty!' but he will be a hound if he take you back again —I'm sure of it! You must tell them to hide you with some friends at once—for I heard the name of Speckland to-day, and that's suspicious. You're trembling."

" A little—I shall be better in a minute."

" And I have crossed the bridge to put you on your guard. You must not be brought back to Choke Street, though it has been the devil's own home since you've been gone. Oh! Bessy, that dreadful bible!"

Bessy looked into Lotty's face as she flung back her veil for breath—paler and more deeply-lined than ever, and yet she fancied not so wickedly defiant.

" That bible you left me, because I was a jealous fool, and did not want you to think of Mary Davis too much—oh, that bible!"

" Have you read it?" asked Bessy, hopefully.

" Part of it," was the answer—" it has been nearly the death of me—it has told me so much. Bessy, do you believe half that is in it?" she asked, eagerly.

" Every word."

" That such a woman as I can be saved, after all I have done in my accursed life?"

she cried—" that for such a woman, with all her sins upon her, there is a gleam of hope ? "

" I believe it—yes !   And you will believe it too ! "

" No, I won't !" was the abrupt reply.

" Not believe ? Oh, Lotty ! "

" It's worse to know that—and to be sure there is no escape for me.   That I am hemmed in—hemmed in—and there is no breaking through to the light."

" There is no power to hem you in, if you believe and trust."

" You have altered, Bessy," said Lotty, thoughtfully regarding her.

" Thank God—yes."

" I thought you would—suddenly, instantly, when the heavy weight of such an example was removed.   I forgive that Parslow saving my life, now ! "

" Dear Lotty, do you mind talking a little more of Mary Davis's bible ? "

" Yes, I do mind.   It has done me no

good—it has shown me water beyond my reach, and I am dying of thirst—it has spoken of heaven, and I am in the clutch of the fiends. Bessy, girl, there is no escape for me—upon my soul and body, not a single chance!"

"Will you go and tell Mr. Parslow that?"

"Parslow is watched, and I daren't go there if I had a wish that way—which I haven't, and never shall have. Where's my chance? If I run away, Bessy, there is not a soul who would offer me the shelter of her home—not an honest man or woman but would turn away from me. It would be the old life over again, with the seven devils worse than the first, that your bible talks of, preying on me."

"We might live together—we—"

"What! your life marred by mine, and your character blasted by contact with it—to offer you a share in my evil name, and rob you of your good one ! Madness and folly ! "

"Do you read the bible still, Lotty ? "

"Yes, that's the worst of it. I have hidden it once or twice, and then I have been curious to make sure if the very, very worst were promised pardon or repentance, and then hardened myself with the thought that I never meant to repent, and there was an end to it."

She gave her old short laugh at this, but looked still anxiously into Bessy's face, as if for a denial to her terrible assertion. And Bessy denied it strongly and indignantly, and told Lotty she was repenting already, and said the time would come when the one chance of which she despaired would be offered her. Bessy would pray for that time, and think deeply and earnestly concerning it.

"I won't hear any more about it!" cried Lotty; "I have stolen out to give you a warning, and tell you that there is no time to be lost—that's the only business that concerns you. Don't trouble your head with Mary Davis's bible—anything that ever belonged to *that girl* won't do Lotty Calverton much good."

It was the old jealous cry, and Bessy sighed.

" Tell your new friends what I have said —if they can't help you, write to Mr. Parslow at once, and he may think of something, though he is a bit of a blunderer. Do they make you happy in this place ? "

" Yes—they are very kind to me."

" There's a girl there, I see," said she, a little sullenly ; " I suppose you think more of her than—than Mary Davis even now !"

" Why should you think that, Lotty ? "

" Because you're a girl of fancies ; and let anyone be fond of you, and you give all your love back in return."

" Is it not natural ? "

" Perhaps it is," she replied, after a pause; "if you don't forget those who loved you before. Bessy, you won't forget me—bad as I am ? "

" Never."

" I don't ask you to love me like Mary Davis—I don't expect that ! "

" But I do love you, Lotty, better than any one in the world."

Lotty suppressed a cry, and walked on in silence. After a time she said—

" I have seen two young men there—do they make love to you ? "

" Love to me !—oh, no."

" Take care of the men—there's no trusting their lying tongues."

" You appear to know the family well, Lotty—you have been here before—and I was beginning to think you had forgotten me."

" Have I anything worth remembering but you ? " cried Lotty; " is there a bright spot in all my life, save that which you have made for me ? Well, I do know all about the

Specklands—I have been in this street twenty times, or more—do you think I could keep away, with the chance I had of seeing you now and then, when that grim-faced fellow bent his head a little over his work? More than once he has frowned me away, and you were sitting at the back, and ignorant how near I was to you."

"My dear Lotty, and you never gladdened my heart by a sight of you!"

"I am a shadow lurking in darkness—leave me there—it is best for us both!"

"But the light shall come, Lotty; I promise it—I am living for it!"

"I'll believe it when I see it," said she, and her scornful little laugh echoed again in that silent street; "you're all confidence—if it makes you any the happier, keep so! But don't think of me too much—*that* can't make you happy. What is the name of the one who goes to church with you sometimes?" she asked, abruptly.

" Stephen."

" He's the best tempered and the best looking brother of the two. Don't let him rob you of your heart, before you're aware of it. You're nearly eighteen years of age now."

" I will take care, Lotty."

" It might be the best thing that could happen, if—but the best or worse will come, and you'll not be able to stop it. I must go now. Write to Mr. Parslow when you are safe, and I shall be able to find you out— God bless you—now go. And," she added, " don't think of me too much—I'm good for nothing !"

She darted away from Bessy's embrace, and went rapidly down the street, leaving Bessy with the tears in her eyes, but with hope in her heart; for there was a change in Lotty, however much she might talk of despair, or think there was no surmounting the great wall of her sins. Mary Davis's bible had roused her at least to thought, and from such thought as her's what good might evolve ? Bessy forgot the danger that threatened her in thinking of the better times of which she had spoken so assuringly to Lotty, till a hand touched her own, and the deep voice of Hugh Speckland said, close to her ears—

" It is a late hour to be alone in the streets, Miss Calverton."

CHAPTER IX.

HUGH SPECKLAND'S ADVICE.

HUGH SPECKLAND did not speak in very soft accents to our heroine; on the contrary, he addressed Bessy as if he were a little vexed at finding her alone, and some distance from home. But he changed his tone immediately she looked towards him, and said—

"You mustn't think me harsh, Miss Bessy, but this is out of your usual way—and it is not safe for young women to be alone at an hour so late. On a Sunday night all the scum of the metropolis floats to the surface, and makes London streets hideous. Are you going home, now?"

" Yes, sir."

" You were standing deep in thought when I came up with you—you do not expect any-one?" he asked earnestly.

" No, I have just parted with my sister."

" Indeed!—any bad news ?" was the anxious inquiry.

" They know where I am at the ' El-Dorado,' " said Bessy with a sigh, " and I must leave you all !"

" No ! " said Hugh impetuously.

Bessy looked surprised, but he continued—

" A hundred times, No, Miss Calverton. Will you tell me all the news, and let me judge what is best—do you mind taking my arm? I shan't bite you," he added, a little satirically, as Bessy seemed to hesitate.

Bessy had not hesitated, she had only been surprised at his request; at the cold self-abstracted head of the family politely offering his escort and protection homewards. She had expected him to make an abrupt little speech and pass onwards, not find him doubtful of her ability to reach home in safety without his protection. True, he had marred his politeness by his last observation—but that was a habit of his, and she did not take offence at it, although of a hasty disposition at times.

"Let us walk slowly and discuss the matter. There will be only argument and foolish reasoning to vex one in-doors. What is there to fear, Miss Bessy?"

Bessy related all that Lotty had warned her of; and he listened with great attention, although he was silent after she had concluded the few remarks that threw a light on the matter.

"May I inquire," he said at last, "if you are tired of us yet?"

"Do you think so?" asked Bessy, with some warmth.

"I am an uncharitable thinker at times—don't ask me."

But Bessy persisted, and he said at last very positively, " No—I do not."

This part of the subject having been definitely settled, he put another question.

" Are you fond of the country?"

Bessy replied in the affirmative.

" Perhaps it may be as well to give your father as little clue as possible," he said; " although I do not fear him—and I doubt if he would put forth a legal claim, if we resisted him stoutly. Still, father and mother will go in the country shortly, and there will be a home with them, if you like to accept it."

It did not appear a very cheerful prospect, although Bessy thanked him. And it did not appear feasible; for how was she to work for her living in the country, where work was scarce—and, above all, this sudden talk of the country was very new and startling. Hugh Speckland observed this, for he said—

" You are the first, Bessy Calverton, to hear me talk of the country. The long struggle I spoke of at an earlier hour this evening ends with a country life for those who have despaired of it so long."

"It seems very strange."

"It is a little surprise of mine—a *coup-de-théâtre*, as the French say. My father, whom time has afflicted and weakened, has mourned many years for a country life, and the last three years I have been working day and night to give it him. His life has been a reproach to mine—but it was not to be helped. I took my share of blame, and said nothing."

"And this was the secret motive of which you spoke one day?"

"Yes."

"It is very kind."

"No—only very selfish," was the reply. "I shall be happier out of the reach of my father's reproaches—perhaps I shall be glad to get rid of the old people, and call the house my own, and feel my own master. Set that down for the motive. If it be not a very high one, it's as near the truth as the other."

" I don't think so."

" Don't you ? " and he looked suddenly at her, and then turned his head away again; " Well, there are motives within motives, as there are wheels within wheels. Practice at my profession has made me, if not perfect, at least sought a little more by publishers and print-sellers; and it has not been very hard work, after all, to save a hundred and twenty pounds, and buy and furnish a little cottage down in Kent for the old people. They have wished it in their hearts all their lives; let us see if the accomplishment of that wish will make them happy—or think better, just a little, of one they have doubted."

" And Stephen and Lucy—are they ignorant of the surprise ? "

" Yes, at present. I may tell them to-morrow, or the next day, if you do not fore-stall me ? "

"Do you think I would deprive you of the pleasure of so agreeable a surprise, Mr. Hugh?—you who have worked so hard for it, too?"

"And spoiled my temper so much in the effort."

"Not so much, after all."

"Ah! will you think better of me as well as the rest, and forgive my fits of petulance, for the sake of the object that caused them? Do you expect now my end is gained—to find me as indolent and easy as that good-tempered brother of mine? No, Bessy, I have something else to work for still; and as I have taken you into my confidence, I'll—I'll tell you that, if you like."

He was looking at her again, and his voice was deep and low—scarcely for the moment articulate. Bessy felt for the moment afraid of him, and half made a movement to withdraw her hand; but he pressed it close with his arm, and would not let her go.

"I must tell you whether you like it or not," said he, a little hastily. "It's a foolish task to beat eternally about the bush, wherein no bird may be ever entrapped. If I take a fancy—have a wish—I seek for some hope to guide me on, or I let it go at once, and turn away. It is an irremediable folly to build a world of hopes on a vapour, that must collapse and let them down. Bessy Calverton, I'm going to ask you to give me hope to call you mine some day."

"Oh, sir! I never thought—I never dreamt of this! Pray, let go my hand, and say no more."

"Will you think of it from this time?—or will you let me know to-morrow, after a night's deliberation? I don't wish to alarm you, Bessy; but I must say, that your presence in my house has made a new life for me, taught me to build on a future that may make me a very different man. Here is a work of reformation for you, Bessy—will you attempt

it ?—will you trust in me ?—will you give
me a right to protect you against those who
had a trust, and forfeited it ?   Will you believe that this grim, hard-worker at your side
has a heart strong to love, and make you
happy ?   There, I have frightened you, leaping forth from the shell wherein all my better
feelings have been buried so long ; but I must
seek hope, or face the worst, and not live on
in uncertainty.   I was never afraid to face
the worst yet."

And he looked very sternly before him, as
though the worst lay beyond in the darkness.
He had relinquished her hand now, and Bessy,
with averted head, was hurrying along by his
side, anxious to escape this embarrassing
position, and alarmed at this new change, so
sudden and fierce.

"Some time to-morrow you will give me
my answer, Miss Calverton," he said ; "that
is but fair to you and myself. And, if you
can give me one more hope to work upwards

for—the brightest my life may ever know."

He proceeded at a slower pace, to allow Bessy to recover some portion of her embarrassment alone, before she entered the home from which her sister had called her with news startling to her peace of mind. But what was that to the news which had come upon her since, and set her heart wildly beating, and thrown every thought into confusion. Oh! let her hurry upstairs to her room, and lock the door on those thoughts, before they betrayed her into an outburst of incomprehensible tears.

CHAPTER X.

BESSY'S ANSWER.

BESSY CALVERTON spent the greater part of that night and the early morning thinking of all that Hugh Speckland had told her. It was her first offer; she was but little more than a girl—and a first offer is always so confusing and exciting. And to add to it all, there was the consciousness of not having thought of Hugh Speckland as a lover—of living a little while ago in a vague kind of dream-land, in which other figures and other hopes had existence. But it was only dream-land after all, and this was reality!

Bessy Calverton had time before her to think, and Hugh Speckland could not have adopted a better course than not pressing her for an immediate reply to his love-suit. Bessy pressed on the instant would have answered no ; but Bessy left to herself was a thoughtful and prudent girl, who had not had much chance in her life of fostering romantic ideas.

Bessy saw a choice between Choke Street and Hugh Speckland's home—life in " El-Dorado" *versus* life in Seymour Street. To Bessy, a wanderer as it were, indebted to foreign kindness for the protection of a home, the offer of Hugh Speckland's was something more than she could anticipate—a rise in life for which she was unprepared. She was grateful for it, pleased in that heart of whose workings she comprehended so little, that her poor self had had charms enough to rouse into action feelings long dormant in the breast of Hugh Speckland. What could he see to love in her, and why did she not feel more happy under the circumstances? Hugh had not sworn her to secrecy—possibly had not expected her to take counsel alone of herself in a case so momentous and critical—she would rise early and visit Mrs. Wessinger, and make a confidant of that motherly old lady.

And despite the late hour at which Bessy dozed off and plunged into troubled dreams, it was only striking seven when she was startling Mrs. Wessinger by her unlooked for appearance.

"My goodness, girl—what is the matter that you look so scared like!" she cried, as her independent right arm continued its labour; "no bad news, I hope."

"I hope not, Mrs. Wessinger," said Bessy. "I'm in trouble, and I come to you for advice—but it's—it's not bad news!"

"It's too early for watchers in the street, supposing that the watch has been kept up, which I doubt," remarked Mrs. Wessinger; "but still this is an imprudent step."

"I don't know that I need be prudent any longer—I saw my sister last night, and you are aware that she came to warn me to choose another home, for my new one she feared was discovered."

"Yes, my dear. I learned that sad news last night."

"But that is not my trouble, dear—it's advice of another kind that I want. Mr. Speckland has—has asked me to marry him."

The shoe dropped off Mrs. Wessinger's hand at this astounding piece of intelligence. She had not been so taken off her guard since her little money was lost and her husband died.

"Stephen?"

"No—Mr. Hugh."

"Hugh Speckland!" exclaimed Mrs. Wessinger; "that obstinate, well-meaning, hard-hearted, hard-working infidel—I beg your pardon, Bessy, but he's all that and more, and there's no telling what sort of husband he would make a young girl like you. You're so very young, and he's thirty at least. But you're a poor girl, and he stands a chance of getting on in the world—and a protector like Hugh would keep you from all dangers that a return to the 'El-Dorado' might bring. But then he's an infidel—a No Church man, and all the rest is worldly reasoning. Upon my word, my dear Bessy," said Mrs. Wessinger, inclined to cry at the host of pro's and con's that suggested themselves; "I don't know what to advise—if he loves you, it is all for the best, perhaps; and if you love him—you know best, my dear, about that—why, I mustn't advise you against your own happiness. And I'm not advising you—I can't. Oh! if Mr. Parslow were only here now!"

But Mr. Parslow was not there, and to seek him was dangerous; good man as he was, how could he advise Bessy in so delicate a matter. He might not have even pressed her so closely as to the state of her heart as Mrs. Wessinger, who had no belief in "good matches," unless love was at the bottom of them. What an old-fashioned idea!

"Go back and think it over very deeply again, Bessy," said Mrs. Wessinger; "trust in what your heart prompts you to do, and I think it will be right. If you are still perplexed, ask for longer time—the match that is made in a hurry never turns out well. Have you told Mr. Speckland that your father is likely to discover you again?"

"Yes."

"We ought to think of something very speedily—if he has nothing to suggest, I shall be round in an hour or two with a suggestion of my own. The grass must not grow under our feet."

Bessy went away as perplexed as she had come, and returned once more to her room to think the matter over—to pray for a clear judgment in this great turning-point of her life. And after a long prayer she woke to the consciousness that she did not love Hugh Speckland—that it would be false and wrong to let him believe that she loved him. She might love him in time, and make him a good wife, perhaps. But if it had been only—— and then she buried her head in the bed-clothes and sobbed, and would think no more of a folly which, fostered too long, might have been the wreck of her happiness.

She went downstairs with a mind unre-solved, and a heart still ill at ease. If she had had but one adviser!

Bessy was surprised to find the old couple not downstairs yet, Lucy still absent, the tall stool at the window vacant, and only Stephen Speckland sitting in a brown study before the fire. Bessy quite started when he turned round, he looked so pale and hag-gard.

"Good morning, Bessy," said he; "I have been waiting here an hour for you."

"For me!" exclaimed Bessy, and her colour came and went strangely.

"Hugh told me a great secret late last night, concerning you and him—a secret that I learned then for the first time," said he; "it's an odd story, of which I never had a suspicion. You are not angry with me for introducing the topic so abruptly?"

"No," responded Bessy.

"Hugh of course is unaware that I rose early this morning to talk the matter over too," said he; "the poor old fellow is nervous for once in his life, and has fled before the bright face of a girl of eighteen. I suppose love makes cowards of us—eh, Bessy?"

"I don't know—I can't say," said she, embarrassed at the question.

"Once upon a time, Bessy, you were inclined to leap at decisions rather hastily," said he; "in Wales there was a dispute about

U 2

a halfpenny, and a run up a mountain in the mist; in London here you had taken offence at a few words of Hugh's, and were thinking of flying back to Mrs. Wessinger's—I hope you will not hastily say 'No' to poor Hugh's one chance of being happy."

"You hope I will not say 'No'?" said Bessy.

"With all my heart, I hope you will not say 'No,' Bessy," he answered earnestly.

Bessy coloured, and looked down at the floor, and felt as if the room were spinning round with her, and rested her hand upon the mantelpiece to steady herself from a shock that she had never expected. Had she been hoping against hope even till that minute, that she felt as if one more tie had been cut asunder that bound her to an illusion?

"I hope so for both your sakes, Bessy," he said, speaking slowly, and looking at the fire again, as though he read his lesson there; "of your own shall I speak first?"

"I would rather not hear any more," murmured Bessy.

"But this is a great crisis, and I ask it as a favour," said he; "I will be brief."

"I am listening," murmured Bessy.

"You will have no reason to fear your father after that marriage with Hugh; you will have one of the best of husbands—for the true nature of Hugh Speckland is developing itself, and it is a good one. You will be very happy—you will make him so. And for Hugh's sake, I ask it, because no one has understood him; and to only one he loves and thinks of making his wife will he soften, and let the noble heart and all its unselfish nature have play. He will be a new man if you accept him, I am sure: if you turn away from him, deterred by the mask he has worn so long—it *is* only a mask!—you harden that nature for ever, and shut him up in himself till his dying day. Hugh may bear his disappointment well in your eyes, but nothing can change him so much, or work so much for evil, as your refusal."

"Why do you plead so earnestly for him?" cried Bessy; "is it not treating him like a child?—treating me——"

"I hope not. It is a strange pleading, I own; but, Bessy, I have a reason that makes me take an office ungracious in itself, and one which Hugh would resent more warmly than you. It is the best of reasons."

"Will you tell it me?"

"Not now," and Stephen compressed his lips and looked more fixedly at the fire, as though the lesson there had become blurred, and hard to read.

"Will you ever tell me?"

"I may some day."

"Ask me to be your brother Hugh's wife, then," said Bessy, with rapidly increasing excitement, "and I will say 'Yes.'"

"I have asked you, Bessy."

"Ask me again."

Stephen Speckland looked up again, and repeated his former words, not altering a syllable.

"With all my heart, I hope you will not say 'No,' Bessy."

"I will make him happy, if it lie in my power, then. If his happiness depend alone upon myself, it would be cruel to say that no—a poor return for all your kindness—all *his* love."

"Yes."

"May I ask whether you had any suspicion of Hugh's secret till last night?"

"Not any," answered Stephen.

Bessy shivered as she dropped into a chair by the fire; and Stephen, as if he had fulfilled his mission, rose and hastily left the room. Bessy did not know how long it was before the subject of the late conversation was standing by her side—it could not have been many minutes, she fancied.

"Miss Calverton," Hugh said, leaning his

arm on the mantèlpiece, and bending forwards to regard her more intently. Bessy looked up as he addressed her, and shrank a little at the dark face so close to hers—it was so unlike a lover's—it expressed so little hope, so much fear, anxiety, even trouble, in the midst of the set sternness that work and thought had rendered habitual to its character.

"I don't wish to hurry you, Bessy," he said; "if there be anything to consider still, pray defer your answer, and leave me in suspense. But—but you *have* thought of all I said last night?"

"Yes."

"And the future life of him standing at your side, Bessy?—is it to be something newer, brighter from this time; or shall I step once more into the darkness, and let the shadows close on me?"

"If—if, Mr. Speckland, it is in my power to make you happy——"

" I_F ! " he cried.

" And if you will be content with one to whom your offer has come with a surprise from which I have not yet recovered, but who will do her best to return your love, and make that future life you speak of, bright."

" Bessy—dear Bessy ! "

It was the face of a lover's then. In a moment Bessy saw what it was in her power to effect, with such a love to work on—saw, too, what a little trouble, a little true affection might make of that nature, whose noblest attributes had been warped by constant labour and no sympathy. In the midst of his own family he had lived alone, and been misunderstood—he had worked and struggled intently for the home in which they had lived, and the roof that had sheltered them all, and been rewarded with no thanks. Only his brother Stephen had understood him a little, and seen more deeply into the inner life, wherein many noble traits of character waited the right word, the right method to leap into existence and make a hero of him. Nay, was there not as much heroism already in this engraver of Seymour Street, Snow-fields, as in the Rolando's and Tirante's of times more remote—he had sacrificed ten years of his life for those who bore his name, and had slaved hard for that cottage, the unattainability of which had been his father's constant source of complaint. It was only now his life was brightening, and the better times advancing—and the young girl trembling there at his side had given the signal of the great change by her timid answer. His was an intense love—for his character was intense—and the sudden change was new to her, and alarmed her a little. But she felt more happy already. Give her time, and this strong man's love, and let the one fleeting vision pass by unacknowledged—and might not her own life take its colouring from his, and the best, brightest days be dawning for her also. She would hope so—she would try to feel happy in the present, by believing so; she would shut her eyes to the fact that it was one step from perfect truth—and that from such a step evil must follow in due course.

END OF THE SECOND VOLUME.

R. BORN, PRINTER, GLOUCESTER STREET, REGENT'S PARK

NO CHURCH.

BY

THE AUTHOR OF

"HIGH CHURCH."

[F. W. Robinson.]

"And as we fall by various ways, and sink
One deeper than another, self condemned
Through manifold degrees of guilt and shame;
So manifold and various are the ways
Of restoration, fashioned to the steps
Of all infirmity, and tending all
To the same point, attainable by all—
Peace in ourselves, and union with our God."
WORDSWORTH.

IN THREE VOLUMES.

VOL. III.

LONDON:
HURST AND BLACKETT, PUBLISHERS,
SUCCESSORS TO HENRY COLBURN,
13, GREAT MARLBOROUGH STREET.
1861.

LONDON:
PRINTED BY R. BORN, GLOUCESTER STREET,
REGENT'S PARK.

PART THE THIRD.

(CONTINUED.)

THE NEW LIFE.

NO CHURCH.

CHAPTER XI.

FATHER AND LOVER.

At the breakfast table of the Specklands that same morning, Hugh, in a very few words, laid before the family his new hopes, and the new plans that were based upon them. He took little notice of the surprise visible on the countenances of most of his listeners, but continued and concluded his narration with an amazing *sang froid*, that said a great deal for his command over his feelings. He spoke of two subjects—of the new great hope of his life, to which other hopes were as nothing, and of that other aim and object of his life that had for years been silently persevered in, and was only then upon the eve of completion. Of the former he spoke first very calmly and determinedly, and his father and mother looked from him to Bessy, and from Bessy to him, and would not have betrayed much greater astonishment had a thunderbolt dropped from the ceiling into the midst of that breakfast tray. Mr. Speckland, senior, looked askance at Hugh, and dodged his great black eyes, which seemed to forbid all reasoning, and muttered at last—

"Well, it's a surprise, and I don't understand it. I can't make out what time you've had to fall in love or think of a wife—but so it is, at all events. It was to be expected, I suppose, and the old woman and I will be two too many in the way. There's only one thing I have to wish."

"What is that?"

"That you'll *amuse* Bessy Calverton rather more than you have me, or a precious mess you will make of your marriage."

Hugh laughed and looked at Bessy, who was too timid to meet his glance yet.

"Bessy will not mind me working for the home that keeps us together. And now of the two too many in the way that you speak of, father."

And Hugh spoke for the first time of the cottage that he had worked so hard for, that was purchased and would be ready in a few weeks for the reception of the old couple, who had been so long recommended country air. He treated it all as a commonplace matter enough, and took no credit on himself for his labour and perseverance; and the old gentleman sat and fidgeted in his chair, and breathed hard, and finally burst into a childish fit of weeping, and possibly understood that stern, grave son of his for the first time in his life.

"I shall be amused in a minute," he sobbed
—"don't anybody speak to me, if you please
—see to your mother! Run for Mrs. Wessinger—there's a fit of the horrors coming—
look at her!"

"I wish to speak of your companion for a
little while," said Hugh—"of the necessity
there is to leave as soon as possible, for
Bessy's sake. The old danger is threatening
her again."

"Ay, and nearer than you think!" exclaimed a voice by the door. Bessy screamed
and started to her feet, then sank into a chair
again, and clutched Hugh Speckland by the
arm. And the faces of the rest were turned
towards the door, whereat stood Richard Calverton, *alias* honest Dick, of Choke Street.

Not a pleasant person to look at, in the
best of times; at this particular season, with
a countenance smeared by yesterday's dirt,
and with eyes bloodshot and half-closed with
yesterday's drink, as arrant a vagabond as all

Whitechapel could produce. The door was half open, and he leaned with his back against it, and swung with it gently to and fro, enjoying the confusion into which his sudden presence there had thrown that little family party. Hugh Calverton had not turned yet in his direction, but kept his hand on Bessy's arm, as if to assure her by his touch that she was safe near him; but he bit his lip, and scowled at the humble teapot of block-tin, and was possibly biding his time.

"A pretty piece of kidnapping all this, I must say," remarked Mr. Calverton, at last; "and no one man or woman enough to offer an apology for all the trouble and expense that it has cost to find my daughter out— and my daughter sitting there as scared as if I were a Guy Fox or a Beelzebub. Bessy!"

The call to his frightened daughter was sharp and peremptory, and Bessy's hands tightened on her lover's arm.

"Bessy!" he cried again; and Stephen looking towards him, said—

"That'll do—you need not make that noise here."

"I'll make any noise I like, in asking for my rights," said Calverton, with a stamp of the floor and one of his favourite oaths; "and there's no one here to stop me—whipper-snapper! Bessy, will you come to me, or shall I fetch you?"

"Will you—" began Stephen.

"Will you hold your tongue, and leave this to me?" cried Hugh Speckland, suddenly leaping to his feet, and making one or two quick steps towards the intruder in his house. The landlord of the "El-Dorado" and the engraver of Seymour Street looked fiercely into each other's face, and the sternness and the unflinching gaze of the younger man seemed a trifle too much for Dick Calverton, who dropped his eyes, and muttered his daughter's name again.

" What do you want here ?" asked Hugh.

" That's a question you can answer as well as I," replied Calverton.

" You are her father ?"

" Don't you see the family likeness ?"

" No."

" It's a pity your shortsighted."

" You are her father, and stand here to claim a father's right—I stand here to dispute it."

" You !"

And Calverton looked at his adversary from head to foot, and indulged in a snort that was intended for a sneer.

" I dispute it ; but I ask you first, if you have the slightest interest in your child's future welfare, to leave her in a home where she is happy."

" She'll come to her own home—I have said it !"

" I say no !"

" You'll have your say—when you're be-

fore the magistrate for abduction, my fine
fellow."

"As her friend and adviser, I say No!—
As her future husband, I say fifty times No!"

"You may say it a hundred times, if you
like—what the devil does it matter to me
how many times you say it?"

"You alluded to the law a moment since,
Mr. Calverton—to the law I recommend you;
face it, if you dare, with your claim to destroy
the soul of your own child. There is no
other answer to your demand to be obtained
in this house. Take it, and rid us of your
presence."

"I want my child—I'll have her."

"Not by force," said Hugh, as he quickly
stepped before Richard Calverton, who had
made a movement towards Bessy; "my
will is law here, and I am accustomed to
obedience. Will you keep back, or shall I
throw you into the street?"

It was Hugh's turn to stamp with his foot,

and to frown at Richard Calverton, and clench his fists. Richard Calverton paused and took in the proportions of his adversary with his evil glance, and thought twice about resistance to a man many years his junior, and a trifle over six feet in height. Dick Calverton was a loud-speaking man, a boaster and a braggart, but he was not a brave man, and the determination visible on the darkling face before him deterred honest Dick from asserting his paternal authority too forcibly just then. Between Hugh Speckland and a little one-eyed quarryman there was a wide difference, and no one was quicker to perceive it than Bessy Calverton's father.

"Ask Bessy if she will come home with me?"

"Oh! no, no—not that dreadful home again!" cried our heroine. "Father, you must let me stop here—if you have ever loved me, wished my happiness, you will not seek to take me back."

"You're not your own mistress by law and —and you don't know what's best for you," he growled.

"Will you leave my house?" asked Hugh, peremptorily.

"I don't know that I will," with a flash of his old surliness; "I don't know that I'm not a match for you, and I'm big enough to take my part, and give as well as take. By —— who are you after all, but a black-faced kidnapper, that shall be transported before I've done with you. By —— you'll find your match if you lay a finger on me— ah! would you?"

Hugh made one step closer to him, and assumed an attitude more threatening, and Bessy screamed and implored him to desist; and Richard Calverton rather hastily stepped back, continuing his vitupera-tions meanwhile, and braving it out to the last. And as Hugh Speckland advanced, Richard Calverton backed step by step into the passage, where, in the midst of his easy flow of powerful language, he backed into the arms of a policeman kindly waiting for him in the passage.

"Hullo!" cried Dick Calverton, wrenching himself from the arms of the new comer, and turning a shade paler through his dirt, "what's this?—what's up?—what have I done?"

"You're Richard Calverton of the 'El-Dorado'—aint you?"

"What of it?"

"Then you're my prisoner—if you're going to ride rusty, say so, and I'll call in a friend of mine who's waiting for you outside."

"Call the devil if you like—I'm an honest man."

The policeman stepped to the door and called Bill, instead of the gentleman recommended; and Bill came clamping into the passage, from which Calverton had hastily retreated.

"What's the charge against me?" he muttered, scowling at the two representatives of the law from under the shabby brim of his hat.

"Gold dust—that's all."

"Gold dust," with a shrug of his broad shoulders; "I know nothing of gold dust, and have never heard of any. I haven't said I'm Richard Calverton yet, so don't be in a hurry. Let a fellow think."

The policeman Bill went to the door and called a third person, who came stealthily into the passage, and crept into the room, with his face half turned to the wall.

"Is that him?" asked Bill of the new comer.

"Yes," was the low answer.

Richard Calverton leaped in the air to give full effect to the double stamp with which he descended and shook the house; then with a fresh torrent of oaths he made a rush towards that man who had been so long his slave, and who had turned at last and betrayed him to the Philistines. But Richard Calverton only ran into the arms of the outraged law—that held him tightly this time, and kept him fast.

"There has been a reward offered—and you've kept me poor, and treated me ill, and trampled on me—and I've turned at last"—said Charles Edwin, with a vindictive glance towards his brother, "was there anything else to be expected?"

"I wish I had you by the throat, for swearing away an honest man's life. Mind you," he cried, as a bright idea suggested itself, "it's all the reward that has turned that cursed viper's fangs against me, and made him tell a heap of lies—all lies, by everything that's holy!"

"You'll come quietly?"

"Of course I will. Innocence can walk uprightly and keep its gallows back straight with the best of you."

He looked towards Bessy, who stood with clasped hands watching him; but the frown which he bestowed on her for her attention was neither amiable nor paternal. The policemen walked him into the street, kindly linking their arms through his; and a crowd of little boys who had been attracted, as street boys are, by a policeman on the lookout, received the *cortége* with shouts, and gambols, and back somersaults, and proceeded to accompany honest Dick and his companions any distance whatsoever under fifty miles.

Charles Edwin remained with his head against the wall in the sitting-room of the Specklands, and it was some moments before his presence there was noticed in the confusion that followed a passionate outburst of tears on the part of Bessy Calverton. When Hugh had calmed her, by reminding her of the dangers from which she had escaped, and of the absence of all share in the crime which that morning's events had shadowed forth, Charles Edwin was observed for the first time.

"You are not wanted here," said Hugh.

"I suppose not—I suppose not," said he, beginning to creep towards the door. "I haven't stopped for thanks; perhaps I don't deserve any."

"Thanks for what?" asked Stephen.

"For saving that girl from him," pointing to his niece—"from the 'El-Dorado,' and all the devilry that goes on there. I don't say that I haven't brooded on my wrongs in my way, and nursed them, and felt inclined to fly at his throat a hundred times—for he was a coward and a knave, and I was his own brother! But I might have only brooded, if he hadn't found where Bessy was living, and swore to bend her to his will, and crush her. And Bessy had been kind to an old man, and given him kind words, and I was grateful for it. I can remember a kindness as well as a wrong; and to save that girl from my brother

was to offer her another chance of living
honest. I've done it for the best, whatever
comes of it. She was worth saving, and he
was good for nothing. That's all."

And the old spy and informer shuffled out
of the room, and gave one more glance to
Bessy before he passed into the passage and
went down the single stone step before the
door into the street.

" 'Another chance of living honest,' "
quoted Hugh—"ay, and of living happy," he
added. " Don't grieve, Bessy—all is for the
best."

" But he is my father, and they are taking
him to prison!" cried Bessy. " Oh! if he
had been a different man, and loved me ever
so little ! "

It was the strange, yearning voice of one
who missed the love and affection that should
have been her right—of one still standing
alone in the world, perhaps, with those to
whom her heart would have clung the most

fondly, holding aloof from it, and passing her by.

Is it not always so in the great world in which we dreamers live?—in which so many hopes are born and wither, and so many vain ambitions burst like bubbles in the sun? Setting out upon the tortuous road, the end of which is veiled, wisely and mercifully, in mystery, how many friends do we meet who judge us wrongly, and think lightly of us, and to whom our hearts will cling the fonder, though we wander on and keep our lips sealed?—from whom, such is the perverse law that rules our human nature, only a word, a look, a sigh, is needed to make us leap towards them, and betray the secret that we mask with smiles. And the world spins round, and we wander on our way; and they are wandering, too, who love us not, and whose names are whispered in our prayers.

END OF THE THIRD PART.

PART THE FOURTH.

TROUBLED WATERS.

CHAPTER I.

LEARNING TO LOVE.

THE gold-dust case was clear against Richard Calverton, and all the protestations of his innocence were coldly listened to by a sceptical judge. The case was intricate, and the counsel for the defence was of a subtle mind and deep in flaws, but Charles Edwin was a witness whose testimony was hard to shake; and Bessy's father was transported for fourteen years, and remained "Honest Dick" no longer. Society had found him out, and turned its back upon him, and all the brightness of his future—that he had worked for, and looked forward to—was shut from him for ever. If he had only stopped short just before that gold-dust robbery, and had no hand in it, and sold the " El-Dorado," and added the proceeds arising from that sale to his own hard earnings, he might have retired into private life, and been the SWELL for which he had toiled, and striven, and prayed. Not such a swell as a few years' more work without a cross would have made of him, but still comfortably off, the possessor of a dog-cart and a fast-trotting horse, the patronizer of prize-fights, the keeper of a safe book for the Derby, the oracle of some snug bar-parlour, the wearer of white hats, and startling coats, and gorgeous velvet waistcoats.

And Fate was hard upon him, and had cut him off in his prime, and he was going to the Bermudas for change of air and scene. He might die out there; or even if he worked his time out, why, fourteen years, added to fifty-two, made sixty-six—a drivelling, toothless old humbug he should be by that time! There was no help for it, however, let him fold his arms and give up grumbling. He shouldn't die happy now, unless kind fortune threw a chance in his way of throttling Charles Edwin; he did not see very clearly how that was to come about, but he would think of such a contingency—it relieved the monotony of his position. If he could only throttle that two-faced brother of his, he would feel more re-signed to the strong current of ill-luck which was bearing him away.

Previous to his trial he had the forethought to make over his "little bit of property" to his wife—neither Charles Edwin nor Bessy, nor Lotty, should touch a farthing of his money. They had been all against him, and opposed his brotherly and fatherly wishes for their good; and Mrs. Calverton had been docile and obedient, and allowed herself to be knocked down almost without a murmur. She would, probably, drink herself to death;

but it was a happy death he thought, now the law forbade him spirituous compounds, or even a glass of porter—or she would marry Joe, the barman, when he was across "the herring-pond." Joe was of insinuating manners, not too particular, and cared no more for bigamy than a brass farthing.

He went away sternly refusing to see Bessy Calverton to the last, and leaving his curse to Charles Edwin in a neat little blasphemous note, which the governor, who objected to swearing, never forwarded to its right destination.

And the "El-Dorado" broke up like a card-board castle when Richard Calverton's sentence was formally pronounced at the Old Bailey, and all its inmates scattered right and left. Joe, of insinuating manners, proved himself not too particular, by absconding with all the cash he could conveniently lay hands on, and left the fascinating Mrs. Calverton to those who had more time and inclination; and

Mrs. Calverton retired into private life, and began the drinking process at once, and quarrelled with Lotty, who vanished her own way, too, and defied all Bessy's attempts to find her out. Charles Edwin, on the strength of his blood-money, emigrated to the West End, and, abandoning postage stamps, set up as "a medium," and found the business prosper on the instant—like a reward and blessing for his many virtues.

Should we be drawing true to nature if we depicted Bessy Calverton as deeply moved by her father's calamity, and deaf to the consolation that would teach her resignation for a parent's loss? Bessy had escaped a great danger, the chance of a return to the past hateful life; and her father had ever been her evil genius, crushing ruthlessly every fair blossom that was put forth to the light. He was a man dead to all moral principle, selfish, heartless, and cruel—he had never been a father to her—was it natural that she should

mourn for him? And yet the name of father
exerted its influence, too; she had seen and
read of other fathers who were kind and
loving, and her bible had taught her to honour
the name, and to offer good for evil. In the
common order of events they were never to
meet again; and she had been anxious
to see him, to waken in him some little
affection for her at the last, to be gladdened
perhaps by some little show of repentance for
all the guilty past. But we have seen that
misfortune had not softened Richard Calverton, and that he went his way stern and
obdurate.

And Bessy, freed from his presence, took
heart again and was learning happiness in
Seymour Street. Life was opening fairly
before her, and Hugh Speckland saw not in
her the convict's daughter, but seemed to
love her more for the trouble she had borne,
and the dangers from which she had escaped.

Bessy was learning happiness, we have said, for she was learning to love Hugh Speckland, whose character under the fair sun that shone on him was developing every day. His had been a transition state, as Stephen had prophesied, and now a great labour was ended and he stood on the threshold of a new life. The cottage in the country had been prepared for his parents, but Hugh was in no hurry to see them depart and take Bessy along with them. So long as they remained with him Bessy remained also, but until she was his wife she could not be left with him, Stephen, and his blind sister. He was anxious to marry at once, and make sure of Bessy and happiness; but Bessy had a will of her own, and would not marry in haste. She felt assured she should soon learn to return Hugh's affection as it deserved to be returned, but until that period arrived she would put off the day that made her his young wife. In the impulse of the moment she had accepted him, actuated by a little feeling of resentment against her adviser, though she did not own that—though she would never, never own that to herself!

But she was learning to be happy now—at present not quite happy, only learning and striving hard to feel more grateful for the chances of life that had been generously offered her. She wished at times she could feel more happy—just a little more able to look forward with a hopeful heart to becoming Hugh's wife. She wished he were a year or two younger at times, or a trifle less stern and decisive—that he was more like Stephen Speckland, in fact. Hugh had altered very much for the better, was seldom irritable or sternly misanthropic now; still he was always grave and thoughtful, and regarded things too earnestly. But, oh! she should love him very shortly now—he was so fond of her, he thought so much of all she did and said. Why, he did not mind *her* interrupting him fifty times a day over his work, in fact he seemed to work with greater spirit if she stood and watched his labours. She only displeased him now in the matter of postponing the marriage day, and her firmness in that respect brought a furrow or two to his high forehead.

"Am I to serve seven years for you, Bessy, as Jacob did for Rachel?" he asked one day.

"No, no, Hugh—only a little while. You must give me time to think—I am so very young still."

"Eighteen years of age—and knowing your own mind," said he; "what is there to wait for?"

Bessy pleaded her youth again; the little time she and Hugh had known each other.

"You fear my constancy, then," said he, gravely.

No, she did not fear that; but she thought it was better to wait a little while, and learn to

study each other's character a little, before
marrying in haste. There was no occasion
for hurry now—they were engaged, and had
faith in each other.

"But this is living in a world of uncertainty, and I am a lover of dates, Bessy.
Give me a fixed time to look forward to, and
I can work patiently towards it, and fear
nothing; but day after day, week after week,
and no nearer happiness, will not suit me?"

"A fixed time," repeated Bessy, blushing
and looking down.

"Choose it yourself, Bessy," said Hugh;
"take any time that seems best—every day
I shall be advancing towards it.   Select your
own time, and I will not complain; but remember, Bessy, to that time I bind you irrevocably."

Bessy hesitated, but Hugh Speckland would
remain no longer in doubt.

"I should like a year—one full year, Hugh.
It is not a long while to us, who are both

young," she added, as his face shadowed a little.

"One year from this day—that will be the 22nd of April, 18—, our marriage day, Bessy Calverton," said the precise Hugh.

"But—"

"But you have fixed your own time, and it is finally decided on," interrupted he, with some little impatience; "is it not distant enough, Bessy, that you again hesitate and turn colour? Twelve long months to test that constancy which you doubt?"

"No, I do not doubt it," cried Bessy, quickly.

"I am glad to hear it," was the answer; "that gives me patience to wait; you shall not hear a word of complaint from me again as to the unreasonable time that keeps us apart. Let me consider it a test by which you would judge the strength of my love, and it becomes a happy time, full of promise."

Bessy sighed, and his searching eyes were bent full on her again.

"You do not fear any diminution in *your* love, Bessy?" he asked. "It is not that which has set my happiness so far away?"

"Oh! no—with every day I shall esteem you more—I feel assured of it," cried Bessy.

He did not relish the word "esteem;" but she was young and timid, and it was natural that she should shun a more forcible expression of her feelings towards him. She loved him, or she would never have said "yes" to his love-suit—and he had made a wise choice, he was certain. In the long winter evenings, when he had sat apart at his work, and before he had given voice to his secret, he had made his choice in his heart, and thought what a bright figure in his home that young girl would make. She was a bright figure then, and he had silently watched her, and prayed inwardly that she might learn to love him some day, and gladden a life that had not till that hour an idea of what true happiness meant. Methodical, grave, and hardworking, this fairy face had beamed suddenly upon him, and changed the whole tenor of his thoughts—lifted the veil from his inner life, and showed him what an ascetic and a misanthrope he had been rapidly becoming. For ten years, dating from his entrance into manhood, he had thought only of working hard and earning money—what was one more year to him now, with Bessy at its expiration, to give him her love, and call him husband? In matters of sentiment he was a child still; and Bessy's manner might have troubled one who had mixed more with the opposite sex; but he was certain that she loved him; she had a quiet way of showing her affection, and he was twelve years her senior, and grave in his manner, and perhaps she was not quite used to him yet. He did not look very grave, however, after Bessy's last warm expression of her feelings, even though she had talked of

esteem instead of love. She had asserted her
confidence, and would love him dearer every
day, and his heart leaped at the thought.

"Why, what a storehouse of affection there
will have accumulated at the end of a year,
Bessy!" he cried; "that is a great prize to
wait for—a rare dowry to bring with you to
the altar. I can understand that happiness
now, which I have read of in books and
shrugged my shoulders at—fully realize that
despair which poets paint in their verses when
such a happiness is snatched from their arms."

"You are not like Stephen, then."

Hugh looked at Bessy for an explanation,
and she reminded him of his own words, that
Stephen would recover from a disappointment in a week.

"He has a light heart, and it takes no very
deep impression, I fancy," said he; "but
I was harsh in my remarks then, and unjust
towards that frank nature which has rendered
this place for so many years home-like. A dis-

appointment would affect him, though it would not break his heart, or alter him very much."

"Would it alter you, then, Hugh?" asked Bessy.

"It would cast me back to darker thoughts than those from which I have recently emerged," said he; "it would destroy all confidence in woman, all hope in a fair life and a bright future; it would render me hard, and cruel and unforgiving. Take care, Bessy," he said, with a smile; "I shall never forgive you if you prove false. Deceive me once, and I am your enemy."

He spoke with a smile, but Bessy shuddered. Looking up into his face, she could imagine how it would harden, and those eyes gather fire, if he were made a dupe of, or woke up for a single instant to deceit. His was a nature that could love warmly; but still it was an unforgiving nature, and she feared it—a jealous nature, perhaps, and from jealousy springs envy, and hatred and distrust.

But she was learning to love him, and the task was growing easier every day. She had spoken from the heart when she had said that with every day she should esteem him more; that task would not be difficult at least.

He was so kind and so considerate now; every little action betrayed some thought of her, and some new interest. He had found her once in tears, and, pressing her for a reason, she had related Lotty's history, or rather all that she knew of that dark life, and of the faint struggles her sister made at times to live better and resist temptation; and Hugh had warmed at the story.

"You will meet her again, Bessy," said he, "and the time will come when we may both be able to assist her."

"You will not turn away from her, Hugh, like all the rest?" she cried; "you will strive with me to save her, when that time comes of which you speak?"

"I promise that with all my heart."

And in a future time, at a period of sorrow
for her of which she dreamed not then, he
reminded her—he who never forgot—of that
promise made during their engagement!

And the engagement continued, and Bessy
continued to learn the lesson she had set herself. She knew now that she had done wrong
in so hastily replying to that question put to
her by Hugh, and which affected her whole
life; but she was striving to make amends for
it, and the effort was no longer difficult. And in
the midst of all she forgot not her old promise
to the minister who had first saved her from
danger; and the result of her efforts in that direction, backed by the love she had gained, was
encouraging, at least. Hugh Speckland laid
aside his engraving of a Sunday—even went
to church with her to hear Mr. Parslow now
—and Mr. Parslow, being neither a High-
Churchman nor a tub-thumper, and having
his say in the pulpit without a chance of being
interrupted by Hugh, made the strong-minded

man below him think, once or twice, if his own
reasoning had been the best in the world.

But he would not own to Bessy that he
was a convert to any particular views yet; he
only laughed when she pressed him to acknowledge that a No-Church existence was a miserable one after all.

"I go to church because it is a pleasure to
accompany Bessy Calverton—to feel her hand
on my arm, and think that hand will be
placed in mine some day, a pledge of love,
honour and obedience. Don't let me take
credit for being a religious man, Bessy."

But the work still remained untouched of a
Sunday, and a good habit, once persevered in,
is as strong as a bad one. Stephen even took
a fancy to imitate Hugh's example, though he
went to a church of his own, and did not
adopt the new plan of crossing London
Bridge every Sunday to hear Mr. Parslow.
And even the old gentleman, caring not to be
left alone in the house, thought there might

be a little amusement to be found at church—
especially about the hymns — and perhaps
after all it was a little unthankful, now he
was coming into his cottage. Bessy had said
so, and Bessy exercised a power over that
household that was second only to Hugh's.
He would go with Lucy and the good lady,
and just try it.

So Hugh and Bessy took long walks to
Whitechapel by themselves, and coming home
again talked a good deal of their future.
Bessy found courage to talk of it soon—and
Bessy thought Mrs. Wessinger was right about
a castle-building family, for Hugh was as
sanguine as the rest now, and piled up fairy
fabrics, wherein no human being, with human
passions, human weakness, could possibly live.

Still it made the present bright to talk of
them, although the future—such as they
painted it—was a fallacy, and the real future
advancing was full of trouble undreamed of.

CHAPTER II.

THE day was finally fixed for the departure
of Mr. and Mrs. Speckland to their little
country home. For the departure of Bessy
Calverton also, whose movements were to be
regulated by the old couple till that momentous twenty-second of April, decided upon
by the matter-of-fact Hugh. The boxes
were packed, and waiting in the passage;
and there were more gloomy faces than one
in Seymour Street, with the idea of separation. Even Stephen Speckland's spirits were
not of the best in the few days before departure;

but then his health was not of the best either, and Bessy fancied that his hollow cough had been more troublesome of late. But perhaps it *was* all fancy, for he laughed when Bessy taxed him with her suspicions, and said he never felt better in his life. He took that opportunity also of alluding to Bessy's coming departure.

" ' When shall we *two* meet again,' Bessy," said he, "after you have left Seymour Street, I wonder? Don't look surprised—I have spent my life in wondering, if you recollect."

"Do you think it will be a very long while, Stephen?" asked Bessy.

"I am busy all the week, and Hugh will expect me to take care of Lucy on Sunday, whilst he runs down by the train to keep you company."

"But Lucy and you will come with him, now and then."

"Lucy may. I had my holiday in the country years ago—that was my first and last."

"Your father and mother will expect to see you sometimes."

"So they will—I forgot them."

He did not appear anxious to continue the conversation, however, and left Bessy perplexed at his evasive replies.

On the evening of that day on which this dialogue took place no less a personage than Mr. Parslow made his appearance in Seymour Street. It was some time before he stated the object of his visit, or paid any particular attention to Bessy, although there was a nervousness and excitability in his demeanour that he found some difficulty to repress.

"So you think of sending Bessy into the country, Mr. Hugh?" he said, addressing that gentleman, as he stood by his side and watched his attention to the wood-block.

Hugh had fallen into the good habit of treating the reverend gentleman with less discourtesy since attending his little church in Whitechapel, and he answered in the affirmative, and asked if Mr. Parslow had any objection to urge.

"No—that is—that is, I fancy that Bessy Calverton will find it rather dull in the country with your parents—that your parents, in fact, are not the most fit companions for her."

"I don't see any help for it," said he; "it is Bessy's wish now."

"I suppose if a home could be found in London for her, it would be more convenient to you—and not very objectionable to your parents, who, it strikes me, will find Bessy just a little in the way."

Hugh turned quickly to the minister with those dark, searching eyes of his.

"If you have any proposition to make, I shall be glad to hear it. There has seemed to me no alternative but that of Bessy's accompanying my mother, until this home becomes hers by right."

"But there is an alternative, if you have

no objection," said he; "I take it that your wish in the matter is to be considered now."

"Thank you," answered Hugh.

"I have not mentioned it to Bessy, because I feel pretty well assured that her heart will jump at the idea too readily; and as it is just next door to impossible to guess what *your* ideas are likely to be, till you divulge them yourself, I thought I would not broach the subject until your consent was obtained."

"I have no wish contrary to Bessy's— mention it to her, and leave her to decide."

"Bless my soul, how very much you have altered!" remarked Mr. Parslow.

Hugh bent his head lower over his work to conceal a smile.

"Love as well as time works wonders—eh, Mr. Hugh?"

"I don't dispute the assertion."

"I had my doubts once what kind of a husband you would make, but I am gaining confidence daily. I shall not give up your acquaintance, sir, for a long while to come now; and when you and Bessy are married, I shall look in very often, if it be only for the sake of a good argument now and then."

"Argument tries the temper."

"But you are 'leaning to virtue's side,'" cried the incumbent; "you come with Bessy to church."

"I would go anywhere with her."

"But you don't mean to tell me it is only for her sake that you come to church, my dear sir? You don't bring your worldly ideas, your worldly affections, into St. Owen's?"

"Sometimes, if the truth must be told."

"You'll never come to any good then."

Hugh laughed.

"Your very love will turn against you and betray you, if you make it your idol."

"It is something new for me to love, Mr. Parslow," replied Hugh; "it is a new sensation, that chases away all my dark thoughts, and renders me susceptible to new impressions—even less of a sceptic. All this is a new world to me, and time will do its best to mould my character afresh."

"Well spoken. Upon my word," rubbing one of his thin hands over the other, "it is pleasant to hear a man of thirty—a man of the world—talk of love with all a fledgling's enthusiasm."

"You would not have me ashamed of my passion?"

"God forbid, my dear sir—it is singular, but it has made you better already."

"I agree with you."

"And that is more singular still. Patience! only to think that for once in his life Hugh Speckland agrees with me! I say, with Dominie Sampson, 'Prodigous!'"

"Well," said Hugh, frankly, "I cannot

say that I am not a better man—that I have not new thoughts, that help to raise me from rather a low estate. Six months ago my greatest ambition was to earn money, gain a higher name in my profession, and rise a little from Seymour Street. I would have been content with that ambition, and worked hard all my life, and scraped money together, and sealed my heart up hermetically. Now I have brighter thoughts mixed with my fame-longings."

" May they endure."

" Surely they will, unless—unless she fades from me, and leaves me despairing."

" What do you mean ? " asked Mr. Parslow.

" I have been used to disappointments all my life, Mr. Parslow—I am not what the world calls a lucky man. The prize before me, and my hand stretched towards it, and lo ! it has withered, or eluded my touch. I build too much upon this love of mine ; I bind with it too many hopes, and I fear sometimes that the God I have turned my back against may punish me now, and snatch her from me when my hopes are highest. It seems too great a happiness ever to think of her as mine—standing by my side, bearing my name, sharing my cares and my joys, my rebuffs and my triumphs."

"It is not my place to say, set your heart on things of this world," said Mr. Parslow; "it is a world wherein trouble and disappointment fall to every man's share."

"I am an enthusiast, and must think of this world—it is nearest my heart."

"I'm very sorry for it," remarked Mr. Parslow; "but I am afraid there are one or two erring mortals in a similar way to yourself. The best of us are of the world, worldly. Still, young man, do think a little now and then of another and better world—it will reconcile you to the disappointments of this."

Hugh took it as a trite remark, to which there was no occasion to reply, and turned the conversation by abandoning his work, and coming to Bessy's side.

" Bessy, Mr. Parslow, I believe, has a proposition to make," he said.

" Just a little one, Miss Bessy," was the reply of that reverend gentleman, " for the consideration of yourself and friends : I have a new home to offer you—the only objection to which is, it is not in the country."

Bessy looked anxiously at Mr. Parslow. She did not care for the country now ; she would have preferred to stay in London, and see Hugh Speckland of an evening. She had begun to think it would be very dull without Hugh Speckland ; very dull spending the long evenings playing cribbage with an old gentleman of variable temper.

" Mrs. Wessinger," was the prompt response of Bessy.

" Mrs. Wessinger has left Snowfields," said

Mr. Parslow, to Bessy's surprise, " and given up shoe-binding for a long time to come. I have been the means of obtaining her a situation as housekeeper to a lady."

" Oh ! dear, what will become of me when my 'horrors' come on ?" was the exclamation of Mrs. Speckland.

" Why, are you not going into the country, my dear madam, where no horrors can disturb you ?" replied Mr. Parslow.

" I'm not so sure of that."

" And is it not enough to get rid of your horrors for ever, to think another hardworking friend has risen a little in life, and likely to do well ?"

Mrs. Speckland sighed. Perhaps it was; but then she had lost that friend who cheered her in lonely moments, and who allowed herself to be scolded when the horrors were surmounted—she had relied on her even in the country, if necessity required it.

" And the lady wants a companion now,

and I thought Bessy might suit her. Bessy Calverton is going to be married some day; and by the laws of courtship in general—see what a deal I know about them!—lovers should not live too far apart from each other."

"And the lady—" began Lucy.

"Is coming here to answer for herself," concluded Mr. Parslow; "I expect her here at eight this evening. It must be nearly eight now, I think;" and his fingers, which had not lost their old habit of straying to his waistcoat pocket, went in search of the plated watch that had flown away to keep its New Year with bad company.

"It struck eight five minutes since."

"Hum," mused the minister, "not so punctual as I should have anticipated. I should have taken her for a very precise, formal little body, who kept telegraph time, and was true to a second. I should have — there she is!"

And a brisk rat-a-tat on the outer door seemed to announce the lady who was in search of a companion. Mr. Parslow ran to open it as though he were used to the business, and presently returned rubbing one hand over the other in a pleasant state of exhilaration, and announced, in an eccentric fashion—

"The lady I was speaking of, ladies and gentlemen."

And the lady, followed by the smiling Mrs. Wessinger, made her appearance, and Bessy leaped up with a cry of delight, and ran into the arms of Mary Davis, late of Aberogwin, North Wales.

"Oh! my dear, dear cousin Mary, how glad I am to see you!"

"And my dear, dear Bessy, how glad I am too—and how you have grown—and I don't think I should have known you—and how you are crumpling all my crape tucks!—but never mind; kiss me again, my dear."

And Mary Davis began to speak hoarsely,

and to shed a few tears in the first moments of meeting.

"I'm not so strong-minded as I used to be," she observed, when she and Bessy had recovered the emotion natural to such a meeting as theirs; "time and trouble have affected my nerves a little."

Bessy looked at her, and the black dress struck her for the first time.

"Uncle Davis?" she exclaimed.

"In heaven, I trust, my dear. He was a good man."

"Poor uncle!"

Bessy Davis had long since forgiven his stern rules, his harsh discipline, and looked back with regret to the Welsh cottage wherein she had lived with him. In the few moments of Bessy's last meeting with him on earth, he had spoken of his love for her, and his heartfelt wish for her happy future, before the grim father had borne her away. Bessy had not thought it a last meeting then; not until

that moment, when Mary Davis's black dress
told the old story, had she given up all hopes
of seeing him and Mary Davis in their mountain cottage again. And now Mary Davis
was in London for good, and uncle Davis had
shaken the dust of the world from his feet.

"I daresay you wonder, Bessy, why, during
the four months of your stay here, I have
only replied once to your letters, and that
very briefly," said Mary Davis ; "but poor
father's was a long illness, occupied most of
my time, and I was anxious to send you the
better news which I promised, and of which I
never had the chance. And now we have met
again, my dear, and this worthy man," indicating Mr. Parslow, "to whom we are all indebted, was kind enough to prepare the way
and soften the shock of surprise."

"Which I did not, Miss Davis, like an unfeeling old scamp, as I am—for I enjoy a
little surprise now and then, and I didn't believe a surprise of this kind would do a great

deal of harm; on the contrary, a great deal of good, I think. I appeal to Mr. Speckland."

"Ah! Mr. Speckland?" exclaimed Miss Davis—"an old friend too, whose good work still remains strong at Aberogwin—a sign of a good workman. I am very glad to see you, sir."

And Mary Davis shook hands with Stephen Speckland, and started a little at the change six years had made in him.

"I little thought, Mr. Speckland, when you and Bessy used to gossip under the porch, that you would ever think of being man and wife. But strange things happen in this world, and you must promise me, her old guardian and friend, to make her the best of husbands."

Stephen Speckland's colour was high, and his voice somewhat altered as he said—

"Miss Davis mistakes—it is my brother Hugh."

"Oh! I beg your pardon—I was giving you the wrong husband, Bessy;" and Bessy smiled faintly by way of response. She felt very dull just then, and it was all Stephen Speckland's fault; had he treated the matter lightly, and turned it aside with his customary laugh, she could have joined in the jest, but his embarrassment startled her, and made her heart sink. In the whirl of fancies with which her brain was troubled there darted at times some suspicion of a truth, which her life was spent in pressing down and keeping hidden; and in that moment it passed like lightning athwart her again, and scathed her. And she felt her cheeks redden when looking up she met the eyes of her betrothed fixed upon her.

"Is anything the matter?" he asked, huskily.

"No, Hugh—what should there be?"

"Miss Davis's mistake has disturbed you?"

"No," said Bessy; "why should it?"

" Why should it, indeed! Miss Davis," turning to that lady, " will you allow me to present myself as the future husband of Bessy Calverton ?"

Miss Davis frankly extended her hand to him.

" Bessy's future husband must be a friend of mine. He will find me a very tiresome friend, always inquiring after her happiness, and interfering if it be not very apparent."

" Miss Davis shall have no cause to complain, if Bessy Calverton's happiness depends upon me."

Miss Davis was soon friends with the rest of the Speckland family; and it was some time before Mrs. Wessinger could find an opportunity of exchanging a few words of greeting with our heroine. Having once secured Bessy in a corner, she launched forth into a stream of encomiums on the new young mistress that Mr. Parslow had found for her.

" Quite a lady, my dear, now," said Mrs.

Wessinger; "she has been telling me all her fortunes and misfortunes, as though I was a lady born and her equal. Her father was a saving man, my dear, and a lucky man, too, for he took to a fancy that helped to ruin the father of that dear good Christian there."

"What was that?"

"Mines, my dear. Regular gambling— and I dare say the old gentleman would have torn his hair at the sight of a pack of cards— but he's dead and gone, and we won't be hard upon him, especially as he was lucky. The few shares he possessed have turned out a nice little independence for his daughter— who deserves it, if ever a woman deserved anything in her life."

"I am so glad you like her."

"So meek, and patient, and gentle!—can I help it?"

Bessy had not found those virtues strikingly apparent when she was a child, although she had loved her and known her to have been one of the best-meaning little souls in the world. Time and trouble had altered her too—and for the better, which time and trouble do not always, unfortunately.

"I fancy, my dear Bessy," said Mrs. Wessinger, in a lower tone, "that the old gentleman died hard at last. It's only fancy at present, but it's my idea that his money troubled him, and he saw that his love for it had squeezed him in a little. I think so, because Miss Davis cares so little for money herself, and seems so anxious to do all the good with it she can, and give it away right and left. A blessed young woman as ever I met with in my life. *Oh!*—"

"Is anything the matter, Mrs. Wessinger?"

"No, my dear," replied that good lady, whose right hand, in the absence of the work to which it had become habituated, had been gently see-sawing all this time—"only—*oh!*"

Mrs. Wessinger was looking straight before her, and gasping for breath.

" I shall be better in a minute, my dear—
don't notice me. My breath's clean taken
away with such a wonderful idea—such a
surprising idea !"

" What is it ?"

" Don't ask me, my dear—you won't know
for a year or two, and then it will all come
true, and I can say, 'there—that's my doing!'"
Then she added, as Bessy still continued to
regard her with amazement—" And don't
look so alarmed, Bessy ; I'm not out of my
mind yet. Oh ! dear," with a sigh, " how I
do miss those shoes of mine !"

Mrs. Wessinger was anxious to turn the
conversation to shoes, and distract Bessy's
attention from the one wonderful idea that
had seized her ; and when " shoebinding " failed
as a topic, she spoke of Hugh Speckland, and
of the life for Bessy that would lie before
her some twelvemonths hence. And Bessy
found that subject more interesting, whilst
Mary Davis was laying her plans before the

Specklands with regard to her, and spoke as
warmly of Hugh, of the change in him and
his thoughts, of his love, and attention and
kindness, as though she had ceased learning
to love him, and knew the lesson by heart, and
was proud of her knowledge. For eighteen
years are not adamant; and a deep earnest
love must affect them if the heart thinks but
kindly of him who casts at her feet all his
hopes.

CHAPTER III.

BROAD CHURCH.

IT was arranged that Bessy Calverton should live with Mary Davis; and the day that witnessed the departure of the old couple for the country — whither Lucy went with them for a few days' change, and to make the parting less heavy—witnessed the installation of our heroine as companion to the lady whom mining shares had raised to something like affluence.

Mary Davis had chosen the quiet little home which Mr. Parslow had recommended for her, in the neighbourhood of St. Owen's.

And Bessy was not long in her new home before
she remarked that Mary Davis was changed:
that she took larger, broader views of religion
and its duties; and that all the little irritable
fits of the past had by some strange meta-
morphosis, been transformed into those virtues
of which Mrs. Wessinger had spoken.   Still
it was the same Mary Davis, but always
in those best moods which had made the
happiest portion of Bessy's life amongst the
mountains, and preserving amidst her prim,
methodical ways, that rapidity of movement which was a family inheritance.

Mrs. Wessinger was a shrewd observer, to
have guessed by the few remarks on money,
its value and uses, that uncle Davis had, as
she termed it, died hard.   Such had been the
case; and in his last illness, when left to ponder
on his ruling passion, he had not spared himself, or the error of his life—for he was a
conscientious and a just man.   He knew then

that he had lived for money, and loved money
too much, and it weighed on him and troubled
him in his last moments. He had even been
hard and unchristian at times with some poor
Welsh tenants who rented some little property
of his in the village, and he felt he might have
acted more up to his preachings had he been
more lenient and spared them. And Mary
Davis, seeing him suffer in the spirit and
hearing his complaints, learned a lesson at
her father's dying bed which in all her after
life was not forgotten. By his hard manner
and close life much of her best feelings, most
of her sympathies, had been kept down, or
had no room to play their part; and now her
life had been proved an error, and she was
a woman on whom such a proof would affect
sensibly, and work marvels. There was some
of the old Catholic spirit of expiation in her
determination to turn that money to a worthy
use; to assist the suffering, the sick, and
feeble, and no longer pass by on the other

side, as she had done for many years. She
found herself, in her own ideas of wealth, a
rich woman—certainly possessed of a larger
income than she, as a single lady with simple
wants and a horror of display, could easily
spend. She had seen how the garnering of
money for its own sake had warped a naturally
devout nature, and had set about the task
of atonement with a zeal that only a good
woman in her best moods has ever the power
or the inclination to persevere in. We of
sterner stuff, men of the world, worldly, as
Mr. Parslow declared, may have our spasmodic promptings to do good for our fellow-
men, and help those who are in need; but the
effort grows slack, and the huge account-books,
or the pleasure-trips in the summer, or the
dinner-parties we intend to give, and take the
shine out of our friends and acquaintances
who give dinner-parties also, rise in the way
and balk us of our best intentions. And the
"weaker vessel," with less strength, less

energy, but with an amount of patience, faith, which few men can possibly possess, perseveres in the good, great works our Saviour indicated, and puts us all to shame.

Mary Davis had chosen a large sphere for the exercise of her mission—that of a great London parish, where destitution and privation abound, and where Mary Davis's fortune was not likely to be of any great service. In her own Welsh home she had been a witness to poverty struggling against a severe winter, but there were few specimens of actual want in her neighbourhood—the Welsh being a provident class, and with a thought for a rainy day. In her anxiety to commence the one task that she had allotted herself, her heart had been touched by the news of the great distress in London, and she had started at once, full of hope in her mission.

And there she was quietly settled down in London, as though she had never known Wales or Welsh people, with all her time occupied in the good work before her. And Bessy and Mrs. Wessinger were trusty *aides-de-camp*, whose London experience could point out the really deserving, and whose hearts were warm enough to assist her in a. variety of ways ; and the Reverend Jacob Parslow, though he objected to Methodists as a class, was frequent in his visits to Miss Davis, having his own suggestions to make, his own deserving objects of compassion to introduce to this ministering woman.

"And what do you think of her, sir?" said Mrs. Wessinger one day to him. "Isn't she an angel, and too good for this world?"

"One in a thousand, at least—we can say that, Mrs. Wessinger," replied the incumbent of St. Owen's.

"And she's a Methody, too."

"I don't know that, Mrs. W.," said Mr. Parslow; "she has been brought up by a Methodist father, and attends a Methodist chapel, but I can hardly fancy her a Methodist myself. Not that the Methodists are anything but a worthy sect, take them all together—a little narrow in their views, that is all."

"If she only belonged to the Church, sir!"

"She does."

Mrs. Wessinger looked at Mr. Parslow for an explanation.

"To the same church as myself, Mrs. Wessinger, which is better than High Church or Low Church, chapel-going or open-air preaching—which is the one and the true, and that's Broad Church."

"Ah! how nicely he always brings it round, now!" said Mrs. Wessinger, with a glance at Bessy.

"It is a wide creed, has love and sympathy for all classes, and shuts the door in no one's face—be he Jew or Gentile. It don't seek to reach heaven by singing, intoning, or high mass—and its worshippers are from all churches, and of all degrees of life. There are not many of us yet, Mrs. W.; but our numbers are increasing, and, with God's help, will increase, till there is peace on earth and fellowship with all men. The barriers between our pride and prejudice are growing weaker every day; and there will come a time—if neither you nor I should live to see it—when its followers will be legion, and all the pomps and vanities and prejudices that pollute the sanctuary be as far removed from actual, working religious life, as the racks and thumbscrews that tried to force a creed in Mary's time."

There had been a listener by the door, who now came forward with a heightened colour.

"Such a Church as that I hope to belong to some day."

"Well spoken, Hugh Speckland. We shall make a man of you yet."

Hugh had called to take Bessy for a little

quiet evening stroll; and Bessy, in a flutter of confusion and happiness, was soon on his arm, listening to that constant topic of his, which always alluded to the 22nd of April, 18—. Let them talk of Mr. Parslow, or Mary Davis, or Stephen, or anything, and that one subject always swerved round, upon which Hugh could grow most eloquent.

Another stroke of fortune had descended on Hugh that particular day he called at St. Owen's Terrace, and he had arrived to communicate the good tidings to his betrothed. His engraving and his sketches had attracted more than common attention of late, and more than one illustrated paper had lately solicited his services, and offered him terms which enabled him to lay by money more easily.

" It is all through going to church," said the enthusiastic Bessy.

" Or practising my hardest, even on Sundays," added Hugh, drily.

" Oh ! you don't think that ? "

" Perhaps you bring good luck with you, Bessy," said he, pressing her arm to his side; " I am inclined to think *that* the true secret of Hugh Speckland's success. You have brought me a better temper, a purer heart, a host of brighter thoughts—why should I not attribute the little fame I am making to you ? "

Hugh was in one of his best humours, or he would not have been so complimentary, or had such faith in the truth of his compliments.

Those were pleasant courting days of Hugh Speckland; they were a fair retrospect to Bessy in the future days when her heart was heavier, albeit there was a dark side to it—for bitter memories are ever attached to dreams that have vanished.

Hugh came every evening to St. Owen's Terrace to take Bessy Calverton for a little walk after sundown and business hours; and though they were a humble couple enough—

the reader by this time has discovered that
we do not deal in fine heroes and heroines; in
fact, they are fast becoming most unsaleable
articles!—and albeit their walks were confined to the London streets, or the bridges;
yet, they were as happy in their humble,
quiet way, as couples of a higher rank, who
have parks to wander through, and talk love
matters in, and who talk them, too, in the
grandest of English, with never a word of
less size than three syllables—that is, if Lady
Amelia Gushington's novels are standards of
aristocratical conduct.

Hugh talked of Mr. Parslow a great deal
on that night, wherein he had listened to his
broad-church doctrines, and confessed that the
reverend gentleman had risen several degrees
in his estimation.

" I had always set him down for a narrow-
minded bigot, hemmed in by class distinctions;
I have a better opinion of Mr. Parslow from
to-night. We will be married in St. Owen's

church, Bessy, and Mr. Parslow shall be the officiating clergyman."

" And you and I will be regular members of his congregation, Hugh ? "

" Some day, perhaps, when he preaches broad-church doctrine, as well as talks of it in private life. Will you tell me a little more of Miss Davis ?—don't be jealous, but I am interested in that young lady."

Bessy spoke of Mary Davis forthwith; of the great task she had set herself to befriend the poor, and sustain, by kind words, and helping hands—so far as lay in her power— the sick and suffering who struggle against despair in the stifling London streets.

" Do you know, Bessy, that has been a wild visionary dream of mine, in which Miss Davis has obtained the start of me. For two years I have had the idea constantly before me, that with means at command, and with my experience of the real, deserving poor, I might rescue many honest souls from the toils that encircle them at such times as you and I were witness to last winter. For the real and the false poor are hard to distinguish; I have known a man starve to death and complain not, and I have been offered three coal-tickets for as many glasses of gin, from a pale-faced trollop, whose wan face was her fortune."

Meanwhile, Mrs. Wessinger, whose knowledge of the true poor was as great as Hugh's, and had been bought with harder experience, after consulting with Mary Davis and Mr. Parslow concerning the names on their relief-list — after the departure of Mr. Parslow also—asked the rather direct question, as to what Miss Davis thought of the reverend gentleman.

" A good and worthy man," was the reply.

" And that is your true opinion ? "

" How could I think otherwise—are not his actions good and worthy, and do not they speak for themselves ? "

"I always fancied, do you know, that Methodists were rather hard upon ministers of the Church of England," observed Mrs. Wessinger; "but you are hardly a Methodist."

"Oh! yes, I am," said Mary Davis, proud of her sect.

"Ah! Mr. Parslow doubts it—he says you belong to broad-church, like himself."

"Broad-church?" repeated Mary Davis; "that means—ah, I see what it means now. Yes, I hope so."

"He's the dearest man under the sun—so gentle, and not one-and-forty yet."

"Yes," answered Mary Davis, absently stirring the fire.

"It's a-coming!" cried Mrs. Wessinger, with a precipitancy that nearly startled the poker out of Mary Davis's hand.

"What is?" she inquired.

"Only a little idea of mine—something that is to happen in a year or two."

"Sufficient for the day is the evil thereof!" quoted Miss Davis.

"Ah!—but not the good. It is comfortable to think of things happening just as they ought to happen—aint it?"

"Yes—but it is folly to build upon them. Don't be too sanguine, Mrs. Wessinger."

"Well, I'll try not," was the reply. "I'll get a bit of needle-work and distract my ideas. My right arm does ache for the want of something to do—sure-*ly!*"

CHAPTER IV.

THE TIDE TURNS.

A GOOD woman is soon known in a poor neighbourhood, however narrow her means, or extensive the size of that parish in which those
means are diffused.   Mary Davis was not long
in discovering that a thousand such fortunes
as her's would, at times and seasons when dis-
ease and   want were paramount, be as the
dew-drop to the wide ocean.   She found the
claimants many at her gates, and the interest
on her mining shares, and bank stock speedily
running low ; and nearly six months to wait
before those pleasant things called dividends

would flow towards her again. In her enthusiasm
she had possibly been a trifle improvident, and
she set herself to repair that task, and exercise
a little more discretion in the distribution
of the few pounds remaining from her reserve
fund. It was summer now, and Whitechapel
was holding up its head again, and most of
its denizens in full work. Mary Davis's advice would effect as much good as her money
now, and she was anxious to inculcate, in those
who had been the recipients of her bounty,
habits of providence and forethought. That
was a harder task than she had imagined;
those people she had studied were of the class
that took no heed for the morrow in its literal
sense, and lived in the present, and let not
the shadow of the winter, which always tried
them more or less, cross their thoughts and
disturb them. They had just escaped one
severe season, let them have the little enjoyment which the summer afforded, and not
annoy them by talking of savings banks, and

the rainy day that might come when they
were dead, for what they knew of the matter.
Let them have fresh air, and excursions by
spring van and railway train on Sundays and
Mondays occasionally; let them spend the
money which they had honestly earned—next
winter they might be lucky enough to keep
in work; and if it were a hard winter, why,
so had been the last, and they had fought
through it somehow! They would hear her
read the bible in their houses, and to their
sick wives and children; a few of them,
touched by her earnest persuasions, would
venture to a church at times; but they would
not save their money—it was a harder task
than working for it.

Nevertheless, Mary Davis felt that a certain
amount of good had followed her appearance
in the parish, and hers was a nature that did
not flinch before a danger or difficulty. In
her noble labours she was encouraged by seeing here and there a fair result, and she had

not hoped to have it all her own way in the midst of a troubled world.

Meanwhile, Hugh Speckland and Bessy took longer walks together now the days had lengthened, although the time seemed to pass more rapidly than in those short winter evenings before Bessy had her lesson by heart. Mary Davis was pleased with her cousin's choice, too, and that rendered affairs still more satisfactory. "He's a steady, saving young man, and will do well," said Mary to Bessy one day after they had canvassed his merits together. "I am glad your choice has been a good one, Bessy; for at your age young girls are generally inclined to accept the most objectionable offer. He is a good temper, I think?"

Bessy thought her cousin should have seen him in the early days, before he gave signs of his love, and when his father was harassing him with his eternal complaints.

"A good temper," observed Bessy, however ; " a little hasty at times, but generally warm in defence of a right, or in the attack of a wrong."

" I daresay he has his faults, like other people," remarked Mary Davis; " but I think you will be happy with him, Bessy. He will make you a better husband than he whom I imagined for a moment was the object of your attachment."

Bessy might think so, too, although she did not reply to the observation.

" He will have a will· of his own all his life, and a man with a will is the best for us weak women, after all. His brother Stephen, whom I set down to you, Bessy, is of a good-tempered and affectionate disposition, I should say, but lacking that strength of mind which is woman's support, however much at times she may think to the contrary."

Mary Davis, who had been busy with her needle during the dialogue, suddenly paused in her work, and looked intently before her.

Talking of Stephen Speckland had perhaps
conjured up the faintest of dreams that she
had had once, when Bessy was a little girl, and
Stephen Speckland had wandered to Aberogwin, and brightened by his genial presence
the cottage up the mountain side. It was
well for her perhaps that he went away so
soon, and that her early training had been
strict. She had been taught to master her
emotions all her life, and keep down all
thoughts verging on romance; and the waters
had flowed on peacefully after his departure,
and the little fancy that had risen in her heart
was dropped to the bottom of it, and
never an one the wiser. Her's was a quiet
life, that made no sign; she bore her trials
uncomplainingly, and faltered not in her way.
She could look back at it all now without a
pang, and think it was a strange illusion, and
wonder how by a thought she had been ever
led to encourage it. Only unhappiness could
have followed any closer relations between her

and Hugh Speckland's brother : it was all for
the best that it had happened otherwise.
And though Mary Davis would not have
accepted Stephen Speckland had he offered
himself to-morrow, yet she sighed—for it is
pleasant to be loved, and Mary Davis was a
young woman still.

Bessy Calverton had reason to be alarmed
that day concerning Stephen Speckland when
she repaired to Seymour Street that afternoon
to see Lucy. She and Lucy were of course
the best of friends, and Lucy looked forward
to those visits, when she could have Bessy all
to herself, and talk of her Harry, still working
for her, and faithful, and keeping the one romance of her life alive—an antithesis to that
romance of Mary Davis's, that had met its
death so early.

In these visits Hugh was left to himself in
the parlour, and only tolerated at tea-time, or
when it was necessary to see Bessy safe home
to Whitechapel. He would have neglected

his work now for Bessy's sake, had Bessy not been firm and reproached him with becoming dissolute in his habits, and losing that old energy that kept home together when remuneration was below *par*. Hugh was saving money for a new home and an extravagant wife, she told him ; and with a smile at her sauciness he would turn to his work and leave her and Lucy together.

Stephen Speckland had been so seldom at home of late that Bessy was surprised to find him that particular afternoon in question lying on the old sofa under the window, looking very pale and ill.

" Ah ! Bessy," said he, as she entered and kissed Lucy; " knocked over again for a little while you see. Pains in the side, and a short allowance of breath, and a cough that gets the mastery over me now and then—nothing alarming, don't look so frightened. Hugh has been foolish enough to leave his engraving and start in search of a doctor—as if I wanted a doctor, or one could do me any good."

"It is nothing serious, I hope."

"Serious—no," was the reply; "am I looking at my last gasp, Bessy Calverton?"

He exhibited a little petulance as he asked this question, Bessy thought; but it was gone in an instant, and left no trace visible.

"You must have another holiday when the theatre shuts, Stevie," said his sister; "go down and see father and mother in the country."

"Ah!—perhaps," was the evasive reply.

"You are fond of the country, Stephen," said Bessy; "at least you were."

"Once upon a time, as your fairy-book said," replied Stephen; "have I not always maintained Wales was my one holiday? Here are Hugh and the doctor—now for a thousand questions to worry me into fever-heat."

Bessy and Lucy went upstairs to talk over the matter of Stephen's illness—it was a subject that dismissed that of the eternal Harry for a little while.

"It comes so suddenly," said Lucy; "he seems to bear up, and hide all sign of it as long as his strength will allow, and then he gives way all at once and frightens us. Poor Stevie will be no better, I fear, until he takes me to Canada. He has made up his mind to do that when Harry writes for me. Do you know," she added, after a pause, "I believe at times that he has something on his mind— he has lost so much of his good-temper, and copies so much Hugh's old reserved manners."

They were talking of him still when the doctor went away, and Lucy's more than usual anxiety made Bessy nervous. Much of her old interest in Stephen Speckland revived as she listened: Stephen was her first friend, and the thought of danger to him affected her strangely. And he *was* altered; when she went down into the parlour at last she shuddered at the contrast presented between the Welsh times and the present— he was but the shadow of his old self now!

Hugh and Stephen were deep in argument when Bessy entered the parlour.

"I tell you I am well enough," Stephen was saying; "and there is no occasion, Hugh, to neglect business for my sake. Do you think I require as much amusing as our poor old father?"

"You are dull to-day, Stevie."

"Not a bit, upon my honour," was the answer; "what can I do to prove myself in the best of spirits?"

"Do nothing—but keep still."

"I shall jump off the sofa and fly into one of your old passions if you neglect that appointment," said Stephen—"if you treat me like a baby, and think I cannot be left alone without falling out of my cradle, and damaging myself somehow. I consider there is another lift in life for you if this magazine starts."

"Possibly."

"Then don't neglect it—you may have a bad-tempered brother to keep, if his strength return not in a hurry. Am I so very ill, that you are afraid to leave me with two women in the house?"

"No," returned Hugh; "but you are low spirited, and Stevie Speckland in bad spirits is a bad sign."

"Have I not denied it, upon my honour?" he reiterated. "Hugh, I'm going to sing a comic song!"

"Don't be foolish. I'm off after this appointment. Bessy," to our heroine, "talk to this refractory young gentleman till my return. I shall not be long."

When Hugh was at the street door, Bessy hastily joined him. He was leaving with a very thoughtful countenance, when Bessy laid her hand upon his arm and looked up at him.

"Hugh, there is nothing serious to be anticipated—is there?"

"God forbid, Bessy."

"What has the doctor said?"

"Nothing particular—he has no great faith in Stephen's constitution, and he has evaded, after the old fashion, a direct answer to a plain question. Still—there *is* hope."

"Has there been a doubt of it?" cried Bessy, alarmed.

"Yes, more than once. But the last physician who saw him said his health would vary a great deal, and that there was no danger—and I have faith in him still. Good-bye, Bessy—talk to him of Wales; it is one of his pleasant memories. I hope to find a great change when I return."

And he went away, little dreaming of the great change in himself, and in the lives of those he loved, that was so very close at hand!

When Bessy returned to the parlour she found, to her surprise, that Stephen was standing by the window, intently inspecting his brother's work.

"Oh! is not this wrong of you?" she asked.

"Not that I am aware of," he said, with the return of his old laugh; "only Hugh harasses himself and me, till I lie in state on the sofa to oblige him. As if I wanted rest, or cared for it! That brother of mine has lost all his old nerve, now his heart has softened. Are you a judge of engraving, Bessy?"

"A very poor one, I am afraid."

"You are not aware that you are to be the future wife of a genius, then—of one who will take higher rank yet than most of his friends give him credit for. His should be a bright future," he said, musingly--" and God bless the old fellow—he deserves it!"

Stephen spoke with some difficulty, and put his hand to his side. The action did not escape Bessy, who suggested that he should lie down again. But Stephen was obstinate, and had a will of his own as well as brother Hugh.

"I hate to look like a sick monkey, Bessy —to be wholly conquered by the powers that battle with my strength. I was talking of Hugh?"

" Yes."

" You are not anxious to shun the topic, Bessy?"

" Why should I shun it?" rejoined Bessy.

" I don't know," he answered; " for no reason that I can see or explain. Concerning this Hugh then, and all the change that has come over him—was I not right in my prophecy?"

" Yes, Stephen."

" Was I not right too in that advice which I gave you a few months ago?" said he;

" have you ever had reason to regret the engagement which dated from that day ?"

" I have never regretted it, Stephen," replied Bessy; "he has been all that is good and kind."

" He will make the best of husbands—and you the best and gentlest of wives," said Stephen. " Let me live to see the day that unites you, and I have played my part out, and Fate may drop the curtain, when it likes."

Bessy looked intently at Stephen. He was regarding Hugh's work beneath his hand still, but his thoughts had travelled very far away.

" You must not talk so gloomily, Stephen —it is unlike You," said Bessy; " you must draw the picture in brighter colours, and let no dark curtain fall between you and the prospect."

" I might wish to watch the progress of your married life—to see Hugh gathering more fame, and growing more happy every day—to have your children dancing round me, perhaps; but Bessy—it is marked out otherwise."

Bessy felt her heart sink. Looking into those eyes strangely mournful and expressive, that were turned towards her, she could believe it for the first time.

" Oh ! don't say that," she murmured.

" I have been making up my mind to tell some one the secret I have kept for a long while to myself," he continued ; " and I fancy, Bessy, you are the best confidant to choose. You know them all so well now, and can prepare them for it better than I, and save me so much pain. With time before you—you can think of all that is best to console Hugh and—and the rest of them. With you at the side of that old friend and truest of brothers, he may not miss me much after the first shock is over. For old Hugh will feel the shock—we have been together so long ! "

"But, Stephen, are you sure—is there not any hope? May not your suspicions be incorrect after all?"

"They are something more than suspicions, Bessy. I did not try to teach myself resignation, until I had sought out those who could read my constitution like a book. I pushed the question home, and would have my true answer, which was—a few months more or less of life, and then an end to me! Don't cry, Bessy; this is for the best, at any rate."

Bessy tried not to make a scene of it, but the tears would silently course down her cheeks, he spoke so earnestly, and so decisively.

"I look my future in the face, Bessy, and am resigned—I expect you to be calm too, and teach them resignation, if it be necessary. All *is* for the best," he reiterated; "I knew it would be when I bade farewell to all my hopes, and sunk them in the sea for ever. And knowing that, I cut them away without a murmur, although their roots were in my heart."

"Stephen!" cried Bessy. For her life's sake she could not have avoided that cry, as the rush of the one great truth came forcibly upon her. She saw it all then; she read much that had been a mystery to her, and perplexed her, and given a false aspect to outward circumstances; and if she loved him no longer, still his noble sacrifice, his abnegation of self, his deep consideration for her, moved her to seize him by the hands, and look through her swimming tears into his face. He had had one great hope in his life; he might have once realized it by a word, and had turned away, and resisted the temptation!

Stephen Speckland's face was troubled beneath Bessy's gaze, but the compressed lips exhibited a firmness that nothing could subdue. It was some moments before he spoke.

"I had intended to keep this a secret to the last," he said—"to have died and made no sign; but I have been rash and betrayed myself. Well, is there any harm, now you love Hugh Speckland, and are to be his wife—now I am standing apart, as it were, with all my interest in worldly cares dying away? It is all over now; and yours is a new life, and—and—" he said, tightening his clasp on the hands that were still confidently in his—"and I did love you, Bessy, with all a strong man's love!"

He would not say he loved her then— would love her to the last, with that intensity and purity that had ever made him shun linking his destiny with hers.

"I knew it!" murmured Bessy.

His hands dropped suddenly to his side, and Bessy felt her own heart sink to a lower depth as she looked up and saw Hugh Speckland standing by the door, a stern, white-faced witness of their interview. Her conscience did not accuse her: in that heart she knew that Hugh lived there, and held now the foremost place; but still it sank, for Hugh had changed so suddenly, and the face was darker and more full of anger than she had known it at its worst.

"Have you finished?" he asked, hoarsely, when his presence was observed for the first time; "or shall I retire, and allow this sentimental dialogue to end in a more natural manner?"

"Hugh—Hugh!" said Stephen, reproach-fully.

"I fear my return for a missing sketch has been most inopportune—let me offer my excuses and begone."

"Not till you have heard me, sir," said his brother, firmly.

"I am anxious to hear all, and end all," he said, between his closed teeth.

"Not in anger, Hugh," said Stephen—"not with the ruling passion gaining the mastery over you, and blinding you to justice ? "

" Well, well—I will be calm," said he— " I am calm."

" Bessy, will you leave us for a moment ? "

Hugh stepped aside to allow Bessy to proceed to Lucy's room. She looked towards him as she passed, but he kept his dark eyes directed downwards. He maintained that same brooding position long after Bessy had left him, and was sobbing her story forth on Lucy's bosom ; and Stephen, who watched him at a little distance, did not intrude upon those thoughts, which he believed would at least bring calmness in discussion. And the signs of anger died out from that darkling countenance, although the shadows settled there as though they would never leave it till his dying day. He closed the door, and advanced into the room, and placed two chairs close to where Bessy and Stephen had been standing.

"Sit down, Stephen; you are not strong."

When they were seated, Hugh said—

"I have been hasty—I have been wrong."

"Well said."

"One moment," he added, quickly — "hasty in my remarks, not in my judgment. You, at least, are suffering and ill, and I will spare you my comments—forgive you all the evil you have strewn around me, in your narrow estimate of what was best for me. I have not heard much of the conversation between you and Miss Calverton—I have no desire to hear more."

"Uncharitable and inconsiderate."

"All is plain as noonday to me, Stephen. I do not reproach you—I will even thank you for your best intentions. But your scheme for my happiness was a false one, and it crumbles away to dust, and leaves a sterner future than before. So be it—man is born to trouble."

"Will you let me speak!" cried Stephen, excitedly—"I must speak!"

" By heaven, I will not hear you ! " ex-claimed Hugh, his hand falling heavily on the table.

" By heaven, you shall ! " and Stephen's hand followed that of Hugh's, and Stephen's eyes glared, perhaps for the first time in his life, a defiance to that brother's will. " Would you judge a case without listening to the truth—or are you a coward, and would shun it ? "

Hugh hesitated a moment ; then he folded his arms on his broad chest, and said—

" Speak, then ; I am a patient listener."

Stephen, as briefly as he could, and in ner-vous earnest language, related the story of his love for Bessy, his struggle with it, his final triumph over the passion that had at one time nearly mastered him. He did not dwell upon his desire to see that brother before him more happy than himself ; he simply told his own story, and how it had ended, and been kept back even from Bessy until that present hour.

"Setting aside the folly of confessing all to Bessy in a weak moment, there is nothing of which I blame myself, or of which you can accuse me."

"I accuse you not," he said, regarding his brother mournfully; "yours has been a harder life than mine, Stephen; but you have groped on blindly, and dragged me to the gulf with you. I have only to see Bessy now—another dreamer like ourselves!"

"You will remember she loves you—you will be careful, Hugh."

"I will not wound her by a harsh word, Stephen."

Stephen seized his hand and pressed it, but Hugh responded not, and the cloud was still upon his face.

"Hugh, for her sake and mine, do not resolve hastily."

"I have resolved," was the hollow answer; "there is no changing me."

"What! will you throw away your happiness like a madman?"

"Like a wise man, who has found the semblance of happiness, not the substance, and wakes up to the truth."

"The substance is with you. You will be the destroyer of your best days if you are deaf to reason now."

"I have been deceived! Mask the truth as you may, produce as many extenuating circumstances as possible, it is a grim truth, from which there is no escape. I accuse no one, but I am firm."

"Will you not think of Bessy's happiness as well as your own?"

"I will act for the best. Will you," he said, with a strange appealing look on his face,—"will you let me think a little while?"

He leaned his elbows on his knees, and took his head between his hands, and was silent; and his brother, anxiously watching him, had not the heart to break upon his thoughts.

Stephen did not remember how very weak and ill he had been that day till the excitement of the last hour having partly subsided, he could feel a greater weakness stealing over him. He crossed the room, and dropped to his old place on the sofa, whence he watched the figure of his brother, so still and rigid, and yet expressive of so much despair. He knew Hugh's love-dream would all vanish now, and that no power of his could stay it; he felt assured the end for which he himself had striven, and had sacrificed so much, was shattered in a moment, never to be replaced and gather strength again !

CHAPTER V.

DISUNION.

HUGH looked up at last, and there was nothing to hope in his face. It was the old face of a past time, before Bessy Calverton was known to him; all its new brightness had vanished away as though it had never been.

He glanced towards his brother, and said—

"Don't you feel so well, Stephen?"

"About the same, thank you."

"I have been forgetful of you and your weakness—you must overlook it for this once.

There are times when we forget everything but the one crushing fact that has numbed our interest in passing things. Keep quiet."

"And let me be quiet," he might have added, as he turned to his work, and sat down to his old place by the window. It required an exercise of all his firm will to begin every-day life again; but he brought it to subjection, and no one but himself ever knew the struggle it was. Bessy and Lucy came down together at a later hour, and he bent more closely over his work as the door opened and admitted them. He had been accustomed of late to look up when Bessy entered the room, and by the studied intentness with which he prosecuted his work, Bessy knew he had not forgiven her. He had said a little while ago that he never forgave an injury, and he had taken her interest in Stephen as an injury to himself, that no love of hers could extenuate. Bessy Calverton had not lost all her high spirit, and her cheek flushed and her bosom heaved at these thoughts. Her first impulse was to return home at once; then a second thought taught her discretion. If all were over between her and Hugh Speckland, why, it was better to part with some semblance of good will; and perhaps her actions were not wholly right, and she had deceived him a little. But she had striven hard to make amends, and been rewarded by his better life and her own lighter heart; and now it was all dashed down, and the shadows were deepening as she sat there.

Yes, she must go home. It was an unnatural position for her, and the blind girl's faint attempts to relieve the depression that had settled on them only made things worse. Sitting there amidst the wreck of so many best intentions, was a mockery to her woman's feelings. She would be glad to depart, and think it all over in the solitude of her chamber, and wrestle with the bitter knowledge.

She was ready to leave an instant afterwards, and to Lucy's faint appeal not to go
away so soon was answering with a lip that
quivered in spite of her. Would it be the
last time, she thought, as she kissed Lucy
passionately, that she should stand within
that room, and be face to face with all those
who had made it like home to her? She
could believe it in that moment. She shook
hands with Stephen, who held her hand for a
moment in his, and said,

"For all the harm I have done, Bessy,
may I ask your pardon?"

"There is nothing to forgive, Stephen.
What has happened was God's will. Good-
bye."

"God bless you," he murmured.

As Bessy turned, she became aware that
Hugh had left his seat, and was awaiting her,
hat in hand. It was no surprise; she felt
that the engagement between them must be
broken formally; and though she inwardly

feared him, and distrusted her own calmness, it was right that his cold words should end it.

"I am going a little way home with Bessy," Hugh said in answer to a glance from Stephen.

"Take care of her," was the low response.

"You will——" began Lucy more passionately, when he interrupted her by saying, "I will not be late—*fear nothing.*"

Deep as his voice was, there was more mournfulness than harshness in its tone, and Bessy felt they would not part in anger.

They went together from the house, and walked the whole dreary length of Seymour Street without a word being exchanged between them. He had offered her his arm, and she had taken it, as if their old relationship existed still, and then they proceeded silently into the broader thoroughfares, where more hearts and hopes were failing than their own.

"Bessy," he said at length, "I have no

long speeches to offer, no reproaches to make;
to be very brief is better for us both. I have
been a visionary, and shown myself, with all
my boasted strength of mind, no better than
the weakest and most foolish. I have been
deceived in myself and my worldly knowledge
rather than in you. For you were a child—
you are a child now, and I am a strong man,
who should have read you differently: it is
all my fault."

Bessy tried to answer, but her voice failed
her. The strange mournful cadence ringing
throughout his words affected her, despite
the efforts she had resolved upon to keep
firm to the end. She had not expected
that he would talk or reason thus, after all
that she had seen and heard that afternoon. His cruel sarcasm had been ringing
in her ears till then, but this touched her
heart and moved her. And yet this told of a
purpose there was no power to move.

"It is all my fault," he repeated; "I

stepped from the life I knew into a crowd of foolish romantic thoughts, that would have shamed a schoolboy's first love—and I have met my punishment. It may be hard to bear, but I have borne hard truths before, and mastered them—and I will master this! Bessy," he said in a lower tone, as the crowd swept by them. "I was too many years your senior, too far removed in thoughts and pursuits, ever to have made you happy—I think we have both been a little wrong in suffering the engagement, but I take the blame for forcing it upon you. All I ask you, is to bear in mind that I had not the power to read until to-day that story of your love for Stevie."

"No, no!" cried Bessy; and then stopped and struggled with her emotion, and drew her thick veil before her face.

"Why deny it at this moment—at this time? Does it matter to me or you now?—can it influence, for an instant, the after-life of either of us? We are parting—we must part!—why should there be a screen between you and me at such a crisis in our fates? Bessy, will you answer me one question fairly—by all that truth in your heart which you possess, I beg it of you."

" I will answer it," said Bessy.

" Did you love Stephen Speckland on that Sunday evening I asked you for my wife?"

It was a cruel question, and struck home. It was a question from which there was no escape—and, even if she had wished it, no evasion. Oh! if he had only asked her at that time and hour, if she loved Stephen Speckland now!

He repeated the question, and she answered, "Yes." He had sought the truth ; and though it quivered like an arrow in him, he kept firm, and the expression on his face did not waver for an instant.

" I was assured of it—and he loved you, and, doubtful of his future health, disguised it till this afternoon. Well, Bessy, thinking it all over now, I see how natural it was, and how wilfully blind *I* have been. Wrapped in my egotism, I left you and him together, and then expected to be loved myself—to ask and have, and never a disappointment in my path to check me. I have merited justly such a day as this !"

"No," said Bessy, firmly, "for you were truthful, Hugh, and I was wrong. I should have waited till the time when I could have answered honestly and from the heart."

"The answer must have been 'No' then— we were so unfitted for each other, and the dissimilarity between us would have suggested itself each day with greater force. It would have been better, however—I see all that, I feel all that. You would not have had the hard task to strive to love me— even to bewilder yourself between a fancied love and common friendship ; whilst I—ah ! no matter that—all's over !"

And Bessy Calverton felt how true it was; that there was no power, no unmaidenly effort of her own, which could change the line of action he had sternly drawn for both. He would not ask then if she loved him; he would not believe in her, or her affection; he set it all aside as beyond question—and her woman's pride resisted her impulse to explain. And had she even explained, he would have crushed her with his disbelief, perhaps.

"May I ask one more question—the last?"

Bessy did not answer, but he took her silence for consent.

"I would wish to know why at that time, when you loved Stephen, when you secretly believed he loved you—your own words confessed that this afternoon!—you accepted me for your future husband, and cast away every hope of your young life?"

"Is it necessary to dwell upon this now?" asked Bessy, a little indignantly.

"I am in the dark—I cannot reconcile the

answer of that morning with the actions of your life—I am very anxious to know all before I go."

"Your brother Stephen pressed me to an answer at once—for the sake of your future happiness, he begged me to say 'Yes.' He spoke of—of—"

"Enough, Bessy, I am satisfied," he said, quickly; "let me not add to the pain of that avowal by listening to another word. I forgive him all the harm he has done in his efforts to bring happiness to me. He was never a thoughtful man, or he might have looked forward to the natural end of such a scheme, and seen the day when it must crumble into dust. It was all based on a lie, and deserved to fall!"

It was Hugh Speckland's one reproach, though he had promised not to hurl it against her. He did not know then that he had uttered a reproach; for in that moment he was but thinking of the cruel waters that had closed round him, and left him alone on the rock.

They were in St. Owen's parish then, and advancing to Miss Davis's. Bessy felt her strength failing her, and envied the firm unfaltering step of him at her side. Nothing would alter him she thought, not even the pang of that separation which must ensue now, and end all. He would have marched like that to his grave, had it been dug at the end of the street, and made no sign. It was better that they should part thus; with so cold and unforgiving a nature she would have been never happy—he was right! They were at St. Owen's Church at last, where he stopped and let her hand withdraw itself from his arm.

"I will leave you here," he said. "I fear I have prolonged your pain as well as my own by accompanying you so far—but it is our last walk together, and there must be no ill feeling at our parting. Let me say once

more—for the last time in life that we may
ever meet, Miss Calverton—that I take all
the blame upon myself, and that I claim it as
my right.   Good-bye."

He extended his hand, and regarded her
intently.   His face changed then for a
moment, but Bessy was looking at the pavement at her feet, and observed it not.   She
only heard the deep unwavering voice
addressing her, as he held her hand firmly
in his own.

"In all your after life may God's blessing
follow you," he said, "and make that life
brighter and more fair than any effort of mine
could have done.   Good-bye—I am not rash
enough to say for ever, although I honestly
believe that we shall never meet from this day."

He reiterated his good-bye, released her
hand, turned away, and went rapidly down
the street, without looking once back at all
the hopes he had quitted.   He crossed the road
and plunged into the maze of streets before

him, and went on at an increased rate in the
direction of his home, as though he could
outwalk all the troubles that crowded on
him, and all the whispers in his ear of
what might have been, of what could never
be again. He had performed his duty, and
cut himself adrift from the ties that bound
him to her; he was alone now, free to act,
and to strike out a new path for himself. It
would not lead to happiness; he had done
with the search from that hour, and no visions
could live after the waking—from that day
never more a dreamer!

As he hurried on through the streets amidst
the crowd of workers like himself—many of
whom had cares like unto his, and many more
deep and self-engrossing, and bore them better
and with a philosophy more pure—they were
not few in number who looked into his face,
and turned to watch him as he hastened on.
For it was a face that betrayed its owner was
ill at ease by that stern set expression which he

considered surmounted all emotion, and made
a man of him.   There were gathered many
idlers on London Bridge, watching the departure of a steam-ship below, and, his progress impeded, he mingled with the mass and
found himself after a time looking over the
parapet and watching with the rest.   He did
not know why he had paused—whether the
thoughts of the busy day had been too much
for him, and brought him to a stand-still.   He
might have been walking in his sleep for the
notice he had taken of events ; and his
thoughts were so vague and confused still,
that he could hardly believe himself a conscious being like those who stood beside him.
He remembered a man speaking to him once
or twice, and his returning a few unmeaning
words for answer ; and he had a vague sense
of wishing that he were utterly alone in the
world, that he might step on board that ship,
and be borne with her to another land, where
he might begin life afresh.   And then he

forgot all about the vessel and his propinquity to a few suspicious characters, and played again the cruel part he had resolved upon, and parted with Bessy Calverton, and muttered his last blessing again so loudly, that his neighbour looked from under his hat at him, and gave a wink to a friend, significant of Hugh's mental condition. The steam-ship went on her way, the crowd dispersed in that mysterious, magical way common to all crowds, and Hugh Speckland still stood there, and watched the water flowing through the arches, and the black night deepening upon its surface, and the faint lights coming out on board ship and from warehouse floors, and shimmering in the restless water.

Deep and soul-oppressing thoughts, from which he finally broke away, to find the night had come upon him, and that some one had stolen his handkerchief and a pocket-book, in which were a few of his best sketches; and that a policeman, puzzled at his long stay there, was suspiciously regarding him. He started once more at the old quick pace, and stopped not till he reached Snowfields.

He entered his home by his latch-key, after pausing for a moment at the door; and, after one glance towards Stephen on the couch, and to Lucy sitting by his side, he walked straight to his bench, and plunged at once into his work. And those who watched him thought how like it was to the past habits, before he had known Bessy Calverton; and felt that that past life, with all the old thoughts belonging to it, had come back once again.

CHAPTER VI.

THE LAST MEETING.

BESSY went direct to her room, and closed the
door upon herself and her troubles. She had
borne up well whilst the eyes of the world
were upon her; she could afford to give way
now the world was locked out, and only the
eye of God could take note of her sorrows.
She felt that she had loved Hugh Speckland
then, and that he, in his selfish obduracy,
which would not believe in future happiness,
had cast her aside, coolly and phlegmatically,
and thrust the best feelings of her heart back
upon herself.

He had never truly loved, or he would have acted in a different manner, she thought; let it end as he wished it, and let her turn to new thoughts and pursuits also, and forget him. He had been too old for her, and she was little more than a girl even now—scarcely nineteen years of age. How could she have expected to make such a man as Hugh Speckland contented with her? It was a whim— a phantasy, that such men as he encourage for a time, and then shake off. Why should she feel more than himself? He had owned, if not directly, still by words which implied that truth, that his confidence was shaken, and he would prefer his life alone: so be it, she thought, dashing the tears from her eyes with a hasty hand; she could bear it, and not give way too much. There would lie duties before her to distract her thoughts, and keep her from brooding too much on the irreparable; a deeper study of lives more wretched than her own would keep the cruel past in

the background, and teach her to forget the
follies and wrongs that belonged to it. And
then those last words of Hugh rang in her
ears again—" It was all based on a lie, and
deserved to fall." They were accusing words,
that struck home, and she could not shut
them from her.

And whilst prostrated by this thought, Mrs.
Wessinger, after trying the handle of the
door, called her name from without. Bessy
rose and opened the door, and Mrs. Wessinger
stood there gazing with no small degree of
amazement on the pale, tear-stained face of
our heroine.

" My dear Bessy, what's the matter ? " she
exclaimed ; " what has gone wrong, my child,
since you and I saw each other last ? "

" Cannot you guess ? " she said.

" Hugh Speckland ? " cried the old lady.

" Yes. Between Hugh Speckland and me
has ended all engagement. We were not
fitted for each other, and we are better apart,

he thinks. Oh! my faithful, best of friends, who has been the comforter of so many troubled ones, will you comfort me now in my turn, and try to make me think as he does?"

She flung herself into Mrs. Wessinger's arms, and they folded round her and pressed her to her breast, as they would have folded round that daughter of hers who had died early and left her childless, and in whom this Bessy seemed to live again.

"But will you think so?"

"Yes—soon!"

"If he were the first to say so, it is for the best, my child," said she; "the man is not worthy of you who coolly asserts so much after your engagement. Will you tell your story to me and two old friends downstairs?"

"Is Mr. Parslow here?"

"Yes—he has called to have a quiet cup of tea with us, Bessy. If anyone can give you comfort, teach you resignation, it is he."

But Bessy shrank from the revelation of

her love story. She did not care to enter
into all the details of that history, now the
book that contained it was sealed for ever.
It had been a strange story—let it remain
buried deep within her, now no good could
arise from its relation.

"No, no," she hastened to add, "there is
no occasion to speak of it. Surely it is
enough to know that all is over between me
and Hugh, and that a new life begins for
both. He is not to blame so much as myself
—you must promise me never to seek him
out, or utter one reproach to add to a misery
that will be ever greater than mine."

"But—"

"But you will promise—will you not?"

And Mrs. Wessinger promised, and began,
after her own homely way, to offer that consolation to Bessy which it was in her power to
bestow. And she had a way of speaking that
always had some effect—for it was from the
heart, and full of faith, and was ruled by

something higher than worldly experience. With a woman's tact she could see that Bessy was suffering, and she did not strive all at once to bring her back to herself, as though a great disappointment could be shaken off like a dewdrop. She preached the homely doctrine of resignation, and trust in the God who in His will was thus testing her, and she had faith in time and Bessy's youth to work the rest.

When they went downstairs Bessy was calm, and it was not till later in the evening that she startled Mary Davis and Mr. Parslow by saying—very hurriedly, for she would not trust herself with the subject —

"I wish you all to know that I am no longer engaged to Mr. Speckland—that we have resolved to put an end to the engagement. I should feel it kind of you if you will both believe that it could not have happened otherwise, and that it has happened now for the best."

Mr. Parslow looked perplexed, and put the end of his forefinger into his mouth, and slowly nibbled it like a morsel that he was choice of. He observed Bessy's agitation, however, and put on his quiet manner, and passed the matter over lightly enough, for her sake.

"For the best—to be sure, Bessy, who doubts it? The sea is full of fish, and there are more in it than ever came out of it, according to some wise man or other, whose name I don't exactly call to mind at this moment. At nineteen years of age one does not give way to despair over the loss of a sweetheart—only in a trumpery novel that is."

Mary Davis thought Mr. Parslow treated the matter very lightly; but she did not know Mr. Parslow yet, and was not so shrewd a judge of character as Mrs. Wessinger. She would have liked to dwell upon the subject, and distress Bessy by probing too deeply into

the matter at that moment; and was surprised
at the rapid manner with which the reverend
gentleman darted away to other topics, chiefly
of a light turn, too, and somewhat unbecom-
ing in a minister of the gospel.   She did not
know, neither did Bessy, nor Mrs. Wessinger,
that he left St. Owen's Terrace for Seymour
Street, after bidding them good night, and
bearded the stern man in his den, and de-
manded with some warmth an explanation.
He found the old Hugh Speckland at his
work—the taciturn, irritable man, whom a
little annoyed—yet the man of granite, that no
earnestness could soften.   Hugh dismissed the
case in a very few words : he took the blame
upon himself, as he had asserted at an earlier
hour of that day ; but he did not conde-
scend to enlighten Mr. Parslow in any degree
whatever.

"I have been mistaken in what I thought
was best for her and me—I have awakened
to the consciousness that I should have only

made her unhappy, and have considered it my duty to apprise her of it. Have you an objection to urge against that line of conduct ? "

" No—no," said the incumbent of St. Owen's, with a little hesitation ; " but might you not have thought of this before?"

" I might—but I did not think. My fault again—I own it!"

" And might not some little explanation make matters right ?"

" Never, sir !"

" And might not—"

" You distress me with your persistence," cried Hugh ; " will you have no mercy on me ?"

Mr. Parslow gave up before the fierce glance and the contracted brow, and returned home to think that Bessy Calverton's life had taken another turn, and to wonder perhaps whither in good time it might lead her.

So Hugh Speckland and Bessy Calverton

parted and went their ways, each setting it down for the best that such a separation had ensued, and growing sceptical concerning any true happiness in the world. If it were all for the best, neither seemed to have come forth the better for the trial, but to have lost some faith in human nature, and some belief in human love. Each flew to work as to a distraction wherein might be sunk a harsh remembrance; and she who, in the common order of things, might have been expected to suffer most, was the first to take heart and learn resignation. For Hugh Speckland belonged to the No-Church class after his disappointment; he lost all faith in prayer bringing him any good. She whose influence had led him to God's house had betrayed him, and in his bitterness he would hear no comfort from the lips of those who preached the divine laws. He was anxious to make his life the true reflex of what it had been before Bessy's face shone on it and distracted

him; let him go back to the past, and forget
that she had ever played her part there. Yes,
she had betrayed him; in his heart he believed
it; in the solitude of his own chamber he
nursed that thought, till it rankled within him
and made him uncharitable. He had spared
her his reproaches in that last interview between them; he had promised Stephen so—
he had desired it for her own sake·—but,
nevertheless, she had betrayed him, valued
not his love, and returned it by a false show
of affection, that made him wince to dwell
upon. To the two questions that he had
asked her she had answered in a manner
unsatisfactory to him and his self-respect, and
he brooded upon the result over his work,
though her name never again crossed his lips.

The reader perceives that Hugh Speckland
is not a model hero—it has never been our
intention to present him as such. Model
heroes belong not to real life; and even novels
are on the turn, and immaculate characters a

drug in the market. It was Hugh's nature to twist and pervert a subject that he dwelt upon, until it became fixed upon his mind, a distortion in which he read an injury to himself and an offence to his pride. From Stephen, who might have given a different aspect to affairs that troubled him, he would seek no further explanation; he would frame for himself one of the darkest colours, and set it up for truth, and believe in it. With every day he hardened—it was but the growing weakness of Stephen that touched him now, for it was only in his case that he gave his heart play. The brain and hand worked diligently, and were seldom still; but the heart, with all its deep feeling, its great thoughts, he kept a weight upon, and would not have it move. It was his study to do that—for the first time in his life it became an especial study.

Perhaps it was wisely ordered that this strange nature should be distracted by his brother's weakness more and more, and that time, with the memory of his disappointment green, should not be wholly left him to brood on one wrong.

Stephen Speckland had made a struggle to return to business again, and then broken down utterly, and been forbidden night air, or any venturing into the streets, except in the warm sunshine, and with the wind in a fair quarter.

"A child at last, Hugh," he said—"dependent on your bounty, and bound to fifty restrictions, that can only save me a few more days at the best. Well, I can afford to be patient now."

If he were inclined to be dull and abstracted Hugh would detect it on the instant, and set aside his work, and go to him. One day Stephen, observing this alacrity, said—

"I am robbing you of your time, Hugh."

" Does it matter much, Stevie ? "

" You must fetch up after I'm gone, old fellow. There will be only sister Lucy to distract you—and you won't forget her now and then ? "

" No."

" I suppose her time will come to leave you too, Hugh," said he ; " for we may believe in this Canadian hero, now."

" Every day is full of uncertainty, and he is a fool who builds one hope on the morrow."

" Still it may occur," reasoned Stevie ; " and then," with an anxious glance towards him, " you'll be wholly alone here, Hugh. That is a picture I don't like to regard very much—for I can't trust you far."

" Am I not fit company for myself—have I not lived in myself for many years ? "

" Still, it is a gloomy picture," mused Stephen ; " this room, deserted by all the old faces, and you sitting yonder under the lamp for ever alone, fostering all the evil, unjust thoughts which turn you against your better self."

"A gloomy picture as you draw it, Stevie," said Hugh, forcing a laugh; "neither a bright nor a true one."

"Cannot you manage your work in the country—live with the old people again?"

"They don't understand me—I never made them happy."

"Wrong."

"I was not born to study others' happiness, Stevie—it is my fate, perhaps."

"I wish you would study your own happiness a little more, Hugh," he said, after a long pause; "may I talk of an old subject?"

Hugh looked fixedly at Stephen.

"Of all but one."

"Ah! but it is that one—it never leaves me now. I am haunted by it, as by an evil spirit."

"Exorcise it by prayer," said Hugh, somewhat scornfully.

"You are your own enemy — you are
suffering."

"Not I."

"Do you think that I have known you for
so many years, that I cannot tell by that face
when the heart is troubled?"

"Romance—romance, Stevie," said Hugh
in reply; "I give you my word that my
mind is resigned to my future, and that every
day I regard it with more composure. Granted
that I sketched a fairy picture once with
vivid figures in the foreground: the picture
is gone—and I am none the worse for having
nursed a folly late in life."

"But Bessy—"

"Stephen," interrupted Hugh, "that name
is the one subject on which I will *not* dwell—
for which I pray your forbearance. I cannot
hear it, even from you, whose wishes in every
other respect I hold sacred, and will obey."

" Ha !"

Hugh hastened to qualify his promise.

" So far as it is possible for my stubborn nature to obey," he said ; " you will not bind me to anything I may blush at as weak and childish ?"

" No ; but I must see *her* again before— the last ! I have resolved upon that. This is your house, and if you refuse me consent, I must drag my way somewhere else."

" There is room for both of us herein ; only —only—she and I must never meet, you understand."

Stephen nodded his head.

" And when the old people come next week—they are talking of it, I hear"—(he did not tell Stephen that he had sent for them)— " you must not let them, with their want of forethought, pain me, or—her."

" You may trust me ; you may rest assured that she—"

Hugh started up with his old petulance.

"You will speak of her, and I have said
'No' to it! Is she a subject of which you
will never tire?"

"Never."

Hugh caught him by the arm, and looked
full in his thin, wasted face, wherein the eyes
had become so preternaturally large.

"Stephen, you love her still!"

The brother did not answer, but he evaded
the glance bent on him.

"You have loved her through it all—is it
not so?"

"Is it worth disguising now?" he asked,
with a faint smile; "will you think worse of
me for confessing it?"

"No."

"Mine is a strange love—it don't belong
to this world, Hugh. I have nursed it in
health and sickness, before and after your
engagement: I have kept it pure and free
from selfishness. She gladdened this home,
and made a change in it—she would have

gladdened you, and made you happy. She loved you."

"Hush—hush—you will speak of her, and I listen like a man, who is spell-bound. Why do you tell me that she loved me, when every word is a mockery, that I can disprove?"

"Impossible."

"Stephen, it will make you happier, perhaps, to know that she has been ever aware of your passion—and God knows why I should begrudge you a happy moment in a time like this."

He stooped down and said, in a voice that trembled—

"She loved you from the first. She loved you on the day she consented to my offer. In our last interview on earth it was her confession, on my honour!"

He crossed the room to his work again, after giving voice to that which he believed would be a solace to his brother, and applied himself to his task with all his old energy. It had been a humiliation to confess it, and he was a proud man—but it ended all argument for ever, and it would make his brother happy. But he was wrong there; it but added to that brother's trouble —for he saw, from the graver complication existing, the utter impossibility of linking Bessy's life with Hugh's.

Before his last resolve to give her up even in thought, Stephen had believed that Bessy loved him; but he had not sought the knowledge, and would have given worlds not to have known it in his dying hours. It distressed him—it showed before him all that might have been had life and health been spared him. And he had been trying to undervalue life, and been long reconciled, as he had thought, to resigning it.

" Hugh," he said at last.

" I will talk of her no more," was the deep answer.

" I have dismissed the subject," said he ; "but it is dull work here alone. Do you mind talking of the old times now, when you and I were boys, Hugh ?"

It was for Hugh's sake that he asked the question, but Hugh did not guess it at the time, and set aside his work for good that evening, and went back to his seat near the couch, on which Stephen lay so often now. And Lucy, coming downstairs a short time afterwards, found the brothers talking of the old times with a fervour and interest that were new to them.

The days seemed to flow speedily towards the end after that confidence between the brothers, and every day left less time for Hugh to wander on his own road, from which, the greater light excluded, the more morbid satisfaction it appeared to afford. The next week there arrived the old couple from the country ; and later in that week Stephen called Hugh to his side, and said :—

" I should like to see her now ! "

" Is it intended to be a long interview ? "

" No."

" To-morrow she shall be written to, and to-morrow—I shall be absent from home."

Hugh kept his word ; and when the morrow came, and Bessy—touched by the few words written to Stephen's dictation, which told his condition, and begged to see her once more— was again in the old home in Seymour Street, the owner of that home was wandering about the London streets.

It was not a long interview between those who might have been lovers once, but it compressed within its narrow limits much of pain ; for there were many associations connected with their meeting, and it was their last interview this side of the grave.

Both were embarrassed, for both had much to keep back, and the name of Hugh was a forbidden one.   Stephen was pained to see the pale face and the sad expression thereon ;

he felt that it was his work, and that his unruly tongue had set her and Hugh apart. If he could but live again from that day, what a different life for his brother and that girl!

"There is nothing in the past which you have not forgiven, I hope, Bessy," he said, when their interview was drawing to a close.

"There is nothing which I have ever had to forgive, Stephen," she replied; "you have been a dear and valued friend of mine all my life, and helped much to gladden it in its saddest times."

"You are very kind to say so."

"I say it with all my heart—do you doubt it?"

"No—not now." Then he added, after a pause, "are you happy with Miss Davis?"

"She does all in her power to make me happy; she is a good woman — a good Christian."

"What a while ago it seems now since the

mountain days," said Stephen—"since I thought what an useful wife she would make a runaway carpenter."

It was his old light tone, but it was a poor effort, although Bessy smiled sadly at it. He was anxious to see her leave him with a smile, however—as if that were probable in such a parting! But he had ever been a visionary, and indulged strange fancies.

"May I read to you before I go?" she asked, in a low tone. "You will pardon me, but you do not seem to think much of your bible at this time."

"The good genius has deserted us," he said, meaningly.

"May I read?"

"Yes—it is kind of you."

Bessy sat down, and read a chapter of the New Testament to him; and he listened attentively, and gave a little sigh as she concluded.

"They are good words, and tell me what

I have neglected—but they do not appeal to me, or rouse me very much. Whatever the fate before me, I can meet it."

" That is recklessness, Stephen."

" No—I think not."

" Will you let me send Mr. Parslow here to see you ? "

" I cannot expect that he will take the trouble."

" I am sure that he will be very glad to come."

" Well then—I will be glad to see him ! "

Bessy reached out her hand and said,

" Shall I bid you good-bye now ? "

" Ah ! it must be that sooner or later—I have been selfish, and kept you at my side too long. Good-bye."

When her hand lay in his, and he was looking at her swimming eyes, he said,

" I am a weak fellow—I have been weak and erring all my days, and the ruling passion lasts with me to the end. Bessy, I am going

L 2

to break a promise I made my brother Hugh, yesterday."

"Oh! no, no—don't do that!" she cried.

"It was a rash promise, and it is merciful to break it. Bessy, you will not remember him with anger?"

"No—why should I?"

"In the far off days will you think of Hugh a little?—for in the far off days I have a dreamy hope still. Should you and he meet in that distant time of which I speak, will you revive my name, and let it be perhaps—ah, perhaps!—a peacemaker between you. There is only one I have ever loved more than him in all my mis-spent life—and Hugh's future is a dark and lonely one, and full of bitter memories."

"Stephen—is not all this futile? Is it possible that my life can ever cross that of your brother's again—both our paths lying so wide apart, and not likely to intersect each other's. Say that they ever cross, dear friend—what then?"

" Ah ! what then ? " murmured Stephen— " we will not talk of it any more. Only think of it occasionally, Bessy, for in the future what may not happen in a world as strange as this ? Say good-bye now—God make your life a happy one, dear Bessy ! "

She stooped and kissed him lightly on the forehead, and then went from the room, he following her with his anxious eyes. The door closed between them, and the last meeting on earth between Bessy Calverton and Stephen Speckland was over.

CHAPTER VII.

FIRM TO THE LAST.

THE Reverend Jacob Parslow did not require twice telling that there was one ill and sorrowing in Seymour Street, and that his counsel might be of service there. His religion was not confined within the bounds of his own parish—it was the creed of a good Christian, and had no limits.

He was at Seymour Street next day, and the next; he devoted the time he had to spare to bringing Stephen Speckland to that knowledge of the truth to which more than once he had approached. And Stephen, of a

nature naturally docile, was not a stubborn
subject under his hand; his fear had been
that his new life had begun too late, and it
only required the kind supporting words of
the good man at his side to re-assure him.
He was grateful for Mr. Parslow's visits, to
which he speedily began to attach an interest,
and anxiously wait for.

"Yours should be a happy life, Mr. Parslow," he said on the third morning, "enjoying the respect and love of so many."

"I am as happy as the rest of the world I
believe," he said; "I have my little crosses
and vexations; I see some of my best
friends thinking too much of the world and
living for it, but I am happy. I build my
faith on things imperishable."

"It must be a hard task for one in health
and strength, with all the world's temptations
to battle against," mused Stephen; "for it is
hard for me, lying here apart from action, to
detach myself from worldly thoughts."

" Why hard ? " asked the minister.

" I shall leave so many unhappy—so many
in the thickest of the fight, on the wrong side,
upholding the wrong cause."

" It is human life."

" But those I leave are my best friends, and
things might have been so different had not
the trials come ! "

" Trials were to teach us endurance."

" And endurance has its limits when the
trials are unceasing.   Do you know of whom
I am thinking ? "

" Your brother ? "

" Yes — and Bessy Calverton.   She had
gladdened his heart, and he was turning away
from the darkness, when the blow fell.   If
I had only died six months ago, and not have
marred all by my rashness !   Mr. Parslow, is
Bessy Calverton happy ? "

" I think she will be.   She has met her
disappointment early in life, and there may
lie before her much to brighten the future.

She is more grave and thoughtful than her years warrant, perhaps ; but that is natural."

" Yes."

" Do you think your brother ever loved her ? "

" More than himself, sir."

" I cannot understand it. Will you tell me the story, if it will not pain you too much ? "

Stephen very briefly related the particulars of the breaking of the engagement, pausing now and then to take breath, and struggle with his racking cough—for he had grown very weak during the last two days. He was no longer one of the family in that back parlour which he had brightened for so many years by his presence, but shut in his own room, where sad figures came softly stealing to his bedside, to ask if he wanted anything —if he felt a little better, or more weak.

Mr. Parslow shook his head at the conclusion ; he could not tell all that was hidden in

Bessy Calverton's heart from the simple relation of the story—he saw only the disruption
of an engagement hastily begun.

"Surely, it is best that such an engagement is ended."

But Stephen held firmly to his opinion.

"They were both happy; he loved her
with his whole soul, and she was learning to
love him—did love him, perhaps: who can
tell? Mr. Parslow, you will do your best for
Hugh when I am gone? You are the friend
who will come in his solitude and seek to
turn him from the darkness in which he
would enwrap himself?"

"I will try."

"Now and then—not too often," said Stephen, ever considerate. "You know his nature, and how hard and exacting it is, and
how, with an undue pressure, it will take the
contrary way, and defy all effort. But now
and then," he repeated, anxiously, "call to
see him here; speak to him of me, and he

will listen, I think. Tell him of all my last wishes — not to shut the door against his chances of a better life."

Mr. Parslow promised.

"I do not say he will ever be a happy man; he has been a man all his life to cling to one thought, and follow it for evil or good. There is only one can ever make him happy even now—you will remember that?"

"Can it ever be—is it possible?"

"I don't know. I have spoken of this to Bessy, and she has answered like yourself; and still the dreamy hope I mentioned to her flashes before me. But then," with a faint smile, "I have spent my life in castle-building. We are all castle-builders, good Mrs. Wessinger has declared."

"So is half the human race," observed Mr. Parslow; "we must look forward, and count the prizes that never fall to our share."

The conversation passed to a topic more serious, which it is not our place to intrude

upon our readers, and the day passed away,
and then the next; and doctors and physicians appeared again, and shook their heads
more gravely than ever as they came downstairs, where Hugh was anxiously awaiting
them. Stephen required now a constant
watcher by his bedside, and Hugh would let
no one take the place but himself, but sat
up night after night, and was as gentle and
considerate with him as a woman. To have
seen Hugh Speckland then, was to disbelieve
in the hard nature that resisted every effort
to soften it, and to find it difficult to believe
that, the last task over, the last duty accom-
plished, he would return to his labours the
same callous being, to whom no lesson had
been taught by a dying brother's gentleness
and love.

No lesson even at the last—on that still
summer night, when the moon was peering
over the black railway arch into the sick
chamber. No lesson ever to be learned by

that man who would hew for himself his own
fate.

Hugh had been sitting by the bedside with
his arms folded on his chest, staring down at
the carpet, and absorbed in his reverie. He
had fancied Stephen was sleeping, until the
brother's thin hand touched his own.

" What are you thinking of, Hugh ?"

" Nothing," answered Hugh.

" What is the hour ? "

Hugh looked at his watch, and answered—
" Twelve."

" Feel my pulse, Hugh—is it weaker ?"

Hugh placed his fingers on the pulse of
his brother, and then turned deathly pale,
and looked anxiously at that wan face beside
him.

" Shall I—shall I call them, Stevie ?"

" Yes—I think I should like to see them
all—again ! "

Hugh left the room, and went from door to
door, knocking softly, and whispering the

fatal news for which they had waited, and
slept lightly many nights—for which we all
have waited and prayed against in our turn,
and hoped against hope, till the tapping at
the door has sounded like the hand of fate on
our hearts.

Hugh re-entered the room, and Stephen,
with a feverish impatience that was new to
him, beckoned him to the bed-side.

"You will not like me to speak of the one
old subject before them—but Hugh, Hugh,
do think a little of what a life you are making
for yourself!"

"I have thought."

"Do promise me to see Bessy Calverton
again? My last wish, Hugh—remember!"

Hugh's face betrayed a strange agitation,
but he compressed his lips, and turned away
his head.

"Will you not ask her to be your wife
again, Hugh?"

"Never."

" She will make you happy."

" Impossible."

" Will you not seek her once again—just once ? "

" No !"

" Firm to the last, Hugh ! " murmured Stephen.

" For her sake as well as my own—for all our sakes," said Hugh, in the same low tones ; " she should have been my brother's wife, not mine. I stood in the way, and marred her life and yours. Better apart."

" You will be ever alone, my dear Hugh," said Stephen ; " there will never come a fair hour, a cheerful thought, to make your work light, or your home worthy of the name. And I had pictured such a home for you once ! "

" Ah ! don't speak of it," and Hugh's lip quivered.

" You will be——"

" Stephen," said Hugh, " you are distressing yourself unnecessarily—you are regarding a future that must be a mystery. Will you believe that I shall be happy in my way— neither grieving, desponding, nor misanthropical, but quietly happy, with a trust in myself that cannot deceive me? Will it be a consolation to know that the first shock is over, and day by day I am nearing recovery —that the world is even treating me with respect, and talking of me and my works, and that, in seeking a name, I shall forget her."

" She is unhappy too—you will think only of yourself! " replied his brother.

" She will be happy in good time—it is woman's nature to shake off a sorrow—if sorrow it could have been, that released her from me. My dear brother, is this a time to talk of her ? "

The door opened as he spoke, and Lucy, white and trembling, found her way to the bed-side, and fell sobbing there, with Stephen's arm resting lightly round her neck.

" You will live for our blind sister, Hugh, and take my place, and let her not miss me too much."

" I will do my best."

" I have nothing to bequeath you, Hugh, but my old cheerfulness of heart. If you would only but inherit it ! "

" I am not worthy of the blessing, Stephen."

" It is a gift that must die with me, then," sighed he; " where is my mother and father? —how long they are—in coming ! "

The father and mother were by their dying son at last, and he stretched both his hands towards them, saying—

" Good-bye. For all the past care and love, your child's best thanks ! "

" Oh ! my poor dear boy—the best of all of them !" sobbed Mrs. Speckland.

" No, no—you are unjust—the best son is there, to remain a blessing and a comfort to

you after I am gone.   Shall it not be so—
brother—Hugh?"

"Yes."

"That is a hearty promise—you will keep
it.   Remembering them a little more, you
will be a better man, old Hugh."

"With God's help."

"Now let me speak to Hugh again, Lucy.
Now, good-bye, sister—a blessing on your
future marriage—it will come, I feel it.
Hugh," he called.

"I am here," said a hoarse voice by his
side, and the stern brother took his hand and
held it tightly within his own.   Not stern, or
hard, or cruel then, but a child in his weak
efforts to conceal his grief.

"Oh! Stevie—Stevie—if *you* had only
stayed with me!   If God had only spared
you, I could have suffered and been strong."

The old—old wish was still troubling the
dying man.   He could not shake it off even

in that hour, or forget the one chance left to make that brother happy.

"Hugh," he said, "you love her still—I am not deceived. For the last time, I beg of you to seek her out—again : you will not say No—now."

"I must."

"It is my last wish."

"*No!* For it is a wish to cast a blight upon my life," Hugh added, after a painful silence—"to fill my own with suspicion and doubt—only think that, Stephen, and do not blame me. Ask me anything else—and I will fulfil it—God be my witness in this awful trial!"

"God be witness to a brighter day than this for you, old Hugh," said Stephen, in a tone more faintly still—"it is my earnest prayer. Now say good-bye, and let me die —thus!"

Hugh whispered his good-bye, and held his brother by the hand, and stooped and kissed him as he lay there, as though he were a little child.

And like a little child he calmly died, with Hugh's hand in his own—and there was mourning in the house of Speckland.

END OF PART THE FOURTH.

PART THE LAST.

VAIN EFFORTS.

CHAPTER I.

MRS. WESSINGER'S MANŒUVRES.

TIME waits for no man, and for no man's griefs. A dear friend, brother, hope, dies every day, and the world takes no heed of the units that drop off with each of its revolutions round the sun. There must be more sorrow than joy in that world too, to teach us of a higher, purer one, where all troubles cease—it is the lot of man to suffer, it is his duty to grow strong.

And Bessy Calverton, encouraged by the good example ever before her, had grown strong also, since the day she bade Stephen

Speckland farewell two years since.   In those two years there were no figures from the past to cross her path; she had mapped for herself a certain track, along which she journeyed, if not with much hope of earthly happiness, still with faith and resignation.   She did not complain that her life was passed with those much older than herself, who had outlived youth and most youthful thoughts, and were grave earnest people, to whom life was a religious duty. Bessy did not complain—had no reason to complain.   She was content with her life— still and even, and a little monotonous; and contentment in these latter days is something for which to be grateful.

Bessy looked older than her years warranted; she had lost much of her bright colour, her features had assumed a graver cast, her full dark eyes sparkled no more with the light thoughts at her heart.   She had bought her experience of human hopes at an early

age, and it had made her wiser, subdued her
spirit, taught her moderation. From the
first day of her acquaintance with Mr. Parslow, we have seen she had begun to change;
her natural disposition run wild, and yet
yearning for the good words and kind help
that might restrain it, had leaped readily
upwards; and now disappointment had tested
it and proved her strong, and the last two
years spent in more constant communion with
those whose lives were good and pure, had
finally moulded her character and ennobled it.

There was much to occupy her mind, and
she did not dwell on the past now. She had
applied herself more earnestly to the task
which Mary Davis had commenced; she
had seen many good results follow her efforts,
and they were incentives to persevere when
here and there her labours proved vain, and
for her love and interest were returned
nothing but selfishness and ingratitude. She
was the right hand of Mr. Parslow and Mary

Davis — she had youth and energy on her
side, and the only fear of her friends, as
she grew paler every day, was, that she would
overtask her strength and give way. But
Bessy Calverton persevered, and in the sick
room, in the homes where "poverty, hunger,
and dirt" held sway, in the schoolroom as
Sunday teacher, poor men, women and
children learned to love her.

The Reverend Jacob Parslow regarded his
protegée with a full heart—from the one step
in the right direction which he had indicated,
it was pleasant to trace the result, to see the
manifold good which had succeeded it. If
one false step—alas, too often!—carry the
weak and erring to the verge of the preci-
pice, it is worth remembering that one step
away from wrong may set the wanderer on
the deserted path, which, following earnestly,
may lead to heaven! There is no telling
what an evil word, falling on soil that nourishes
things evil, may result in; but God be

thanked, there is no guessing either the illimitable good which the one right word may
work in that strange mystery, the human
heart. It is well and encouraging to know
that midst the throng of wilful mortals seeking their own doom blindly, there pass them
working upwards to the light some hopeful,
trusting pilgrims, with confidence in the
glorious Hand that guides them on their
way.

During two long years Bessy had seen
nothing of her sister Lotty. Since the
break-up of the "El-Dorado" she had vanished in the crowd, might have even died,
Bessy thought sometimes, with never a friend
at her side, to give her comfort in her last
hour, or whisper hope to her. And thoughts
of Lotty troubled Bessy Calverton in times
that were not unfrequent; the uncertainty of
what had followed their last meeting would
often add to her depression. Were they
ever to meet again, now there was no danger

to be warned of? Was Lotty still reading
Mary Davis's bible, and striving against the
hard fate that kept her down—or had she
given up, and fallen to a lower depth. She
prayed not every night; but Lotty, as an
answer to her prayers, appeared not before
her.

From the Reverend Jacob Parslow she
heard now and then of the old love; he who
might have been married to her now, had the
adverse current not borne her away from
him! Mr. Parslow had not forgotten his
promise to Hugh's brother, and made a point
of calling now and then, in conformity
with it. Hugh received him with some
degree of courtesy, but the incumbent of St.
Owen's was never satisfied with the result of
his visit. There were times when he fancied his earnest words, his urgent appeals,
touched the man who silently worked and listened to him, and said nothing; but there
were times also when the nether millstone

might have been a fitting representative of
the state of that man's heart. Hugh would
talk of Stephen, of himself, of his father and
mother in the country, of the blind sister—to
whom, as Stephen's charge to him, he was
strangely kind and gentle — on only one
subject would he decline discussion; and
Mr. Parslow, knowing the pain to ensue
therefrom, seldom intruded it before
him. Hugh, Bessy learned, was no longer
living in Seymour Street, but rented furnished
apartments further west, where he was nearer
to the great publishing houses that required
his services. Bessy read of his name occasionally; and in books and papers that by
chance came to her hand the name of Hugh
Speckland beneath an engraving or an etching set her heart beating once or twice.
But she was glad he was well known and
gathering fame; he had been, to a certain extent, an ambitious man, and perhaps the name
he was making for himself had long rendered

him happy, and forgetful of her. She missed
Lucy Speckland more than she owned to the
kind friends with whom she lived, although
she knew that only pain could follow their
meeting. She could believe that Lucy had
not forgotten her, although they were divided
from each other, and never a word passed between them. She thought often of Lucy's long
engagement, and whether it would end like
hers in some distant day, despite the faith
that still existed in that Harry, who was so
long in coming for his blind betrothed; knowing human weakness·better now, and having
less belief in heroism, she feared the end of
Lucy Speckland's one romance was fast approaching. But there are exceptions to every
rule in life ; and though heroes are scarce
amongst the ranks of men, there are still one
or two to keep our trust alive. Bessy Calverton, whose hero proved but of common
stuff after all, may be not a fair judge in this
matter.

And, perhaps, we all have our heroes to set
on our pedestals, and make much of, till they
are tried in the furnace, or the pedestal
shivers, and the idol we have worshipped
topples down in the dust. Even Mrs. Wessinger had her hero ; and though a gentleman
of forty-two, with ill fitting habiliments, and
a wrinkled countenance, may be but a sorry
specimen, still there was something of the
self-denying hero in him, and there were many
worse judges of human excellence than Mrs.
Wessinger.

Good Mrs. Wessinger was still prosecuting
her one mysterious idea, although rather perplexed that it made but little progress. She
was only living to see that idea brought to
perfection, she said, to die happy and comfortable.

And the opportunity to still further develop it came one day suddenly and unex-
pectedly.

Mary Davis, Mrs. Wessinger and our

heroine, were together in the little drawing-room of St. Owen's Terrace one evening, and Bessy had just finished her usual custom of reading a chapter of the bible aloud after supper, when Mr. Parslow made his appearance.

"You'll excuse me intruding upon you at so late an hour, ladies," he said, "but I am the bearer of good news."

"And good news is always welcome," said Mrs. Wessinger; "sit down, my dear master, and let us be the first to hear it."

"To a certain extent it is good news," remarked Mr. Parslow when he was seated, and engaged in nervously buttoning and unbuttoning his shabby kid gloves, "although at present I am not so exhilarated or thoughtful as I might be. Dear me, what a great deal it requires to satisfy us. Here is a rise in life for Jacob Parslow, and Jacob ungrateful and inclined to feel morbid. Here is a snug living in a country town offered me by an old college friend, who has turned up in the most romantic manner—a nice little income of four hundred pounds a year waiting for me."

His auditors hastened to offer their congratulations, although more than one face was shadowed at the news.

" I don't know what makes me feel so dull about it," said he; " perhaps our council of four, that has lasted now these two years and a half, had its attractions, and to break it up suddenly gives me a little pain. And then all my old parishioners, whose ways I have grown accustomed to, and who are now accustomed to mine—it will be a struggle to part with them, notwithstanding my successor, whoever he may be, will do his duty by them as well as myself. But it does seem strange to give up St. Owen's."

" Ah! and all the old faces," remarked Mrs. Wessinger.

Mary Davis, who had been listening gravely to the news, looked up and said—

"Will it be long before you enter upon your new duties, Mr. Parslow?"

"I am expected almost immediately—the rectorship is now vacant, and the curate is doing all the duty.   Poor young man, I hear he complains a great deal, as if two services a day were enough to ruin any constitution ; he should be incumbent of St. Owen's for a little while.   And," turning to Mrs. Wessinger, " what was that which you said about all the old faces, my dear lady?"

"I said it seemed strange to give them all up."

" Yes—but, but—bless my soul, I must not be left entirely alone.   I have been so used to seeing you all, that I cannot part with every face for the sake of four hundred a year and a home in the country.   You at least, Mrs. Wessinger, I have set my heart upon having for a housekeeper again."

"My dear master !" cried she, leaping in her chair, and then sinking back again, and extinguishing suddenly the radiant expression of her countenance—" it is very kind of you, but—but I cannot leave Miss Davis. I am engaged till Christmas-twelvemonth as her companion, Mr. Parslow."

" Bless my soul," again repeated Mr. Parslow, in dismay.

" Mrs. Wessinger need not fear my——," began Mary ; and then she stopped, bewildered by an extraordinary pantomimic action on the part of Mrs. Wessinger, which being perfectly extempore, and the performer thereof out of practice, merely suggested the idea that Mrs. Wessinger had gone out of her mind.

" I am quite determined to stay in London," said Mrs. Wessinger, at last, " and I won't have any agreements cancelled, or anything. Don't say any more, Miss Davis, but leave me to explain to Mr. Parslow at another opportunity. Until Miss Davis is married, I shall not leave her—a poor little Welsh girl, as she is— to the mercies of the London ragamuffins."

" Married !" exclaimed Miss Davis, blushing and bewildered at this assertion ; " how very foolish you are to be sure, this evening, Mrs. W. ! "

Miss Davis had not expressed herself so petulently, or felt so much annoyed, since her peevish days at Aberogwin. As for the incumbent, what with the flat refusal of his old and faithful servant, and the after-comments with which she had accompanied it, the Reverend Jacob Parslow was too confused to give utterance to anything save the usual benediction on his soul and body.

" Many funny things happen there are no guessing at," she said ; " I shouldn't be surprised so very much myself. Why, you are not more than thirty I suppose—a sensible, marriageable age, when all the girl's nonsense is over, and one can judge wisely and well. Of course, I don't suppose you are going to be married to-morrow, Miss Davis."

Mr. Parslow here came to the rescue, and

contrived to turn the conversation into another channel, with something like effect. But it was a dull hour during which he stayed there and talked of his new living, and it was with a sense of relief that he rose to bid them adieu till the morning.

"I shall call to-morrow, Miss Davis," said he, "and talk a little more of the old pensioners I am about to commit to your charge. It is a subject that cannot be dismissed in a moment."

Leaving Mary Davis still somewhat confused, he went slowly along the narrow hall, preceded by Mrs. Wessinger. At the door he looked very gravely at his ancient housekeeper.

"Mrs. Wessinger, Mrs. Wessinger," he said, shaking his head at her reproachfully, "I can't make you out."

"Why not, sir?"

"I thought you would have been glad to be my housekeeper again—you are used to my ways, and could have studied my bachelor habits."

"And leave Miss Davis all alone, sir?"

"She will have Bessy—a more fitting companion for her than yourself."

"Bessy is not such a cheerful girl as she used to be," commented Mrs. Wessinger; "and Miss Davis will want rousing after *you're* gone."

"Rousing, eh?—why rousing?"

"Do you think everybody can bear a parting as stoically as yourself, sir. It isn't everybody that's made of iron, and has no nerves, and can go away for ever, as if it were for only next week."

"Why, you don't mean to try and persuade me that—that Miss Davis is likely to miss me—eh?"

"Oh! but I do," said Mrs. Wessinger, heartily.

"Bless my soul and body, if you weren't a truthful woman, I should think you were hoaxing me almost," said he; "I—I—good evening to you."

"You won't think any more of a poor old soul like me for a housekeeper, Master Parslow?"

"I shall think of that amongst other things with which you have disturbed me this evening, Mrs. W.," said he.

"You should think of being happy, sir, in your new home—of taking a wife for a companion now—I'm sure you're not a bit too young."

"I'll wish you a good evening, Mrs. Wessinger," cried the scared incumbent. "A good evening to you!"

And the Reverend Jacob Parslow, after being shut out in the street, went slowly down the steps, and paused at the bottom one, and nibbled at the finger ends of one of his gloves as usual.

"A most remarkable woman," mused he, half aloud; "if I had not known her so well and so long, I should have certainly fancied she had been drinking this evening."

He moved on at a slow rate of progression, and turned up his own steps at a few paces distant, and halted on the top one, and thought of Mrs. Wessinger's eccentric behaviour again.

" She's generally a sensible woman," thought he ; " she must mean something. She always means something."

He opened the door with his latch-key after this second soliloquy, and repaired to his room, lighted his table lamp, adjusted the reflector, and sat himself down to compose one of his sermons for next Sunday, now a leisure hour presented itself. A nice night for composition, with St. Owen's more quiet than usual, and a less number of carts rumbling about the streets, and no boys whooping to and fro, and clattering up and down the steps, and giving runaway knocks. His MS. paper was beneath his hand, the pen was between his fingers, his little reference bible was handy for a text, the light shone on his thoughtful, amiable face as he stooped over his purposed work; a scratch or two with his pen, then he set it aside, and looked round his lonely room, and thought of " that remarkable woman's " eccentric behaviour. " It is not everybody that can go away for ever, as if it were for only next week." A strange remark, that indirectly accused him of a want of feeling, as if *he* could leave them all, and not be affected by the separation! " Think of taking a wife for a companion now, sir." A wife! He who was going on for forty-three, and growing older every day —why, whom could he take for a wife?— who would care for him or understand his old-fashioned ways? Years ago it might have been different; when he was a very young man he fell in love and was jilted. That was his time to think of a wife, and he had let it escape him. And yet, now he came to consider it, that was *not* the time; for his father was ruined after that, and he had become the incumbent of a poor parish, with an income of a hundred and forty or fifty pounds per annum—what an income for a wife, and what a home for her! She would have never been happy, unless she had been a quiet, religious woman, with strength to bear adversity bravely—just such a woman as Mary Davis, in fact.

Ah! she was a good little woman that Mary Davis; the only one he had known in his life-time who united to much sound common sense, an abnegation of self that was out of the common. A good woman, who gave nearly all she had to the poor, and lived for them and their sorrows—what a wife for a clergyman!—what a helpmate and a companion in his labours! And that remarkable woman who had come out so that particular evening—he could think of no words more expressive than " come out " just at that moment—had talked in the most natural manner of Miss Davis marrying some day in the future, quite as a matter of course!

The Reverend Jacob Parslow did not succeed very well with his theological studies that night; he bundled his manuscript and pens out of the way, and left his seat at the table, and took to pacing up and down the room, with a slow regular tramp, that worried his landlady almost to death in the room underneath.

He arrived at the determination that it was all very foolish speculation, however, and went to bed confirmed in that opinion, and woke up and seasoned his breakfast with it, and went early next day to Miss Davis's to sketch that little plan concerning his parishioners which he had spoken of last night.

He did not know how it was, but Mrs. Wessinger required Bessy's company very particularly in the upstairs room that morning, and he was left to discuss his plans, and

talk of going away with Mary Davis all
alone! And then Mary Davis, it struck him,
looked paler and more sad than usual, a fact
which necessarily led to inquiries about her
health, and then—and then—the Reverend
Jacob Parslow, in a moment of excitement,
in a formal, but in a tender gentlemanly way
for all that, offered his hand and heart to the
little Methodist, and was accepted, after
much blushing and a great deal of emotion.

"And we four shall not be separated, after
all," said Mr. Parslow at a later hour, when
Mrs. Wessinger and Bessy were in the room,
and he had, to the surprise of one, at
least, stated the overtures he had made to
Mary Davis; "for we shall require a housekeeper in the country, and Bessy Calverton
will not be too proud to live with her cousin
Mary till we can find a good husband for
her?"

Bessy murmured that he was very kind,
and the tears swam in her eyes to think of

the good friends she had gathered round her, and of all their kind offers. She did not know then how near she was to another change from all this—she whose life had been made up of changes.

CHAPTER II.

"SHOULD AULD ACQUAINTANCE BE FORGOT?"

"IT was all my own idea, Bessy, my child," said Mrs. Wessinger, confidentially, the evening of the same day. "I can say now, 'it's my doing,' as I prophesied when I first saw them together."

"Did you think of such a marriage all that while ago, Mrs. Wessinger?" asked Bessy.

"Ay, my child, I did," was the reply; "when I saw Mary Davis for the first time, heard her talk, saw her anxiety to do good, I said, 'That's my dear master's wife some day.' She talks and thinks like him, and he's

about the only man that's fit for her. It's all
come true; and what a happy couple they'll
make, Bessy—the happiest under the sun,
I'm sure of that! To think I should live to
find a wife for that dear young master of
mine, after these many years!"

Mrs. Wessinger took all the credit to herself, and perhaps Mrs. Wessinger was right.
Since she had been in Mary Davis's service she
had spent her leisure time in eulogizing her
" young master;" talking of his many virtues,
relating all those anecdotes in his life that
had ennobled it, and which he had had too
much modesty to allude to himself; and
Miss Davis had listened, till Mr. Parslow
had become her hero as well as Mrs. Wessinger's.

And now it was all settled, and they were
to be married in a fortnight; two who understood each other so well, and had been friends
so long, did not require a formal engagement after having once made up their minds.

It was a busy fortnight, and Bessy and Mrs. Wessinger found their own labours almost doubled, now Mr. Parslow and Mary were thinking a little of themselves for a change, and speculating in furniture, to be sent down in advance to the rectory. So love, with even the best and most disinterested, will interfere with " good works."

The engagement was a week old, when Bessy was returning late at night from a long round of visits to the sick and infirm of St. Owen's, Whitechapel. She was returning home somewhat dull, for she had had the painful task of breaking the news of Mr. Parslow's departure; and not all the assurance of the virtues of his successor seemed to comfort those who had known and looked up to Mr. Parslow for the last four years. They had grown used to his ways, been sustained by his ministry, and it would be hard to part with him.

Bessy was thinking of the ill news she had

diffused that day; and there was mingling
with her thoughts the new country life before her, which she fancied she should not
like so much as life in St. Owen's, Whitechapel. Add to this, that she was reflecting
also on the nature of her position in the future, and thinking if it were not possible to
be her own mistress, and less dependent on
Mr. Parslow's kindness—and it may be imagined that her mind was fully occupied.
Therefore, it was not until she was within a
dozen yards of her home that she became
aware of some one crouched upon the door-
steps—some one whose sex it was difficult
to distinguish, so dark was the night, and
so huddled was the figure against the area
railings.

Bessy was somewhat surprised at the appearance of a beggar or a wanderer at so late
an hour, till the idea that it might be
Lotty returned to see her after so long an
absence, dismissed all the old thoughts, and

brought a train of new ones in their stead.
And yet Lotty in that place, at that hour, in
that strange huddled position, betokened a
fall lower still from all that was right, and
honest and womanly. If it were not Lotty
she would feel relieved, however much her
heart might yearn to see her sister.

And she drew a long breath of relief
when she stood before the figure, and saw
it was that of a man who, with his hat battered, as it were, over his eyes, had fallen
asleep from sheer fatigue on the doorstep.
Bessy touched him lightly on the arm, and
he sprang to his feet with an alacrity that was
too much for his strength, for he clutched
at the iron railings to keep himself from
falling.

"Have you no home, my poor man, that
you sit here at so late an hour?"

"No home—starving!"

"Starving!" exclaimed Bessy; "will you
wait a moment, please?"

She had one little foot upon the steps, when he stretched forth a long claw-like hand, and caught her by the mantle.

" You live here, then ? "

" Yes."

" You are Bessy Calverton ? "

" I am.   Why do you ask ? "

Bessy felt her blood icing in her veins. The voice was not new to her; the figure seemed to develop itself in the darkness to that of one from whom she had fled years ago, and from whom she had believed herself for ever free.

" Because you may help me; are the only one that can help me, and without you I must die here in the streets.   Don't scream —you know me now !"

He pushed back his disreputable hat, and disclosed the face of Richard Calverton—a face that had altered so much, was so pinched and ghastly, that it might have been his ghost's, and looked no more unnatural.

" You are Richard Calverton—my father ?"

" Ay, your father—don't say the name, for God's sake, or I shall be carried back to gaol, and killed by extra work and chains to my leg.   I'm not here to harm you now—all that's gone and past; and I *am* your father, girl, and starving in the streets."

" Oh, this is awful ! " cried poor Bessy.

" Walk with me a little way up and down here.   I have been waiting for you the last two hours."

Bessy hesitated.

" You needn't be afraid of me now," said he, with a harsh laugh, that Bessy well remembered.   " My life's in your hands, and a word of yours can send me back to the Bermudas.   See how a father trusts his child in such a moment as this."

Bessy trusted him, and he passed his arm through hers, to support himself as he walked. And, cruel as had been his conduct towards her, and close as she had been to the wreck by his own guilty acts, she felt for the first time in her life that he was her father, when he needed the support of her arm along the streets that night.

"It is strange that you should come to me," said Bessy, as they walked slowly on.

"Whom else could I come to, Bessy?" said he, in a half churlish manner, and a half whimper; "who else wouldn't have fastened on me like a blood-hound, and sold me for the reward that's on my head? I've been a long while making up my mind to come to you; I didn't know if I could even trust you—I don't know now."

He was looking eagerly into her face, and Bessy answered—

"You may trust me."

"That's spoken like my own child," said he; "it was a toss up whether you would help me, or turn against me, and pay me out for old scores—and I chanced it. Why, I had nothing else to chance," he said, betraying his hand more to Bessy, although she was too agitated to detect the utter selfishness that lurked in the remark; "it was a last hope to come to you, when I was dying of want, and next to death's door. And that wife of mine has all my money, and I can't go and ask for it, lest some devil or other should make a grab at me."

"Hush—hush!"

"Bessy, you must help me in some way or other. You have got a little money—have you not?"

"A little."

"You're a good daughter—I'm sorry now I treated you so ill. Upon my soul, I am!" he answered.

"How did you escape?" asked Bessy.

"I was driven to it by hard usage—they treated me like a dog, Bessy. They worked me to death in those cursed Bermudas all day, and sent me on board ship all night to sleep, where I caught a fever—two fevers—

and was worked as hard as ever before I was well again, and brought to skin and bone. You should see the arm a Christian government has left me—it's a splinter, that a baby could snap in two," he added.

" But you are sorry—you *are* really sorry for all the guilty past, father ? " asked Bessy, anxiously ; " you have come back to tell me that, I hope ? "

" Oh ! yes—I'm sorry," he responded, with alacrity — " and so awfully hungry, too. What's to be done with me, Bessy ? "

" I am thinking."

" That's a good girl," he said—" think away your hardest."

They had turned by this time, and were retracing their way down the street.

" Are you known to be in London ? " Bessy asked.

" No—I think not. They're," with a childish laugh, " all in the fog about me. Three of us escaped one day—poor old Bob

Jones was shot at, and hit—clean through the head—such a mess! Jack and I ran for it, different ways—Jack was caught, and I hung about the woods for a time, and found a friend, who put me on board a ship where they were not too particular; and, after a hundred shifts and chances, here I am. What's to be done with me, now my life's in your hands."

"Here is money—all I have," said Bessy, thrusting it into his hands; "that will at least save you from starving for a time, should we not meet again just yet."

"Where are you going?"

"To ask of those who love me, and are, perhaps, becoming anxious about me, what is to be done."

"They'll transport me, sure as a gun. My dear daughter Bessy, you'll never tell them you have met me to-night?"

"They will not harm you, father. For my sake, I am assured that they will keep your secret."

" Parslow is one of them."

" Yes—how do you know that? How have you been able to discover me?"

" It's another long story," grumbled the father " I went to that place in Seymour Street first, and then to the West End, and all to no purpose—for *he* was a single man, living with a blind sister, I heard. Then I thought of the parson, and came crawling back to Whitechapel, and heard that he was going to be married to a Miss Davis—all the parish knows that—and that Miss Davis had a Miss Calverton living with her. That's all—I'm dead beat with so much talk on an empty stomach, girl. And now—are you going to trust Mary Davis and the parson with your father's life? For mercy's sake just think again, girl, before you do anything rash. They'll be glad enough to get rid of me, at any cost, remember."

" Tell me that you honestly repent the past life?"

" On my honour," affirmed the veracious Richard Calverton.

And Bessy, who was anxious to believe, felt her heart thrill at his assertion.   To have honestly repented of all the past sins, and to be striving to amend in the future—what a hope for him even at the last !

" You may trust my friends," said Bessy ; " will you wait here till my return ?"

" Ay—somewhere here."

Bessy withdrew her hand from his arm, and ran back lightly towards St. Owen's Terrace, whilst he remained at the corner of the street watching her.   Were there any pangs of conscience, as he watched, for all that guilty past he feigned to deplore ; any regrets concerning the evil into which he had thrust that daughter, now returning good for it, and striving for him, and interested in his safety ?   It is doubtful !—the nature of Richard Calverton was iron, and the true feelings—if he possessed any—difficult to move; and in his whole career he had thought of nothing, cared for nothing, but himself. Even then, with Bessy's money in his hand, with Bessy's words vibrating in his ears, he did not seem to be thinking of her much, for he muttered "I'll chance it," as if he had been calculating the pros and cons respecting his own safety after his daughter had communicated to those who could bear him no love, the startling fact that he was once more in England.

Yes, he would chance it. He removed himself from the lamp-post against which he had been leaning, crossed the road, and walked slowly up and down the street. At the corner of the opposite street there was a policeman standing, and his presence there gave him a turn and brought his heart to his throat, although his nerve carried him past that guardian of the peace in the Whitechapel district. The policeman did not regard him suspiciously, however—rags and feebleness were not scarce in that neighbourhood, and as sorry figures as Richard Calverton flitted to and fro all night and day, creatures of evil omen.

Calverton took a *detour* round a back street and purchased a loaf at a baker's, and was eating it ravenously when he came in sight of St. Owen's Terrace again. The policeman had gone on his way by that time, and he was left alone in the dark streets, with a drizzling rain setting in, that would soon soak him through. What a time they were to be sure! —did it augur ill or well that they should be such a long time, knowing how poor and helpless he was? Why don't they give him shelter, and not leave him standing out there; they ought to know as well as he that he dare not show himself at any of his old haunts, lest the love of gain should tempt his friends of " auld lang syne " to sell him.

The door was opening at last—he would have thanked God if he had thought of it !—

and Bessy and another female were descending the steps. That looked well; he would not have cared to see the parson just then— he had always hated parsons awfully! Bessy's companion was thin and gaunt, and a person whom he had never seen—well, he must trust in strangers, he supposed, especially when strangers carried a basket that might contain some cold meat and a bottle of beer perhaps—and a little brandy. He hoped to God—he suddenly thought of his devotions then — that there was some brandy in that basket!

They crossed the road towards him, and for security's sake he turned into a narrow street that led to a wilderness of streets, and courts, and alleys, where all classes lived and tried to live. Bessy and the woman followed him, came up to him, when he stopped and looked curiously at Bessy's companion, and flinched a little from the steady gaze directed towards him.

"You're Richard Calverton then?" asked Mrs. Wessinger, abruptly.

"Yes."

"You've broken the laws of your country and defied them, and come back here and expect friendship from us," said she; "well, are you a better man?"

"I hope so," muttered Calverton.

"Ah! it's as well to be doubtful," said Mrs. Wessinger. "Here, take this basket— you'll find some food and drink there."

"Where's the parson—he knows I am here?"

"Yes, and was at first anxious to see you. I stopped that."

"You?" said Calverton.

"Do you think I would let a good man risk his name, and get into disgrace for aiding and abetting a man to escape the punishment he deserves? Do you think my young master was to lose all chances in life— however much he might feel for Bessy's distress—by such an action?"

"Bessy," said Calverton, regarding Mrs. Wessinger, with no small alarm, "who is this —good person?"

"I'm Mrs. Wessinger, once of Seymour Street, whose house you watched when you wanted Bessy back; I've been Bessy's friend from that time—I mean to keep so."

"You're very good."

"Ah! that's more than you are," returned the plain-spoken old lady; "although Bessy thinks you may be some day. If there's a chance of that I shall not be sorry to have helped you, Richard Calverton, and have run the risk of being transported in my old age, perhaps, with this rash daughter of yours, who has been weak enough to be touched by your—repentance! She calls it repentance, mind."

"It's a kind of repentance," explained Richard Calverton, who thought the old lady before him not to be easily impressed; "I can't say that I feel much the better for it yet."

"Well, that's not a bad sign," said Mrs. Wessinger; "and now, do you want me to find you a safe place to sleep, or will you trust to your own discretion?"

"I'm afraid of the lodging-houses—there are too many people that I know in London."

"Come with me, then—Bessy, bid your father good-night."

"What is she going away for?"

"Because she is better at home—and must not risk too much. Because she has promised to be guided by her friends, if we take this matter up. Because," she touched Calverton's arm, "we cannot trust you yet."

"Well," said Calverton, with a sigh, "why should I be trusted?"

"If you have any love for your daughter, any regret for the evil you have caused, and the further evil you might have caused, you may come and bid her good-bye to-morrow night at nine, before you go away for good."

"Where am I to go?" asked Calverton.

"We may talk that over to-morrow—Bessy, I and you. Think of your plans, and we may try to aid them. You'll see no one else, you understand."

"The fewer the better."

Bessy bade her father good-night, and held her hand towards him. Calverton did not perceive the movement till Mrs. Wessinger said—

"Your daughter wishes to shake hands with you—sign of a better trust in her, which you will not abuse."

Calverton placed his attenuated hand in hers, and wrung it with some warmth.

"Good night, my girl. For all your kindness, many thanks. Good night."

Bessy watched her father walk feebly along by the side of Mrs. Wessinger, and whispered a prayer after them, that the first sign of a great change in him whom she had feared throughout her life might not grow less with time.

"Whereabouts are you going to take me, Mrs. Wesleyan?" inquired Calverton.

"Only a few doors down the next street," was the reply; "can't you walk faster?"

"I'm eaten up with rheumatism."

"Take hold of my arm, then," said Mrs. Wessinger. "Good Lord!" she added, in a lower tone; "to be walking about Whitechapel arm in arm with a housebreaker."

Dick Calverton's quick ears caught the words, and resented them.

"I never broke into a house in my life; I never raised my hand against a fellow-creature; I was an honest man, except for one little mistake, in minding a parcel for a friend."

"Ah! we all make our little mistakes," said Mrs. Wessinger, drily; "will you take care and not make a mistake of the instructions I am going to give you?"

"Trust me."

"The little house I am about to take you

to belongs to a poor workman at a factory, who leaves at five in the morning, and is seldom home before nine at night. His wife is busy all day at her own work of weaving, and attending to a bed-ridden father in the front room. The wife is from the country, and cannot recognize you—the workman and father you are not likely to see. They have a room to let, and I am going to hire it for one night."

" It seems all safe. Do they know Bessy ?"

" She comes and reads the bible to the father sometimes."

" Ah ! that's awkward."

" Why—she is not coming to see you?"

" No," said Calverton, after a pause ; " but the name is strange, and there may be a likeness !"

" Not the slightest," cried Mrs. Wessinger, indignantly.

" If anything should happen, I am Mr. Richards, then."

" And a gentleman from foreign parts," added Mrs. Wessinger.

Richard Calverton thought there was a great deal of humour in Mrs. Wessinger; even had an idea that that estimable lady was a trifle unfeeling, considering his position, his misfortunes, and the grinding pains that were driving him mad. And Mrs. Wessinger at that moment had not a great deal of sympathy for the *ci-devant* honest Dick ; she was a woman of the world, and read human nature correctly. She had her own suspicions of the true state of mind of Mr. Calverton, and believed that had there been another friend in the world to aid him and give him money, no fatherly affection would have brought him to his daughter's side. And she hinted that fact pretty plainly, after she had prepared the way for the reception of Richard Calverton as a lodger, and she and that gentleman were standing in the passage of the house of refuge.

" With a wife, brother, and another daughter living, and with fifty old friends to lay your hand upon, you find only one poor girl to trust in at this time. Be thankful that she is left you, man—that she has been spared to return you good for evil— that in her dear young heart there is still some affection, of which you are not worthy yet. Try and think of that to-night—if you ever prayed, man, in your wasted life, try and pray to-night, and remember that one friend in your prayers as she will you."

Mrs. Wessinger spoke warmly, and he cowered before her, as the shadow of things evil must cower before the light and force of truth. Mrs. Wessinger puzzled him, and set him thinking till his head ached. She might have even touched him for a moment, till astonishment got the better of his feelings, as he pondered it all over in the back bed-room which she had procured for him. It was not a very elegant remark which he gave utterance to, over his cold meat, with the door locked against intruders, but it expressed his astonishment pretty clearly.

"She IS a rum 'un!"

CHAPTER III.

"THE DEVIL A SAINT WOULD BE."

THE following evening the inhabitants of the little house in St. Owen's Terrace, together with the incumbent of St. Owen's church, waited, with no little anxiety, for the hour of nine to strike. He who had suddenly intruded upon so much of quiet happiness, had been the subject of considerable discussion that day. What was to become of him?—when would he rid them of his presence, and relieve them from that sense of responsibility, even of danger, which his stay in that neighbourhood engendered? Bessy alone had not these

thoughts, for she was not fearful for her
future ; she could only think of the sick
father, who had suddenly emerged into the
every-day world again—of the change that
was in his appearance—of the greater change
which she believed was working in his heart.
Had he returned with the old brutal scowl,
the harsh threat, the threatening gesture,
she would have turned to her friends for
shelter—or, strong in her innocence and
maturer years, have resisted him, and bade
him go his way ; but to come back weak and
helpless, and to throw himself upon her love
and charity, was to affect her sensibly. After
all, he was her father; and a child's duty was
to befriend him when he needed help, and
trusted in her to bestow it. In her belief of
his repentance, she could look forward to the
time when he would return again some day, a
wiser, better man than last night ; or write
to her from a foreign land, and ask her to
join him in some little home he had created

for his latter days—a home where God's
word should not be excluded, and the
darkness of the "El Dorado" never again
existent. It was a strange scene to draw, a
strange future to almost look forward to, as to
the crowning happiness of her life.

The clock struck nine at last, and no Richard
Calverton. The room in which the interview
was to take place remained still empty, and
Mr. Parslow, whom Mrs. Wessinger and Mary
Davis would not have connected with the
secret for an instant, had retired to his lodg-
ings in vain. Half-past nine—the pendulum
of the little time-piece on the mantelshelf
slicing its inroads into another half-hour, and
no sign of him they had met yesternight.
Mr. Parslow had promised to return at ten,
and hear those particulars concerning which
he was extremely anxious, and in due course
Mr. Parslow and a little boy with a note came
up the steps of Mary Davis's house at the
same time.

Mrs. Wessinger was putting her bonnet and shawl on to go round in search of Mr. Richards, when the note arrived. A consultation was held at once in the front parlour, and the note, which was addressed to Bessy, delivered to our heroine.

Bessy hastily opened it, and read the lines aloud :—

"Dear Miss Calverton.   Very ill.
                              "RICHARDS."

"Humph! not too ill to have his wits about him," remarked Mrs. Wessinger.   But Bessy had sprung to her feet with pallid features.   He was very ill—he was her father, and alone in the world—her duty was plain enough, and she did not flinch from it.

"I will go to him at once!" she cried.

"My dear Bessy, do let us consider a minute," said her cousin Mary.

"I must not forget whose child I am, at such a time," said Bessy, with excitement; "and forget what power there may be to bring him to repentance."

" My dear child," said Mrs. Wessinger, " you have been always ready to act upon the instant. It is not wise—it is not proper. I appeal to Mr. Parslow."

Mr. Parslow was deep in thought, and attentively regarding Mary Davis's carpet.

" It confuses matters somewhat," he said, thus appealed to ; " and Bessy is young and inexperienced—and he—well, well—he is ill now, and it is extremely hard to advise."

" I'll run round and see first if he is very ill," said Mrs. Wessinger. " Bessy, you'll excuse me, child, but I cannot trust your father yet."

Bessy sighed. Could she trust him herself?

Mary Davis and Mr. Parslow, approving of this suggestion, Bessy was forced to curb her impatience, and allow Mrs. Wessinger to depart on her mission. It seemed a long while before she returned, with so moody an expression on her countenance, that the general idea that Richard Calverton had robbed the house and decamped immediately suggested itself.

"Is he not ill?" asked Bessy.

"He's ill enough—yes, its truth. And he's lying on his back there, groaning and calling for you and a doctor, and thinking he shall not live till the morning! Awfully bad sure enough he looks. I suppose you must go, Bessy."

"Unless Bessy be afraid," said Mary Davis; "she must not risk her health and strength for him who morally can have no claim upon her. If she have any fear—"

"I have only a fear that I may not be of use to him—of service to that God, who has perhaps brought him here to die."

"Not to die—we won't think so badly as that, Bessy," said Mr. Parslow.

"Mayn't it be the best thing that can happen?" whispered Mrs. Wessinger.

" Hush—it may be. God's will be done, Mrs. Wessinger—we cannot oppose it."

Bessy made a hurried inquiry concerning a doctor, which was responded to by Mrs. Wessinger, who had already sent for one; and then she was hurrying, a messenger of love and charity, to the house in which her father lay ill.

She found Richard Calverton tossing to and fro in his bed, and replying to the numerous questions of a tall slim gentleman in green spectacles.

' Ah! Miss Calverton," said the father, his face lighting up at Bessy's approach, "this is kind of you. You know Miss Calverton, doctor?"

"I have heard of her very frequently," said the doctor with a bow; "her name is a household word in this parish, Mr. Richards."

"Ah! she's a good young woman, by all accounts. Always ready to help the sick and the unfortunate. Oh! Lord, doctor, will you ever be able to get rid of this *screwing* pain?"

"I hope so."

"Make haste with the stuff, if it is to do me any good!" he groaned.

Bessy followed the doctor from the room, and asked if the sufferer were in any danger.

"I do not anticipate any danger," said the doctor; "he will require a patient and careful watcher, that is all. It is possible that he will be delirious to-night; give him the composing draught very regularly, Miss Calverton. Good morning."

When Bessy re-entered the room her father was sitting up in bed nursing his knees, and rocking himself to and fro.

"What does he say, Bessy?—wilful murder?" he asked, eagerly.

"He says there is no danger to be anticipated."

"What did he look so serious about, and frighten me out of my life for, then?" he said. "Does he think a man burning alive and touched up with red-hot irons is strong enough to lie and bear it? Bessy, I'm going to die—I'm sure I am going to die, with all my sins thick upon my head, and all the imps of darkness sitting round my bed, waiting for a scramble after my soul. Don't leave me!"

"I will stay with you to-night."

"There's a good girl," he said, lying back in his bed, and beginning to toss to and fro once more; "you'll be a comfort to me yet, and be rewarded for it in another world—oh, this screwing! It's like that damned complaint I caught in the mountains years ago, when I first met you, girl. And it's a judgment!—and—don't leave me!" he cried again, and it required a reiteration of Bessy's intention to remain that night to satisfy him.

Richard Calverton, really ill for the first time in his life, was a coward. He had boasted too much of his strength, and been too much a bully, not to give up all at once when laid low and left helpless. He was not grievously ill, but his excited imagination saw the grim king of terrors at his bedside, and the sands in the hour-glass running low. Better to have stopped in the Bermudas and worked his time out, than have fought his way by sea and land to die like a dog down a back street in Whitechapel. It was his usual luck. He had thought once upon a time, when he did come to die, that he should die like a Swell in the state bedroom of his little shooting-box down in the country somewhere —and look at him now! Why, he might not even die peaceably, if his secret once escaped that stifling sick chamber.

When the night grew late he became delirious in his sleep, as the doctor had prophesied, and raved of old times at the " El-Dorado," and counted his gains, and wrangled over his share of the spoil in that back parlour, wherein he and " his school" used to lock themselves.

When he broke from his troubled dreams, he gave the old cry of " Don't leave me, Bessy !" and required his daughter's assurance once more repeated before he closed his eyes and re-commenced raving.

Mrs. Wessinger called at a late hour to hear what arrangements had been decided upon, and found Bessy firm in her intention of nursing her father, and resolved to sit up all night with him, and have no one to share her watch.

" He is my father," was her reply ; " he will learn to love me now. He will submit himself to my teaching, and let me read the bible to him, and learn a lesson therefrom. Can I have a task before me that can give me greater satisfaction, Mrs. Wessinger ?"

" No," replied Mrs. Wessinger, gazing ruefully at the future penitent, who at that moment was swearing his hardest, and knocking an imaginary Charles Edwin Calverton—to whom he was a little indebted—from one side of the " El-Dorado " to another.

So Bessy kept her place by her father's side, and nursed him from day to day, till he was able to sit up, and be reasoned with and read to. And Richard Calverton took Bessy's reasonings and readings in much the same manner as he took his medicine— with a wry face, and a distaste for that which he thought might be good for him. He had a vague dreamy idea that all this bible reading would work some miracle in his favour, and that Bessy would never leave him again so long as he said he was sorry for the past, and intended to live honestly and soberly if he were spared.

In his peculiar position he felt himself entirely dependent upon his daughter; she had friends who had money to give her, and he had altered sufficiently to find Bessy good company. Nay, when he began to think of Bessy's sacrifices for him, of the willingness and cheerfulness with which she had come to his side in her trouble, he was a little grateful. He felt it threw a new light on Bessy's character, but it did not teach him to be a better man. When he was stronger he did not say, " Go back to your friends, and leave me to fight my own battle ; do not link your life with that which may mar it for ever ;" he simply preyed on Bessy's feelings, and feigned to be rapidly improving in his morals; and, to interest her more in his unworthy self, he even made an effort once or twice to struggle through a chapter or two of that bible which Bessy was always putting in his way.

And Bessy's natural shrewdness of perception was deceived, inasmuch as she was anxious to deceive herself, and believe that her father was repenting of all his past sins. She had felt a void in her heart for a long, long while now—and her's was a loving nature, which required love in return. The affection that her friends in St. Owen's Terrace bore her was not the affection that she craved — and here was a tie, that should have been naturally the strongest, forming for the first time between her father and her. Could she sever it of her own free will, when such a chance to do God's work was offered her?—was it natural or right? He was in trouble, poor, afflicted and disgraced—let her bear all with him, and be a comfort to him in his declining years.

Praiseworthy were these intentions, though misplaced on their object; who, however, did his best to encourage her in them, not by pressing her too much on the point, but by showing her how useful she was to him, and how he looked to her for everything. He was weak still; he did not believe he should ever regain his old strength—and who was to take care of him if Bessy forsook him? He could not even seek relief at the workhouse without owning his parish, and giving his real name and address—and then, hey for the Bermudas and that accursed convict-ship, which had laid the groundwork of all his complaints!

Bessy resolved to live with him, and work for him. Well known in the parish now, and clever with her needle, she had little fear of not obtaining sufficient work, until such time as another plan could be resolved on. Her father had the idea of a little shop in a quiet neighbourhood, where Bessy could serve the customers, and he could lie snugly out of harm's way in the back parlour, and smoke his pipe, and read his paper, until the night came, when she and he could go for a little walk.

"He should not trouble any one a great while longer," he said, when delicately hinting his suggestions for the future; "if his daughter, whom he loved, could only stay with him, keep him good, be at his side to close his eyes when it pleased the Lord to take him—that was all he wished!"

Bessy felt at times that all was not true in his speech, and that her father thought more of his own comfort than hers; but they were early times yet, and she trusted to see with every day an improvement. She communicated her wishes, her intentions, to her old friends the night before the marriage of Mr. Parslow with her cousin; and they listened sorrowfully, although they knew not what to suggest for a plan that was better. They had all great faith in Bessy Calverton, and were good Christians, whose hearts warmed at the thought of one sinner coming unto repentance. They might have their doubts of Richard Calverton's sincerity, but still there was a probability of Bessy's influence working the great change—for Bessy had energy and power, and her heart in the cause.

"Well, Bessy," said Mr. Parslow, "I am sure you would like our consent to your plans, but there is one condition attached to it."

" And that ? " inquired Bessy.

" Is, that you take from me and my dear future partner in life, a loan of thirty pounds to begin with. We must not have you working yourself to death for him, and marring the good effort; we must see you in some little business—in the country, if possible—that will bring in sufficient profit to keep you both. And pay back the loan too, of course," added he, seeing that she hesitated.

" You are very kind, sir. Oh! my dear Mr. Parslow, shall I ever be able to repay you all your kindness and thoughtfulness? I have been indebted to you all my life."

" My little kindness has been long repaid by your confidence in me—by a daughter's, or a sister's love. Which shall we say ?"

" A sister's, to be sure," added Mary Davis, who objected to her future lord and husband being made older than he really was.

" So it is settled," said Mr. Parslow, with a sigh that he could not repress   " I hope it is for the best.   I'll go round to your father to-day."

"No!" said Bessy, firmly ; "the share of the danger in screening him from justice belongs to me now.   Mrs. Wessinger has been right in keeping you from meeting him. Whatever happens, the minister of St. Owen's name must not be coupled with our illegal acts."

"But the minister of St. Owen's knows all about it, and is legally blamable for withholding his knowledge," said Mr. Parslow.

"But there is no one to blame you," said Mrs. Wessinger ; "and there is some one to think of now, besides yourself, sir."

"To be sure," with his face brightening, as he turned to Mary Davis.

"And although that some one appreciates your good intention, she objects to your running into danger," added Mary.

"Thank you, Mary—thank you !" said the incumbent.

But though Mary Davis objected to the danger to which Mr. Parslow might expose himself, she took the trouble that evening to excuse her absence for a little while, and surprise Mr. Calverton and daughter — for Bessy was again at her father's side—by her appearance before them.

"I have come, Richard Calverton," she said, "to make sure that you appreciate the trust we place in you, by leaving this innocent girl behind us."

"Mary Davis may trust me," he said, making a faint effort to rise, and sinking back in his chair again; "times have altered, and I have altered with them."

"For the better?"

"Yes. I," with a little snort that might have been intended for an appreciation of his own remark, "could not very well have altered for the worse!"

"You read your bible now," with a glance at the book that lay on his lap.

" Yes—a little, Miss," was the humble answer.

" The study of it will make you a good father and a faithful friend. Be that to my dear cousin Bessy, sir."

" I will," responded the father; and Mary left him with more confidence in Bessy Calverton's future, despite the dark turn it might take at any instant.

" You will come to my quiet wedding to-morrow, Bessy ?" said Mary Davis ; " I must see my old friend, the little girl I loved at Aberogwin, at St. Owen's."

" Yes, I will be there to offer you my wishes for a long, long life of happiness with the worthy man you have chosen for a husband."

" Ah !" sighed Mary, " he is too good for me. If my poor father were only living now !"

" He would be a little surprised at your change of religious opinion," said Bessy, with an arch look at Mary.

"Religious opinion is one thing and true religion another," said Mary, sententiously; "does it matter of what sect we are, if we love God and keep his commandments?"

"Ah! you belong to Broad-Church now!" said Bessy.

"Yes—I hope so!" and Mary Davis went home thoughtfully, to think of it.

Bessy Calverton repaired to St. Owen's church on the following morning, and saw Mr. Parslow take Mary Davis for better, for worse. Bessy offered her hearty blessing on the marriage too, and poured a host of well-wishes into Mary's ear as she kissed her after the ceremony and held her to her heart. She felt that it might be a long parting between them after that day; that the time might never come when they should meet again. Marriage separates friends and kindred every day, and a new road in life ever starts from the altar. Bessy felt that Mary Davis's happiest life was coming, and amidst her own hopes there was some doubt whither her own journey might lead.

" I shall look out for a little place in the country near us," said Mary Davis ; and Bessy smiled and thanked her, though she thought it was not likely ever to be realized. And Mary Davis, before she left that church, slipped into Bessy's hands the thirty pounds that they had spoken of ; and Bessy, with a heightened colour, took it, and resolved to pay back every farthing of the money as soon as possible. It was her first loan ; and the first loan gives always an unpleasant sensation to the borrower.

Bessy parted with them all at the church door, and received manifold blessings on her head : her father was fidgety in her absence, and she would be glad to return to him, although it was a step that might be taking her from her best friends for ever.

There was a crowd of idlers round the church doors, and she pushed her way through

it in her haste. For a moment, as in a
dream, she fancied she was face to face with
Lotty ; but the face vanished away before she
could recover her surprise, and try to see
more clearly through her blinding tears. She
gazed anxiously round, but no sign of the lost
sister presented itself. At the corner of the
street leading to her father's lodging she
paused again ; but there was no Lotty. The
old friends were coming out of church, and
the people were hustling each other to see the
bride, and wish joy, one or two of them, to
their minister, as she turned and made her
first step on the unknown road.

CHAPTER IV.

U P - H I L L   W O R K .

WAS it hallucination, that face of Lotty Calverton's in the crowd round the church doors
of St. Owen? It was strange; but Bessy
could not shake off the impression when she
reached home, or refrain from blaming herself
for not making further search. It must have
been fancy, she thought, despite the idea that
began to suggest itself that it was the face of
Lotty, with two years more care impressed
upon it, and yet not two years more of that
recklessness which, from her long silence,
might be feared. Ah! it must have been

fancy, she resolved at last; and in the sober, stern reality before her, she must indulge no more in fancies!

It had been a morning of fancies, for the matter of that, and the events that had taken place within it had engendered them. She could imagine how differently things might have been, had it not been ordered otherwise by the Ruler of all events that sway our lives, and make or mar us. What a different wedding there might have been in that old church, and what a different part she might have played in it!

But she had a new part to play now; and she turned to it with her characteristic energy, and flagged not, despite the adverse current that set in at times, and would have borne one of weaker faith away. The great task was before her, and the stubborn scholar did not care to learn—perhaps grew more callous as his strength and old selfishness came back.

Richard was almost himself again a month after the departure of the newly-married couple to their country home ; a little shaky at times about the knees, and subject to a swimming in the head, which aggravated him and made him swear. He kept up appearances still, if in a less degree ; for Bessy Calverton was useful to him, and he could not see his way clearly without her help and guidance.

Bessy and her father were then living in the little shop for which the thirty pounds were borrowed—a poor specimen of a fancy repository, that Bessy thought might make a stand, and realize an independence some day. Bessy had had time to practice fancy work during her stay at St. Owen's Terrace, and specimens of her crotchet work and embroidery filled the window, and were offered in vain to the denizens of a poor neighbourhood, Tothill Street way—a strange place for a fancy repository, where fancy abided not, and all the graces of life had been starved out by those who strove hard to keep the wolf from the door.

Still, it had been necessary to leave White-chapel; the propinquity to the locale of the "El-Dorado" rendered Richard Calverton nervous, and he would prefer a neighbour-hood where Bessy was not better known than himself. He breathed a little freer when he was living near Tothill Street, and had per-suaded Bessy, much against her will, to paint the name of Richards over the door.

"Fancy writing up Calverton in capital letters," he said; "isn't it as bad as saying, 'Here's the man who ran away from the Ber-mudas—step in, and collar him'! Richard's the name, Bess."

"We begin with a falsehood," said Bessy.

"Well, try the other if you like, and see how soon a policeman will call to ask if Mr. Calverton's at home."

There was force in this reasoning, and Cal-verton was not a very common name; so

Richards was painted over the shop-front, and Bessy began business.

Richard Calverton kept to the back-parlour all day, and only ventured forth of an evening, as he had promised himself, when all things were settled. He was very content just then, with nothing on his mind, no business to trouble him, and a daughter who studied his little wishes, and tried to make him comfortable. She worried him with that bible of hers, and the questions she put to him afterwards to make sure that he had been paying attention—and how she did talk of his future state to be sure, as if it were not his business more than her own, and she could not leave it alone! He had not been prepared for a pious daughter when he first went in search of her after his abrupt departure from the hands of a paternal government; she had not been so full of texts, and psalms, and hymns when she ran away from the " El-Dorado "— whom on earth did she take after ? It was

not himself or her mother, who died in Brixbank Prison—he supposed it was that one-
eyed Methodist fellow, on whom he stole a
march so many years ago. Well, he supposed
he must put up with it, and pretend to
be interested and pious — it seemed to
please her; and "if she took the huff," as
he expressed himself, why she might leave
him in the lurch at last.

Bessy, who had long been in the habit of
making her own dresses neatly and with good
taste, began to think, as the "fancy articles"
became brown in the windows, that she had
better "do a little dressmaking" to keep the
home together, and her father applauded the
motive, and thought it very praiseworthy.

Bessy announced that new branch of business on an embossed card in the window, and
as the terms were moderate, even for Tothill
Street, and people in Tothill Street must
dress in some sort of fashion according to Act
of Parliament, why Bessy found work accu-

mulate on her hands, and the time less at her disposal for the moral education of him who lived on her labours.

"You must read the bible to yourself now, father," said Bessy, "whilst I work at my new profession."

"Certainly, Bess—pitch it over here, girl!"

And Richard Calverton, having the bible in his hands, feigned an intense interest until his eyes grew heavy, and his head made sudden dives, and the bible fell at last with a crash into the fender. Bessy asked him to read aloud after that; but he still nodded, and dropped the book, and it was a hard effort to keep him attentive. Bessy sorrowfully acknowledged to herself, that the result of all her efforts was not quite satisfactory, when three months had been spent in that shop, and the first quarter's rent came round. She was working hard to make up the rent; and it was not till five weeks in the new quarter that the landlord's claim was satisfied, and the receipt proudly filed and hung up in the back parlour, along with the poor's rate and house duty.

" We're out of debt, father."

" Hum—yes."

" I don't know what we shall do for the next quarter, though," said Bessy, with a sigh; " here are five weeks gone already."

" But there's plenty of work," said Calverton; " and you are not the girl to be afraid of it ?"

He had not observed how thin Bessy was becoming, and how all her colour had long since vanished away from her cheeks. He thought Bessy wanted encouragement, and he gave it freely with all his heart, and smoked an extra pipe of tobacco that afternoon as a tribute to the satisfactory manner in which his daughter had squared the rent.

" No, I'm not afraid of work," said Bessy, in answer to his last question.

" And there are your rich friends in the

country, to stand another thirty pounds, Bess."

"But I have not put by one pound off the first loan yet," cried Bessy, indignantly; "and am ashamed to write my apologies with every letter that I send them."

"They never expected that thirty pounds back, you may depend upon it, Bess," said Calverton. "I would not say anything more about it."

Bessy did not reason further with her father; her heart was heavy that afternoon, consequently her reasoning faculties somewhat dull. She had toiled and striven hard for Richard Calverton, and her reward had not arrived yet, although she prayed for it every night at her bedside. She was not beginning to despair, for she was a young woman of great faith, and she knew what a hard nature she had to deal with. But if only he would show some signs to give her hope; even a greater interest in her—a greater proof of the love she was so anxious to win! She was content to sacrifice her life for him; she had chosen her path, and would follow it to the end; but if some hope for all her labours were to shine upon her as she toiled along the weary up-hill road, with how much greater cheerfulness of heart would she proceed thereon!

Bessy became despondent after a time; he seemed to go still further back, despite her struggles, his hypocrisy. More than once, lately, he had mourned the past " El-Dorado" times; and though he suffered Bessy's reproof, he did not show any signs of being impressed by it.

" If there were only a little more money coming in to make you comfortable, Bess," he said, one day.

" I do not want money!" cried Bessy, almost petulantly.

" To think of the little bit of money I had once," moaned he, " and the little bit I was putting by; and now the old woman drinking

it all away, and I daren't try and stop her for
an instant! It's all that two-faced devil's
fault—that brother of mine, Charles Edwin.
I wish I had him by the throat over a deep
river!"

"Father, I will not hear it!" and Bessy
started up with a flushed cheek and heaving
bosom. "Am I working and suffering to
see your past brutal nature become more apparent every day? I will not hear it!—I
will not have it!"

Richard Calverton was never destined to be
his old self again; he cowered before Bessy's
honest indignation, and whimpered forth that
he did not mean what he said; it was only
his fun, just to try Bessy—she did not mind
him having a little bit of fun now and then
—it wasn't often that he felt in the humour.

Bessy cried herself to sleep that night—
might have cried all the next day only business was brisk, and she was required on a
dress-making expedition to a tradesman in

the neighbourhood, whose daughter was going to an evening party, and wished to surprise her friends and acquaintances with a dress that a duchess would have thought twice about purchasing if she were of an economical turn of mind.

Richard Calverton always objected to these dressmaking missions away from the business; he had never surmounted his aversion to the daylight—it was unconquerable. Bessy was sometimes absent four, five or six hours, and during that time he had to attend to the shop, and wait on the customers that strayed in occasionally. Certainly, take one day with another of Bessy's departure, and the average of customers was about two—sometimes a dirty little girl with a mania for fancy work, and a contempt for shoes and stockings, would purchase a penny crotchet-hook; or a servant maid would bring in her new piece of merino, and state that she would call in the evening to be measured; but there was nothing to

alarm Mr. Calverton. Nevertheless, he saw
Bessy depart that morning with evident re-
luctance; he did not see that a few shillings
more or less mattered so much, that he should
be exposed to public gaze for six or seven
hours, and perhaps be recognized by some one,
and walked off to a place that he inelegantly
termed "quod." He even swore once about
it, to make his remarks a little more forcible;
and Bessy left with tears in her eyes, and
with a something like anger in her heart.

She mastered her anger, however, and
came back to kiss the old brute, and to hope
he would not think she was unmindful of his
anxiety, although she did not believe—she
added assuringly—that there was any just
ground for his fears.

Richard Calverton, left to himself after
Bessy's departure, smoked sundry pipes of
tobacco, and then wandered about the parlour
and the two upstairs bed-rooms, looking for
the remains of a bottle of brandy, that Bessy

had put away somewhere for cases of emergency. He discovered the bottle at last, in a cupboard in his daughter's room, and tilted it to the light, and swore fluently at the paucity of fluid which it contained, and which was disposed of at one gulp. Then he managed to neatly pick the lock of Bessy's private drawer, and count the little store of money she was putting by for next quarter's rent; and being honest Dick no longer, to surreptitiously extract two shillings from the small hoard, by way of pocket-money, of which she kept him awfully short.

Proceeding down stairs with the two shillings in his pocket, he wished some juvenile customer would come in now, that he might induce him or her to fetch him a quartern or a quartern and a-half of brandy, just to keep him lively till Bessy came back. Once his love for brandy so nearly overcame his discretion, that he put on his hat and went to the door with the black bottle under his arm; and then a glance through the glass-door at the bright daylight beyond, sent him shuddering back to his arm-chair, wherein he ensconced himself for just a little think before dinner.

This little think, or the drop of brandy, or the extra allowance of tobacco with which he had indulged himself, brought on a state of somnolency that jerked his head divers ways, till it finally fell forward on his chest, and reposed there in a quiescent state of ugliness. And whilst thus reposing, the street-door was opened, and some one came quietly stealing in, and, after closing the door as quietly, advanced towards the parlour and peered over the little blind at the sleeping man, for whose repentance Bessy Calverton was slaving out her life.

After a long survey of Bessy's father, the handle of the door was turned, and the intruder passed from the shop to the inner sanctum, and stood a few paces from the sleeper, whose time to waken had not come yet.

Richard Calverton was indulging in a very pleasant dream, when a thin hand was put forth to touch him on the shoulder—a dream of an impossible future, with himself the grand Swell that he had fancied once upon a time would be the apex of his fortunes. Heavens! what a tiger and a cabriolet he had, and how he was dashing along Regent Street, with other swells on the pavement putting up their eye-glasses and regarding his "turn out" with envy. Everything conspired to render that a happy dream; Charles Edwin had fallen on his back crossing the road, and he was about to ride triumphantly over the pit of his stomach, when the hand fell on his shoulder, and he started up, glared at the face looking closely into his, and sank back again, as though at the presence of a danger which as yet he did not clearly comprehend.

"Lotty —Lotty!" he gasped twice, and then sat speechlessly regarding her.

CHAPTER V.

NEMESIS.

It was a strange meeting, after three years of separation between that father and daughter. It foreboded evil to the ease and comfort of the former, that father felt assured, as Lotty stood there looking at him. Richard Calverton had not paid much attention to his daughter's looks in the last days of the " El-Dorado," but it suggested itself then that she was deathly white, and that her great fiery eyes alone had life in them.

" You know me?" she asked, in a low tone, and with her lips compressed, as though repressing an effort to speak with greater force; "I have not changed so much but that you recollect me?"

"I recollect you," answered Richard Calverton.

"Do you recollect the new part I played at the 'El·Dorado' after your daughter Bessy came from Wales?"

Calverton looked dreamily at Lotty, but did not comprehend.

"The part of her saviour, defending her feebly, but with all the moral strength that you had left me, from the dangers into which you thrust her, from the villany and temptation that cast me on the streets before *her* time. I don't think, man, I played that part so badly, considering that I foiled you."

"You were always against me," said he, in the tone of a man who had been injured; "but what do you want here?—how did you find me out?"

"I have not lost sight of you for nearly

four months now," replied Lotty; "day after day I have watched your house and dogged your steps. Since I discovered Bessy was left in London by her friends—and rare friends they were to have left her there!—I sought the reason, and found *you*."

"Well!" asked Calverton, with a half defiant, half anxious glance towards his daughter.

"You had broken from the hands of justice and escaped," said Lotty, losing more self-command, and betraying, by her agitated face and trembling hands, the passion that consumed her; "with a price upon your coward's head you came to London, and, like a coward, sought help from one you had striven hard to injure; and by some lie or other—it must have been a lie!—touched her young heart, and led her to believe in your repentance. You were never a man; and there is something so beneath all manliness in living here, and letting her kill herself by inches to support you, that I have come to stop it!"

"You!" and Richard Calverton, with an oath, sprang to his feet and looked dangerous.

"You would murder me if you dared!" said Lotty, standing her ground boldly; "if I had not a friend waiting without, to whom I have given directions how to act, do you think I should have ventured here alone? Do you think I have forgotten," she cried bitterly, "all the love and kindness and fatherly affection you have borne me from a child?"

Calverton sat down again, and clasped one hand within the other, baffled. His fierce looks vanished, and his colour changed, and his heart—it *was* the heart of a coward—beat faster with his fear.

"Have you come to give me up to the police," he asked; "is it so bad as that—my own daughter!"

"I have come to save Bessy Calverton," said Lotty; "whatever consequences may lie in the way, I shall not consider them for one.

Say that, to set her free, I have to ask the law to take you prisoner again, do you think for a moment I should study you in saving her?"

" Your own father," reminded Calverton.

Lotty stamped with her foot as he said that; his new airs of sentiment, that had had some effect on his younger daughter, only enraged this woman, who stood there his Nemesis.

" I disown you!" she cried—" I will not have you for my father! You cast me from your love years ago, and gave me hate, and taught me hatred in return! There is only one I love in all the world, and for her sake I'm here!"

Richard Calverton made no reply to this. He was dumb-foundered—he could not understand her reasons yet. The first surprise over—the first impulse, perhaps, to save his life at any cost, quelled by Lotty's firmness—he sat there stupefied. He could not believe that she had come to give him up to justice; she would not have prefaced that intention with so many hard words—she would have not stood there in that room. But he waited anxiously for the true meaning to resolve itself from all this wilderness of words.

" For the sake of Bessy Calverton, who struggled longer than myself against temptation, having been taught God's word in a youth more innocent than mine—for the sake of Bessy Calverton, who offered me her love, and tried to love a wretch like me—who turned me from a tigress to a woman! To her I am indebted for a better, purer life, if one more hard and killing—and for her sake I come back to sweep from out her path the shadow of her life ! "

Calverton caught at a chance here greedily.

" Bessy loves her father for his own altered state. It is her study to see him profit by her teachings—to stir up in him, Lotty, thoughts of repentance. Oh, such thoughts ! "

Lotty's brow contracted more.

"You were, at least, no hypocrite when I knew you," she returned; "your own brutal nature paid best, I suppose. I don't believe in your repentance, for I have watched you narrowly of late. Do you remember this day week, when Bessy was too ill to take her walk with you, and you went out alone at nine o'clock?"

Calverton drew his breath spasmodically.

"Do you remember lurking round the house of the man who trades in human weakness still—the man who calls himself Calvertini, and lives at St. John's Wood? How much would his life have been worth had he taken a walk that night down his dimly-lighted road? Don't talk to me of repentance after that—don't speak again, but put on your hat and follow me."

"Where?" was the question.

"Away from this place, where innocence is dying for the sake of guilt, and blinding itself to believe in reparation—away from the daughter you will never see again in this life —mark my words!"

"I—I have nowhere to go!" and Richard Calverton's face blanched more and more, and his teeth chattered in his head.

"Will you come? — or shall I proclaim your lurking-place to that world which will be glad to hunt you down?"

"You—you wouldn't do that?"

"I'll have no mercy!" cried Lotty, flinging open the parlour door and stepping into the little shop. "If you hesitate a moment, I'll proclaim you. If you ever dream for a moment of coming back here, I'll proclaim you. If you try one scheme to thwart me in the purpose I have formed, I'll give you up, so help my God!"

Calverton rose, took his hat from a peg behind the door, and followed her into the shop.

"I shall be known in the streets now—if you will only wait till night!"

"There is a cab-stand a few paces off, and I will not wait a moment."

"Where are we going?"

"You are going abroad — you leave to-morrow."

"Damn——" began Calverton.

"You leave this evening for Australia. I have abused a trust placed in me, and made use of money given for another purpose to buy your passage out. You are entered by the name you have placed over this shop-front, and you are behind time now, the rest of the passengers being aboard. You will be watched till the ship sails; at Gravesend and Liverpool you will be watched also, and if you step on land one instant you will be arrested. I have sworn it, and I will keep my oath!"

"I've no money," he muttered; "what am I to do in Australia without money?"

"This is all I can spare," and she placed a few sovereigns in his hand; "it will keep you for a day or two, until you procure work."

" I shall die of starvation."

" Will you come ?"

" Lotty there *is* a little money upstairs,"
he suggested, in a husky voice; " and if Bessy
knew I was going, I'm sure she'd give it
cheerfully. Oh! dear, what is to become of
your poor old father abroad !"

" You must take your chance, like men
more honest than yourself," was the stern
reply; " there is no lack of work there, and
you are well acquainted with the country.
Are you coming ?"

" But the money upstairs ?"

" Shall not be touched."

Calverton groaned, but he made no further
effort at delay. He followed Lotty to the
street door, where she beckoned to a little
girl of ten or eleven years of age, and told
her to mind the shop till Miss Richards's return, and not forget the letter; and then she
passed her arm through his, without a word.

What a difference to that other daughter's gentle manner, when she walked out with him—and what a walk to take! It was all over with his luck now—fate set in dead against him, like a sea, and swamped him utterly! He had no power to resist, with that terrible threat hanging above his head, and that terrible oath, which assured him how sternly, how remorselessly, that woman would keep her word, ringing in his ears. He gave in, and submitted, and thought no more of struggling against her. He sat in the cab by her side, and reflected on the duty of children to their parents, and "the serpent's tooth" that had buried itself deep in his heart. It was not so bad as it might have been—bad enough as it was. If so wild and reckless a daughter knew the secret of his stay in London, why he was better beyond the reach of the law; and Australia would be a nice place for him—if he did not die of sea-sickness on the passage out: he should never forget that journey to the Bermudas to the longest day of *his* life.

Presently he was in the close, narrow streets bordering on the Thames ; finally, stumbling his way about the London Docks, very nervous at each glance directed towards him and his companion. In that broad daylight, with so many people passing and repassing, he felt it would be salvation to reach the ship and settle down.

He crossed from ship to ship, and went nervously and in haste along the planks between them, and reached the Australian vessel at last, and breathed again, and took off his hat to wipe the damp sweat from his forehead.

" Are you safe now ?"

" Yes."

" The steward will tell you Mr. Richards's berth. Here is your claim to it, and your board." And she thrust some papers in his hand.

He did not answer ; the rapidity of her movements had bewildered him too much.

"I am going now.   You will remember all I—I have warned you of?"

"You will not say anything against me now?" he muttered.

"Whilst you are here—you are safe."

She laid her hand upon his shoulder, and looked full into his face. He did not know her then, she looked so strangely at him.

"You and I will never meet again—shall we part as friends or enemies? If in this parting it will do you any good to hear I forgive all the past, I say that freely. If parting thus you can believe that I might feel more happy to hear you say, 'I believe you did it for the best'—say it!"

"No," and he turned away, stubborn to the last.

"Shall I take your thanks to her who is an angel on earth compared to you and me, for all the sacrifices she has made?"

"She has done me no good—why should I thank her?"

Lotty moved away, and he followed her, saying, in his old cringing tone, " You are not offended ? If you're going off to split upon me, I'll say, ' God bless you, and forgive you.' I'll send a thousand thanks to Bess."

" I will not take your blessing, or your thanks now, father," was the reply ; " they will do no one any good, when they spring from fear instead of love. I'll keep your secret—sleep peacefully on that assurance till you dream of treachery."

So the strange father and daughter parted, never, as Lotty had prophesied, to meet again. From that day the man, whose heart no love could touch, passed on his way to the new world, and was heard of no more by those who have their names enrolled in this history. Lotty, firm and resolved in her purpose, waited all that day near the Docks, till a steam-tug took the ship down the Pool ; went by train to Gravesend, and waited there, distrustful of her father, till the ship sailed

away; again repaired to Liverpool, and spent
five days upon the quay, wandering up and
down, and asking questions of those who
came on shore concerning Mr. Richards, who
kept so closely to his berth, and objected so
strongly to the daylight. But Mr. Richards
had faith in Lotty's obduracy of temperament,
and, fearful of apprehension, made no struggle
against the destiny that took him from his
native land.

CHAPTER VI.

SISTERS.

BESSY CALVERTON, arriving home late that evening, paused in the shop with her hand to her heart, and gàzed with a look of dismay at the little girl behind the counter. She had given one hasty glance towards the parlour, where the well-known figure of her father was not, and then stopped to collect her ideas, and prepare herself for the great shock that she felt was in store for her.

"If you please, are you Miss Richards?" asked the child.

"Yes—yes—what has happened?"

"I have been told to mind the shop till you came back, but no one has called, Miss Richards."

"Who told you?"

"Lotty Calverton."

Bessy panted with this new surprise. Was it all a troubled dream?—and should she wake up presently, and find that she had fallen asleep over her needlework, and that her father sat in the old place before her? No— it was not a dream, albeit the incidents of her waking life were strange and perplexing.

"I was told to give you this letter, Miss," said the child; "Lotty Calverton lodges with mother, and she wrote it before she left this morning."

"Did—did Lotty Calverton go away with Mr. Richards?" asked Bessy, as she took the letter with a nervous hand.

"Yes, Miss," was the answer.

Bessy broke the seal in haste, to arrive at the solution of the mystery, and her eager eyes devoured the contents of the hurriedly written missive.

It ran as follows :—

" DEAR BESSY,—I have made up my mind to end your present unhappy life. It is a mistake—it is killing you. I, who know our father so much better than yourself, know there is no changing him—that he was born bad, and will die so. It will be all altered when this note reaches your hand ; it will be all explained when we meet in a few days. Have patience, and trust in me. God bless you.   " LOTTY."

Bessy sat more bewildered than ever after this letter had been read; it suggested so much, and threw light upon so little. That Lotty had stepped from the crowd in which for so long a time she had been lost was certain ; but whether for good or evil, she dared scarcely ask herself. Certainly not for good, for she had stepped between her and the one task for which she was working hopefully, believing the reward for all her perseverance would come some day—God's blessing on her labour. She had lost all thought of self in that task, and to have it snatched from her was disheartening—was even cruel, for she should have been warned, and asked if she had wished it.

And now her father was gone, and the labour ended, and she left to mourn his absence and the futility of all her efforts to save him. She had never sounded to the depths of that father's character, and did not know how vain all those efforts would have been—she saw herself, in the first moments of grief, deprived of one who she fancied might have learned to love her and believe in her had time been mercifully given him. For an instant the thought that Lotty had betrayed him to justice seized her, and stopped her heart beating; and then she turned away from so cruel a suspicion, and did Lotty Calverton more justice.

But it was terrible to remain passive, and wait days for the clue to the mystery by which she was surrounded.

Still there was no help for it, and Bessy struggled with her anxiety, and counted every hour of the long days. She bought a newspaper every morning also, and scanned eagerly its columns, and breathed more freely when the name of Richard Calverton, *alias* Richards, appeared not there to affright her.

Bessy could never afterwards remember those nine or ten days which were spent in that deserted house—how they passed, or in what manner. They were days of fear and suspense, wherein her needle lay idle, and in which her thoughts were confused and troubled. No incident, not even a new customer, occurred to relieve that monotony of uncertainty which robbed her of her appetite, and turned her paler that before.

Lotty came at last. Late in the evening,

when the boy who called to put the shutters up had fulfilled his task and departed, this strange sister, who had for so long a time been lost, suddenly appeared as Bessy was crossing the shop to shut the door.

Bessy Calverton had been so long alone in that house, shut up with her own thoughts, that she gave a cry of joy at seeing Lotty, and ran into her arms. In the first moments of meeting, she could feel no anger against her who had acted for the best in her own judgment.

"Oh! Lotty, Lotty, why did you keep away from me so long?" was her only re·proach, as she clasped her wandering sister in her arms.

The first emotion subsided, the street door closed, and the sisters in that little back par-lour, Lotty placed a hand on each shoulder of Bessy and held her at arm's length.

"Let me see how you bear the world's rough work, and how the task you set your-self has altered you. Don't speak!"

They looked at each other for a moment intently, sadly—both could see a change. Bessy alone felt that the change in Lotty was for the better. The face of Lotty was pinched and worn, but the defiant look that had been its characteristic had departed, and in its place were a sadness and a deepness of thought which rendered her less stern.

"Well, Bessy, are you not going to heap upon me all your reproaches? Let me have them, and recover from them before I explain."

When they were seated together, with Lotty's hand on her sister's arm, Bessy said—

"Let me know what I have to reproach you for, Lotty? All is darkness and mystery with me yet."

"Coming back from Liverpool this afternoon, I thought if it would not be better to keep away from here, and spare you such a meeting. I could but give you pain, I reasoned, and the first shock over you were learning resignation."

" I was dying with suspense," said Bessy.

" Well, I came on, Bessy," said Lotty; " I could not resist the desire to see you for the last time."

" The last time !"

" Ay—but I will talk of that presently. Now of Richard Calverton."

Bessy, with suspended breath, had clutched Lotty's arm in her turn, and changed colour. She was to know the very worst then, and she had feared it and held back.

" Richard Calverton has left for Australia," said Lotty—" at my wish—forced by my will, which held him fast, and would not suffer him to turn."

" He wished to stay then ? Oh, Lotty ! "

" Yes, he wished to stay—to be kept by you, and worked for and caressed in his old age, as though he had been a father or a friend to you all his life."

"But, Lotty, he *had* altered," said Bessy; "he was no longer the father we feared—he was learning to repent."

"He was learning to deceive you!" cried Lotty; "nothing better or more noble was in his thoughts than that. Had I believed there was a change in him—there was even a hope of change—I might have paused; but there was no hope, and you were dying for him."

"I would have died happy," said Bessy— "for there *was* hope, Lotty; and in your precipitation you have deceived yourself."

"You were giving up your life for him," cried Lotty, with the old vehemence; "all your youth, your future, was being cursed by him, and I said weeks ago it should not be. I had not helped you to fly from him in times past, to sit patiently down, and see all the evil from which you had escaped surrounding you once more. You were in danger, and I have saved you from it. I don't expect you to be grateful," and that short disagreeable laugh of times past grated on Bessy's ears again.

"Lotty," said Bessy, gravely, "how did you know there was no change in him? Could you see so much better than myself into the workings of his heart?—you at a distance, and I so near?"

"You were blinded by your wishes, and I was distrustful and ever on the watch," said Lotty. "Months ago, when I found you left in London by the minister and that Mary Davis you have always thought so much of, I knew no good could come of it, for I knew that father of ours was wholly bad and could not mend. Still, I watched and gave him time; and when I saw him drifting back to all his old bad thoughts, despite your efforts, Bessy, I stopped it."

"His old bad thoughts?" slowly repeated Bessy.

"In the nights when you were busy here, and he left this house alone, I have dogged his steps and seen how vile he was. I have followed him from gin-shop to gin-shop, where he has spent the little money he could beg or steal from you; and I have seen him lurking round the house of his brother, praying—I could swear he was praying!—for a chance of paying off the grudge he has borne him for three years."

"Oh! Lotty, Lotty—not that!"

"He knew his address by some means; he went there more than once; he hid in the shadow of some trees that overhung the foot-path opposite his brother's house. Was it love that took him there?"

"Oh, my God! after all my prayers and hopes!" cried Bessy, bursting into tears, and rocking herself to and fro like a child.

"Ah! it's hard," said Lotty—"hard to know it, hard to tell it. And I don't spare you, because you won't mourn for him after the first shock's over, and you'll see that he was no less a wretch than when he tried to

blight you first of all. He would have mur-
dered me the day I came here in your defence; he would have robbed you of your
savings, had I consented to it."

And Lotty related those particulars of her
interview with her father detailed in our preceding chapter, sparing not Bessy, as she
had said, and showing, in her passionate
words and by her excited manner, how the
recital affected her, and roused her angry
feelings.

"And it's all done now," she concluded;
"and, thank God, there's no help for it. I
have striven hard to take that blot from your
path before I go—and you won't thank me,"
she added, fretfully.

"You think not of the blow it has been
for me; you are not sorry for me. You
exult over all the evil in our father's heart!"

"Bessy, I can't be sorry that you are quit
of him," said Lotty; "and I can't feel any
love for a man who has never been a father

to me. I forgave him all the injury he had done me before I left him—and that was more than I thought I ever should do in this life."

" You did not part in anger, then?" asked Bessy.

" No."

" And what did he say of me before you left him ?"

Lotty answered evasively; that last instance of ingratitude she would have spared Bessy, had Bessy not pressed the question, and implored her to tell all. Then the truth came out, and Bessy covered her face with her hands, and cried bitterly again—she saw the hopeless nature of that task which she had set herself, and how it would have ended for her.

"Lotty, you will not leave me to-night, with all these dark and cruel thoughts," she said, after a pause.

Lotty was sitting with her hands clasped

before her, dreamily regarding the fancy fire-paper that Bessy had made.

"I am misunderstood."

"No, no," cried Bessy, "I can understand your motives, Lotty—they were all actuated by your love for me—but I cannot rejoice over them, and I can only thank you for that love."

"That's all I want; and if you don't think it best to be rid of a bad father—you will when you think of it more quietly. Perhaps he will succeed in Australia," Lotty suggested, as a thought likely to make matters a little less gloomy; but Bessy shook her head, and replied not.

"I have no particular work at home," said Lotty; "I'll stay here till to-morrow, and postpone our last parting."

Bessy thanked her.

"To-morrow I must talk about you, Bessy, and what is to become of you."

"If we were to live together, Lotty, you and I—I think——"

" Ah ! another wild idea of reformation," cried Lotty—" another shadow to darken your life—that's like you ! But, Bessy, my life's planned out—I am going to America."

" I will go with you !" cried Bessy ; " what have I to live for here ? I am entirely alone."

" You will get on better alone than with me for a companion," was the answer. " I may have altered—I *have* altered—but I have not your thoughts, and my path must be a different one to yours. I may be a better woman somewhat—just a trifle—but I shall never be a good one."

" How have you lived ? " asked Bessy, timidly.

" For the last two years I have been a needlewoman—working day and night for little else than bread and water," answered Lotty. " I chose it of my own free will, perhaps, as penance, like the Catholics—perhaps because the old life was awful and murderous—perhaps because I had a sister who I thought might love me more if I were better, instead of turning against me when I acted for her good !"

It was the old jealousy of the " El-Dorado" time, but it was not its sullenness and hardness. There was anxiety to be loved in the tones, not a reckless indifference to any one's affection.

" Dear Lotty, I *do* love you more ! " cried Bessy.   " Oh! Lotty, I must have some one to love—you will not go abroad ? "

" We'll talk of this to-morrow," said Lotty, as Bessy's arms stole round her neck ; " you are tired and distressed, and I'll say no more to-night.   You wouldn't think now," with the forced laugh again, " that I wanted to sit up and read a bit, after such a journey from Liverpool as I have had ? "

" Read ? " repeated Bessy.

Lotty drew from her pocket a small dogs-eared, discoloured volume, and held it towards Bessy.

" Mary Davis's bible !" cried Bessy ; " and you read it still, Lotty—you have not set it aside, as you threatened ?"

" No—I couldn't do that—I tried once or twice, but somehow, it wouldn't do, girl," was the answer ; " and when it began to give me hope that even the worst of us can be saved— I suppose nobody thought of Richard Calverton when this was written—"

" Hush, hush !"

" When it began to give me hope," continued Lotty, " I stopped short in my sins, and said, I will try something else, and if I die over it I'll die the better for it."

Bessy's arms tightened round her.

" And when I thought I was dying of starvation, I read the one chapter where all is promised that I speak of, and thought I should be glad to die. I always read that —nothing else but that—and I am going to read it now."

And Bessy left her reading it, and went up

stairs to wait for Lotty, to thank God for the change in her, and to pray that a time might come to him who was now upon the seas, when God's word should teach him even yet the love and penitence against which his heart was steeled.

CHAPTER VII.

LOTTY DEFENDS BESSY.

LOTTY CALVERTON did not part from her sister the next day, or the next. Bessy was ill and weak, and required help; and however firm Lotty might be in her resolves, she could not leave Bessy with those wan looks, which were almost akin to despair.

On the third day, when Bessy seemed stronger, Lotty spoke of both their futures —of her own in the first instance.

"I said I was going abroad, Bessy," she said; "perhaps I spoke in the heat of the moment, and without much thought as to my chance. For I have had my chance, and thrown it away."

" What do you mean ?"

" Nothing—nothing. Thrown away in a good cause, and the friend who offered it will believe so, hearing my story. I may not go abroad now, for I must not expect two chances in life ; but I cannot live with you, Bessy. Whatever happens, it is not right."

" Tell me why, Lotty," urged Bessy ; " all the old reasons cannot avail now."

" There is so little true penitence in the world," said Lotty, " that I can't expect the world to believe in mine—I don't ask it. But I *can* expect, if you and I were to become sisters, Bessy, that world to point its finger at you, and give you a share of its sneers and its lies."

" I am not afraid of the world," said Bessy, proudly ; " and in a world across the sea we may—"

" We may *not*," interrupted Lotty. " Do

not reason with me on that which cannot, *must* not happen, for the sake of Bessy Calverton. Your life will be a brighter one without me."

Bessy shook her head.

" You have passed through all the dark troubles that have beset you, and the light must come now—you have waited patiently, and God will reward you, Bessy."

" A sister's love and confidence be that reward, Lotty," cried Bessy; " I wish none other now."

" You will join Mr. Parslow in the country—he and his wife will give you a home, and make you happy. When the minister's wife was that Mary Davis you were always happy with *her*."

Lotty saw Bessy's colour change at this half reproach, and said hastily—

" You must not mind all I say, Bessy— I never could get over that girl, although I tried hard not to be jealous of her love for you. There, she's a good woman—and never a word against her will you hear me utter again. She has been a friend to you, and I am grateful—though its my nature to be a little jealous—Bessy ?"

Bessy looked towards her.

" You said once you loved me the best, though—that *was* true, Bessy—eh ?"

" Yes."

" Well, though I don't deserve it, I'm your sister. And you have said it again ; and when we are apart I'll think of it, and feel happy for the thought. Now, Bessy," said Lotty, " understand that we can't live together—it is impossible. For your own sake—God knows, not for mine !—I wish it. Still, I must trust you by yourself in London for a few weeks, till you hear from me — I wish that, for a reason of my own."

Bessy said she had no intention of leaving London yet awhile; and added, that if there were an opportunity of earning her living in that neighbourhood, she would stay there and be independent of her friends.

"No—you are too young to live here alone," said Lotty.

"My knowledge of the world began early."

"This is slavery."

"But it is independence; and if you turn away from me, you must leave me to follow my own path."

Lotty regarded her silently for several moments, then she said—

"We will talk of this in the next meeting— that may be possibly our last. Don't speak, I say only possibly now. Bessy, I want to speak of something else before I go." She drew her chair closer to her sister's, and let her hand rest lightly on her's. There was something in the action that startled Bessy, and aroused her interest.

"When we met last in that street in Snow-fields, Bessy, I had a hope that your home was fixed for ever there; that one or other of those brothers might have taken a fancy to you—I cannot think why they did not!—and asked you for a wife. I could have imagined then your settling down by the side of some honest, hard-worker, and making him happy, and being happy in his love. I was so sure that it might happen, that I did not seek you out for sixteen months; and then I went to the same house, and found it deserted, and heard from the neighbours that there had been great changes. Even then, Bessy, I had a belief that you were married, and sought out the Specklands instead of Mr. Parslow, and heard that you were living with Mary Davis, and had left them for upwards of a year. The brother told me that—a tall, dark-skinned, dark-eyed man, with a face that had seen sorrow, or I am no judge of sorrowful faces."

"Indeed!" responded Bessy.

"And he turned pale when I mentioned your name, Bessy—and had some trouble to become the stern hard man, whose equal I have never met—and, Bessy, then another fancy seized me."

Bessy did not answer, or ask what it was.

"That other fancy was that you and he had been engaged to be married once, and that something broke it off. And that disturbed me, till one night, when he was absent, I called at the house again, and saw his blind sister—and asked that one question, and"—her hand tightened its hold on Bessy—"found it a cruel truth!"

Bessy looked down to hide some tears that would brim over and run over her pale cheeks, and Lotty watched her nervously.

"Did he speak of me?" she murmured.

"Never a word, Bessy," was the reply; "he did not know that I was your sister—at least, he has never asked my name."

"Have you seen him more than once then?"

"I have met him more than once," she replied, somewhat evasively; "and always with the same dark looks, that stopped all questioning. But now, Bessy, will you tell me why the engagement was broken off—how it all began and ended?"

" Is it not sufficient that it has ended, and that he thinks no more of me?"

" Bessy—you love him!" cried Lotty, catching her in her arms—" I see that, and am sure of it. Tell me this story before I go— let me hear how the one chance that came to you was thrown away and lost. Is there any reason why I should not hear it?"

" No, no—but it is a painful story, and has been ended long since."

But Lotty persisted; and Bessy, after a short struggle, related the whole tale that she thought for ever to have kept a secret, from the day when Hugh Speckland gave her up. It was opening an old wound, and she drew her breath with pain more than once during its recital, although she gathered firmness as she proceeded, and spoke in a voice less faltering and weak.

"He did not know—he will never know," she added in conclusion, "that I loved him with my whole heart, when he thought it best to part—that knowing then the depth of his character, and all its nobleness, I could but love him. He did not seek that knowledge, but in his pride and stubbornness cast me from him, and went his way. And I had my pride too—and I—I should have never been happy with him when he had once lost confidence. I did deceive him at the first—and he was a man who forgave not."

"Ah! a stern man, who would resent a wrong, but who would pardon a weakness," said Lotty; "it is a pity that you were separated. I think you would have been happy with him. He cast you off too readily, Bessy—but he has not found happiness himself."

"How do you know that?" asked Bessy, quickly.

"I see him in my neighbourhood now and

then," said Lotty ; " I hear him spoken of occasionally He is a man who is trying to do good in his way, and with his money ; but it is a strange, unsympathizing way, and I fear he gets few thanks. He has an unmerciful way of doling out his alms, that grates with more than one or two who have been assisted by him."

Bessy said no more concerning him—on the contrary, made haste to quit the topic, and talk no more of that which, rising from the grave of the past wherein past hopes were buried, had so disturbed her with its reminiscence. The sisters spoke of parting again ; and the clock was striking nine when Lotty, disregarding Bessy's wistful appeal, put on her bonnet and shawl.

" I have work to do, and must live by my own labour," said Lotty ; " you will not wish me to remain idle here. Some day hence— perhaps before this week is ended—you will hear from me. Don't feel too lonely about

such a wretch as I am—and believe in the
light that must come to you, as I have prophesied !"

But Bessy's heart was heavy, and not inclined to believe in anything brighter than her
present lot when Lotty went away that night.
Understanding and appreciating as she did
the reasons for Lotty's inflexible resolve to live
apart from her, she, with her heart yearning
for something to love, and study, and beat for,
could but regret it, and wish her sister's firmness had been less.

Bessy did not know how much Lotty had
kept hidden, or what a struggle it had been
to preserve that firmness, and not acquiesce.
Lotty knew that Bessy was offering to her
that which would make her life a blessing
to her; but for Bessy's sake she had repressed all sign, and let the offer pass,
though it told of faith, and charity and
human love. Lotty did not abandon the
neighbourhood of Tothill Street immediately ;

she returned to the house five minutes afterwards, and looked anxiously towards the parlour, to make sure that Bessy was not utterly prostrated; and did not leave till her sister was sitting quietly, if thoughtfully, over her work. Then, as if actuated by some new thought, or by some old one that she had repressed till that time, she hurried away, swiftly and surely, on some secret mission. Passing quickly through the crowd upon the footpaths, taking the road when any extra attraction brought people to a standstill, taking short cuts down dark streets to broader thoroughfares, she continued her progress until she stood in one of those turnings out of Oxford-street where the houses are large and imposing, and were rented by well-to-do people before Kensington rose a second time into fashion.

At one of these houses she knocked, and asked of the maid-servant who responded to her summons if Mr. Speckland were within.

Mr. Speckland was at home, but very busy at present; would the young person please to state her business.

"Tell him that Charlotte Calverton has called to speak with him for a moment," said she; "I think he will see me."

The maid went upstairs to the first-floor, rented by Mr. Hugh Speckland, engraver, and returned a few minutes afterwards to state that Mr. Speckland would see her if she would step up. Lotty followed the servant into the room, and having been announced, was shut in with that man whom we left last at a dying brother's side.

It was a large, well-furnished room, having a table by one of the windows, as in the old Seymour Street times. Lotty cast a hasty glance round the room in search of his sister, but she was alone with the worker, who sat intently at his engraving, with the light of the table-lamp full on his face as he pored over his wood-block. A face that had not altered much, in which the lines might have been deeper perhaps, and on which the old expression of energy, resistance, obduracy— whatever it might be—had settled and hardened.

He looked up for a moment as she approached, and then turned to his work again and said, "Well?"

"I have come to say I give up the idea, Mr. Speckland."

"Indeed!" was the brief reply.

"That many things have happened that compel me to give it up—sore against my will—and with a hundred thanks to you, sir."

"Against your will, and yet give it up?" said Hugh.

"It seems strange, but it can't be helped," said Lotty; "shall I explain?"

"Yes."

"In the first place, you will think all your trouble in seeking me— all your kindness after that search was successful—very ill repaid—for, with the exception of two pounds, I have spent all the money which you lent me for my passage and outfit."

"Well, well — I thought I could have trusted you. No matter." And Hugh, who had expressed his surprise by leaving off his work, resumed it again.

"There are the two pounds," said Lotty, placing it at his side; "some day I may be able to work off the rest of the debt."

She placed on the table beside him a little packet of money, which he swept off with a hasty hand. As it fell at her feet, he said—

"Do you think I give and take, that you so coolly fling the gift back in my face? I tell you again," he added angrily, "that there is no place in England for you, and that in Canada you may begin a new life, and will have those near to watch and encourage you."

"I have betrayed your trust."

"No matter, I am used to it," said Speckland; "I shall trust you no more, but act for myself. I shall pay for your passage out to-morrow."

"Your sister?"

"Was married to-day, and a week hence will leave for Canada. You will be a foolish girl to reject my offer—you shall not reject it?"

"You are very kind," murmured Lotty.

"Have you altered your mind?" asked Speckland—"you thought the offer a good one when I made it last."

"I thought it salvation—I think so now," said Lotty; "and—and I will take your offer, if you will hear my story, sir, of how that money was lost."

"I am busy," he said, by way of an excuse.

"But you have lost trust in me—you own it," urged Lotty; "and as the money was spent in a strange cause, I should like your opinion of it. Will you hear me, sir?"

"If you wish it," said he; "take a seat."

"Thank you—I will stand, sir."

She moved a little nearer to him as she spoke, as if to watch the effect of her disclosure; and he, ignorant of the strange turn that revelation was to take, sat and worked on calmly.

"You were good enough to lend me thirty-five pounds; and as you sketched before me a means of repaying that sum by small instalments, I was weak enough to borrow it. The greater part of the money went a few days since in purchasing a passage out for my father."

"Your father!" and Hugh leaned back in his chair, and regarded her with astonishment—"your father in London!—I do not understand."

"He had escaped from the Bermudas; I found him living with—with a sister of mine," she continued hurriedly; "he had flattered her into a belief of his repentance, and was living on her bounty, and suffering her to work her life out to keep him in idleness. She had taken a little fancy repository near Tothill Street, under a false name, and was dying by inches in his service. Was it wrong to save her?—to compel him to abandon the hold he had upon her, and work on for himself?"

"No—you are a brave woman," he said; and he bent more closely over his work, so that she could see only the masses of hair, that had turned of an iron grey since we met him last in Seymour Street.

There was a long silence, and Lotty with a half-sigh felt the interview had ended. She was moving away when he repeated—

"Dying by inches, Charlotte Calverton! Where is Mr. Parslow?"

"Married, and living in the country."

Until that time he had never mentioned her name, or appeared to have known it or her history. He turned to his work again, and seemed to forget her presence; for after a while he looked up, and was surprised to find her standing there.

"Oh!—good evening to you," he said; "I did not know you were here still."

"When shall I see you again, sir?"

"Next week. I shall let you know by letter when the ship sails, and shall meet you on board. Good night."

"Have I forfeited your confidence now, sir?"

"No," he answered; "I judged hastily."

Lotty caught at the words, and came back with a hurried step, and, leaning both hands on the table, looked full into his face. The action struck him as singular, and he looked back at her for an explanation. They were two strange faces at that time.

"You judged hastily once before, sir—I must say it, I will say it, if it lose me my one chance, and all your kindly help. Until to-day I have never known your true history, nor my sister's. I know it can't be helped now, sir, and that all is over and gone; but it was still a hasty judgment, and it darkened your life—and you were wrong!"

"What do you mean?"

"She was my sister, and you loved her. She would have been your wife, and made you happy—only your pride, and anger, and sense of injury thrust her away at the time she loved you best—ay, loved you best on all the earth, sir—I call my God to witness!"

"Woman!" shouted Speckland.

"It is the truth, sir—if I pain you, I can't help it. You have a right to know it, for the sake of her good name—for the barren life which, with all the light crushed out by you, has fallen to her share. There—I have told you, and am going!"

"One moment—how do you know this?"

"I heard her story to-day for the first time, sir—I wrenched it from her, after a hard struggle to keep it back."

"She loved my brother—did she not tell you that?"

"Ay, she loved him for a while, until she knew you better, and could esteem you more.

And then you blighted her whole life—not willingly, not knowingly, but in a weak moment, when your good angels were away, sir."

" Will you leave me now ? " he asked, in a low tone.

Lotty went out of the room at his request, and shut the door upon him, and on the trouble in his heart she had left. And he sat there, silent and motionless, after she had quitted him, as though the shock of the truth had stricken him to stone. It had been a strange, unreal day to him before. His blind sister had been married to the old love, who came from Canada to keep his word, and take her to the home he had made for her ; and his' estimate of human nature had risen somewhat higher. He had left Lucy happy, and returned to his solitary work, his solitary labour, and the companionship of many thoughts, that were no less bitter for being nourished by himself and in his heart. And the day

x 2

had ended in as strange and unreal manner as it had begun—and there he sat struggling with himself and an accusing past.

He took up the graver at last, and balanced it on his finger, and looked at his work; then he made a movement as if to bend his will to it. But the will was weak that night, and there was a rush of old thoughts and bygone hopes, to sweep upon him and hurry him away from the present. He gave up his task, and buried his head in his arms, and groaned as with a heavy weight upon his soul.

CHAPTER VIII.

IN WHICH THE HERO OF THIS STORY MAKES HIS
FIRST APPEARANCE, AND SEVERAL CHARACTERS
THEIR LAST.

BESSY CALVERTON spent a dull week in that
shop near Tothill Street. For the first time
in her life she felt wholly alone in the world.
Great as had been her troubles in times past,
many as had been the homes which had sheltered her, or from which, for lack of moral
shelter, she had been compelled to fly, she had
ever had a friend to cling to—some one to
comfort and console her in her saddest hours
of trial.

And now all was altered, and no voice gave her assuring words, and no face but the stranger looked into hers. The present was the true picture of her future now—dull, and spiritless, and lonely, with never an one to love. Those she loved best had all parted from her, and she remained to battle for existence alone, with a crowd of unsympathizers round her. If Lotty had but only stayed with her, and they had shared life's troubles together — Lotty, her own sister! They were true companions, and they loved each other, and there was not a great dissimilarity of thought now: why should Lotty have studied so much what the world would say, she who had defied it for so many years? If for Bessy's sake alone, was it not her wish? —and had Bessy ever found the world so great a friend, so charitable a master, that she should sink her one chance of happiness, and live on in loneliness for its sake?

Bessy had many such thoughts as these,

mingled with others concerning her father, Parslow, Mary Davis, and the Specklands— all parted irrevocably from her, and to whom, in the common order of events, there could follow no reunion. For her father had passed from her to his unknown life, and Mr. Parslow and his wife's hospitality she could entrench on no more; and the Specklands—or rather he who ruled them, and was the head thereof —had cast her off, and crushed her self-esteem. Let her live alone, then. The first shock over, would she feel entirely alone with the Father of all to watch her, and His book at her side to offer solace in her hour of need?

Bessy was beginning to think that she should not hear from Lotty again, when a letter in her handwriting reached her. Bessy opened it, and eagerly read its contents. For the first moment she thought there might be some hope therein, until it more plainly developed the firm determination with which she had left her seven days ago. It spoke of Bessy's loneliness, her sympathy with it, her trust that it would shortly end; but it spoke also of a wish for a last parting in the emigrant ship, "The Queen," on board of which waited Lotty, to bid her good-bye before she went away in search of a new home. Bessy shed some bitter tears over Lotty's letter: to talk of hope, and pity her loneliness, and then to so firmly prove that there was no love sufficient to conquer the writer's determination, was a mockery to the poor girl, who struggled vainly that night to teach herself submission.

Bessy Calverton shut up her shop the next day, and went by train to Gravesend; the ship was to sail at three in the afternoon, and Bessy's appointment was for one. And it was striking one as, with a heavy heart, the boat rowed her to the middle of the river where the ship was moored, and where, amidst all the bustle and confusion, it seemed impossible to find her sister Lotty. Amidst the boats that passed and repassed, taking and bringing back disconsolate friends—few of which were to ever meet again by the adamantine laws of separation—Bessy's waterman fought his way, exchanging polite abuse with those who rowed against him, and as dead to all feeling for the sorrow in his track as if he had been Charon rowing souls across the Styx. They are a hard-hearted race, those Gravesend boatmen.

Bessy, after some difficulty, was on board, pushing her way amidst a crowd of friends, relations, and acquaintances, coming up or going down to the between decks where Lotty was to meet her.

It seemed a long, 'long time before she was in Lotty's arms at last, and Lotty was struggling to be calm as Bessy sobbed upon her bosom.

" You are the first who has ever cried for me, or cared for me—and I'm not worth it!"

said Lotty, hoarsely, as she strained her closer;
" what does it matter what becomes of me?"

Bessy looked up with a strange fear on her.
It sounded like the old reckless tone, and she
cried—

"Not going away like that, and with such
thoughts, Lotty!"

"Well, no," with an expression that softened
as she regarded Bessy; "but I want to console you—not to see you broken down like
this."

" You have your bible with you?"

" Yes."

" There is nothing there that says, ' What
does it matter what becomes of you'—you
will remember that, Lotty, when you feel to
turn against yourself? And—will you remember, dear, my faith in you, when we are
parted, sometimes?"

" I will remember it for ever," said Lotty;
" it made me what I am—please God, will
make me better. But don't cry again—I have

so much to say, and the signal for sailing is already flying, Bessy."

Lotty did not appear to have much to say when Bessy had somewhat recovered her composure; she spoke of the life that lay before Bessy, and her confidence that her young sister would find it brighter than she deemed— but it was strange talk at that time, and gave no comfort.

" I can still hope for you, Bessy. And now, my dear, dear sister, I have kept you too long to myself, and there are friends here waiting to say good·bye also."

She smiled at some one near her, and Bessy turned round and saw Hugh Speckland, a tall, sun-burnt stranger, and her old friend Lucy.

Bessy was conscious of changing colour, and leaning for support on Lotty's arm, as they came towards her—conscious of trembling very much, and feeling her heart beat faster as the hand of Hugh Speckland was the first extended to her.

"Miss Calverton, I am glad to see you," he said, in a voice as deep, if not as firm, as usual.   Bessy fancied not as firm.

Bessy murmured some inarticulate response, and placed her hand in his.   Did she think in all her life that it would come to this again ?— that he would ever hold her hand thus, and look so strangely at her !   But he was going away, and she could forgive him then, and wish him, in that heart which throbbed so wildly, a better home, a brighter life, than he had found in England.   And he asked for her forgiveness, too, in a low tone, that was audible to her alone—and Lotty, Lucy, and her husband seemed to move a step or two away.

"Bessy, for all the past in which I wronged you in my thoughts, I have to ask your pardon—for all my rashness, sternness, self-conceit ? "

"No, no—don't ask it now, sir.   The past and all that happened in it is a dream !" cried Bessy.

" Will you forget it like a dream, and pardon me ?"

" I bear you no malice, sir—I was to blame for my share in it. I would forget it all. If there be anything to forgive—I cannot see it!—you have my forgiveness, and my wish that you will be happy in Canada."

" Thank you."

Bessy fancied that he smiled, as though her wishes were of little moment to him. Well, well, there was a time when he thought differently, and its memory would be less sad to her after that day !

" You and Lucy will see my sister now and then, and sustain her in her efforts, Mr. Speckland," said Bessy ; " it is fortunate for her, as well as strange, that you leave England in the same ship."

Lotty was at their side again, and Hugh was frowning at her. Alas ! even at such a time, thought Bessy, his bad temper must obtain the mastery.

" I must explain, sir," said Lotty, in answer
to his frown. " You have been my bene-
factor, counsellor and friend, and I have a
right to own it. Bessy, it is to this generous
man "—he was going away, when she caught
him by the arm and held him back, despite a
deeper frown than ever—" that I am indebted
for this hope of a new life. Will you thank
him with me now ?—your thanks are of more
value to him, perhaps."

Bessy, in the whirl of ideas that beset her,
did not for a moment think of Lotty's pero-
ration; then her colour mounted, and had it
not been a parting for ever, she could have
frowned too at so cruel and mocking a speech.
Still she thanked Hugh Speckland, and held
her hands towards him—this time of her own
free will—and let him wring them in his own.
He was embarrassed at her thanks, and
murmured—

" Lucy was leaving for Canada with her
husband—I had seen your sister by chance—

I — I thought — that is — *it was an old promise !* "

Bessy had never seen Hugh so confused before; she was troubled herself, and felt relieved when he turned to Lucy, and, after a few words with her, hurried on deck. An old promise!—and he had remembered it during those years of separation—and this was his noble proof of memory. He must have remembered her too, she thought, and not have wholly closed his heart against her ! And she was glad of that, now he was going away for ever—she could remember him now with feelings that would pain her less.

But the minutes were speeding away—there was little time for reflection—and there was Lucy Speckland to kiss, and shed a few tears with, and congratulate on her marriage.

" Ah ! and you must let me introduce you to that hero of mine, whom you and I have talked so much about—you see we are not all castle-builders, Bessy," said Lucy.

"Thank God, no."

"Harry," said Lucy, touching her husband on the arm, "this is Bessy Calverton—my sister, my more than sister. Is he not a fine fellow, Bessy?" added the blind girl—"they tell me so; and he's a conceited young man, and inclined to that opinion himself."

And Harry laughed, and shook Bessy heartily by both hands; and Bessy thought he was as fine a fellow outwardly as so true and constant a lover deserved to be.

Were it not for the sake of that kind reader who has so far borne us company, we would endeavour to sketch this Harry. And as he *is* a fine fellow, we could wish the reader had made his acquaintance, and that the current of our story had brought him to the fore ground at some earlier period than the last chapter of this history. Our experience of novels assures us that this is the first time the hero of a story has made his appearance in the last chapter; and we take the credit of the novelty of the arrangement, and leave our lady-readers to sketch him after their own *beau-ideal*.

And time sped on still more swiftly, and the order sounded at last, from a Rhadamanthus in pea-jacket and sou'-wester, to clear the ship. And then the last partings took place between many aching hearts, and it was raining blessings on everybody's head.

Amidst the blinding mist which swam before her eyes, Bessy took her leave of them— of Lotty, Lucy, Lucy's husband, and of Hugh, who had returned—and then of Lotty again, who cried like a child, and kept her arms locked round her till the last minute.

" God reward you in good time for all your kindness, love and charity, to me—I feel your best time will begin from this day."

" I cannot think that, Lotty."

" I feel so—I believe so—you will leave me praying for it. Good-bye."

" Good-bye—remember Mary Davis's bible,

Lotty—write to me often—God bless you!"

And so the sisters parted ; and Bessy went up the ladder with the rest of those who were warned to go ashore, and who had experienced partings as severe as hers, and felt the shock as deeply. Looking back, she saw how anxiously their faces were turned towards her still—all but the face of Hugh, who stood holding Lotty and Lucy's hands, as though restraining them.

She could have wished to see him turn and look towards her once again ; he had softened much towards her in that final leave-taking— if he would only turn once more, and look good-bye ! But he retained his old position, as though forcing his will thereto, and showing much of that firmness which in mistaken moments had been the curse of his life. 'And so we part,' thought Bessy, 'friends in heart at least, and bearing each other in more kind remembrance.' She could whisper a blessing on his life, too, as she went away.

Bessy was scarcely seated in the boat, when, to her amazement, the object of her thoughts followed her, and took his place beside her.

" Mr. Speckland ! " exclaimed Bessy.

" Don't be alarmed, Miss Calverton. It is all a mistake. I am not going to Canada myself—I have not thought of it."

Bessy was at a loss to understand him in the first emotion that seized her ; at a greater loss to guess why he took his place by her side, as though it were the old times back again, and he had a right to sit there. She felt her colour rise and leave her, and rise again, and with a faltering hand she drew the veil down before her troubled face.

Hugh Speckland was silent for several moments, as the boat rowed away from the ship at his signal.

" The ship will sail almost immediately. Shall the boat put us ashore, or shall we watch its departure here with greater ease ? "

" I—I don't know, sir."

But Hugh Speckland knew, and the boatman received a second signal, and rowed more slowly to and fro. They were sitting in the stern of the boat, where a low voice could not be heard, and Hugh Speckland spoke in a very low voice, that vibrated in her heart, and made her tremble. A summer afternoon, with the sunshine streaming on them; with the busy life around them on the river; with the emigrant ship unfurling its sails, and the voices of the sailors at their labour.

" When your sister told you, Miss Calverton, of the little task I had set myself concerning her, she did not mention that she had repaid it a thousand-fold by a few words that showed how falsely I had judged you, and how cruelly I had shut my heart against the truth. But you have forgiven all the past ? "

" Yes," answered Bessy. He had waited

a long while for that answer, and asked the question twice—and when it came at length, he said, with a wild impetuosity—

" Will you trust your future with me once again, Bessy? I have marred it once, and am not worthy of your confidence; but the brighter life may come—with God's help, I believe it will, if you say Yes. Ah! you shake your head, and my poor brother's dying words are ringing in my ears again : ' There will never come a fair hour, a cheerful thought to make your work light, or your home worthy of the name?'"

" Did he say that, Mr. Speckland?" she asked in an agitated whisper.

" Yes."

" And is it true—you so clever, so famous, with all the best prospects in life opening out before you? Oh! Mr. Speckland—remember what I am, and how our engagement ended years ago. How can I make you happy?"

"By saying that which will set our lives together in one track, instead of each journeying along the solitary path, strewn with the ashes of our dead affections. Bessy, is there no power to make that affection live again?— no past memory that will endear us one to another, even yet? Is this true forgiveness, if you turn from me at the last?"

She kept her head averted from him, but it was to hide her tears; he stole his hand beneath her shawl and clasped her own, and though it trembled in his, it was not drawn away. There were words of Stephen Speckland ringing in her ears too at that time: more hopeful words—more true—than those which Hugh had uttered.

"In the far off days will you think of Hugh a little, for in the far off days I have a dreamy hope still. Should you and he meet in that distant time of which I speak, will you revive my name, and let it be perhaps a peacemaker between you?"

"You will love me," he continued; "take me for your husband, become my teacher, guide and confidant again, set my steps aright and see they falter not as they turn away for ever from the No Church path—you will do this, dear Bessy?"

"I will do my best—dear Hugh!"

His arm stole round her waist and pressed her to his side, and he would have kissed her, in defiance of the wooden visaged waterman facing them, had Bessy allowed such impropriety. But he pressed her to his heart still, and though the boatman might have his suspicions—for he was a man who had seen life—he could not be exactly certain that Bessy's waist was encircled by Hugh's arm. Those shawls are comfortable things, and handy on the water!

They were looking towards the ship again, where were a crowd of faces now. The sails were being spread, the friends on board were waving their adieux to friends in the boats and upon shore, a faint cheer broke out here and there from those whose hearts were not too full, or whose powers of endurance were more strong; the bright sun shone on all this busy scene.

Full in the sunshine, with his arm round her still, the lovers stood up in the boat, and looked towards the voyagers so dear to them; and one poor sobbing woman never missed that blessed gift of sight so much as then.

"I promised, Bessy, if you were to make me happy to let them know it, e'er they went away. We were to stand up thus, and wave our hands towards them, and, setting out on their new journey, they would wish God speed to ours!"

And as the ship with all its sails spread began that journey, Hugh and Bessy waved their hands; and those who had been watching anxiously, and she who had not watched but listened to Lotty's hurried exclamations, wished God speed to them, and prayed that all their troubles ended with that memorable day.

And are there any earnest, heartfelt prayers ever listened to in vain?

THE END.

R. BORN, PRINTER, GLOUCESTER STREET, REGENT'S PARK.